Escape to the Turquoise Seas

ALSO BY CARRIE WALKER

Escape to the Swiss Chalet
Escape to the Tuscan Vineyard
Escape to the Northern Lights

Escape to the Turquoise Seas

CARRIE WALKER

HEAD ZEUS

An Aria Book

First published in the UK in 2026 by Head of Zeus,
part of Bloomsbury Publishing Plc

Copyright © Carrie Walker, 2026

The moral right of Carrie Walker to be identified
as the author of this work has been asserted in accordance with
the Copyright, Designs and Patents Act of 1988.

All rights reserved. No part of this publication may be: i) reproduced or
transmitted in any form, electronic or mechanical, including photocopying,
recording or by means of any information storage or retrieval system without
prior permission in writing from the publishers; or ii) used or reproduced in
any way for the training, development or operation of artificial intelligence (AI)
technologies, including generative AI technologies. The rights holders expressly
reserve this publication from the text and data mining exception as per Article
4(3) of the Digital Single Market Directive (EU) 2019/790.

This is a work of fiction. All characters, organizations, and events
portrayed in this novel are either products of the author's
imagination or are used fictitiously.

9 7 5 3 1 2 4 6 8

A catalogue record for this book is available from the British Library.

ISBN (PB): 9781035919871; ISBN (ePub): 9781035919833

Cover design: Gemma Gorton

Typeset by Lumina Datamatics Ltd
Printed and bound in Great Britain by Clays Ltd, Elcograf S.p.A.

Bloomsbury Publishing Plc
50 Bedford Square, London, WC1B 3DP, UK
Bloomsbury Publishing Ireland Limited,
29 Earlsfort Terrace, Dublin 2, D02 AY28, Ireland

HEAD OF ZEUS LTD
5–8 Hardwick Street
London, EC1R 4RG

To find out more about our authors and books
visit www.headofzeus.com
For product safety related questions contact productsafety@bloomsbury.com

For my beautiful cousin Samantha.

My favourite, funny Brummie and the original dancing
queen. You have the biggest heart of anyone I know.
Always smiling, chatting and shining your light on
others, and one of the few people who can
make me laugh until I cry.

You will forever be the best one xxx

One

Monday 17th May

'Kat! Thank *God* you're back. Can I grab you for a sec?'

'Absolutely,' I said, forcing a smile. I'd only been in the office twenty minutes, and Heidi was already on me. I'd been mass-deleting emails with half a mind to 'select all' but didn't want to miss any major news. Most problems had burnt themselves out but I liked to scan for red flags just in case, and I was only halfway through. I wasn't sure if the team were being extra diligent or winding me up, but they'd copied me in on every single email – like *all of them*. PR was the worst for overcommunication. Pre-meetings, post-meetings, meetings about meetings. It was a wonder we ever got any work done.

'How's everything been?' I breezed, following Heidi into her office. I'd had a boozy fortnight in Los Angeles with my HIIT friends Sara and Abi – not that we'd done any exercise, obviously – and I was still in super-chilled holiday mode. 'Any dramas?'

"

'Just the one,' she said, closing the door. 'But a big one.' My smile dropped as I sat down and braced myself for a bollocking. Heidi wasn't one to exaggerate.

'Excalibur have appointed a new chief marketing officer.'

Heidi paused to let the words sink in, but my mind was already three steps ahead at what that might mean for the agency and the team… *and me*. Excalibur Cruises was my account and the biggest in the agency, worth well over two million pounds a year. Twenty of us worked on it full-time to make sure they got their money's worth in publicity, and any shift in the status quo was big news.

'Have *theyyy*?' I said, slowly processing the information. 'When? Why? *Who*?'

'Greg called last week,' Heidi said, quietly. Jesus. This was serious. Greg was the big boss and rarely spoke to us directly. 'An American venture capitalist firm have come on board and the new CMO is part of the deal. Brooke Harris – quite the mover and shaker by all accounts – and she's already made it clear she'll be reviewing the terms of our contract.'

'What's Fran had to say about it?' Excalibur's marketing director had been there for five years – almost as long as I'd been at Northstar PR – and would give us the inside track.

Heidi slid a finger across her neck. 'Gone. It was as much a shock to her as everyone else, by all accounts. Nothing she could do about it.'

I thought back to the missed calls while I'd been in LA and was glad I'd ignored her voicemails. There was always some crisis or other happening at work and I hadn't wanted to get sucked into whatever it was. But this was next level. This was the kind of crisis that would have worried me to death and ruined my holiday entirely.

'One thing I do know, is that our new client – and *your* new best friend – has an impressive business background. Apparently she's known in the industry as the *Queen of the Cruisers*.'

'Now there's a title,' I said, arching an eyebrow.

'Isn't it. Ex-Sunseekers according to LinkedIn. She worked with them in Miami before the VCs sent in their head-hunters and her brief is to…' she read off her notepad '…*Popularise cruising among the British middle classes*. So, the exact same brief we've always had: to acquire new customers and make them more money.'

I nearly laughed out loud. They already made *tons* of money. Hundreds of millions in profit last year alone. The cruise ships were like floating cities, and Excalibur's money was on display wherever you looked: thousands of stylish cabins, Olympic-sized swimming pools, multi-screen cinemas and a cabaret space on every ship. Money, money everywhere. Not to mention the food on board… there was *so much* food. A never-ending buffet, fine dining, à la carte; Italian, Greek, French – every different type of cuisine you could imagine. No sooner had one meal service finished than the next one began. There were plenty of efficiencies to be made if Greg wanted to up his profits. *We* were not one of them.

'Have you spoken to her yet?'

'Very briefly on Friday but she wants to meet us both in person, so we're going over at eleven.'

'Today?' My stomach clenched in panic. Talk about dropping me in it.

'Yes, Kat, today. I did put it in your calendar – and I tried to call you several times over the weekend, but your phone was off.'

Heaven forbid I try and put some boundaries in place, but now wasn't the time to say it. Heidi looked unusually pale, so I swallowed my own worries down and gave her a reassuring smile. These sorts of situations were always the big fear. We were only ever three phone calls away from having to shut up shop, but this was particularly bad timing as I'd been gunning for a pay rise, and it was meant to happen kind of now-ish. If my account went out the door, there'd be no money for a raise – more likely, I'd be going with it.

'Let's not panic yet,' I said, already sweating.

'No, there'll be plenty of time to panic after the meeting,' Heidi quipped. 'Can you dig out the latest creds deck and be ready in half an hour? Jules has booked us a cab.'

I looked down at my jeans and sparkly boots, heart racing – I wasn't really dressed for a client meeting. Especially not an ASAP-new-client-type meeting. Luckily there were a couple of dresses hanging on the coat stand, which doubled as my emergency wardrobe at times like these. Along with a freshly dry-cleaned jacket and my smart shoes. Such was the way in PR; you could be hauled in front of the client on a whim or asked to represent the agency at an event last-minute and suddenly you're off to a champagne reception or a film premiere.

This glamorous London life was worlds away from my scouse roots, although my accent still popped up occasionally. I'd left school at sixteen to join a local PR firm in Bootle as an office junior, doing anything and everything I could to ingratiate myself with the team. I knew PR was going to be my industry from the moment I walked through the door. The wild ideas from the creatives were so exciting to my teenage self. Cleverly thought-through headlines with intricate illustrations and serious debates over how long a nose should be on a cartoon character. Was a bum crack inappropriate? Should she have boobs?

Then once I had my own client projects, I really started to fly. I was working on all sorts of products – cars, cereals, washing powder – my boss would point me at a brief and within weeks I'd be selling in ideas for a new campaign. I loved being part of the PR machine when it came to crisis comms as well: learning how to polish up a bad situation and spin a story in the clients' favour. It was one of the many reasons Excalibur Cruises loved us so much – we did all that for them and more. At least I'd thought they loved us. Now I felt like I'd been cheated on while I'd been on holiday, betrayed by the only life partner I'd ever had. Fran must have been even more devastated.

I changed into my stretchy turquoise dress and stepped into my heels, then brushed my teeth and smooshed on some lipstick. Luckily, we had GHDs in the ladies' loos, so I gave my ponytail a quick going-over to shine up the blonde and clip-clopped back to my desk. Andy, our head of design, gave me a whistle.

'Look at you!' he said. 'Interview is it?'

I laughed. 'No chance. You're stuck with me here, I'm afraid.'

'Promotion on its way, I heard,' he said with a wink. I gave him a quick smile and shoved my jeans in a drawer. Ever the consummate pro, Heidi obviously hadn't shared the bad news with the leadership team, otherwise Andy would have said something. It made sense to keep it on a need-to-know basis until we understood the severity of the situation, assuming it was bad news of course. Which it surely must be. Brooke would have her own way of doing things and would understandably want her own PR people in. *No. Stop it.* I was spiralling. I sent a note to the team telling them not to disturb me under any circumstances and googled her. Prior to Sunseekers she'd worked in Las Vegas at The Bellagio and was responsible for a refreshed mix of water dances in their fountains and the residency deal with Adele. What else had this woman done? Invented cheese? Clearly she was a big-ideas person, or a lover of them at least. I suddenly felt anxious about meeting her. Maybe we weren't as cool or creative as the American agencies? Maybe I didn't know what I was talking about? I doused myself in Chanel, slid my laptop and a couple of creds decks into my bag and ran downstairs.

Heidi sat with her eyes closed the entire journey, gathering herself together and creeping me out, while I stared out the window, not wanting to disturb her process. We'd taken Excalibur on as a mid-market brand with zero personality and repositioned them as the 'Tardis of the Seas'. *Step aboard and be transported.* Everything taken care of, your gateway to a smorgasbord of fantastical places. We'd had so many successes as a client-agency team, with award-winning campaigns, record sales and the share price increasing fourfold since we'd started working together. I mentally rehearsed my facts, so they'd be front of mind in the meeting. God only knew what Heidi was doing, but this was my account and my opportunity to make a good first impression with Little Miss *Cruising Queen.*

The Excalibur office loomed large above us as we got out of the cab, dominating the skyline. A skinny metal building with a square head, which we'd nicknamed The Spatula. I'd walked through these revolving doors thousands of times over the years and felt as much at home here as I did back at the agency. The security guards gave me a friendly wave as I beeped us through the barrier. They saw me just as often as the Excalibur staff and had issued me with a pass to save the daily admin of signing me in.

'Off we go,' I said, as the lift launched us up to the tenth floor. Heidi took a deep breath, her eyes now wide open as we catapulted through the building then shuddered to a halt.

'Let's do this,' she said, as the doors slid open, more to herself than me, and the pair of us marched out and nearly collided with Greg Excalibur and his entourage.

'Hold the doors!' he called, and I wedged my foot in as they started to close. He had an air of James Bond's dad about him and still dressed sharp and smart despite being in his late sixties. Lithe and dynamic, his beautifully tailored Armani suit singled him out as the captain of the ship. It was clear he was the boss.

'Morning, Greg,' I chirped, as he strode past me, followed by his PA, his EA and two men with open laptops. All of them far too busy to put the work down for even a second.

'Ladies,' he said, acknowledging us with a curt nod. 'Enjoy your meeting with Brooke.'

'How are you, Greg? It's been too long…' Heidi started, as the doors slammed shut.

Greg Excalibur had been passed the family business by his father, who'd been passed it by his father before him. Three generations of men who loved being in front of the camera and the sound of their own voice on the radio.

Greg wanted Excalibur to be the by-word for cruising. Like Sellotape or Hoover or Jacuzzi. To be in the dictionary and part of the British lexicon as his family legacy. For cruisers to say *we're off on an Excalibur* and for people to know what that meant. The teams on both sides had been working hard to make it happen and we were finally starting to get somewhere, so a new boss coming in to shake up the strategy would really throw them.

Heidi put her laptop on the reception desk with an over-zealous smile. 'Heidi Caddel and Kat Brennan for Brooke Harris,' she said to the man beaming back at us. He was wearing full crew uniform, as were all the front-of-house staff. Everything but the sailor's hat.

'Absolutely,' he said. 'Ms Harris is expecting you.'

Were people still saying Ms? I'd tried it on for size instead of Miss at one point, but both titles sounded ridiculous at thirty-four years old. But then I wasn't a Mrs either. So many words to let people know your marital status as a woman, but only Mr for men. Typical. The mahogany doors opened automatically – a replica of the dining room entrance on the very first Excalibur cruise ship – and a tall, perma-tanned lady with a head of blonde hair appeared in a flurry of green.

'Brooke Harris, delighted to meet you both,' she said, smelling zesty and fresh. My new best friend was all business, with a firm handshake and intense eye contact, the exchange only slightly softened by her southern accent.

'Pleasure's all mine,' I said, imitating her style. 'Kat Brennan, Business Director at Northstar PR.'

'And Heidi Caddel, CEO. Great to meet you in person.'

My face already ached from all the smiling as we followed Brooke into the boardroom. It was an enormous space, with views across the city, and the wooden table was polished to gleaming with tiny goldfish swimming up and down the centre section. I'd been to many a product showcase session in this room and knew it almost as well as my own flat. Greg would use the big screen to reveal the latest cruise liner to the leadership team and their agencies, with platters of Pret sandwiches and buckets of beers on the table. This was the first time I'd ever felt out of place in here. The atmosphere was awkward and uncomfortable, and I wasn't entirely sure how to behave. Ordinarily I'd have helped myself to a coffee, made one for Fran, and got going with whatever we needed to discuss, but not today. No. Today was the Brooke show, and Heidi and I sat quietly, waiting for her to speak.

'Thank you so much for coming in at short notice,' Brooke beamed. 'I've been looking forward to meeting you both so much!'

'And us you,' Heidi said, fawning over her. 'Congratulations on your new role. This has been quite the surprise announcement… for all of us.'

Brooke leant back in her chair. 'I know. Internally here too, of course. There's been a lot of work going on behind the scenes to push the deal through, so I'm glad to finally be through the other side of it.'

'Fran will be missed,' I said, hoping to get some kind of reaction or gossip out of her. 'We've worked with her for years.'

Brooke played it cool, with no sign of emotion as she answered. 'So I hear. Yes, Fran has been great for the business, but you know what they say – a change is as good as a rest. She felt it was time to move on and who were we to stand in her way? All very amicable of course.'

Fran would never have suggested moving on – amicably or otherwise. Excalibur was her everything. They must have paid her a chunky wedge to just pack up and leave like that.

'She'll be snapped up soon enough,' Heidi said. 'These kinds of situations inevitably lead to growth opportunities if you keep your positivity glasses on.'

'Right?' Brooke said. 'I'm glad you see it like that, Heidi, as that's very much our thinking on the situation we have here with you gals and Northstar.'

The room went a different kind of quiet as Heidi and I realised we'd been talked into a trap.

'Is it?' I asked.

'Absolutely! There is a *huge* growth opportunity when it comes to our PR strategy and I'm here to make it happen.'

'Alleluia. That is music to my ears,' Heidi said, and I wasn't sure if she was deliberately misunderstanding. 'Between us, Fran was never very ambitious for the brand. We have loads of ideas we'd like to present. We are here and ready to supercharge the PR with you.'

Heidi kicked me under the table and I jumped.

'Yes! We'd love to talk you through some of our highest-performing case studies,' I said, keen to get her on side, 'and give you a sense of how we operate.'

Brooke dismissed me with a wave. 'No need, I've seen it all. You guys have been real troupers in putting us on the cruising map that's for sure, and we're hella grateful for that,' she said, talking like she was the founder, not someone who'd been in position for less than a week. 'And so, I won't dilly-dally, as you Brits say – I'll cut straight to the chase.'

Heidi's leg started jiggling under the table and I froze.

'I want to vamp things up a little around here,' she said, leaning in conspiratorially. 'And having the right agency by my side is the first step in doing that.'

Heidi plastered on a smile. 'One hundred per cent. And we are incredibly proud to be that agency.'

Brooke cocked her head. 'I don't know which agency is right just yet,' she said, lightly. 'But I'm sure as hell gonna find out.'

And there it was. She'd fired her first shot and I felt sick to my stomach. The air was thick and stifling, but I couldn't help an involuntary shiver. I'd been deferring to Heidi until now but it was time to get involved. I needed clarity on what she was saying.

'Sorry, Brooke, do you mean you'll be doing a review?'

'Nothing to be sorry about, sweetheart. Yeah, *kinda*. More than a review though; I'd like you to re-pitch for the Excalibur Cruises business, against one or two other agencies – I'm seeing a selection this week for a meet-and-greet.'

'For the whole account?' Heidi asked, incredulous. 'Everything?'

'That's right, cookie,' Brooke replied. 'We want to see what you've got.'

'I can show you what we've got, right now,' I said, flipping my laptop open. 'We've got a presentation to talk you through and loads of ideas to keep the PR fresh and moving forward.'

'My team have briefed me on everything you've done to date. And it's nice and all, but the business is entering a new phase and it needs a turbo boost, y'know? Our cruise ships are bigger and better than ever; we've got huge stars on the line-up, the best facilities, unusual routes – it's not just a big boat trip anymore, it's a holiday sensation.'

I scribbled as she talked, wanting to capture her exact words. This sweet-smiling American wasn't taking any prisoners. We had to be on our A-game and get her on board ASAP.

'Do we really need to go down the route of a competitive pitch?' I asked. 'Could we not have a stab at the brief first and then call a pitch if you're not happy?'

Heidi nodded frenetically. 'We've been running your PR for over ten years at Northstar! No one knows you like we do. If you give us a sense of the new direction you're looking for, we can take it away and work on it immediately.'

'Which would save you a lot of time and money,' I added, sounding desperate.

'Don't you worry about all that. We've got the rest of our lives, don't we? Plenty of time to make sure we've got the right partners by our side. And as you say, you know us best... which puts you at a huge advantage, so I'm sure y'all will do just fine.'

Heidi and I had the same stunned expression as we nodded. This was a serious situation. Seriously shitty. Half the agency worked on Excalibur and if we lost the account, they'd lose their jobs. *I'd* lose my job. The thought of it made my insides shrivel. I'd worked like a trojan my entire life and there was no way I was starting again from scratch.

Two

Two weeks later

Heidi and I sat in the boardroom and dialled into the update call with Brooke. We were two coffees in, with a third on the go, wide-eyed and wired and prepared for bad news. The phone clicked to connect and an automated voice announced us: *Northstar PR has joined the conference.* I slapped on a smile as apparently you can hear it down the phone, but I didn't feel very smiley inside. Waiting two weeks to have this call had felt like forever and the pair of us were on the edge of our seats.

'Hello?' Heidi fake grinned as she spoke into the spider phone.

'Well, good mornin', Northstar PR!' Brooke's voice came through, clear as a bell. 'How're you gals goin' over there?'

'We're GREAT,' I cheesed, side-eyeing Heidi. 'How are YOU?'

'Gorgeous day for it!' Heidi added. 'Can't believe it's June tomorrow.'

Brooke laughed. 'You Brits and your obsession with the weather! The sunshine is fabulous of course, but the heat makes me miss Texas.'

'It must be strange being so far from home,' I said, dragging out the small talk.

'Yeah… but at least I can get my summer wardrobe out now.' I kept on smiling. This was painful. 'Anyway, let's get to it. I've seen half the PR agencies in London, and I've come to a decision.' Heidi frowned anxiously into space. 'It's only fair to have you guys on the shortlist as the incumbent agency, and I'd like you to pitch against Amplify.'

There was silence as I looked at Heidi and she pretended to headbutt the table.

'No way! We love those guys,' I said, through gritted teeth.

We hated those guys. They'd pipped us to the post on the pitch for Dinky Drinks last year and it still stung.

'Leo Kendrick is CEO there now and Zach Evans is their creative director – I believe you know each other?'

Heidi folded her arms with an animated eye roll but kept her voice steady. 'Yes, we know them.'

Amplify were fast becoming our PR nemesis. We'd pitched against them eight times in three years, and they were beating us five-three. But that was all *new* new business. We'd never pitched against them for one of our own accounts. What was that even called? New *old* business? Whatever it was called it was a new level of low, even for them.

Leo Kendrick had gained himself quite the following in the PR press and was forever spouting his opinions next to his overly quiffed headshot. He'd recently been promoted to the chief job at Amplify and been listed as one of Forbes' forty under forty. But his entire new business strategy seemed to involve snapping at our heels, and I could just imagine his Cheshire cat grin at the thought of taking our biggest account.

'Yes, we like to support start-ups,' Heidi said, pulling herself together. 'Their creative director used to work for me, in fact. Back in the day.'

'Oh, really? Zach?' Brooke sounded delighted at this unexpected kinship. 'He's got some pretty wild ideas on how we can shake things up around here.'

'I bet,' Heidi said, shaking her head. 'Yep. Zach Evans. He was my protégée when he first started out – it's good to see him doing so well.'

'A pitch rivalry,' Brooke breathed into the microphone, and I could practically hear her drooling at the idea. 'I love it!'

'Hardly,' I said, lying through my teeth. 'They're an interesting choice to pitch us against, but we don't see them as rivals – and especially not when it comes to the cruising industry. Even they would admit we're the experts.'

'Oh, quite the contrary. They told me you often compete for business, but they usually come out on top.'

'They did *not* say that!' I blurted, before I could stop myself. *The audacity.*

'Oh yes they did!' Brooke squealed with glee. 'Those cheeky boys think they've got it in the bag.'

'There's plenty of something in their bag, that's for sure,' Heidi said, mouthing the word 'bullshit' at me. 'But there's a fine line between overconfidence and bare-faced lies!'

I tried to maintain a dot of decorum. 'Well, we look forward to showing them – and you – how uniquely positioned we are when it comes to your business.'

'Well, ain't that just wonderful to hear?' Brooke sing-songed. 'Nothing wrong with a little healthy competition between friends now, is there?'

'Nothing at all. Bring it on,' Heidi said, her voice strong and steady despite her deflated body language. 'No one knows Excalibur like we do.'

'That may be true,' Brooke said, 'which is why this pitch process is such good timing. My knowledge of the cruising industry is *unrivalled* – as you gals can imagine – but when it comes to the Excalibur business specifically, I'm still getting my head around how it all hangs together, y'know? I can talk to the team until the cows come home but there ain't no better way to find out about it than to discover it for myself.'

'One hundred per cent,' Heidi said, nodding vigorously. 'You have to know it to sell it – that's what I always say, isn't it, Kat?'

She glared at me then pointed to the phone.

'It sure is,' I said, loud and clear into the microphone. 'You've gotta see it to be it, right? Love it and live it to… give it.'

Heidi pressed the mute button. 'Stop now.'

Brooke cleared her throat. 'Quite. Anyway, on that note, I've decided to get samplin' the goods as soon as I can to get me up to speed across our cruise portfolio.'

'Makes sense to get out there and experience it,' I said, slightly jealous of that kind of induction.

'As you both know, we have a new flagship product, the *Esmeralda*, set to sail to Portugal in three weeks or so. She is a cut above our other cruises as we look to acquire a bigger share of the market and as such I'd like you both to join me on board. It'll give us chance to get to know each other while we witness our latest holiday proposition first-hand.'

'Really?' Heidi gave me a thumbs up across the table, eyes shining.

It had been a while since we'd gone on an Excalibur Cruise – we'd been on and off the different ships while they were docked, for a quick photo shoot here and there, but it had been a couple of years since we'd had the full passenger experience. *Ye bloody ha.*

'Oh yes, really. The pitch will be all about the *Esmeralda*, so you'll need to know her inside and out. What makes her different? What makes her tick? Talk to the guests, understand how they think and what would bring them back. I'd like to set a pitch date of July twenty-first, here in the boardroom at Excalibur head office, so you'll have a couple of months to prepare.'

'Understood,' Heidi said, leaning forward with a wicked smile. 'And will the Amplify team go on the trip after ours?'

Brooke chuckled. 'That wouldn't be very fair with the overall timeline now, would it? It's a two-week cruise! No. They'll be coming too so both agencies can experience the *Esmeralda* at the exact same time. No favourites.'

Two weeks? I swiped through my calendar to check what I had in. Work gatecrashing my personal life wasn't something I normally tolerated, but it didn't look like I had much choice this time. I'd miss Mum's birthday lunch with Dad and my sisters, but I could make that up to her. Then there was the weekly pub quiz and softball in Regent's Park and those three coffee dates I'd managed to bunch together into consecutive half-hour slots: Toby, Terry and Tim.

Dating by first letter made as much sense as anything else these days. But no, none of my plans were immoveable.

'How very generous, Brooke. Let me RSVP immediately for both of us, and say we will *absolutely be there*,' Heidi said, with no regard for anything I might have planned.

'It'll be more work than pleasure this time I'm afraid, but we might sneak a couple of cocktails in somewhere, hey, gals? That settles it then. I'll see you both harbour side on the big day and my PA will be in touch to arrange the details.'

Brooke rang off and Heidi slumped down in her chair.

'Amplify again! I can't believe this is happening!' I said. 'Although at least we're still in the game I suppose – maybe we should be grateful for small mercies.'

Heidi shook her head and covered her eyes. 'This is a nightmare. I should probably tell you…' she started, then hesitated. '…that Zach and I do not get on. We had a fall-out when he worked for me years ago and we never really got over it. It's no biggie but best you know before we all head off on holiday together.'

'Interesting,' I said, intrigued. 'What happened?'

I watched her struggle as she weighed up what to say. Heidi was never lost for words.

'I don't want to sully his reputation or be unprofessional…'

What? This wasn't like Heidi at all. Gossip was her thing. Her daily bread – she loved nothing more than a good speculation session and an opportunity to dish the dirt. And never *had she ever* cared about being unprofessional before – which she was all the time.

'Did he do something illegal?'

She shook her head. 'Let's just say there was a dispute over the source of one of his ideas and in the end he had to go.'

I winced.

'I know. Mega awks, right?'

'You sacked him?'

'No… he resigned, eventually… but it was all under a cloud.'

'Somewhat of a biggie, then. For him, at least.'

'I was young and inexperienced, and who knows, maybe I made the wrong call, but that's by the by. Do you think I should disclose the situation to Brooke? There's a clear conflict of interest if we're working on the same pitch.'

I nearly choked on my coffee. 'Absolutely not. You're on opposite teams! Fair enough if you were the client, but not the competing agency?'

'Hmm, yeah, you're probably right. And I can't imagine Zach or Leo flagging it from their side.'

'Exactly.'

'That Leo has a reputation for being a total slag when it comes to pitches as well, so we're in for a real treat with the pair of them.'

The mention of his name made me stop.

'Does he? Client-side or agency?'

'Both. He's one of those PR pretty boys who thinks everyone fancies him.' Heidi looked disgusted. 'Not my type *at all*.'

'He is very pretty,' I said, thinking of his chiselled features and piercing silver eyes. 'I know him, remember – we interned together at Engelman when I first moved to London.'

'Did you?'

'You know I did,' I said, exasperated. 'I tell you every time you mention him – which is on the regular.' Honestly… she didn't listen to a word I said.

Leo and I had applied for the same internship in our early twenties and both got it. It was the summer after he'd graduated and I'd just moved to London. I'd been firing out my CV to PR agencies for months and couldn't believe it when one of them finally replied, let alone one of the big five. I'd been so excited walking through their flashy front doors on my first day and signing in. Engelman was in the heart of the action on Soho Square, and it had felt like a dream to be sat waiting in their huge white reception, sipping on a matcha latte. The only flash of colour came from the elaborate vase of wildflowers on the glass table, until fancy-pants Leo Kendrick walked in. There was only one permanent job on offer at the end of the internship and the second I saw his floppy black hair and easy smile, I knew he'd get it.

'Morning,' he'd said, sitting opposite me. 'Reception said you're interning too. I'm Leo.'

'Hey,' I'd said, feeling instantly shy. 'I'm Kat.'

He'd seemed so much older than me, like a real grown-up, not a student, and he had an innate polish to him I could never have matched. He'd been to a real university and I'd been to the university of life, and you could tell. Everything about him screamed class and sophistication, from his tailored suit to his manicured nails. I'd sellotaped my hem up after it had unravelled on the bus and felt like a shambles in comparison.

On our first day we were briefed to review the Engelman PR and judge how successfully they were promoting themselves as a company. It was our special project to do alongside the real job and we'd worked on the presentation for months to get the thinking just right. I'd secretly hoped they might find two permanent roles so we could both work there, but when it came to the day of the meeting, I was off sick. I'd stupidly eaten a hot dog from a street vendor the night before and been vomiting all morning. I still had the text I'd sent when I'd realised there was no way I could go in.

Me: I'm so sorry to abandon you.

Leo: Don't worry, I'll represent.

Me: Yes, make it clear it's both our work. Keep saying my name.

Leo: Got it :)

Leo presented our analysis and ideas to the bosses and however many times he'd said my name, he got the job. The panel had loved the analysis and ideas, but without me there, they must have seen it as his success alone. When they told me I hadn't made the cut, they said it seemed like I hadn't been pulling my weight and might be better suited to an assistant role somewhere. I'd been so frustrated and angry at the unfairness of it all. I had no idea what went down in that meeting, what Leo had said – or not said – to sway the board in his favour, and I didn't stay around to find out. I was going to find it hard to stay civil for two whole weeks on this cruise.

'Those Amplify boys are double trouble as far as I'm concerned and I plan to avoid them as much as possible.' Heidi stood up, a determined look on her face. 'I suggest you do the same.'

'Understood,' I said, drawing myself up to my full five foot five. I didn't need telling twice; this was a nightmare double-date scenario, but we weren't trapped together in a cupboard, we'd be on a thousand-foot boat. Plenty of room to avoid each other – if we saw each other at all.

Three

Wednesday 23rd June

The journey to Dover was hit by weather chaos every step of the way and it was a relief when the taxi finally pulled into the harbour. Hurricane-level rain as we'd thundered through the Surrey Hills on the train, then sunny as you like on the south coast with the calming slosh of waves leading us towards the boats. Enormous seagulls circled overhead, cawing loudly and dive-bombing tourists as they tried to tuck into their fish and chips.

'Look at the size of it!' Heidi cried, ducking as one swooped past us, scanning for food with angry, yellow eyes.

'The seagull or the ship?' I said, staring up in horror at *Esmeralda*.

The cruise liner completely blocked the horizon, the sun bouncing off the windows as hundreds of black dots moved around the decks. The crew must have been scrubbing for weeks for it to shine so bright, with both the Union Jack and the Portuguese flag at full mast, fluttering in the wind. I had a full-on *Titanic*-panic as

I looked at my holiday home for the next fortnight. How did it float? HOW? I'd convinced myself the ship would be so big it wouldn't feel claustrophobic at all. But standing here next to it, feeling so small and insignificant, was giving me palpitations. It was four times the size of their other ships and I'd be sleeping in a tiny tin bed, inside a tiny tin bedroom aboard a gigantic TIN BOX that somehow floated on the water. With no one to help if anything went wrong. The boat version of Russian dolls. My breathing went shallow and the volume of the world suddenly went quiet, replaced by a ringing in my ears. I was going to faint.

'Kat? Are you OK, love? You've gone slightly green.' Heidi put her hand on my forehead.

I gave her a weak smile and nodded. Excalibur Cruises was *my* account, and nobody was taking it from me – not without a massive fight, at least. I was getting on that boat no matter what, and I'd be sleeping in that teeny, tiny tin bed.

'I'm just hot,' I said, using my hand as a fan and looking around. 'I need a drink.'

'You and me both,' Heidi said, swiping two champagnes from the meet-and-greeters at the bottom of the ramp. The crowd were mingling while they waited to check in, and there was a day one party going on, with a DJ and drinks. Checking in and getting on board was a whole event in itself and the soon-to-be cruisers bobbed along to nineties tunes in anticipation while they stood in the make-shift queue. Champagne wasn't the kind of drink I'd had in mind, but I made the best of a bad situation and knocked it back, clocking all the fifty-somethings nudging forward eager to get on the ship. My soon-to-be holiday besties. There was clearly a cruising *look* – and neither Heidi nor I were wearing it. The men were in navy jackets and pink trousers, with boat shoes and no socks, while the women fluttered around like excited butterflies in floaty dresses and Panama hats. Purples, greens, pinks and yellows – my black shorts and matching jacket were stuffy and dull in comparison.

'I'm overdressed,' I said, nodding at them.

'You're dressed to impress, which is exactly how it should be,' Heidi replied. 'We're working, remember – this lot are all on holiday.'

I was always in awe of the perfectly buffed women with manicured nails and swishy blow-dries when they arrived on holiday. That was occasionally how I looked on the flight home, once I'd had a fortnight's peace and time to think about myself, but never on the way out. It was hard to commit to appointments when I was on client-call twenty-four-seven. I'd cancelled the hairdresser so many times over the years that they wouldn't let me book anymore; I could only go on standby. My holidays these days were all about powering down and recuperating, which usually started with a solid day of sleep. I'd crawl exhausted onto the plane, looking a total wreck, with a plan to beautify myself once I'd arrived. A plan that worked less than five per cent of the time.

'Kat! Heidi!' A bronzed hand with bright red fingernails and adorned with gold rings waved above the crowd, and Brooke's face appeared through the melee. 'There you are!' she gushed. 'I've been hunting everywhere.' She was wearing a burnt-orange dress, with gold sunglasses and sandals to match. A willowy flame with a feathery white cape, and certainly not dressed for work.

'Morning!' Heidi and I sang in unison, then kicked into profesh mode, speaking over each other in our rush to ingratiate ourselves.

'We're so excited to be here!'

'The ship looks amazing!'

'Thank you so much for having us.'

Brooke waved away our platitudes with a fan she'd flipped out of nowhere. 'Not AT ALL. You need to understand the product to sell it – right? You should be on these cruises once a quarter at the very least. How else can you keep your ideas fresh and relevant?'

'It's a good point,' Heidi said.

'And I'm sorry but the recent PR has been looking anything but.'

'Do you think?' I said, slightly shocked at her blunt delivery.

Brooke beamed, as if she wasn't delivering devastating news. 'That's why Fran had to go if you want the truth. But we don't know for certain that she was the problem – it might have been you guys for all I know. Hell, maybe it was a combination of y'all, but we'll find out soon enough.'

A sucker punch delivered with a spoonful of honey. The *cruising queen* was a total sociopath. I mirrored her smile with an uncomfortable nod, despite myself.

'Morning, Brooke,' a throaty voice said over my shoulder. I turned to look and there he was. The super-smooth PR-star who had ruined my life.

'Leo Kendrick! There you are!' Brooke drawled, giving him a double air kiss.

'Here I am,' he said, lifting his sunglasses with a grin. I'd forgotten how handsome he was with his thick, jet-black hair and dimples. 'How are you Brooke? Excited for the trip?'

'Hell, yeah. It's everything I love all at once. The ocean, travel, work – and competition.'

Leo laughed and held out his hand. 'Speaking of which. Good to see you again, Heidi, and Kat… it's been a while.' His palms were cool and solid like a professional businessman. Mine were hot and sticky like a grubby gremlin and we held on a fraction too long making eye contact for the first time in years.

'It has,' I said, a convincing smile concealing the irritation I felt at being in his presence. 'How have you been?'

'Very well, yeah. Incredibly busy,' he said, raking a hand through his quiff. 'You know how it is in agencies – there's either too much work and not enough staff or too many staff and not enough work. Right now, it's the former, so we're recruiting.'

'Nice problem to have,' Heidi said. 'And Dinky Drinks have settled in?'

It still stung to have lost that pitch to them. Our campaign had been so bloody cute. A school sports day of kids dressed as fruits racing for the win, then drinking their Dinky Drinks together in wholesome harmony. Amplify had gone down the organic, fresh fruit angle – which put the focus on the parents, and the client had loved it.

'Yes, the ads go live next month,' Leo said. 'Feels like we've been to every fruit farm in Europe these past few months but we're happy with the result.'

'And now you're off again!' Brooke said. 'You're in demand! Everyone wants a piece of you.'

'I don't know about that,' Leo said, abashed. 'But I'm very glad to have every piece of me here. We are delighted to be pitching. I'm looking forward to adding the Excalibur Cruises logo to our website.'

I flashed him a filthy look and he laughed. 'Let's not get ahead of ourselves, shall we?'

'Now, now, children,' Brooke interjected. 'Play nice.'

'Are you travelling on your own?' Heidi asked.

'I hope not. My creative director, Zach, should be here somewhere.' Leo arched his nicely moisturised neck to look around the crowd as *Esmeralda* gave a prolonged blast of the horn and sent a shit-tonne of smoke into the atmosphere. 'Ah, I see him.' Leo put his fingers to his lips and whistled, and Zach ambled over like a well-trained dog, wearing baggy shorts and carrying a large leather man bag.

'Alrigh'?' he said, in a Welsh accent, giving us all a slight nod.

'Zach, you know Heidi and Kat from Northstar PR,' Leo said. 'And Brooke, of course.'

'Of *course*,' Zach replied, shaking our hands in turn. 'Good to see you again.'

We'd crossed paths briefly at the Dinky Drinks pitch, when they'd arrived early, presumably to check out the competition. The pair of them walking in was an impossible image to forget – both well over six foot, Zach with his bright blond perm and wire-framed glasses and Leo super clean-cut in his sharp blue suit. They were renowned in the industry as a formidable team and a well-oiled pitching machine, and once we realised we were up against them, we knew we were in trouble. But I wasn't going to let history repeat itself. This time, we'd be ready.

'Well, ain't it just peachy that y'all know each other?' Brooke trilled, delighted. 'Just a bunch of good old pals goin' cruisin' together.'

We side-eyed each other and laughed. More like a bunch of angry snakes trapped in a bag together.

Esmeralda sounded her horn again and there was a kerfuffle at the front of the crowd as trays of empty champagne flutes were marched back up the ramp and onto the boat. An over-tanned man in a captain's uniform blew a whistle and everyone went quiet.

'Welcome, ladies and gentlemen. My name is Thiago, and I am your captain for the next two weeks aboard the beautiful *Esmeralda*.' He waved up at the boat, gleaming in the sunshine, and everyone cheered. Leo was already filming on his phone, and I felt immediately on the back foot as I scrambled to do the same. The game had already started, and we weren't even on the ship yet.

'It is my humble pleasure to have you as my guests as we sail to the Azores, Madeira and on to Lisbon. Thank you for your patience as we all board the ship; we have one more hour until we set sail, so please be ready with your ticket information while my team help get you onto the *Esmeralda* and show you to your cabins. Thank you and *bon voyage*!' The crowd cheered as Thiago pressed a button and a confetti cannon exploded.

'Right, you four – follow me,' Brooke said, taking control. 'Let's check-in – we don't need to queue.' She marched us to the front of the line and flashed her ID badge.

'Let the fun begin,' Heidi murmured, as we ran after her.

'VIPs coming through,' she barked. 'Brooke Harris from head office, plus agency guests.'

The check-in lady was dressed in lemon feathers and had the energy of Big Bird with her kind smile, and equally gentle demeanour.

'Welcome, Brooke, it's so lovely to have you on board with us,' she said. 'I'll just get Mr and Mrs Binns here checked in, and I'll be right with you.'

An anxious-looking lady in a pale blue dress peered out from behind Zach and her husband pulled her forward. 'This way, my love. We were here first,' he said, firmly, avoiding eye contact as his cheeks went red.

The lemon lady handed them each a plastic card attached to what looked like a real fish. 'Here are your keys,' she said, delighted with herself. 'You are in our Sardine Suite, with a panoramic ocean view, a Jacuzzi, sauna and your own private butler.' *Wow*. If that was what the ordinary punters were getting, I couldn't wait to see what they had in store for us VIPs. 'Our concierge will show you through and we hope you have the most fabulous stay with us.'

Brooke gestured for us to follow as the pair stepped onto the ship. 'No need to go into the full spiel – just tick us off your list and I'll take them through.'

'I'm afraid I can't do that, Ms Harris,' she said, gently asserting her authority. 'We've had strict instructions from head office for you and your guests to get the full *Esmeralda* experience where possible, so Arlo will escort you to your rooms.'

'Fine, that's fine,' Brooke said, impatiently, rolling her eyes. Leo was now taking photos and Zach seemed to be surreptitiously recording the check-in process, while Heidi and I nosed in on the conversation. Gah! I'd missed it again. I was holding my handbag, a tote, my passport and my tickets so I'd have to scribble some notes down later. I couldn't wait to chuck all my stuff on my emperor-sized bed and jump in the Jacuzzi. This competition was going to be mercenary, and I needed to be on my A-game.

Four

Arlo led the five of us up the ramp and onto the ship. The engine continued to pump out clouds of diesel, while the propellers lurched and churned below. I'd been on a fair few Excalibur cruise ships over the years, but *Esmeralda* was something else. We walked through one of the lounges, which looked more like a floating palace than a boat, with its glossy white walls, lavender sofas and gold rugs. Huge straw lightshades swung from the ceiling and a flowery scent had been spritzed all around. I took a couple of snaps while the boat was empty, as we wouldn't get this chance again. The breakfast room was particularly impressive, with its precisely laid tables, bright blue tablecloths and gleaming silverware. The chefs and serving staff were lined up in uniform, full of smiles and happy nods to greet us.

'Good morning. Welcome!'

'*Ciao! Buongiorno.*'

'*Hola!*'

Leo gave one of the chefs a high five, then took a selfie with the whole line waving in the background. 'Good to meet you guys. Pleasure to be here,' he said.

'The pleasure is all ours,' a ginger tank of a man replied, his chef hat starched to attention. He could have been hiding a pint under there. Or a pineapple.

'Great to see you again, Gus,' Brooke called.

'You too,' he said with a wink.

'We used to work together in Miami,' she murmured as we continued down the corridor. 'He can butter my biscuits anytime.'

'You'll get the full tour later today,' Arlo said. I was mesmerised by his moustache moving around like a little caterpillar as he enunciated. An unusual choice for a bald man. We walked past one of the cabaret lounges and I couldn't resist a quick nose in, even though the door was shut and covered with a curtain. I opened it just a fraction, while the others went on ahead, and it was like peeking into a different world. A stage with heavy crimson curtains either side dominated the space, with rows of velvet chairs laid out cinema-style for the audience. A half-dressed drag queen walked the floor, lip-syncing to 'Pink Pony Club' and stopped mid-strut when she spotted me.

'Stop the music, Dahlia. Stop it… STOP!' she barked, in a broad Lancashire accent, glaring at a curly-haired girl with a headset. 'There's an unexpected item in the bagging area.'

'What? Where? Sorry, Barb, I thought that door was locked,' she said rushing over. 'It should be.'

'I *know* it should be. Are yer lost, love?' Barb bellowed across the dance floor. 'Guests aren't allowed in here, I'm afraid.'

'I'm not a guest – I'm staff,' I replied. 'Sort of.' Heidi appeared behind me, then Brooke pushed past us both and Barb looked about ready to explode.

'How many of you are there?' she said, adjusting her hair net. 'Pardon me, ladies, but "sort of staff" aren't welcome, either. This isn't a Tupperware party.'

'Calm it, lady,' Curly said, with sass. 'Brooke? Is that you?'

'Dahlia! Sure as hell is, sweetie-pie.' They screamed and ran to each other for a hug.

'Guys – this is Dahlia Jackson, our new head of entertainment and all-round legend. I managed to poach her from The Bellagio, and we go waaay back.'

Dahlia laughed. 'Now, now. What happens in Vegas, remember...'

'Yes, that's as much as you'll ever know,' Brooke said with a mischievous grin.

Leo, Zach, and Arlo had followed us in and there were now six of us standing inside the door. It was decidedly plush with its polished floors and mirrored tables, and a cocktail bar that ran the full length of the room. Barb surveyed the situation from the stage, then pointed a pink talon at me.

'You don't work here. I've got a nose for the staff and I've sniffed them all. Explain yourself.'

'We're here with head office,' I replied breezily. 'We're your PR agency.'

'For now,' Leo murmured, with a twinkle in his eye.

I ignored him. 'And you must be this season's star?'

'Barbie Queue, at your service. Loves a good banger.' She slut-dropped then twerked her way back up. 'Singer, dancer, compère – you name it, they've got me doing it. For no extra pay, obviously.'

'Queen of the Cabaret,' Heidi said. 'We'll be cheering you on from the front row.'

Not another one. How many queens did one boat need?

'NO PHOTOS!' Barbie Queue shouted, as Zach clicked away. 'Flamin' 'eck! No one wants to see this Hokey Cokey abomination. One leg in and one leg out. Delete them right now and come back when I'm in full hair and make-up.'

'Apologies,' Zach said, raising his hand.

Arlo coughed politely to remind us he was waiting. 'If I can show you all to your rooms? There'll be plenty of time to meet and greet the team once you're settled in.'

'Sorry, Arlo, sweetheart,' Brooke said. 'Come on you lot, he's got a boatload of people to onboard; we shouldn't waste his time.' As if it wasn't her faffing about and gossiping with Dahlia. She gave her one last hug then ushered us back to the door. 'This way, everyone. Out we all go. See you gals later.'

The corridor was pine-scented with a velvet pile carpet, soft and thick underfoot. Everything was so shiny and new. Some might say *untested*. I tried not to think of the *Titanic* again, but it was like trying not to imagine an orange elephant – the mind could be very annoying when it wanted to be. I closed my eyes and tried to gather myself. Panicking was pointless; I was here now and had to get on with it. Besides, I'd be panicking a hell of a lot more if we didn't win this pitch.

Arlo stopped next to a sign that said *Suites* and I was back to feeling excited again.

'Ms Harris, you are staying in our presidential suite, which is in this lift, straight to the top floor and on the right.'

'Thank you kindly, Arlo, that sounds about right.'

Brooke pressed the button and the lift doors pinged open to reveal a smiling bellboy in a white shirt and navy chinos.

'Ms Harris? Welcome on board the *Esmeralda*,' he said, with a quick salute. 'Look after her and she'll look after you.'

'Why thank you so much, sailor. And you are…?'

'I'm Oliver and I'll be your bellboy, your butler, and everything in between during your stay with us.' The Aussie accent went perfectly with his windswept curls and dark tan. There was a free spirit trapped in that staff uniform, and by the looks of his bulging arms and legs it was trying to get out.

Brooke glanced back at us and giggled. 'This is me then. Off I go! Arlo will settle you all into your rooms.' Oliver took her bags and she snuggled into the lift with him. 'Let's meet on the Sun Deck in an hour, shall we?'

'Sounds good,' Leo said.

Brooke was eyeing Oliver up, like a hungry polar bear. 'Actually, make it two.'

Leo and Zach exchanged a look while Arlo sped us to our rooms. Now head office were taken care of, he was less concerned about the chilled vibe.

'Here we are. Ten eighty-five for Amplify times two,' Arlo said. 'And ten eighty-six for you ladies.'

I'd foolishly assumed with such an enormous ship, we'd be on a different floor to the boys, or at least in a different wing. But no, we were next door to each other. All four of us. The neighbours from hell.

'Pop over anytime,' Leo called, as he disappeared inside with Zach in tow.

Arlo pushed our door open and waved us in. I'd seen enough Jane McDonald documentaries to know what came next: a large suite with two double beds, a balcony overlooking the ocean, a Jacuzzi with champagne on tap. I took a deep breath, ready to be wowed, then realised why Arlo had made us go in first. There wasn't space for all three of us. The room was the size of Mum's old shed, with bunk beds, a slim wardrobe and a window I could just about see out of if I stood on tiptoes. Not a butler or minibar in sight. A sliding door revealed a wet room with a tin toilet, and a shower head where you'd normally have a light.

'Your en-suite,' Arlo said, unashamedly. 'Which is self-cleaning.'

He said it like that was a good thing.

'There must be some mistake,' Heidi said, eyeing it with horror. 'This can't possibly be for the two of us. Not for a fortnight?'

Arlo nodded earnestly. 'These are the on-board staff cabins, which is all we had left when Ms Harris requested you join us. The rest of the staff quarters are below deck if you'd prefer to be down there?'

An image of peasants behind bars flashed through my mind, knee-deep in water. The *Titanic*-panic was back. Absolutely not.

'We'd prefer to be in a guest room, Arlo,' Heidi said patiently, as my heart raced. 'We aren't teenage holiday reps.'

Leo appeared in the doorway. 'Little snug next door for me and Zach I'm afraid,' he said. 'We're going to need separate rooms.'

Arlo's moustache twitched involuntarily. 'There aren't any other rooms. The ship is fully booked and I'm sorry but it's above my pay grade to—'

'Don't worry, Arlo,' I interrupted. 'You carry on checking people in and we'll sort this out with Brooke.'

He scurried off as an impatient whistle sounded overhead. The captain was getting ready to roll and there was no turning back. I'd slept in nicer skips after a night out and wasn't convinced I'd be able to squeeze into either bed – they were clearly designed for children, or yogis with full-body flexibility. My breathing dropped and the blood rushed to my ears. We were trapped inside a trap, inside a trap, and we couldn't book ourselves into a hotel, like we usually would. We were at the mercy of Brooke, who must have known this was all they had and was clearly looking forward to pitting us against each other.

'It's OK, Kat,' Heidi said, holding both my hands. 'They either find a room big enough for both of us or we'll get one each.'

'Amen,' Zach called, out of sight. 'There's no way I'm sleeping in this mouse hole. It gets sorted or I'm getting off.'

'Chill, OK? I've said I'll sort it.' Leo tried to smooth his ruffled feathers as I snapped the elastic band around my wrist and took a swig of Rescue Remedy.

'You do that,' Zach huffed. 'I'll be on the top bunk if you need me.'

'Listen.' Leo stood in our doorway, his arms holding up the frame and I tried not to look at them flex. 'We're all in this together, right? We stand strong as a four and she'll have to listen.'

Heidi nodded. 'Agreed. I thought we'd be getting the full VIP treatment – how can we appreciate the guest experience from inside a staff bunk bed? I'll speak to Brooke though, Leo – it's kind of you to offer but we don't need you to be our spokesperson. She's our client.'

'Understood. In which case, I'm happy for you to represent us too, so we're not both on her case at the same time.' Was he being genuine, or just cleverly outsourcing a sticky client conversation? 'We're in competition, but there's no reason we can't be pleasant about it.'

'No reason at all.' Heidi looked at him deadpan.

'Why don't you both go?' I suggested. 'Then she can't play you off against each other.' *And you can't play her off against us*, I thought silently, taking in Leo's relaxed pose and cashmere clothes. He had some serious laughter lines, in contrast to my ever-deepening elevens, so he must still have *some* sense of humour. We'd had so many laughs when we'd worked together at Engelman, however hard I'd tried to keep it professional. We'd been work besties from day one and gone everywhere together. Six months of being a mini-team, working on the same briefs, helping each other work out problems, sharing lunch and trying to fit in.

'Good idea. Let's go,' Leo said, jumping as Heidi marched past him. Fingers crossed they could sort it. Brooke was likely already in her Jacuzzi with a glass of champagne, or face-down on a massage table covered in hot oil. Hopefully, she'd take pity on us and get us upgraded somehow. There was no point unpacking until they got back, so I pulled out my phone to check my emails. The team would be in the office by now and there was always some drama going on.

HIIT Girls Group Chat:

Abi: Hey girls, I miss your faces. Come back and see me soon!

Sara: I'll come to LA anytime. I love your condo, your man and your little dog toooo mwahahaha #couplegoals

Abi: You've got a hot man and double dog combo yourself if I remember right.

Me: I'll take the double man and hot dog combo instead please, if we're putting our orders in.

Sara: Lolz. Are you on your cruise yet? Another one living it up!

Me: Cruising, yes – living it up, no.

I sent them a photo of the cabin to prove it and could just imagine their faces when they opened it. If I was running an anti-PR campaign, this would work as the hero shot.

Abi: Woah. You don't get paid enough for that.

Sara: I heard they have prisons on those big ships. Are you in solitary confinement?

Kat: I wish – I'm sharing with Heidi! Don't get me started.

I heard footsteps stropping down the corridor and poked my head out.

'Back already! How did it...?' I trailed off as Leo shook his head.

'Apparently, we have no choice,' Heidi said, with a face like thunder, as Thiago announced our imminent departure over the Tannoy. 'We just have to suck it up.'

'Oh well, first-world problems, amiright?' Leo winced. 'Poor us, having to cope with a single bed on this seven-star cruise. Millions of people would trade places with us in a snip.'

Heidi's eyes looked like they were about to pop out of her head as she ignored him and barged past me into our room. Leo disappeared next door with a wave and there was a lot of disgruntled grumbling from Zach as he calmly explained the situation. I was sure that if I put my ear to the wall, I'd be able to hear every single word. So much for avoiding the pair of them.

'This was such a bad idea,' Heidi said. 'We haven't even set off yet and I'm already regretting coming. We should have booked our own cabin and billed it back – at least then we'd be getting the full customer experience from start to finish.'

'Well, we're here now so let's make the best of it. I'm happy with either bunk, so you choose,' I said, eyeing up the mini curtains on the lower bunk that were presumably there to give the staff an inch of privacy. It was ridiculously cramped.

'I know it'll be difficult, but let's stay as far away from those guys next door as we can,' Heidi said, folding herself in half and posting her body into the bottom bunk.

'Hmm-mm.' I found a packet of Haribo in my bag and offered her one. She needed some sugar and coffee and then maybe a wine. 'We won't be in here much, anyway – let's just use it for sleeping.'

'That was Brooke's suggestion too, when we were eventually allowed in to speak to her. Seeing the size of her suite makes *this* even harder to tolerate,' she said, looking around in despair. 'She's got a wrap-around ocean view and a rotating bed, lounging around like Lady Muck while we're packed in here like pickled eggs. We need space to get ready and do our hair and paint our nails. And to relax. And *breathe* for fuck's sake.'

She kicked the mattress above her in fury. It was my turn to calm her down.

'We'll be OK, Heidi, don't worry,' I said, but even I didn't believe it. 'We can book daily appointments in the spa and hairdresser's and charge it back. I'll make friends with Barbie Queue and maybe she'll lend us her dressing room to get ready in.'

She stopped for a second at that. 'Do you think she would?'

'Sure, why not? Let's leave our bags for now and go and find the bar. We'll feel much better after a decent Bloody Mary and a bacon sandwich.'

Heidi nodded quietly and picked up her purse. She was well-known to have the occasional strop, but hers weren't panic attacks; they were impatience and entitlement. It was hard to accept a clear no when you always got your own way.

Five

We squirrelled our clothes away when we got back from the bar and stashed both suitcases under the bed, exploring all the nooks and crannies the cabin had to offer to see what we could fit where. The room was impressively space-efficient considering its size, with hooks on all the doors and secret storage everywhere. Brooke had said there was a chance a bigger cabin might 'come up' but I couldn't see how if all the guests had already checked in. If there weren't any spare rooms now, then there weren't going to be, unless there was an unexpected Man Overboard situation, which seemed a bit extreme to hope for. I didn't mind some short-term inconvenience and discomfort for the greater good, but Heidi was going to be a challenge. We'd have to find some workarounds to make it bearable for her. Maybe we could pop an 'Out of Order' sign on the ladies' loos and commandeer them to get ready in. *Esmeralda* would be dropping anchor in the Azores, Madeira, and Lisbon, so we could book into a hotel on those nights, unless Thiago had to count us back onto the boat each night.

Brooke had set up a group chat to connect us all and named it 'Life's a Pitch'. *Hilarious.* Her original suggestion had been 'You better work, Pitch' in honour of Britney, but the rest of us weren't keen. A message flashed up to say she'd be waiting on the Sun Deck once we'd finished freshening up. Our 'air conditioning' was an angry fan clunking in the corner, and I was feeling anything but fresh as Heidi and I squeezed around each other in our rush to get ready, both desperate to get outside.

'Ready to go?' Heidi asked.

'Yup. Tits and teeth,' I replied, with big eyes and a winning smile. We do-si-do-ed the door to leave the cabin, just as Leo and Zach were slamming theirs shut.

'The first summoning,' Zach said, with a wry smile.

'Seems that way,' Heidi replied, po-faced. She obviously didn't want to waste her tits and teeth on him.

Leo was carrying an open laptop, as if he was working on the go, and I hadn't even brought a notepad. I'd been expecting a 'welcome drinks' kind of vibe and only had my lipstick and phone.

'May the best women win,' I called, as they walked ahead.

'We'll see about that,' Leo shot back. 'You might want to start putting the feelers out on LinkedIn. What's that flag they have again, Zach?'

'Open to work,' he said.

'You'd know,' Heidi quipped as she strode after them. 'You've used it often enough.'

'Still stalking my social media after all these years, eh? You need to move on, Heidi.'

The Sun Deck didn't look like any deck I'd ever seen before. It was more like a glamorous rooftop bar, with its white tables and rattan chairs covered in floppy, green cushions. Brooke was already on the bubbles when we walked in, sat on a sofa-swing, looking chic in lilac silk.

'There y'all are. What took ya so long?' Her dress billowed in the breeze as she rocked to and fro, with both bikini straps on show.

'Sorry to keep you waiting, Brooke,' Leo said, swooping in for an entirely unnecessary double kiss and making it awkward for the rest of us. Should we line up and take it in turns to kiss her hand and curtsy? I decided a quick wave would suffice and Heidi followed suit.

'Hiiii! Wow!!! Look at this place,' I breathed. 'It's beautiful!'

'Isn't it just?' Brooke turned her face up to the sun.

'It shouldn't even need PR,' Heidi added, laying it on thick.

'Oh, but it does me darlin.' *Uh-oh*. She'd walked straight into that one. 'The Cool Cruisers campaign just ain't workin' for the young ones.'

Zach guffawed under his breath. We'd been running Cool Cruisers with top-performing influencers for the past three years, and it absolutely *was* working, but it was difficult to challenge her without looking defensive. The campaign followed couples who shared their holiday stories to demonstrate how cruising the Excalibur way was far superior to anything else. OAPs being treated like royalty, forty-somethings celebrating birthdays and partying like it was 1999, and adventure-seekers wanting to visit maximum countries in minimum time. It showed the full spectrum of customers and meant people could always see themselves as the target audience. It wasn't just for the newly wed, overfed and nearly dead.

'Excuse me?' Brooke clicked her fingers at a passing waiter. 'Can you pour my friends some champagne too, please?'

'Not for me, thanks,' Leo piped up. 'I'll take a water.' *Oh no*. He was one of those.

'Two waters, as well, please,' she said, pivoting easily, and the waiter strode off. 'Are you low or no alcohol?'

'Neither,' Leo said, eyes sparkling. 'But if I start on the champagne now, I'll be asleep before dinner.'

A cruising four-ball meandered past us, squealing with laughter as they carried an ice bucket and two pints to the sunny side of the deck. The women looked glamorous, yet full of mischief and the men were cracking jokes, their neatly parted hair thick with gel. It felt strange to watch someone else's holiday from the sidelines. Being on a cruise with people I'd never normally hang out with, or eat with, or sit next to in a swimming costume. My inner voice told me to relax as I inhaled the salty sea air and the smell of coconut sun cream. But I couldn't. I had to stay on guard. Amplify were the enemy, no matter how friendly and casual Leo tried to play it. I'd fallen for his tricks once before, and I'd be damned if I let it happen again.

'OK, ladies and gents. We are gathered here today to witness the...' Brooke laughed. 'No. Let's get serious. I want to talk you through how the next two weeks are gonna go. It's important you have a good time on the *Esmeralda*, without having *too much* of a good time, if you know what I mean.'

I didn't know what she meant. And from Heidi's face, I could see she had no idea either. Was she implying we'd be getting boozed up and playing naked Twister with the guests? Throwing up over the sides? What was her version of *too much*? I daren't mention the cabins again, but the thought of any jiggy stuff happening in those bunk beds was ludicrous.

'You are completely free to explore the boat and enjoy the *Excalibur Experience* in whatever way you please,' she said, which was music to my ears. Heidi and I could indulge ourselves without worrying about having to entertain Brooke or hang out with Leo and Zach. 'And we'll have dinner together in the evening to touch base. I've already booked us onto the captain's table for Friday night.'

'That's incredibly kind,' Heidi gushed.

'*So* kind,' Zach echoed and she gave him a look. 'Almost too kind,' he said, innocently.

'But we wouldn't expect you to host us every single night,' she continued, wrapping up rejection in concern for Brooke's time. Heidi didn't fancy fourteen client all-nighters in a row, and neither did I.

'What an honour,' Leo interjected. 'We'll be there with bells on, won't we, Zach?'

Zach gave a fractional nod and mustered a smile.

'As will we,' I said, quickly matching him. 'Thank you for the invitation.'

'If you're sure you don't mind,' Heidi added, trying to course-correct.

'Not at all, honey. It's already arranged. We'll have other guests with us as well, to give us all chance to get the inside track.'

'Great idea,' Leo said, sipping his water. 'Insights in real time.'

'Then in addition to dinner, there are one or two activities we've arranged,' Brooke said, with a glint in her eye.

Zach frowned. 'What kind of activities?'

'Dahlia, who you met last night, has put a fantastic schedule together, to make sure you maximise your time here and see a variety of entertainment. The ship is so big, it's easy to miss out if you're not careful.'

As if on cue, Dahlia bounded over, her big curls bouncing around her gold hoop earrings. She was in a sporty version of the Excalibur uniform: a mint green sports bra and matching joggers with the tiny sword logo gleaming gold.

'Hey there, VIPs,' she sang, full of enthusiastic pep. 'Fancy running into you guys again!'

'Dahlia, honey, tell these good people what you've got in store for them, will you?'

'Sure thing,' she said, referring to her clipboard. 'Each day there will be cruise ship entertainment for you to get involved with. Does anyone have any aversion to anything? Any dodgy knees? Allergies? Foods you can't eat?'

We collectively shook our heads. Although I wasn't a fan of mushrooms. Or snakes.

'Here is a map of the ship, along with your timetable,' she said, handing us each two sheets of paper. 'We'll start tomorrow morning with aqua aerobics after breakfast.'

Bloody hell. No rest for the wicked. I scanned through the schedule, and it was gruelling. Water polo, drag cabaret, swimming with dolphins, salsa classes, karaoke... the list went on. And worse than that, all four of us were down to do everything together. If we stuck to this schedule, we'd be stuck with the Amplify bros day and night.

I could see Zach having the exact same thought and he nudged Leo.

'This is incredibly thoughtful,' Leo said, smiling slowly. 'It's rare to get such a thorough induction.'

'You're so welcome,' Dahlia said. 'You guys are in for a lot of fun.'

'But wouldn't it make more sense,' he said, pretending to think, 'for the agencies to do the activities on different days? That way we can throw ourselves into it without qualms.'

Dahlia looked between us, confused. 'What's the difference?'

'Without the pressure of the other team watching?' He flashed me a smile. 'No offence.'

'Absolutely not,' Brooke called over, having downed her champagne. 'I am responsible for the due diligence of this pitch and it's important there is a fair and robust process. If you all do the same thing at the same time then nobody can accuse me – or any of us – of special treatment. Both teams need to have an identical experience.'

'So, other than mealtimes – and the activities between mealtimes – we are free to do exactly as we please,' I whispered to Heidi.

'Free as caged birds,' she seethed.

If the Excalibur account wasn't so important we'd have both thrown ourselves overboard by now and started swimming for the shore. But no, we had to work out how to sell these cruises differently, and quick. Brooke didn't rate the Cool Cruisers campaign. *Noted.* So we needed something new that would sell more and do better. And the best way to figure out what that might be was to *become cruisers* and immerse ourselves in the experience like method actors. Whether we liked it or not, we were all here and in it together, and we had to get on with it.

'Any questions?' Dahlia asked, staring us down like an officious PE teacher. We shook our heads.

'Excellent. In that case, ahead of us getting started tomorrow, I was gonna give you a real quick orientation of the ship,' Dahlia said, her blue eyes shining.

'Fantastic!' Leo and I said at the same time jumping up, and even with his head bent down to read the map, I could see Zach smirking to himself.

'Have fun, kids!' Brooke gave us a wave then settled down to sunbathe as Dahlia led the way. 'See you at dinner!'

'Anything you wanna know, you go right ahead and ask. I'm new here, but I'll be getting up close and personal with the guests – I always do. It's my job to keep them entertained, and there's nothing more satisfying than transforming their vacation with an activity they love. The light changes in their eyes, you know?'

The Sun Deck went on and on, with cocooned daybeds for two, where the odd pair of legs poked out from snoozing cruisers. I'd expected it to be more like an Alligator Park, full of writhing bodies on packed sun loungers, fighting for space, but it was much classier than that. Dahlia opened the doors to another restaurant and we followed her in.

'I'll just do you a quick whistle-stop for now to help you get your bearings – we'll be walking around for a week otherwise. Where you'll eat and drink and where you need to meet me tomorrow for aqua.'

'There's plenty of time for us to see it all,' Leo said, staring up at the crystal chandeliers, which twinkled in the sunlight. The dining room was swanky and modern, with pale concrete tables and plum chairs. *Esmeralda* was taking the brand up a notch, that was for sure. Gone were the cheap wooden trestle tables and multicoloured carpets; the floors were now a textured stone and the ceilings were edged in intricate coving. Greg was serious about trying to attract a different type of customer.

'Exactly. So here we have the fine dining restaurant, where you'll eat at the captain's table. Dinner is served at eight on the dot and the food is divine.'

'Black tie I presume?' Leo asked.

'Oh yes. The guests go all out to impress. Tailored tuxedos, kilts and sporrans... the works. Some of the dresses and shoes I've seen wouldn't be out of place at the Met Gala.'

Heidi looked my corporate work wear up and down, and I could see her changing her mind. None of the outfits I'd packed were particularly Oscar-worthy. I'd have to go 'Gaga' and make a dress out of salami from the breakfast buffet.

'Tell me you've got something appropriate,' she murmured, and I nodded. There was no point both of us worrying about it.

Then on to the main bar, which was like stepping into the rainforest, with panoramic views of the ocean. The air was fresh and balmy, with evergreen trees marking out the pillars and wisteria hanging down from the beams. A barman poured out porn star martinis and banana smoothies and guests were lounging around on the sofas enjoying them and making themselves at home.

'Help yourselves to drinks,' Dahlia said, and we all picked up a glass. 'This is one of twelve bars on the ship, but the one we imagine a lot of people will use in the evening as it's so close to the main restaurant. The drag cabaret will be in here as well, with our resident queen Barbie Queue, who you briefly met earlier.'

We all tittered and I wondered if she might be an interesting front for our campaign.

'The salsa classes are in the ballroom, through those double doors,' she said, pointing to the next section of the boat. 'But let me take you downstairs and show you the activity pool where we'll be doing aqua aerobics and water volleyball.'

We finished our drinks and followed her down the spiral staircase and out onto the deck. When she said whistle-stop, she meant it: I could barely keep up. The pool was already teeming with people, splashing about and enjoying the swim-up bar, which seemed like a recipe for disaster to me.

'Are we OK to observe the aerobics? It's not really my thing,' Zach said.

Heidi jumped straight in. 'Same here.'

Dahlia looked embarrassed at the question. 'Sorry, guys, I'm under strict instructions to make sure you're fully immersed, and Brooke wants you to take part.'

'I'm happy with that,' Leo said, with a winning smile. 'I *love* activities.'

'Me too!' I said, not to be outdone.

'That's er... great,' Dahlia said, giving us a strange look. This trip was going to be hell.

Six

Thursday 24th June

Heidi and I made it down to breakfast in record time. Neither of us wanted to spend a second longer than necessary in the bunk-bedroom, and we were up, showered and dressed in twenty minutes. I decided on my red trouser suit with the big sleeves, which I realised was a mistake almost the second we left the room. Heidi had already relaxed into holiday mode in a flowery halter-neck and oversized shades while I stood out like a sore thumb, literally, as neither cruiser nor crew. The dining room was mayhem, with an overflowing buffet full of every possible type of breakfast: fresh fruit, pancakes, waffles with bacon and syrup, cheeses and meats with an array of different crackers. So much food and so many people. Waiters buzzed from table to table, serving, clearing, pouring coffee and delivering freshly whipped eggs. I hoped we could at least enjoy our breakfast without bumping into the others, as I sidled over to the juice bar, but no such luck. Leo was already up and at 'em, and three ahead of me in the queue.

Heidi's phone started bleating and she tutted loudly at the screen, then put on a big smile to answer. 'Darling! How are you?' she cooed, walking off.

'I'll take a kiwi refresher,' the man in front of me said, as I hung back.

'Coming right up. And for you, miss?' The juice man was small and wiry, with a sharp nose and an oversized apron.

'Orange and pineapple crush, please,' I mouthed.

'Sorry, can you speak up?' the man called, causing Leo to turn.

His face lit up when he saw me and I couldn't help but reflect his good vibes. He was still annoyingly handsome; there was no getting away from it.

'The tropical crush,' I stammered, giving him a professional nod and standing up straight.

'Good morning,' he said with a shiny smile, gesturing for the people behind him to go ahead. 'Day one and all's well, eh? How did you sleep?'

I didn't want to have to speak to him, but two weeks in this situation was going to be impossible otherwise. I'd just keep it short. 'Terrible,' I said, rolling my shoulders. 'I feel like I've slept in a drawer. You seem bright and breezy, though.'

'As breezy as a crisp packet blowing in the wind.' Leo laughed, then yawned, looking like a dishevelled little boy. 'Sorry. I'm shattered. The last time I bagsied top bunk was twenty years ago at cub camp, and I was only four foot tall. I just about fit in the bloody thing. Zach gave up in the end and slept on the floor.'

I relaxed a little at his honesty. Maybe he wasn't trying to catch me out. 'It was pretty bad, wasn't it? The ceiling was an inch from my face. I was scared to go to sleep in case I sat up in the night and knocked myself out.'

'There must be somewhere else we can sleep,' Leo said. 'I'll try Brooke again later.'

'We could all pile in with her,' I said, sassily. 'The presidential suite is plenty big enough for all five of us and being able to sleep would be far more conducive to thinking up pitch ideas.'

'Your crush?' the barman said, pointedly.

'No?' I looked at him confused, then at Leo, who cracked up, his eyes twinkling with mischief. He was obviously a morning person. 'Oh, right. Thanks.' I took my juice feeling like a right idiot.

'Shall we sit together and exchange ideas?' Leo teased.

'Sorry, no can do. Heidi wants to catch up privately,' I said, piling my plate with croissants and jam while Leo opted for fruit. *Ugh*. A *healthy* morning person at that. He was too much. We carried our trays to the coffee station and then over to the seating area, where I scanned every table for Heidi. Where the hell had she gone?

'Good morning sir, madam, table for two, is it?' The waiter ran on ahead before we could answer, then waved us over. It seemed churlish not to follow when everywhere was so busy. Heidi had disappeared and I couldn't hog a table for two on my own. 'Here we are. Last table by the window,' he said, flapping out the napkins and laying them on our laps.

'Wonderful, thank you,' Leo said, palming him ten euros.

'My pleasure, sir. Enjoy your breakfast.'

He was such a smooth operator. That would probably get him the best table every morning for the entire trip.

'Alright, moneybags. Tipping already?'

'Always,' he said, turning serious. 'I've got an American mindset when it comes to service, and I like to share the wealth.'

I nodded. 'Very noble of you. Must be nice to have it in the first place.'

His smile faltered for a millisecond and then the mask returned as he chopped a slice of watermelon into chunks.

'Listen, Kat, I'm glad we've got a few minutes to ourselves, as I thought maybe we should talk sooner rather than later.'

'About what?' I said, feigning ignorance.

'You know what. There's no way we can avoid each other the whole time we're on this ship so let's get the Engelman chat out of the way.'

'Let's not,' I said, immediately clamping up.

He frowned. 'Really? Why?'

'It's in the past, let's just forget about it.'

'Can't we please at least have a conversation? Please? I didn't ever get chance to explain or apologise… or anything, and I really want to. I need to.'

'What's to explain? We both know what happened. You presented our ideas to David Engelman as if they were your own and you got the job. You waited for your chance and the second I was off sick, you took it. Have I missed anything?'

'Yes. Just about everything. It wasn't like that at all.'

'Well, you would say that. It's my fault really, I was naïve and stupid, hoping they might find us both a job at the end, and you were just looking out for yourself.'

He looked miserable, but I didn't care. Even talking about it after all these years upset me. 'Am I allowed to tell you my side or are you wedded to the version you've made up?'

'It's a little late for your side now, don't you think? About ten years too late.'

'No, *I don't think*. It'll never be too late as far as I'm concerned.' He was staring at me in disbelief and frustration. 'I tried to explain at the time, for weeks... months, but you wouldn't hear it.'

'What was the point? The decision had already been made.'

He sighed. 'Come on, Kat, we need to clear the air, otherwise every day of this cruise will be a misery – for both of us.'

'We're not here together, Leo, we're on opposite teams, remember? We don't even need to talk to each other.'

'You know what I mean. We've both seen the schedule.'

I took a sip of my juice and stared through the kaleidoscope of salt smatterings on the window. Miles of ocean in every direction. What if we sank? I flicked my elastic band and closed my eyes. *I am safe, I am safe, I am safe.*

'Are you OK?' Leo asked, interrupting my inner spiral and bringing me back to the table.

'Yes, fine,' I said, quickly, pulling apart a croissant and dolloping it with jam. Maybe having 'the conversation' would be a good distraction from the worry of being eaten by a shark. I set my knife down and sat back. 'Go on then. Say what you have to say.'

'Right. Thank you, I will.' He took a mouthful of coffee then paused. His anxious eyes were back. 'Firstly, I want to say I'm truly sorry for what happened. It was honestly outside my control.'

I was already raging and he'd barely started.

'We'd worked for weeks on that presentation, and it was truly terrible luck that you happened to get sick on the day we had to show the bosses.' He looked at me with big, sorrowful eyes. 'I did ask if we could push it off a day or two, but you know how it is.'

'Lucky old Leo. In the right place at the right time.' I'd meant it to sound sarcastic, but it came out caustic and bitter.

'Please don't. You're acting like I deliberately sabotaged you, but it was no one's fault – we both worked hard for that job and the stars aligned for me on the day. It could just have easily been the other way around.' He looked genuinely devastated about the whole situation. And it was true, what could he have done, really? It wasn't his fault I was off sick, or that PR is a man's world and men like to hire men. 'Honestly, it wasn't easy for me either, you know. I didn't want to present without you, but I had to. I made it clear it was both our work.'

'But out of sight, out of mind, eh?'

'I get it. You were disappointed, just like I would have been if you'd got the job. Which is genuinely what I thought was going to happen – you were much more talented than me. You probably still are.'

I snapped the elastic band again, this time out of habit. 'Yeah, but you looked the part, with your big quiff and expensive suits – which is half the battle in PR.'

'It was luck of the draw; I honestly believe that. We were both qualified and more than capable – either one of us could have got that job. It just so happened it was me.'

What else was there to say beyond that? He was so measured and mature – but then, maybe I'd be more confident and reassured, if I'd got the job.

'There you are!' Heidi rushed over interrupting us in a frazzle, dismissing Leo with a nod.

'Morning,' he said, biting into an apple.

'Sorry, Kat, I'm not going to make it to aqua aerobics.' Heidi waved her phone at me, as if no further explanation was needed.

'Why? What's happened?'

'The cat's been rushed to the vet and Sam is a wreck.'

'Righttt,' I said, not clear how that gave her a free pass.

'I need to be on FaceTime for the appointment,' she said, as if it were obvious. 'Penfold needs his mummy, Kat. Have some humanity!'

I caught Leo's eye as he smirked into his apple then instantly regretted it as I tried not to laugh. She was losing it. Or lying. But fair play. I didn't much fancy jumping around in a pool with lots of strangers either. 'Of course he does. Say no more.' I'd sit out the next activity and let her take one for the team. Two could play that game.

I couldn't remember the last time I'd been to an aerobics class, or in a swimming pool for that matter, and I was not looking forward to a combination of the two. Aqua aerobics was for old ladies and toddlers, not for thirty-something Londoners. But if I was worried about my street cred, it was nothing compared to how the boys must have been feeling. I spotted them limbering up on the other side of the pool, and without Heidi to hang out with, headed over for moral support.

'Ready for it?' I asked, as I put my beach bag down and whipped off my sarong. I'd picked up the wrong sized swimming costume in my pre-cruise panic-shop but apart from a few wrinkles in the middle, you'd never know.

'I was born ready,' Leo said, lowering his froggy goggles. 'Bring it on.'

'Can't wait,' Zach scowled. 'Heidi's binned it off, then? Course she has. She's far too important to be swimming with the plebs.'

'No shade please, her cat's not well, so I'm representing us both.'

The music was already pumping, and Dahlia stood in front of the pool clapping in time to the beat.

'Aqua aerobics is starting in FIVE MINUTES,' she hollered, holding her hand in the air, then dropping into a lunge.

The pool shimmered turquoise as people catapulted in from all sides. Diving, bombing and slithering in to get involved in the session. It was a huge relief as I'd been worried it might just be the three of us, while everyone watched us, cringing. Zach and Leo did a running jump, while I lowered myself into the icy water with a shudder. I'd been sitting in the sun too long and had overheated. Several lines had already formed in front of the 'teacher', so we had to join at the back and tread water in the deep end.

'Good morning!' Dahlia shouted, whooping as the music got louder. 'Shall we do this?'

She didn't wait for an answer before starting the routine, stamping her feet and waving her arms to 'Wake me Up' by

Avicii while everyone copied the moves. Except me. My legs were too short to stamp, and I needed my arms underwater to stay afloat.

My swimming costume was now ballooning around my boobs, and I sneaked a glance at Leo and Zach who were enthusiastically following the actions, switching from the wave to draw a loop above their heads as they turned. Fifty pairs of eyes were suddenly on me as the class did a slow one-eighty, while I thrashed about like a cat in a bath and nearly lost a tit.

'You alright there, Kat?' Leo called, as I tucked myself back in and bobbed through the bouncing bodies to the shallow end.

It was impossible to answer him without getting a gob-full of water, so I kept moving, relieved when I could finally feel the floor beneath my feet. I stood next to a woman who was taking it very seriously and did a half version of her movements for the rest of the class, grooving to the rhythm in my own little world. There was something surreal about exercising in a pool, on a boat, in the middle of the ocean and I wondered if there was anything pitch-able in it. It was the epitome of *dance as if no one is watching*. We were all doing something we could never have imagined, with people we'd never met before and were unlikely to see again. Although – wasn't that the same as every holiday anyone ever went on? We launched into star jumps and I could see Leo at the back diligently aerobic-ing while Zach sat on the edge of the pool taking photos, his muscles flexing as he tied his hair back and grabbed his vape. The pair of them seemed so cool and focused, while Heidi FaceTimed her cat and I nearly drowned in the pool. We needed a much tighter game plan if we were going to storm this pitch. Amplify were not behaving like the underdog in any sense of the word and we couldn't afford to let them get in our heads – or more importantly, Brooke's ear. This account should be ours to lose, but it didn't feel like that anymore. We had a fight on our hands, and if that meant playing dirty to win, then that was precisely what we'd have to do.

Seven

'Strategy-wise, I think we'd be smart to get to the captain's dinner early tomorrow night and stick to Brooke like glue,' Heidi said, lowering her voice. 'We want to be sitting either side of her during the meal.' We'd been brainstorming in the Japanese zen garden for over an hour now and both our notepads were full of scribbles.

'Can we choose where we sit?' I said, thinking there'd be no way Leo and Zach would let us get away with that. Or Brooke for that matter. 'Due diligence' and all that. 'There's bound to be a table plan. They can't have any old random sitting next to the captain.'

'A-ha. The early bird switches the place settings,' she said, tapping her nose. 'We're only interested in where Brooke is sitting in relation to us so it's a double switch at most.'

'Sneaky tactics. I like it!' I didn't particularly fancy a client sandwich for dinner, but we needed time to understand what made Brooke tick and get a sense of what she might be looking for.

We had the rest of the day off to experience the cruise through guest eyes and enjoy ourselves. But while I'd planned to sit by the pool with my book and a bottomless pina colada, Heidi had other ideas. She wanted to map out creative territories for the pitch and feed them back to the studio in London. There was a game of croquet going on and cruisers running around enjoying the sun and instead of the creamy cocktail I'd envisaged, Heidi and I were sharing a calming pot of jasmine tea.

'Did you see the dress code is chess-themed?' she said. 'I read it on the app.'

'What? No? As in black and white or dressing up as pawns?' My mind went to the denim dress I'd planned to fancy up somehow for dinner and how I might still make it work. 'I thought it was *dress to impress*?'

'I know. I got it wrong. Can you wear your "impressive dress" and go as a queen? What colour is it?'

I hated being on the back foot. Any theme-related changes would have been useful to know when I was at home, packing. 'Pink,' I blurted out, knowing she'd freak if I said denim. However cool or glamorous I'd planned to make it look, Heidi was very anti-jeans. 'I could put a paper crown on and go as a fairy queen?'

'Or pretend you misunderstood and go as a prawn?'

'What are you wearing?' I asked, getting palpitations.

Heidi flushed with pleasure at the question, desperate to talk me through it. 'I've got a black lace gown, with a full skirt and petticoats and a fitted bolero jacket.' As you do. 'I just need a crown to go as the black queen. I've been keeping an eye out for something to repurpose.'

'Like a lampshade?'

She rolled her eyes. 'Possibly. If it's a small one. If I can't find anything appropriate then I'll plait my hair in loops and cover them in necklaces.'

'Awesome,' I said, my brain whirring. *What the hell was I going to wear?* And more importantly, who takes a bolero jacket on holiday? This was giving me a headache. 'I'll have a think about how to play it – don't worry.' Like I didn't have enough going on.

Heidi had loads of dresses and hadn't offered to lend me one, so she couldn't be that bothered about my outfit. Her eyes narrowed. 'As long as you don't show me up.'

'I've got plenty of options,' I said, mysteriously, which was a lie and having seen some of the outfits being flaunted on deck as daywear, I had nowhere near the right level of glitz for the occasion. 'In fact, I might just pop back to the room now and have a look-through.'

I could feel panicked tears coming and tried not to blink, waving my hands in front of my face to dry them out. I needed to stay focused and logical and work out what to do. I kept my face hidden and raced down the corridor towards my cabin, turning a corner too fast and colliding with Barbie Queue. She was dressed in green velvet with long blonde plaits and a thick fringe, and even without the stage setting and the microphone was still a force to be reckoned with.

'Hey,' I said quietly, with a half-nod.

'Ey up, cock!' she called, striding past, then stopped sharp and turned. 'Are you OK, love?'

'Fine,' I muttered, speeding up.

'You might want to tell yer face that. You've not been cryin' 'ave yer?'

I rubbed at my cheeks, embarrassed. It would sound superficial and vain if I admitted I didn't have anything dinner-appropriate to wear and I didn't want her to think I'd be so pathetic as to get upset over something so trivial. But it was deeper-rooted than just the dress – it reinforced my imposter syndrome when I tried so hard to fight it. Proof that I didn't really belong in this world, even after all this time. That I wasn't properly prepared and didn't know how to act. This would never happen to the likes of Heidi or Leo. People with money were always prepared. They instinctively knew what to do in every situation and that was what set them apart.

'It's silly, honestly, please don't worry.' I quickened my step to try and get away, but she rounded on me and blocked the path.

'Hey, hey, *hey*… this don't look like nothin' to me! What's goin' on?' she said, catching me up.

I felt like a right prat now.

'I don't have an outfit for dinner at the captain's table tomorrow night. I missed the memo about the chess theme.'

Barbie's concerned frown switched to an eye roll, her eyelashes fluttering. 'You're crying *actual tears* because you need a dress?!' she said, incredulous. 'I can sort that out for yer in two minutes flat. Come with me.'

'Can you?' I felt a rush of relief as I trotted after her. Although the green monstrosity she had on wasn't going to cut it. 'I'm not sure your… er… *look* will be quite right to be honest, Barb. No offence.'

'Fear not, *mademoiselle*, you ain't borrowing this one. This is me Broccoli Spears frock, for Britney,' she said, pulling a coniferous hat from her pocket and putting it on to sing. 'I'm not a girl, not yet a woman...'

I smiled. 'Brilliant! How many identities have you got?'

'Oh, hundreds. Well, at least ten. I'm well known as Jackie Potato at Funny Girls in Blackpool so there's a whole farmer's wife sketch for that, but they wanted something more mass-market for the ship, so I decided on Barbie Queue. Keeps it clean for the oldies, you know?'

'And gives you loads of Barbie options for frocks. Perfect.'

'Naturally. I've got all the classic Barbie costumes. Binge-drinking Barbie, Lap-dancing Barbie, Boxset Barbie, and my personal favourite, Barbie Robs Banks. She's a bugger, that one.'

'Count me in for that show,' I said, giggling. 'Ahh, thanks, Barb, you've cheered me right up.'

'I thought about calling myself Dry Jan, but I couldn't quit drinking for the character, unless it was a different kind of dry of course. Then they asked me to consider a water theme, but Sue Nami seemed in bad taste.'

'Well, Barbie Queue suits you.'

'Thank you. And it means I get plenty of sausage, so I'm happy. Now then. Back to your dress dilemma.'

'It needs to be chic and boring ideally. Have you got anything in black or white?'

She gave me a look. 'Of course I have! I've got every colour of the rainbow in 'ere. My wardrobe isn't just pantomime costumes, twinkle toes; I've had all sorts over the years from the great and good of the cruising world. Jane McDonald gave me a dress once. A slinky green number with a red sash. And there was that yellow and black abomination from Dame Edna Everage. *Enormous* of course, but I couldn't say no.' She frowned. 'It might fit you, actually.'

'Charming!'

'I've got necklaces from both the Kylies – Jenner *and* Minogue – Madonna's beret, an eye mask from Cher...'

'Really?'

'Oh, yeah. I've got all the divas on my Snapchat and they're always sending me stuff. My room is a veritable dressing-up box, sweetheart. Don't you worry – I'll find you something dinner-appropriate.' She steered me past a handwritten sign with 'ENTER AT YOUR OWN RISK' scrawled in black marker, and into an Aladdin's cave. Rainbows flickered on the walls as the sun shone through a porthole and reflected off the sequins and sparkles. It was more fancy-dress *ugly sisters* than a *fancy dress* for dinner, but it was worth a shot. I eyed the bustier and flamenco skirt hanging from the wardrobe and Barb clocked my expression.

'Trust me, Cinderella, I have excellent taste. Outside of this,' she said grabbing a handful of the red satin. 'And this...' she said, gesturing to her costume. 'What size are you? Twelve? Fourteen?'

'Give or take,' I replied, wiggling my waistband, which was tourniquet tight. I'd give her size fourteen a whirl. It would no doubt be some highly flammable number, made of cheap, itchy material, so I was very prepared to reject it before I had to go through the indignity of trying it on. She started rifling through the dresses, eventually disappearing into Narnia in a poof of faux fur.

'Now then, where are they?' she muttered, screeching through the coat hangers. I could only imagine the horrors she was hunting for. Hopefully not the yellow fishtail with the black dots I could see hooked on the mirror.

'Aha!' Barb said, holding a dress bag in the air, victorious. 'Here we go.'

She unzipped it and pulled out two dresses. 'I've got these beauties in black: a floor-length velvet batwing and a skintight bodycon with gold buttons.'

It was such a relief to see normal-looking dresses that had potential. If they fit me of course. I held them both up against me in front of the mirror and imagined myself as the black queen. Heidi would be seething if I turned up in one of these when she'd suggested I go as a prawn, but beggars can't be choosers. Either dress would be fabulous and I couldn't wait to try them on.

'And then finally, one in cream...' She held up a full-length shimmer of gorgeousness on a silky hanger, and I instantly fell in love. 'They've all got names and this one is *Ivy*.' It was the most beautiful off-the-shoulder column dress in satin, covered in a zillion Swarovski crystals.

'Wow,' I said, completely gobsmacked. 'OK, you've got me. I'm impressed. Any one of these could be the one, but *Ivy* is my favourite.'

She gave me a knowing smile. 'Told you! AND she stretches so she'll fit like a dream.'

I couldn't bear to hope it might, as Barb gestured me inside a makeshift changing room. 'Try her on and let's see,' she said, closing the curtain behind me.

My clothes were off in half a second and I stepped inside the dress, the cool satin material easily stretching around my sizable arse. Borrowing dresses from drag queens was the way forward it seemed. *It. Was. Stunning.* I pulled the curtain back and Barbie whooped.

'Seeeeeee!' she said, doing a happy dance. 'A perfect pour. Move aside, Gok Wan, Barb's coming for yer job.'

'Does it look alright?' I said, admiring myself in the full-length mirror.

'Absolutely bangin', babe. I wouldn't even bother trying the other two on. Hilary and Delia can go to someone else. You just need a touch of jewellery to finish the look and you're done. I've got tiaras, headbands, earrings – clip on, obviously – bangles, turbans… knock yourself out.' Barb grabbed accessories from every crevice of the room and laid them all out on the table. Pearls, diamantés, silk scarves and feather boas. It was like the haberdashery department at Liberty's. I chose a silver headband encrusted with coloured jewels and a matching clutch. I'd never looked more glamorous.

'Like an absolute queen,' Barb said, clicking her fingers. 'Not a drag queen, though, obviously. *That* takes real effort.'

'A chessboard queen, as per the brief – and long enough to hide my trainers underneath.'

'Ideal if you fancy a quick jog around the running track between courses.'

I laughed. I felt so much better about everything all of a sudden and my stress headache had subsided. 'Leave everything here and you can come back tomorrow to get ready,' Barb said, untangling the remaining necklaces and hanging them on the doorknob.

'Thank you so much,' I said, hugging her hard. 'You're a lifesaver – and it wasn't just about the dress.'

'It never is sweetheart.' She bopped me on the nose with a long green talon. 'You'll fit right in, don't panic.'

I was such an open book. I tried to breathe the tension out and smiled. I'd been holding on tight to the panic in my stomach, and I couldn't believe it had been so easily sorted. Thank God for Barb, she'd seen right through me.

'It's nice to have a friend on board. Let me know if I can ever return the favour.'

Eight

Friday 25th June

Ilay on the top bunk, gearing myself up for the dreaded pre-dinner small talk. Barbie Queue had been so kind and generous with her time, and I wondered if there was a way to work this feeling of relief into the pitch. She could easily have walked on by and ignored my distress, but she'd gone out of her way to help me out. I barely knew her, yet I felt genuinely cared about. There was a kernel of an idea in there about the connections people make on a cruise. A transient group who know nothing about each other, holidaying together for a fortnight and all the shared experiences before you disembark and go your separate ways. I closed my eyes to think. A cruise was so many things. A million different realities, every type of holiday in one, the cruise-connection, the fortnight-family... my head was spinning with ideas as I drifted off to sleep.

I woke with a start and my Apple watch was blank, with no USB point to charge it in the bedroom. I scrabbled about for my phone which said 18.35 and gave me just enough time to get ready and down to dinner if not quite as early as Heidi's plan. She'd taken her outfit to the hairdresser's to get ready after her appointment. I nipped along the corridor to Barbie Queue's dressing room to change, then made my way down to the fine dining restaurant. A pair of suited men in white gloves opened the double doors to reveal the bustle of pre-dinner drinks in full swing. A bevy of black and white dresses surrounded by men in penguin suits engaged in vibrant conversation and laughter.

'Uh-oh, someone's in trouble!' Leo said, overtaking me with a smirk, immaculately dressed in a white suit and bow tie. 'Although that someone is looking a million dollars tonight, hey?'

'Oh… thanks,' I said, automatically breathing in. 'Do you mean me?'

He stopped and looked me up and down. 'Of course I mean you.'

'Why am I in trouble?'

'I'll give you a hint – Thiago is about to make his evening speech.'

My stomach flipped. 'Is he? Really? I'm not late, am I?' I hurried after Leo, checking my phone which flicked from 18.59 to 19.00 as the grandfather clock started to chime.

I felt the heat from Heidi's glare zapping me across the room on the eighth bong and I gave her a confused smile.

Leo shrugged. 'I'd call it perfectly on time, but Heidi's on the warpath for some reason. That woman is never satisfied.'

A deep voice sounded over the microphone. 'Ladies and gentlemen, please take your seats for dinner.'

Shitttt. So much for being early and cornering Brooke. I pushed through all the Champagne Charlies and made it to the captain's table, with Leo in tow, as the second mate tapped his fork against a glass. Heidi gaped at my dress, beaming at first, as if I were a guest, and then giving it a double take when she realised it was me wrapped in cream silk.

'Where *the hell* have you been?' she hissed as I slid in next to her. Our tag-team approach on Brooke would have to wait.

'I'm so sorry, my phone must still be on London time,' I whispered, sounding like a twelve-year-old who hadn't done their homework. She glared at me as Thiago cleared his throat.

'At least you look the part,' she muttered. 'Where have you been hiding that?'

'Good evening, ladies and gentlemen,' Thiago started, and I was grateful for the distraction. 'I hope you have all had a wonderful first day aboard the *Esmeralda*. My team are here for you day and night, around the clock, to ensure you have the best holiday of your life.' He stopped with a smile to acknowledge the smattering of applause. 'We have three days of sailing to enjoy before we reach Terceira Island and we should reach the port in time for breakfast on Monday morning.' There were lots of oohs and aahs, and a tinkling of champagne flutes in appreciation. 'For now, please enjoy your dinner. As we say in Portuguese, *saúde*, or in English... *cheers*,' he said, raising his glass. The crowd chorused back with a mash-up of *saúde*, and *cheers* and the humdrum of chatter continued.

I sensed Heidi side-eyeing my dress. The knowing of a woman being watched. But I hadn't expected to catch Leo's eyes on my neckline from across the table as well. After all this time. Men could never *ever* get away with a sneaky look at the cleavage; they *always* got clocked. Although who could blame him? *Ivy* was pristine and the girls were bursting out of the bodice nicely. I caught his eye and raised my eyebrows, and he quickly turned to Brooke, his button nose in the air. His profile had barely changed in ten years. I'd zoomed in on a much younger version of that face when he'd updated his LinkedIn with the Engelman job, scribbling non-stop in my diary: *Why??? What has he got that I haven't?* I was a straight-A student, with a gold Duke of Edinburgh award, no less. I'd taken guitar lessons and learnt recreational Spanish. I'd done everything my teacher had suggested to make sure my application stood out. *Prove you're fully rounded,* she'd said. *That you're accomplished as well as academic; that you have a personality.* By the end of the process, I had an entirely new personality, and it was as round as a freshly grown peach.

'Why are you staring at Leo like that?' Heidi asked, interrupting my thoughts as the red mist started to swirl.

'Sorry,' I said, shaking myself out of it.

She nodded towards Brooke. 'Time for some client schmooze,' she said and I whirred into action like some kind of sleeper cell PR bot. Brooke was laughing with Leo, and I leant over and joined in, planting myself in the middle of the conversation.

Brooke stopped in surprise. 'Are you OK, Kat?'

'Ahhh, yes,' I said, sipping my wine. 'I'm just having the BEST time. I've been on a lot of Excalibur Cruises, but this one really is exceptional. *Esmeralda* has taken the brand to a whole new level. Don't you think so, Heidi?'

'Couldn't agree more,' she said, nodding vigorously.

'Have you boys been away with Excalibur before?' I asked, widening the circle to bring in Zach – and knowing full well they hadn't.

'Nope,' Leo shot back confidently. 'Which I'm really pleased about, because we're the exact target audience Brooke and Greg want to attract – new-to-the-brand cruisers.'

'Nothing beats fresh eyes for thinking up fresh ideas,' Zach added, with a wicked smile.

'And while we haven't been on an Excalibur cruise, we've been on plenty of others: P&O, Fred Olsen, Virgin… so there's a wealth of knowledge between us. First-hand experience of the competitor brands for the strategic mapping,' Leo said, with a smug smile. 'And it's clear to see where Excalibur fits in the market.'

'Interesting that you've never been on an Excalibur before, when you're both such active cruisers,' Heidi said with a fighty glint in her eye.

Zach held her gaze and shrugged. 'I'd not heard much about them.'

Brooke shrieked with laughter. 'Doesn't say much for the PR then, does it?!' Heidi turned beetroot, furious to have walked into Zach's trap. 'Just kidding – we've been badly let down by our media agency, so I'm switching them out as well. Who cares how good the messaging is if the punters don't see it. Right?'

'Right,' I said, feeling sick at her slip of the tongue. *As well?* A blur of waiters placed our starters down and we waited for Thiago to begin, like the proverbial bride, then tucked in. Butterfly prawns with a lobster bisque sauce, sundried tomatoes, and onion croutons. Dahlia was right, the food was incredible – delicately flavoured seafood to rival the best restaurants in London.

The waiters reappeared to take our empty plates, leaving Heidi's next caustic remark on the tip of her tongue. We had to be better than this. Brooke watched the ping-pong with a wicked smile, clearly enjoying the show, but putting her in the middle of a childish bitch-fest was not the way to win her heart. We needed to show her a good time while convincing her we were good people. Her wanting to work with us was almost as important as her buying into our ideas. Whatever they might be.

The waiters went from table to table presenting delighted guests with their main courses. More fish. Which was to be expected. They were probably reeling them in over the side of the ship day and night. There must have been five hundred people eating at once – maybe more – and the maths was mind-boggling. How was it possible to cook so much food to such a level of perfection? They must have a hundred ovens down there or fifty chefs, or both.

'Thiago, who is in charge of the ship while you're eating with us?' I asked, keen to understand the magic behind the performance.

'It'll be on autopilot,' Zach quipped.

Thiago smiled. 'It's a good question and as you are our special guests, I will tell you my secret. I am the face of the captain on the ship. I do the hosting and the speeches, the photos and announcements. I am here for reassurance and to manage the customer service side of being a captain, if you will. You are right to ask how I can possibly then steer the ship at the same time and the answer is, I don't.

There is a second captain, my brother, Matthias, who runs the wheelhouse, with the help of our second mate, Stefano, here.' He slapped Stefano's tattooed arm and he gave a gappy nod. He didn't speak English – he was just here to tinkle his glass and eat.

'Interesting. So you would be the captain for our photo shoot if we need one?'

Thiago flexed his muscles. 'Anytime. Add model to my duties, no problem.'

'Giving away your ideas, Kat?' Leo said.

'Help yourself,' I replied with a saccharin smile. 'If taking a photo of the captain is something you haven't considered.'

'It's an old PR trick I learnt years ago,' Heidi added, sardonically. 'I think they call it *showing the product to the customer*.'

Brooke squealed in delight. 'They've got you there, Leo!'

I put a chunk of fish in my mouth. Yeah, *Leo*, I thought, spearing a potato with my fork. The food was unbelievable. Dover sole and roast potatoes with green beans – not so far away from the beige dinners of my childhood. Fish fingers with smiley faces and peas proudly served by Mum. Home-cooked microwaved dinners had been her specialty.

I had a roast potato stuffed in each cheek and was desperately trying to chew my way out of the situation when I felt a tickle in my throat. I swallowed and the tickle turned into a scratch. *Oh no. No.* A fishbone. I coughed discreetly to try and dislodge it, and took a mouthful of wine, but it was too late; it was already in my throat and stuck. I gulped down some water then spluttered as it met with a more assertive cough and Heidi flashed me an irritated look as I tried to clear my throat again. Leo locked eyes with me across the table and offered a discreet thumbs up as I launched into a full coughing fit. I shook my head and he sent a glass of red flying as he ran around the table and dragged me out of my chair. Suddenly waiters were rushing at me from all sides, and I caught sight of my face turning puce in the mirror as someone slapped me hard on the back.

'What's happening?' Heidi stood up, then froze. I tried to take a breath, but there was no air, and just as I started to really panic, Leo's arms grabbed me around my ribs and Heimlich-manoeuvred me off the ground. On the third jump the tickle disappeared and a tiny bone shot out of my mouth as I bent over gasping, flooded with relief.

'Thank you,' I whispered as soon as I'd caught my breath, my heart thumping. *Jesus Christ*, this cruise was turning out to be a lot more stressful than I'd imagined and I couldn't even retire to my cabin for a bath.

'Are you OK there, doll?' Brooke asked, concerned.

'She's fine,' Heidi replied on my behalf. 'Aren't you, Kat?'

I nodded on auto-smile and sat back down. It felt like the whole room had stopped to watch and one by one they slowly turned back to their food. '*Totally fine,*' I croaked. 'Sorry, I had a frog in my throat.'

'Which is now on the carpet.' Zach sneered, pointing to a blob of green phlegm.

'Oh.' I grabbed my napkin and covered it up, mortified.

'I'm a qualified first aider,' Leo said, solemnly, 'and I think – no, I *know* – you need some space and a lie-down after that. For the shock. You should pay a visit to the nurse.'

I smiled gratefully. 'Thanks, Leo, I think I will. I do feel quite shaky.'

'But you'll miss dessert?' Heidi said, her undertone clear.

'I honestly couldn't eat another thing,' I replied, smiling sweetly around the table. 'Thank you for your hospitality, Thiago, and for the invitation, Brooke, and for your er… help there, Leo.'

'For saving your life, you mean?' Zach piped up.

'No need to exaggerate,' Leo said, putting him in his place.

'Who knows, maybe you did,' I said, standing and gathering up my dress. 'Thank you Leo.'

'Anytime.' His face was full of concern. 'Should you have someone walk with you to the medical centre? Heidi, perhaps?'

She snorted. 'Nice try Leo. Trying to get rid of both of us now?'

'I'll be fine. I just need some air and to get out of this dress.'

Leo's expression changed and I felt myself go pink.

'Anyway. Goodnight everyone.'

I hurried off and couldn't work out if it was the shock or something else that was making me feel light-headed, but my knees were wobbling and I didn't want to embarrass myself any further. I'd forgotten about this side of Leo. He'd been a caring soul back in our internship days and always made sure everyone got home safely on team nights out. That I'd got home safely. And I'd been grateful for him. He had a gift for anticipating problems and had seen I was in trouble before anyone else. Thank God his instinct had been to leap into action.

Nine

Saturday 26th June

My stomach lurched as *Esmeralda* motored on out to sea. The heavy thrum of the engine was no longer registering, but the up and down, *upppp* and *downnnn* was starting to take its toll. Abi and Sara told me to keep my eyes on the horizon and take ginger for the nausea, so I had a second slice of carrot cake and tried to distract myself.

'How about "A Whole New World"?' Heidi suggested, looking up from her notepad. 'We could superimpose celebrities and influencers onto a magic carpet and fly them from ship to ship, then film it with a drone?'

I nodded encouragingly. There was no such thing as a bad idea when it came to brainstorming, but a Disney song and a flying carpet would send our production manager into a spin. I could just imagine her face. Besides, there was no way Walt Disney would let us use that song. We'd end up with the Katie Price and Peter Andre version – not quite the vibe Brooke had briefed us on.

'Love it!' I lied. '*The whole world at your fingertips.*
Excalibur Cruises – where the world is your oyster... and
lobster... and whale... We could shoot big, then zoom in on
the food, the chefs and the marine life? *Under-deck, over-
deck, out on the sea. The cruisers of cruising-don, common
are we.*'

Heidi nodded thoughtfully. 'There could be something in
it, write it down. What about: *You're never too young to
start cruising?*'

I sniggered and Heidi looked at me blankly. 'Erm... could
that be misinterpreted?'

'OK, what about: *holidays for the modern, multi-tasking
family. See it all. Do it all. At once.*'

'*Travel the world. Efficiently.*' I scribbled, then crossed it
out with a frown. 'No.'

'*Around the world in eighty cruises?*'

I laughed then whispered in a throaty voice, '*The ultimate
threesome. You,* Esmeralda *and Phileas Fogg.*'

'Would young people be familiar with Phileas Fogg?'
Heidi mused, sitting back in her chair.

'Unlikely,' Zach said, walking past with a coffee.

Heidi snapped her notebook shut. 'Do you mind? This is
a private conversation.'

Zach rolled his eyes. 'I'd want to keep those ideas private,
too. Is this your big pitch plan? Phileas Fogg?' he scoffed.
'The brief is about modernising cruising, remember.'

'Come on now, Zach – nothing says modern and fresh
like an old man from the eighteen hundreds,' Leo chipped
in with a smile.

'Go away, please. We're just throwing ideas around.'
They were getting on my nerves.

Leo whistled. 'Charming.'

'Believe me, we don't want to hang out with you either,' Zach said, following Leo over to the window. 'But it doesn't look like we have much choice. Dahlia's got the four of us whale-watching after lunch.'

'Back together so soon,' I said, drolly, but I could feel the excitement bubbling up. I'd never seen a whale before and couldn't believe we would be so close to them. I'd always loved animals, marine life especially, and been devastated when my fairground goldfish had gone belly up. Goldy Lookin' Fins had been off-colour for a few days and in my seven-year-old wisdom I'd popped half an aspirin in his water. Dad wouldn't let me get another one after that, but once I had my own place, I bought a colourful tank and three fluttery goldfish to keep me company. They didn't give much back, but they were the only pets I had space for. From that to this, I was beside myself.

'Will they be blue whales?' Heidi asked.

I nearly choked on my cappuccino. 'They'll be blue, but not *the* blue whale.'

'Of course not,' she said, quickly.

'An accidental flick of the tail and we'd be full steam to Honduras, otherwise. They'll be humpbacks I'd imagine.'

'But we don't have to swim with them?'

'I bloody well hope not. I'm committed to my job, Heidi, but not enough to swim in whale-infested waters. However good the photo opportunity might be.'

'Write that down too,' she said, nodding.

My notebook was a mess of scribbles but there was a thought or two worth exploring. I glanced across at Leo and Zach deep in conversation and wondered what they were talking about. It all just seemed like such a laugh to them – I suppose they had nothing to lose, whereas we had half the agency on our minds. Twenty people back in the office with mortgages and children, and lives to pay for, relying on me and Heidi not to fuck it up.

Arlo revved the engine as he traversed the catamaran across the waves at full pelt. The boat seemed quite small in comparison to a whale – and presumably there'd be more than one – so I hoped they were friendly.

'How far out do we have to go?' I shouted as I held on to my hat. The boat bounced aggressively over the waves and my plait whipped me on the back.

'Twenty minutes,' he said, pointing towards the horizon. The five of us held on tight to the cool leather seats, inadvertently jumping out of them every time the boat bounced. Zach was filming through a GoPro, while Brooke tried to hold her skirt together, which was flapping about in the wind.

'Shall we go inside before your parachute takes off?' Leo said, standing up and offering her his arm.

Oliver was behind the bar pouring out glasses of elderflower spritz.

'Is there room in there for a vodka, Oli?' Brooke cooed.

He grinned. 'Sure is, Ms Harris. Anyone else?'

Everyone nodded except me. Adding alcohol into the mix was not a good idea. Arlo had dished out the seasickness tablets as we'd got on board and all this focus on vomit prevention was making me feel queasy.

'Looking a little green around the gills there, Kat,' Zach said. 'You feelin' alright?'

I gave him a tight smile as the boat lurched forward, then ran into the toilet and locked the door behind me. There was a small mirror above the sink and my face was pale and clammy, with mascara smudges under both eyes. I splashed my cheeks with cold water and tried to hold it together. I'd rather be sick and get it over with than carry this constant feeling of nausea, but my body wouldn't play ball. *Come on, Kat, sort yourself out*. Breathe and focus. Breathe and focus. The pep talk helped a little and I prised myself out of my safe space to rejoin the group. Leo and Brooke were engrossed in conversation while Heidi and Zach stood by the window with their cocktails.

'Hey, Kat, you OK?' Leo asked as I staggered over.

Brooke looked at him adoringly. 'Ain't you just the cutest? Looking out for the competition. You didn't slip something in her coffee now, did ya?'

He laughed. 'No chance. I always like a clean fight. There's no pride in winning otherwise. Let me get you some water.'

'Thanks,' I said, my voice weak. 'Any whales yet?'

'Not a sausage,' Heidi said. 'And the more of these I drink, the less I care!'

There was a kerfuffle above us on deck and the klaxon sounded.

'Jesus, is that a... a shark!?' Zach stammered, and we all ran to the window. A sharp fin was slicing through the inky water, heading straight towards the boat. My stomach roiled with fear before a bottlenose poked out. 'No, it's a dolphin, two dolphins... three!' Snouts were popping up all over the place as a pod of dolphins propelled themselves through the water. We had a clear view as they chased each other alongside the boat, taking it in turns to bob up and down and occasionally leaping in the air.

The five of us stood mesmerised.

'Are they talking about us?' Leo whispered. It did look like they were gossiping, giving us the side-eye with their big, cheeky smiles.

'It's all part of the show, I reckon. Putting on the ol' razzle-dazzle for the tourists,' I said. 'Being paid in fish by Greg.'

'First come the dolphins and then come the whales,' Brooke squealed in delight. 'Shall we go up top to watch? I'm sure Arlo will let us into the captain's cockpit, or whatever it's called.'

There were maybe twenty people on the boat in total, taking photos – or trying to – of the dolphins. Brooke went upstairs with Heidi and Zach, but I wasn't keen to be stuck in another enclosed space, so I knelt up on one of the seats to get as close as I could to the action.

'Mind if I hang down here with you?' Leo asked, appearing next to me.

'Do I have a choice?' I said, irritated.

He turned and frowned. 'Have I done something to upset you?'

'No.' My cheeks reddened as he called me out on it.

'I saved your life last night, remember?'

'True. Thanks again for that,' I said, embarrassed. 'Sorry, I'm feeling seasick and salty – and we're back in competition mode, remember.'

'It's a friendly competition though, right? PR is a small world, there's nothing to gain from being enemies – we probably know a lot of the same people. Can't we just be friends?'

It was ridiculous and small to say no. 'Sure, why not.'

I wondered how many more people we'd both know if I'd have got that job at Engelman instead of him. Posh old Leo would have walked into a job with Daddy's contacts anyway, but no, he'd snatched the opportunity from under my nose and it had taken me a while to reboot. And now he was a CEO, and I was a dispensable employee. He'd taken one job from me and there was no way he was going to do it again.

The chattering caws of seagulls reached a crescendo as the boat started to slow. Gulls sat on top of the water, watching as their friends skidded in, taking it in turns to dive underwater and grab a fishy lunch.

'The whales must be close,' Leo said, pulling out a pair of binoculars. 'The seagulls know what they're doing.'

'Ooooooh,' a lady next to me let out a piercing cry. 'I can see one!' There was a shimmer in the water as a whale broke the surface, and then another and another.

'Humpbacks,' someone shouted, among the whoops of excitement. The enormous blue lumps were way ahead of the seagulls, gliding through the water, then taking it in turns to disappear, before bobbing back up.

'Oh wow,' I said, too stunned to take a photo. They were so much bigger than I was expecting. I thought I could see the whole thing, then realised it was just his head; his tail was miles away. The dolphins were tiny in comparison.

'The size of them!' Leo said, offering me his binoculars. 'They must be permanently hungry.'

I could see the whale's eyes and long nose snorting out of the water, the ridges across his back undulating blue and grey. I'd never seen such a huge creature in real life.

'Is it a family, do you think?' I asked, spotting the second whale who was slightly smaller and then the third who was half the size.

'Looks like one. I can't imagine you can leave your giant whale baby at home while you go out to find a shoal of fish for dinner.'

One of the whales waved his flipper, then nosed up and twirled in the air, splashing down into the water below and sending waves in our direction.

'Breaching in the wild,' Leo said, with a low whistle. 'Incredible. You don't see this every day.'

'Are you into… whales then?' I asked.

'Not whales per se; I'm into all animals. I wanted to be a vet when I was little.'

'You wouldn't have seen many whales as a vet, I wouldn't think?'

'Then I changed my mind to marine biologist, and then good old PR.'

I frowned. 'I don't see the connection.'

'There isn't one – they're my two passion areas. I've always been good at telling stories and getting attention. Editor of *The Mancunion* at uni, wasn't I?'

'Were you? Is that a local fanzine?'

He gave me a withering look. 'The student newspaper. Animals are more of a hobby for me now. I've got two dogs, three cats, a cockatoo and a tortoise.'

'Two cocks, eh? No wonder you're always smiling.' He rolled his eyes. 'You could start your own petting zoo with that lot. Sounds noisy.'

'Not at all. They all get along. The cats and dogs are rescues and they kind of look after each other – almost like they know, you know?'

'No?'

'The shared trauma binds them together and now they're safe, they like to stay close. All in the same bed and all that.'

I wrinkled my nose. 'You let them sleep in your bed?'

'No, just one big cat and dog bed for all of them. Not the tortoise, obviously.'

'A blended animal family.'

'I think if you've been abandoned in life, it makes you cling onto the good stuff when you find it.'

'Like this…' I said, as another whale appeared.

'Exactly. Underwater life is something else. We don't even know for a fact that the blue whale is the biggest animal on earth. There could be loads of other things down there.'

'I hope not! The blue whale is plenty enough to worry about without imagining anything bigger. We all know what happened to Geppetto.'

Leo laughed. 'True. Although he survived in the end.'

I sighed. 'I thought PR would be fun and glamorous. Not the hard slog it is these days.'

'Yeah, it's relentless,' he said, swiping us fresh martinis from Oli's tray as two whales breached simultaneously to rapturous applause.

'Obviously this kind of thing isn't difficult, but this is the first PR trip I've been on in a while,' I said, taking a swig. *Oof!* This one tasted like it had a large gin in it. 'This can't be a normal workday for you either, surely? I'm usually either glued to my laptop or trying to get across London on a sweaty tube. Not exactly living the dream.'

'It's much more fun than that at our place,' Leo said, with a wink. 'If we win the pitch, you can come and work for me – how's that?'

I laughed. 'Yeah, right.' The audacity of this guy. He was so obviously used to getting everything he wanted in life. He just had to ask for it. 'You couldn't afford me.'

'With an extra couple of million coming in, I'm sure we could.'

'Sorry, but I'm taken.' I turned my back on him, my gaze laser-focused on the whales.

All three whales breached at the same time and there was a collective clicking as everyone tried to get the shot. Except me. I watched as these magnificent beasts propelled themselves out of the water, then smashed back down, sending waves in our direction. Why were they doing it? Were they putting on a special show for the cruise ship? Was it some sort of dance or were they just playing? This was a once-in-a-lifetime moment that could only happen right here and right now. Being this close to breaching whales with a cocktail in hand, was nothing short of magic. *An Unimaginable Moment.*

Ten

The party had more than started by the time I got there. It was supposed to be a silent disco, but there was plenty of noise as people bopped away together around the swimming pool. It was too late to join in now, surely. Maybe I could give it a miss – would anyone *really* notice if I had an early night? I scanned the crowd, and Dahlia caught my eye across the pool, immediately running over with a set of headphones. *Damn.*

'Oh, hey! Thanks, Dahlia, but honestly, I'm not really a disco kind of person...' She ignored my protest and popped them over my ears. The soulful depths of Kate Bush plugged straight into my brain, and I couldn't help but start running up that hill. Brooke was swaying with her eyes closed on one of the podiums, both arms in the air, on her way to The Upside Down, and the room was alive with flashing headsets in electric blue, acid red and luminous green. Heidi was shimmying in the corner, slurping a dirty martini full of olives and Barbie Queue was quite the spectacle in a black and white ball gown, complete with turtle dove head-dress. The music was all-consuming and took me straight back to the multicoloured dance floors in sticky Bootle nightclubs. I felt a tap on my shoulder and turned to find Leo holding out a glass of fizz. My heart jumped at how handsome he looked in double denim, giving cowboy vibes with his brown leather belt and boots.

'HI!!! THANKS!!!'

His eyes twinkled as he put a finger to his lips. 'You're shouting,' he mouthed.

'AM I??!! SORRY.' I gave him a pained look and pointed to my headphones. Kate Bush, champagne and zero conversation. Yes, please.

The music switched to the *Grease* mega mix and my fingers automatically started clicking. Leo and Zach joined in, but were weirdly awkward, jerking out of time and missing the beat, while I pointed around the room to 'Greased Lightning'. Leo did a couple of robotic moves, then watched me for a second, clearly bemused. Maybe he didn't know the dance. Surely he did? Everyone did. He tapped his headset changing it from blue to green then mirrored my movements, throwing himself into the pointing while Zach moonwalked off to the bar. I nodded encouragingly, trying to show him the next move each time so he could join in, and laughed as he jumped on the spot for the speed-clapping finale. And I thought *I* was high energy. The moon grinned overhead as the song reached its *Summer Ni-hiiiights* crescendo and Leo pulled the straw out of his Tequila Sunrise and pointed it up at the stars. Clearly a move he'd done before as he stood still for dramatic effect. I looked up at him lovingly, *à la* Sandra Dee, to stay in character.

We were both panting from the effort of the performance as I slipped off my headphones to take a breather and Leo grabbed the champagne to refill my glass.

'Thanks,' I said, out of breath.

'Courtesy of Excalibur Cruises,' he replied.

'I mean for pouring. It's nice to be looked after for once.'

'That'll be my rigorous client service training,' he said with a wink. 'Keep everyone topped up – that's what my old boss used to say. In every possible way. Tea, drinks, laughs. Marketable PR insights…'

'Wow, he sounds fun.'

'Massive extrovert with a massive brain.'

'Much like myself then – thanks for the tip.'

He laughed. 'Or it could just be my natural Northern hospitality gene.'

'I thought you were from Chelsea?'

'Haha, I wish. I live in Chelsea now – or close enough, at least. No, I'm a born and bred Mancunian.'

'Are you?' This guy was full of surprises. Every time I thought I'd got the measure of him, he threw his cards in the air again and told me something new. 'They say the Mancs are the friendliest people in the UK.'

'I like to think so. Friendly, charming, hilarious…'

'Let's not push it.'

'And excellent hosts,' he said, with another wink, pouring the remaining champagne into an empty glass. 'Speaking of which, my soon-to-be client seems to be without a drink.'

Leo marched off towards Brooke as Zach returned with a freshly poured pint and sat down. 'Was that a hot new take?'

'Was what?'

'That dance you were doing. A hot new take on "Thriller".' He flicked his fringe, pulling a blond curl out of his eyes. 'I don't remember there being so much thrusting.'

'Why would I be dancing to "Thriller"? It was from *Grease*?'

Zach pointed around the pool at the silent dancers, moving around like confused woodlice. 'Different colours for different decades. Seventies green, eighties blue and nineties red. Me and Leo were in the zombie graveyard.'

'Oh,' I said, looking down at my luminous green neck. Leo was laughing with Brooke, probably at my overenthusiastic teaching style, and I cringed. Of course he bloody knew 'Greased Lightning'. He just couldn't hear it. He'd switched from his own song to dance with me.

'Nice of Leo to play along,' I mumbled. Zach raised his eyebrows and took a mouthful of his pint. 'Is he a big John Travolta fan?'

'Not that I know of.'

'Hey, you two!' Heidi launched herself on us out of nowhere. 'Isn't this brilliant?'

'No,' Zach replied.

'Oh, come on, Elfie – live a little. You used to be fun.' She grabbed his cheeks and squidged them together, nearly losing her balance.

Elfie?

'I'm still fun, don't worry about that,' he said, with a smile. 'Depending on who I'm with.'

'Is Elfie a code name?' I asked, too curious not to, and Heidi snorted with laughter.

'It's because of his ears,' she shrieked, pulling them out from under his hair. 'Elfie Evans we used to call him. See how pointy they are?'

Zach's curls had been covering his ears, but now she'd popped them out, I could see what she meant.

'Hands off the Spocks, Gizmo,' Zach said, putting his hands on hers. 'We can't not mention your nickname, now can we? You always were a nightmare after a drink.'

Heidi rolled her eyes. 'I don't remember you complaining before. Who wants another?'

'Not me,' I said, waving my champers.

Zach gulped half his lager down and stood up. 'Go on then. I'll come with and check out the cocktails. An espresso martini might be in order.'

I took another look at my 'dance partner', who was back to glowing blue and Voguing in sync with Brooke. Leo had made them head mics out of straws and his gaze was on her completely. The same old off-the-shelf razzle-dazzle he'd given me. He obviously *wasn't* my dance partner, or Brooke's for that matter. Not really. He was a schmooze-fest for hire and would likely dance with anyone given half a chance and a chunk of their business.

I put my headphones back on as Arlo walked past and I grabbed his hand. Everyone had someone to dance with except me, and the champers had removed any sense of self-respect or shame that might otherwise have stopped me.

'Is everything OK?' he mouthed widely, his moustache on the run as I vigorously YMCA-d at him. 'Sorry, I haven't got…' He pointed to his naked ears with an apologetic shrug and tried to walk past, but I put my headphones on him to share the joy of the Village People. He looked very confused and possibly slightly… scared.

'Fancy a dance?' I said, taking his hands and giving him a jiggle. I side-eyed Leo and Brooke who were arm in arm with their backs to me. This was ridiculous. How was I meant to win at the silent disco if they weren't even watching?

Arlo played along while I launched into the letters. Y-M-C-A. Y-M-C-A. Performing enthusiastically to no one in particular.

Arlo looked pained to interrupt. 'I can't be up here. Chef sent me to get some clotted cream.' I took my headset back and released him into the wild with a thumbs up.

'NO WORRIES! CHEERS!' I shouted, re-immersing myself in the seventies as he gave me a hurried smile and ran off. He must really hate dancing, or guests, or the Village People. There were a couple of other greens nearby, so I wandered over and joined in. The blending of solitude and togetherness made dancing with strangers less weird as we were all in the same green gang.

Minnie Riperton's 'Lovin' You' started playing and we joined arms and swayed together, mouthing the words to each other. I was between two tall men, all three of us bobbing to a slightly different beat, until it struck me that I should be over there dancing with Brooke as well! Maybe this was all part of the Amplify plan: to ply me and Heidi with alcohol then use Zach as a distraction while Leo cosied up to Brooke. I switched my music channel to blue, painted on a smile and skipped over.

'...which is why I think it's about venturing into the unknown – but in safety,' Leo said as I joined them, stopping abruptly when he saw me.

'Talking shop at the disco? Surely not?'

'I know, right?! He's such a bore.' Brooke giggled, nudging him.

Leo held his hands up. 'Guilty as charged – I was just floating some ideas.'

I rolled my eyes. 'Is that a boat joke?'

'It wasn't, but I'll take it.'

His grin was infectious, full of cheekiness and confidence, and I felt myself being drawn in – even knowing I was being played. Did he turn that same smile on with everyone to get what he wanted? Did it matter? He was clearly doing it here: turning on the charm offensive as part of his pitch strategy. I needed to stay focused on the task in hand. Now was not the time to get distracted.

'I'm happy to step back if you want to chat some ideas through as well?' he said. 'In the interests of a fair process.'

'How incredibly gallant,' I said, with an edge.

'Jesus, Leo, no! I don't wanna hear any more ideas tonight, from either of you. Or while we're on this trip, even. What're you tryin' to pull here? Save it for when we're back in the office, where it's calm and quiet. When we're not drinkin' and dancin' and YELLIN'!'

'That makes much more sense, Brooke, thank you.' I nodded smugly. 'And I promise there'll be no sneaky idea-sharing from our side before that. You don't want to be bothered with every passing thought we have.'

Brooke looked horrified. 'Absolutely not.'

'At *Amplify*, we like to involve clients in the ideation stage of the process as part of the team. It's hands down the most efficient way to work.' Leo sounded like he was reading off a ChatGPT script.

Brooke nodded enthusiastically, confusing us both. 'Wonderful, Leo, thank you.'

'Perhaps that comes under "ways of working" *if* you are appointed,' I said, through gritted teeth. 'Clients aren't normally asked to think up the pitch ideas. They've got enough to do.'

Brooke glanced between the two of us.

'It's more about setting them up for success in the boardroom,' Leo shot back, eyes flashing. 'We like our clients to be a step ahead of their bosses when we present, so they have time to consider the work in advance.'

Brooke tilted her head in thought. 'You both make good points.'

Leo and I eyeballed each other over Brooke's head. He was kind of sexy in professional mode, using his powers of persuasion and a finely tuned turn of phrase to present his argument. NLP in full swing.

'Then we're all agreed,' Brooke said, giving him a run for his money.

'Yes,' Leo and I said at the same time, then laughed.

'Now if y'all will excuse me, I need to go to the little girls' room.' She flounced off, her silky kimono glittering in the lights, leaving us both feeling like winners.

'Nice try, cosying up to the client and trying to get her on side,' I said.

He frowned, exasperated. 'Chill! We were just chatting and it came up. I want this to be a fair process too, you know. We're the new boys, remember. We're the ones on the back foot.'

'It doesn't feel like that.'

'I'm also finding it increasingly difficult to concentrate with you constantly in my periphery.'

I tilted my head, confused. 'Are you? In what way?'

'In every way. This is why I don't mix business and pleasure.'

'Neither do I!'

'At least we agree on that, then.'

I put my headphones back on and Leo's face was a picture as I stormed off. What was he even talking about? How dare he! Did he expect me to disappear so he could wave his work willy at Brooke without challenge? Cheeky bastard. He'd have to get used to me being in his *periphery* for another week or so, at least, whether he liked it or not.

Eleven

Sunday 27th June

Esmeralda left Ponta Delgada in the afternoon, and we were already well on the way to Terceira Island by the time we'd finished dinner. Another gorgeous day on the Portuguese seas, and the warm breeze tickled my shoulders as I sipped my Amaretto on the rocks. I could almost pretend I was on holiday if I closed my eyes, until Heidi appeared out of nowhere.

'There you are! I was about to press the man overboard button. Now. Where are we up to with pitch ideas?'

She looked at me expectantly and I put my drink down with an inward sigh. By *we* she meant *me*.

'Nothing beyond what we discussed yesterday,' I said. 'I'm letting my brain percolate the ideas for a while.'

'OK, well let's percolate together!' Heidi said, clearly having no idea how percolating worked. But there was no appeasing her when she was like this. I repositioned my umbrella and sat up.

'We need to appeal to a younger audience,' I said, confidently.

'Yes, yes, agreed.' Heidi wrote *youth* on an *Esmeralda* coaster in capital letters.

'And the key to unlocking a great campaign is working out what's stopping young people booking a cruise right now and meeting them where they are. Leaning into their reality.'

What's their problem? Heidi wrote next to it. 'Uh-huh, sounds good. Which is what?' she asked from over her glasses. 'What exactly is their reality?'

'It's obvious from the data, isn't it?' She nodded and wrote down D-A-T-A. 'The young people think it's too expensive and for old people and we need to convince them otherwise.'

'Well, yes. That's the brief. But how?'

'That's the part I'm percolating.'

She clicked her pen off, exasperated. 'Well, let me know when you've got something. We haven't got forever.'

There was a flurry of excitement as Barbie Queue emerged poolside in full *Bridgerton* regalia: a pale pink bustled-up skirt and a corset that left little to the imagination. She lifted her petticoats to walk through the bar, then delicately cleared her throat.

'Alreet, kids?' she shouted into a megaphone. 'Who's lookin' the business then, eh? Maureen – that tan's comin' on super, love. And them yellow speedos are gorgeous, Eddie; wish I was wearing my bikini. It's bloody hot in this get-up I can tell yer. Now then, why am I here? Oh yes, touting for customers to come to my show. Anyone fancy enterin' the DRAG DEN? It's like *Dragon's Den* but the roles are reversed.'

There was a lacklustre cheer from around the pool.

'You're the ones with the cash and I'm the terrified, sweaty one trying to remember me lines,' she called, faux-dramatically, staring off into the distance. 'Stood all alone, desperate for one of you – just one – to give me a smile. And then inevitably… all yer money.'

There were a few smiles at that.

'Youuu miserable bunch!' she said, throwing up the Vs. 'Forget it then. If you can't be arsed to join in, why should I bother? I'll take Marge Simpson's wig off and save me-self the trouble.'

Everyone laughed then gave a collective 'aaaaaahhhhhh' in sympathy.

She pretended to strop off then turned. 'Is that really what you want?'

'No!!!' they shouted.

'What you really, really want?'

'No!!!' they shouted again. She had them in the palm of her hand now.

'You'll come then? For the love of a good sausage?'

'Yes!!!'

'I should bloody well think so, too, yer lazy lot. Get dressed and I'll see you upstairs in half an hour.'

She flounced off, her platform boots thundering along the deck as people rose from their sunbeds like the walking dead. It was impossible to see the man behind the act in amongst Barbie Queue's costume layers. Lashes on top of lashes and contouring to such a degree that her face looked like an envelope. It must be like having a split personality to put on that level of showmanship – and make-up – day after day. I couldn't wait to see the full act.

'That's tonight's entertainment sorted then,' I said, finishing my digestif. 'There might be a pitchable moment in there somewhere.'

'Really? What?' Heidi asked, desperate for a confetti cannon of creativity to explode so she could write down an idea.

I shrugged. 'Impossible to know in advance, but there'll be something. That's the beauty of a holiday like this. Is there an angle in Barb's *joie de vivre* vibe? The freedom to be whoever you want to be. Feeling free in every way. Free to travel, free to do as little as you like?'

Heidi snorted. 'I could not feel any less free right now. We're trapped. There's nowhere to go and hide and rest. And so many people are filming – it's putting me on permanent alert. I daren't close my eyes in case I end up as the accidental star of some creep's TikTok.'

'Yeah, I get it. It hasn't been very freeing *for us*. You've also hit the nail on the head for why a lot of people won't fancy going on a cruise. Getting stuck with the same people day after day and not being able to get away.'

'But you can end up having dinner next to the same annoying family every night in a hotel in Crete.'

'What if we flip that thought to a positive. The possibility of new friends, new experiences, who knows what might happen – that kind of thing? The ultimate adventure.'

Heidi rolled her eyes. 'Worryingly interpretable. You could end up overboard... left behind on an island... eaten by a shark – who knows? Anything goes! Hashtag ultimate adventure.'

Life's a Pitch Group Chat:

Brooke: Drag supper is starting soon. Where are you all?

Heidi: Just coming!

Leo: At the bar behind you ☺

Zach: Oh no we're not.

Leo: Oh yes we are.

Heidi and I ran up to the top deck, which had been transformed into a palace, with gilt-framed portraits hanging on strings and a gold carpet leading up to the stage. A chandelier twinkled from the ceiling and there were candelabras on every table. Barbie Queue sat on a throne of sausages with her eyes closed as everyone took their seats. We were the last in and I spied Leo and Zach at the very front, sitting either side of Brooke.

'Sorry, sorry. Excuse me, sorry.' Heidi and I squidged through the maze of chairs, knocking into every single person on the way.

'Just in time, gals,' Brooke said, with a bright smile, as we took our seats.

Zach held up a bottle of champagne and we both nodded as the pianist plinky-plonked a pub-style intro to 'Dancing Queen' and it was a relief to be in and settled before the show started. The five of us cheers-ed then sat back to enjoy the show. Leo looked relaxed in his Pink Floyd T-shirt and tailored jacket, smashing his image as

'PR man on cruise' while Zach was giving out Oscar the Grouch in sage green.

There was the ting of a triangle and Barbie Queue opened her eyes, smiling broadly before she stood up and twerked into the audience, showing us all her bloomers, then launched into the song.

'Who fancies a dance?' Barbie Queue shouted and everyone cheered. The waiting staff were circling with mini sliders, halloumi kebabs and hot dogs, to complement the champagne, and we all scoffed happily while she taught us the dance for the chorus.

'Digging the Dancing Queen looks like THIS,' she shouted, pretending to dig a spade into the garden, then putting her hands on her head. 'Now YOU TRY. Go!'

We had a one-handed go while we held on to our food and drink, then sat back down for the next instruction.

'Stop, stop. This isn't working,' Barbie Queue said, exasperated. 'You're not getting it quick enough. I need some volunteers up front.' She stalked around pointing a sharp talon at innocent people. 'You, and you, then the lady with the pink blouse, yes you, and the gentleman with his mouth full? Both of you, please. And one final lady...' She scanned the audience until her eyes landed on me. 'Kat! Perfect. Up you come.' I swallowed a chunk of halloumi and felt it stick in my throat. I didn't want to be a spoilsport, but I wasn't really one to put on a show... I was more of a behind-the-scenes type of dancer.

Heidi gave me a nudge and Brooke started clapping. 'Go girl!' she called as I found myself standing up.

'Show us how it's done!' Heidi shouted, while Zach slow-clapped and Leo whistled.

There wasn't much freedom in this situation, that was for sure. Trapped and forced to dance, but I had to show willing for the client's sake. I faked enthusiasm as I danced onto the stage and started copying Barbie Queue's moves.

'Get up off yer seats!' she shouted, and everyone jumped up as the chorus played again and I danced and jived with the other 'volunteers' and everyone followed along. Leo caught my eye and dug at the same time as me and we both laughed. He looked quite cute, throwing himself into the dancing and I felt myself thaw a little. Barbie Queue clapped her hands like an angry gym teacher, in-between hitting the high notes. I tried to concentrate on the moves, but my gaze kept wandering back to Leo, laughing with Brooke and Heidi as his hair fell in his eyes.

'Alreet, that's enough of that!' Barbie Queue hollered, and the music stopped.

I jumped down, gratefully and shrank into my seat. No more public dancing for me.

'You're a good sport, Kat,' Brooke said, gleaming.

'Ladies and gentlemen, I've got a lovely little surprise for you this evening. Because not only do you get my glorious voice in your ears, but for one night only I am being joined by my backing singers. Please give it up for… The Cruising Crustaceanssss!'

Arlo, Oliver and Dahlia coughed their way through the smoke machine in identical lobster outfits. They each stood behind a microphone, looking distinctly uncomfortable, while Barbie Queue whipped off her top layer and transformed into Cher.

Leo wolf whistled as she belted out the first line of 'The Shoop Shoop Song', and The Crustaceans did their best to harmonise the chorus. Within seconds we were up and shooping left to right like one big happy family. After three champagnes even Heidi cracked a smile and I was stuffed full of burgers when Barbie Queue came to do her finale.

'This is my favourite song, this one.'

'Aaaaaahhhhh!' The audience were really getting into it now.

'No! It is, like. As you can probably tell, I'm from up north... near Leeds. Ilkley Moor baht 'at for those of you who know it. And growing up as just a small-town girl, I had a massive crush on that there Robbie Williams.'

'Wooooooo!' we all chorused childishly.

She raised a pencilled eyebrow the ugly sisters would've been proud of. 'D'yer know him?'

'Yesssssssss!' I glanced at Leo who was joining in enthusiastically.

'I've got a song I like to sing that reminds me of him. Can I sing it for yer?'

'Yesssssssss!'

'Alright, alright, if you insist. I must give the people what they want, after all,' she said, a hand to her forehead, resigned to her duty. 'I'll need a volunteer.' Leo's hand shot up before she'd got the words out, keen to earn his volunteer credits. 'Yes my love, you with the thick hair. I love a man with nice thick hair. All the more to grab onto, amirite, ladies?'

We laughed as she beckoned Leo up on stage and sat him down.

'Now there are just one or two props that'll help me to... er... get myself *there*, if you know what I mean?'

There were a few sniggers, but Leo nodded innocently, and Barbie Queue popped a halo on his head and slipped a pair of wings over his shoulders. He easily pulled off the angelic look with his chiselled face and cherubic dimples. Clean-cut and clean-living, like a grown-up choirboy.

Barbie Queue launched into 'Angels', crooning intensely in Leo's face as he stared adoringly into her eyes. He could certainly put it on, that was for sure, and he barely flinched when she straddled him. *Was that allowed?* I side-eyed Brooke who seemed to be enjoying the show.

'Should we rescue him?' I asked, lightly.

'Hell, no, he's having a great time. Look at that smile.' She waved over coquettishly while he put his hands under the chair. He was starting to look uncomfortable, which wasn't surprising – Barbie Queue must weigh at least fifteen stone. She got off him eventually and picked up an armful of fairy-lit halos for the last chorus, spinning them out into the crowd and one by one the audience put them on and turned into angels. Glowing and happy and singing along.

Twelve

Monday 28th June

The rest of the Azores were now fully in view, and we were chugging steadily towards Terceira Island. The harbour looked far too small to accommodate the size and heft of *Esmeralda* – something else for my worry list – but presumably Thiago and his brother knew what they were doing. Passengers lined the balconies, waiting patiently in the sunshine as the ship grunted and groaned its way into port, eventually dropping an anchor, or ten, to hold it in position.

Bing bong. 'Ladies and gentlemen, we have now arrived at Terceira Island, and you are free to disembark. You need to scan your cruise card as you leave, so please ensure you have it with you before making your way onto the bridge.'

It felt like we'd been sailing for months and I was desperate to feel land beneath my feet again. Solid, dry land. The greens and blues of the Azores were breathtaking, and it felt like we'd landed in the rainforest, without the flies and the humidity. Fresh, sunny air and a gorgeous mediterranean breeze. I spotted Heidi at the other end of the Main Deck and doubled back down the stairs to avoid her. I wanted to explore on my own for a few hours and listen to my self-actualisation podcast 'You're already there'. I hurried over the bridge, pulling my cap low as Arlo scanned me out.

'Kat! Wait for me!' Heidi called from the back of the queue, but I ignored her and jumped in the nearest taxi.

'*Olá,*' the driver said, turning down the radio.

'*Olá! Angra, por favor.*'

'*Sim.*'

'*Obrigado.*'

That was the extent of my Portuguese – *hello*, *please* and *thank you* – so I was relieved when he switched his light off and put his foot down. No messing around. The guidebook described Angra do Heroísmo, or Angra for short, as one of three capital cities in the Azores and the perfect place to disappear. It was a half-hour drive and it felt good to be in a car again, safely belted into the back, on wide, empty roads. The breeze tickled my neck through the window as I took in the lush forestry and the Mediterranean blues. The air was fresh in a different way to the cruise ship. Less salty and more... green – the diet my doctor was always recommending. Ornate buildings with elaborate windows whizzed by, giving Gothic fairy-tale vibes as we arrived into Angra's historic centre. The grand church stood watch over the main square, a pale blue triumph with duomo-topped turrets either side of an ornate clock. Rows of white villas ran along the beachfront with sandy-tiled tops and colourful shutters, in turquoise, lime and cherry red.

The taxi pulled up in the harbour, outside a cosy coffee shop, and I went from sitting in the car to sitting in the sunshine. Peace. At. Last.

'*Olá*. You are very welcome. What can I get you?' A chunky man in a white shirt and jeans fussed around the table and presented me with a menu.

'Good morning. *Café con leche, por favor*,' I said, hoping my Spanish was close enough to Portuguese and desperate for some caffeine. 'Do you have any pastries? Or something sweet to go with the coffee?' I didn't know the Portuguese for that.

'*Sim* – but of course! You must try our local specialty – the Dona Amélia,' he said, with pride. 'Delicious, I promise you. Honey and cinnamon... mwah – one is never enough, huh?'

'Sold,' I said, closing the menu and handing it back. I looked out across the harbour and felt my shoulders drop in relief. The water slapped gently against the fishing boats as they returned with their morning haul, and tourists were taking photos and milling about, waiting for their boat trips to the other islands. A pair of tanned teenagers in vest tops and shorts stopped in front of me to stare at their phones, seemingly unbothered by their enormous red backpacks.

'It's this way!' one of them huffed, pointing at a road sign with *Monte Brasil* in clear type. The highest point on the island was just beyond the city and jutted out into the ocean. Apparently the views were magnificent from the top but I couldn't think of anything worse than hiking all that way in the heat.

The waiter reappeared with my coffee and a lumpy fairy cake covered in icing sugar, and I slipped on my headphones and closed my eyes. Pure. Bliss. Nobody wanted anything from me – well, they *did*, they *always did*, but they couldn't ask me unless they found me, and nobody would find me here. I could listen to my podcast in peace. Bryce Donnelly had been pepping me up with his words of affirmation for over ten years now. Well known as the 'Aussie Gu-roo,' he was the master of self-actualisation. When I'd been ghosted by dates in the past, Bryce was the only man who could snap me out of my misery. His message was one of control and empowerment. Apparently men ignoring me was a good thing. Every ghosting took me a step closer to finding the right one and becoming myself. Bryce said I could have anything I wanted – and what I currently wanted was to win this pitch.

The music started and I felt myself get into the zone. 'Whatever it is you're dreaming about, whatever it is you want. Imagine you already have it,' Bryce lilted softly, in his hot, Aussie accent, then paused for effect. '*You've got it*. Say it with me. *I've got it. It's already mine.*'

'I've got it. It's already mine,' I repeated, mouthing the words as I exhaled.

'Louder!' Bryce could be very persuasive when he wanted to be.

'I've got it. It's already mine!' I said to no one in particular.

'Now say I've done it; I'VE WON,' Bryce cried.

'I'VE DONE IT; I'VE WON.'

I felt a tap on my shoulder and jumped. Leo was standing over me, and I nearly knocked my coffee over, whipping off my headphones.

'Can I help you?' I said, astonished to find him once again in my earhole. How had he found me here?

'Sorry to interrupt, I just thought you'd be annoyed if I sat within listening distance while you did your affirmations and didn't make myself known.' He couldn't resist a smirk, which riled me even more.

'They aren't affirmations, I was on the phone. Can't you go to one of the other coffee places?'

'Easy, easy,' he said, holding his hand out like a horse whisperer. 'Sure, I'll get out of here. I didn't want to be rude, that's all, and I didn't see you until I sat down. I was gearing myself up to climb the mountain.'

'Fine. Sorry.' He'd caught me unawares and I was being unnecessarily harsh. 'I was thinking of doing the same,' I said, not to be outdone, having been doing nothing of the sort. I'd been gearing myself up to eat a cheese platter for two and a carafe of white wine, once my coffee and fairy cake starter was out of the way.

'Great minds,' Leo said, following my gaze. 'Fancy a race?'

My coffee had been quite strong, and I felt some latent competitive rage rear up inside me. He was laughing at me again. He didn't think I had it in me. I'd show him.

I shrugged. 'Why not?' Knowing even as I said it that my aptitude, attitude and attire were all in short supply. I sat up and eyed my maxi dress and trainers. No teeny tops or weeny shorts here.

'You're on. After you've eaten your cake, obviously.'

'It's required eating, apparently. The Dona Amélia – a local delicacy.'

Leo shaded his eyes, salivating as I tucked in.

'I'll leave you to it and be back in ten,' he said, walking off along the waterfront. An old man with a leathery tan wobbled in on a fishing boat and was trying to lasso his rope over a wooden post. The boat was laden down with nets of silvery fish, their rainbow bodies glinting in the morning sun. Leo whistled then held out his hand to help, catching the rope and pulling him in.

'*Obrigado*,' the fisherman called gratefully, revealing a gold tooth. Leo waved and strode off like the everyday hero he was, while I snaffled down my Dona Amélia. It was as sugary and delicious as promised, and I hoped the solid carbs would fuel my enthusiasm levels before my hike. What had possessed me to agree to it? I could barely walk up the stairs these days, let alone up and down a mountain in half a day. I was supposed to be enjoying some R&R with Bryce and getting back to myself for a few hours. I drank the rest of my coffee, my eyes fixed on Leo as he made his way around the harbour, shaking hands with the shop owners and petting a fluffy dog. The gelato lady offered Leo samples of different flavours, before he eventually settled on what looked like chocolate. Caffeine-fuelled annoyance coursed through my body as I watched him eat his ice-cream, savouring each tiny shovelful. He eventually looked up and caught me staring, waved his plastic spoon and walked over.

'Chocolate ice cream, eh?' I called. 'Can't beat a classic.'

'No, it's Black Forest and pistachio,' he replied, showing me the pale green bottom layer. 'I like to try whatever they say is selling well to stay on top of the trends.'

Hmm.

'Zach didn't fancy the climb then?' I asked, changing the subject.

'Nope. He went with Brooke and Heidi to the Uzu Yacht Club. Thiago is a member, and he offered to sign them all in.'

I felt a pang of jealousy. Bollocks. The Uzu was yet another money-can't-buy experience. That'd teach me to ignore Heidi when she called.

'Lounging around and drinking gets tiresome after a while,' I said, annoyed at myself. 'I prefer a more authentic experience.'

'Agreed. We can drink champagne anywhere – this might be the only chance we ever get to scale the mighty Monte Brasil.' Leo tightened the elastic on his shorts and adjusted his backpack. I was woefully unprepared in comparison. I paid the bill, and we set off, falling into an easy rhythm as we walked through the harbour towards the mountain.

'Do you hike back home?' I asked.

'Occasionally,' he replied, giving me a three-fingered salute. 'Ex-Boy Scout with a silver Duke of Edinburgh. I get out in nature whenever I can.'

'Only silver, eh?' I said, furious that my gold Duke of Edinburgh hadn't set me apart enough to get that bloody job. 'I'm a gold so I should probably take charge.'

'Fair enough,' he replied. 'Send my regards to the duke when you see him.'

He gave me a stiff smile and upped his pace, forcing me into an almost-trot to keep up; luckily the fire in my belly fuelled my competitive spirit. It had been a few years since I'd dragged myself up Snowdon for charity. Heidi had suggested we do it as a team-building exercise and it had been hellish. But the facts were the facts. I was gold and he was a silver and there was no way he was beating me to the top of this mountain. My upper lip was sweaty, and I unglued my dress from my back. The two backpackers were already halfway up, their matching red bags zinging bright against the pale grey rock. A man sat in a portacabin at the foot of the path, handing out maps and taking money.

'Ten euros,' he called on repeat as a steady stream of tourists ploughed through the turnstile.

'Two, please. I mean, *por favor*,' Leo said, going first and paying me in.

'You didn't need to do that,' I said and instantly regretted my tone.

He gave me a look. I hadn't meant it to come out quite so rude. 'It's kind of you, though, thanks,' I said, trying to backtrack. I wasn't used to men paying for me. I wasn't used to men doing anything for me.

'It's a business expense,' he said, nonchalantly. 'Makes no odds who claims it.'

I smiled. Of course it didn't. He wasn't thinking about me at all; it was one of a hundred receipts he'd be adding to his bill for Brooke to pay at the end of the pitch process. Rich people didn't think about money in the same way as us mere mortals. It was all just admin to them.

He opened the map and handed me one side so we could stare at it together.

'Let's do the short circuit,' I said. 'I don't want to take any chances getting back for the boat.'

'Agreed.'

'The Igreja São João Baptista – Miradouro Santo António. This red line, here,' I traced the route with my finger embarrassed at the state of my nails.

'Less than two miles, which won't even take an hour. We're already on the trail in fact… looks like it started in the car park.'

'Even better!' I said, delighted. 'Saves us rushing.'

'It won't be much of a race if there's no rushing,' Leo said, good-naturedly. 'Unless you want to walk to the top together, then sprint back down?'

'Erm, yeah... good idea.' *Another terrible idea.* Walking was one thing; sprinting was something else entirely. I hadn't done that since my last school sports day – twenty years ago.

Thirteen

We followed the crowd along the shingle path, which was virtually flat and easily walkable – nothing like my recollections of Snowdon. The views were already fabulous and presumably would look identical from the peak – everything would just be smaller and further away. Was it really worth all the effort to get to the very top? Leo spritzed himself with sun cream and the coconut reminded me of the pool party Abi had taken me and Sara to in LA. So many fit men – and women, annoyingly – but *the men*... the LA lifestyle was strict but worth it – for them, obviously, not me. Say what you like about plastic surgery, but everyone looked picture-perfect – if a little surprised.

Leo lifted his T-shirt to wipe his brow and I got another glimpse of his abs, which he must have drawn on with eyeliner. How was he working in London full-time and maintaining a six-pack? It didn't make sense.

He offered up the sun cream and I slathered myself, gratefully. I'd been shadow-hopping behind a tall, wide man, but I didn't like to get too close and the sun was grilling the back of my neck. I shouldn't even be in this blazing heat – I should be drinking bellinis under a large umbrella with Bryce whispering reassuring nothings in my ear.

We walked up the mountain without even realising it, but my glutes started to twinge as we reached the highest point and I pushed to keep up with Leo. *Mind over matter, Kat.* That's all this was.

'Selfie to prove we made it?' he said, holding up his phone. I was red as a beetroot with my cap stuck to my head, like wee Jimmy Krankie, as I smiled for the camera.

'Easier than I thought it would be.'

'And quick,' Leo said, checking his watch, already keen for the next challenge. 'I don't see how we can run downhill through all these people, though; we need a different kind of race.'

We were in the middle of a walkathon crowd, with all the keenos pushing behind us to get to the peak, and hundreds of slow plodders in front of us on the trek back down. Neither direction could be any kind of a race – unless we were snails.

'Let's just say you won,' I said. Not that there was anyone to announce it to. PR News were unlikely to run the story. 'I'm happy for you to take the glory.'

We rounded a corner and Leo stopped with a smile. 'Now, *that's* what I'm talking about.' I followed his gaze up to the sky, where a packed gondola was steadily making its way over to a second volcanic crater. 'What do you think?'

I shrugged. 'Sure. Show me how we race each other in that.'

'The racing part is on the other side,' he said, his eyes full of fire. 'Volcano boarding.'

Ah. Had I accidentally agreed to something sporty? 'And what exactly is that?'

'Surfing down the side of the volcano on a plank of wood.'

I gulped. 'That sounds terrifying.'

'We can do the scree sliding instead if you'd rather? The beginner's version. Where you go down on your feet. You can walk it, but it's quicker to slide and the stones hold your weight as you go.'

I nodded, glad there was an easier way.

We followed the signs, then our fellow sliders, until we reached the giant cable car, and wedged ourselves in next to a family of four. There must have been a hundred of us in the lift, each person stood straight and still; like one among many in a box of matches.

'Hold on kids,' their dad yelled, and the two boys screamed in delight as we took off into the sky.

'I'd love to be that excited,' Leo whispered, standing far too close, but with no other option. His body shielded me from the rest of the group, and it felt like I had my own personal bodyguard travelling next to me. My breathing slowed to match his and I tried to look anywhere but in his eyes as we juddered along.

'Are you not living the ecstatic life you'd hoped?'

He shook his head and pretended to look sad. 'I try and smile once a week, but other than that I'm dead inside.'

I laughed. 'I can see. It must be hard being so rich and successful.'

He raised one of his perfectly arched brows. 'You think I'm successful?'

'Yes. Aren't you? Did Forbes get it wrong?'

'Oh... that.' He shrugged. 'I spent weeks on that application but I think it was the CEO promotion that clinched it.'

'Sounds like success to me.'

'And as for being rich. Two words. Ex. Wife.'

'That's one word,' I said, looking at his Ferrosi climbing gear and struggling to feel sorry for him. The aviators holding back his twinkling bouffant were Hugo Boss and looked brand new.

'OK, clever. *My* ex-wife.'

'Are you having to cope with three million instead of six?'

'I wish. She pretty much cleaned me out.' His smile faltered and his eyes turned dark.

'Sorry, I didn't mean to pry,' I mumbled.

I was saved from putting my foot in my mouth any further by the cable car shuddering to a stop. The midday sun was now roasting hot, and I could feel my skin burning as we took in the view of the Azores scattered across the ocean. The volcanic crater below us was vast. Tiny people stood around like ants on the edges, and those who had made it down were now nothing more than dots. Beyond the crumbly rocks were green edges full of pink flowers, and piles of white villas heaped together like sugar cubes on the edge of turquoise waters. The Azores were truly breathtaking. Waves were breaking out in the distance, giving the cerulean seas an occasional sliver of white, as speedboats zipped back and forth. I slipped my sarong over my shoulders and put my cap on to shade my face.

'Ahh! I'd forgotten you were a fellow red,' Leo said, waggling my cap in an overly familiar way.

'Of course. Bootle born and bred. Are you a Liverpool fan too?'

'Till I die,' he replied, lifting his sleeve to reveal a tiny liver bird.

'Snap,' I said, pulling my precious liver bird pendant out from under my top. 'I assumed you'd be Man City or United.'

'Nah. Gran used to take me and my brothers to Anfield when we were kids.'

'How many brothers have you got?' I asked, in thick Scouse. 'Your poor old gran with all *youse* men!'

'Two. Oscar and Max. The three of us still go to the match whenever we can and take Gran if she's up to it. She loves to swing her scarf and give the referee a piece of her mind.'

'I haven't been for years – I miss it,' I said wistfully. 'Can't beat a good old singalong at Anfield.' Some of my best memories had been made in that football ground. 'Right then – better get down this volcano hadn't we? I'll set an alarm, so we don't lose track of time.'

'Me too. We've got two hours before we need to be back on the boat.'

We synchronised Apple Watches like a pair of PR nerds, then walked past a woman in freshly ironed camel shorts bellowing into a loudspeaker: 'The cable car down is to your *right*. Steps for hiking are to your *left*. Surfers go straight ahead!'

'It shouldn't take more than an hour to get down, should it?' I said, peering over the side. Having a bit of junk in my trunk was going to be a distinct advantage here, as well as all those early morning bus rides balancing my bags and laptop, with no spare hands to hold on.

I took a photo of the view, zooming out to show the sheer size and depth of the crater and the volcanic rock in all its glory. Lava stones in different shades of black and grey, peppered with spicy reds, leading down to the milky green lake at its centre. I noticed Heidi had added to her stories and was sat with Zach and Brooke on a rooftop cabana, about to tuck into an enormous paella. The three of them were holding up smoky, pink cocktails with an animated arrow pointing to the *Esmeralda* in the distance. It looked lush. And here were Leo and I, about to plunge to our deaths. I followed him to the top of the volcanic surfing section and peered over. Too late for fear.

'Ready?' Leo asked.

I nodded and dropped straight over the edge without hesitation to get a head start. However scared I felt, my overwhelming urge was to win.

'Last one down buys the drinks,' I shouted over my shoulder as I slid into the volcanic shale. It was like skidding down a sand dune and I tried to slide while watching the others to pick up tips. The kids were flying along, completely fearless, leaning back and going for it. I was stopping and starting in a panic, pulling up whenever I went too fast, scared I might never stop. Leo hooned past, using his huge flipper feet like a skateboard.

'You went too early!' he called, as he whizzed past. 'That's a disqualification.'

'You don't make the rules.'

I had no choice but to go, go, *go*. Leaning back and sliding as fast as I could, ignoring my screaming glutes. I was gaining on him, but then he somehow sped up even further. He narrowly missed colliding with an elderly couple who were shuffling down the middle of the mountain, then fell on his face. Hahaaa!

I sprayed tiny stones at his back as I thundered by, my dress putting me at a slight disadvantage and ruining my aerodynamics. I felt a rush as the base of the volcano came into view and there was still no sign of Leo. I was a woman on a mission and nothing was going to get in my way – super-surfer Kat Brennan, going for gold.

The thrill and exhilaration of the ride down had pumped my veins full of adrenaline, and it was a good ten minutes before I thought to wonder where Leo was. I'd taken some photos and checked all my socials, then tried to spot him on the volcano but there was no sign. He should have been down by now, surely. I wandered over to the wine bar near the exit, which was a sun trap for us surfers to enjoy a nice cold drink. It was a makeshift bar with big umbrellas and folding chairs that could be packed away at a moment's notice, and the menu was on a small blackboard. There were pictures of green grapes, red grapes and pink grapes and on the right a wine glass and six euros. Gotcha.

'Two white, *por favor*.' I pointed at the green grapes and watched as the lady behind the bar poured me out two glasses. She held the bottle vertically as the wine shot out, both landing on the 250ml line. Pour-precision-perfect. I'd have bet she could pour a glass spot on with her eyes closed. I sent Leo a text then sat down to enjoy my wine while people whooped and shrieked their way down the edge of the volcano. The sun was warm and comforting as I moved onto Leo's wine and I closed my eyes to enjoy its rays for a few undisturbed minutes. The alcohol and heat mingled together, masking the ache from my tired limbs after flinging myself down the mountain. And then the shingle started to shake as the unmistakable pulse of a helicopter appeared overhead, flying low then hovering as it lowered something down and out of sight.

My stomach flipped as I thought of Leo. I hoped he hadn't hurt himself. I stretched my neck to see. It looked like someone had been strapped into a zippy bag and was being winched up into the helicopter, but I couldn't see enough detail to know if it was Leo or not. I took a photo and the lady behind the bar tutted in disgust.

'No, it's my friend. Erm… *amigo*,' I said, as I zoomed in on the photo. I couldn't make anything out other than a spiky blonde ponytail, but that was enough and I felt my breathing steady. It wasn't Leo. He wasn't hurt. I was still scanning the photo in close-up to see if he was somewhere else on the volcano when he appeared behind me.

'Worried about me?' Leo shouted in my ear, making me jump.

'There you are! Take your time…' I snapped my phone shut and chucked it in my bag.

'Sorry, a lady fell over in front of me,' he replied. 'I think she's broken her leg.'

'That lady?' I asked, pointing up at the helicopter.

'Yup. They'll have her at the hospital in half an hour and can get her plastered up.'

'I'm starting to think you're jinxed. Do you normally encounter this many *accidents* when you go away?'

Leo laughed. 'Are you suggesting I planted that fish bone in your throat?'

'Just seems odd,' I mumbled. I didn't want to seem ungrateful, but who knew what else might happen. 'Anyway, you've been gone ages. Shouldn't we be getting back to the boat?'

Leo checked his phone. 'Jesus. YES! It leaves in half an hour.'

I downed the rest of his wine and followed him out onto the single-track road in front of the volcano, which was dusty and empty.

'No Uber here, or black cabs likely to drive by,' I said, looking up and down the road.

'It will take us ten minutes to walk back to the harbour, then it's a twenty-minute drive,' Leo said, totting up the timings in his head.

'Perfect,' I replied.

'Not really Kat,' he replied, testily. 'The boat *leaves* in half an hour, which isn't the time we should be skidding into harbour.'

'They won't go without us,' I said, hurrying after him as he broke into a jog.

'I'm pretty sure they will,' he said. 'And they'll take our luggage with them.'

'I'll call Heidi and get her to hold it for us,' I said, confidently. Leo looked at me like I'd completely lost the plot.

'What are you talking about? They won't delay thousands of people on holiday for us. We're not even real guests. We're head office – the worst kind of guest, hated by the staff above all others. They're convinced we are spies.'

I heard the gentle thrum of a car engine behind us.

'Quick! Take your top off!' I shouted to Leo's back as I stuck out my thumb and lifted my dress to the shin. I'd never hitched before, but I was pretty sure that this was how you did it. A packed family Volvo drove by with the kids in the back and one of them blew me a raspberry with his thumbs down. Little shit.

'We're not in Ibiza,' Leo said, irritated. 'Getting your legs out won't get us a lift here.'

'OK, smart-arse, what's your idea, then?'

'To RUN!' he shouted over his shoulder, taking off towards the harbour.

After a hike, a volcanic surfing sesh and two large glasses of wine, I wasn't at my athletic best and I wasn't a runner on a good day. I followed as fast as I could, speedwalking like an overzealous New Year's Resolution-er but I didn't feel hugely motivated, if I was being honest. I half wanted to miss the boat and have a break from Heidi's scrutiny for a little while. We could catch them up tomorrow. By the time I got to the harbour Leo was tearing his hair out with no taxis to be seen.

'Do your best, mate,' he said into his phone and hung up. 'Zach will try and buy us some time, and there's a guy inside calling us a cab.' He pointed into the coffee shop we'd been in that morning where the waiter was shrugging into his landline and shaking his head.

'In twenty minute, taxi comes here?' he called out as a question, lowering the handset to ask.

'We need it quickly. *Vamos?*' Leo pleaded.

The man shook his head. 'Iz no possible. Iz twenty minute.'

Fourteen

Twenty minute was twenty minutes too long and by the time we arrived back at the port, there was nothing we could do but watch as *Esmeralda* slowly chugged away. Heidi was easy to pick out on the top balcony, her hands on her hips, clearly seething. I did an exaggerated shrug then waved with both hands, as she glared at me.

'We can catch them up in Madeira,' I said, with a big cheesy smile while Leo squinted at his phone.

'Already on it,' he said, speed-scrolling, then stopping to read. 'Here we go. The ten o'clock flight tomorrow morning will have us back with them for lunch.'

Wow, so soon. We'd be back before they even missed us. 'In plenty of time for more aqua aerobics.'

Leo frowned, then continued scrolling. 'Or we could get the midday flight?' he suggested, a smile on his lips.

'Hmm…' I nodded slowly, pretending to think. 'Yes, that sounds better. It wouldn't hurt to give everyone some alone time – some *thinking of a great pitch* time.'

'Agreed. Send me your passport details then and I'll book for both of us.'

He handed me his business card with *Leo Kendrick* etched on the front in metallic blue ink. Clearly a man used to people doing exactly as they're told.

'Thanks, but I can book my own flight. There's no chance Brooke will let us claim this one.'

'Don't worry – I'll cover it,' he said, with a shrug. I wasn't enough of a big shot to write off the cost of a flight like that, but it didn't feel cool to make a thing of it. He stopped tapping and looked up. 'I insist. It's entirely my fault we're in this situation. I should have kept an eye on the time.'

'You were being a Good Samaritan. It shouldn't cost you money on top.'

'Honestly, it's fine.'

'OK, but if we win the pitch, I'm paying you back.'

'And if you don't?'

'If we don't, then it'll be the least of my problems, and I'll accept your generous gift with grace and gratitude.'

'Deal.'

I shuddered at the thought of cobbling together an updated CV *for whomever it may concern* and trying to find another job. Working for a new – likely worse – version of Heidi. No, thanks. Losing this account was *not* an option. I texted Leo my passport details, relieved I'd brought it with me. He couldn't scam me if he was paying, surely. My photo was nearly nine years old and I barely recognised myself: thick black eyeliner and a long blonde plait over one shoulder, with messy wisps around my face. Freckles and a fast-fading tan from a week in Devon. I'd realised far too late into the summer holidays that my passport was out of date, so we'd postponed our sisters' trip to Greece and gone to Torquay instead. We didn't need a passport for the English Riviera, and we'd stayed right on the seafront in The Torquay Grand, with a three-course breakfast every morning. Orange juice, honeydew melon, a full English fry-up and toast and jam for dessert.

I'd renewed my passport while we were there and my eyes were full of smiles despite my straight face. The twins had grabbed my legs under the curtain as the final photo countdown had started and I'd been stuck with it.

'I recognise that face,' Leo said.

'Yeah, that would have been the summer before we interned together. I haven't changed that much have I?'

He stared at me as if to check. 'Hmm, no. You've still got it.'

'Erm… thanks. I think.' I smoothed down my hair, feeling my face flush. 'At least let me organise the hotel,' I said, googling furiously. It was nearly four and we needed somewhere to stay.

'Chris has already sorted it.'

'Chris who?'

'My assistant.'

'Oh. OK, well that's kind of him. Where are we staying?'

'At the Harbour Club,' Leo said, smoothly, pointing up at the five-star hotel set into the hills behind us. The infinity pool was built out over the rocks and glistened aquamarine as the sun shone through it.

'Really?' Good old Chris – whoever he was – I'd have booked us into a bargain BnB. My stomach bubbled with excitement, and I was double glad we were getting the later flight.

'Yep. We deserve some luxury after sleeping in those broom cupboards for a week.'

A new cruise ship had arrived to replace the *Esmeralda*, and the harbour was back to heaving. The tourists poured off and scattered, immersing themselves in the local vibe. In and out of the shops and bars, keen to explore the island in the few hours they had. I couldn't wait to have a shower or bath – or both – in my five-star room.

'I'm going to swing by the supermarket and pick up a few essentials. Want anything?' Leo asked. I had a perfume miniature and a lipstick in my handbag and that was about it – I needed more than a few essentials. I needed clothes and knickers and… everything.

I remained relaxed and casual. 'I'll come too.'

There was something so shiny and clean about supermarkets on holiday. Air conditioning, deli counters full of meats and cheeses, pyramids of perfect-looking potatoes, glossy tomatoes and huge green beans. But I couldn't wear a green bean for dinner. I'd have to buy a new dress to throw on – this one was sweaty and muddy, and I couldn't wait to take it off. We headed for the toothbrushes and deodorants and bought a pink and blue of each. His and hers. I hadn't been supermarket shopping with a man for years and putting my cucumber-fresh Dove next to his Sure Maximum Strength for extra manly-men felt embarrassingly intimate.

I tried to laugh it off. 'Do we need anything else, love? Kitchen roll? Fairy liquid? A new mop head?'

A woman ushered past with her toddler and Leo smiled. 'I think we're good.'

'I could actually do with something to change into,' I said, eyeing the clothes shop through the window.

'Me too.' Leo grinned. 'I'll sort this lot, and you go get whatever you need. Let's meet in the hotel reception in an hour and check in?'

'Done.'

What a treat. A whole hour to myself to mooch around the shops and meander about. I just needed a cheapy cotton dress and some flip-flops and that'd be fine. A bell tinkled as I walked into the one and only shop that sold clothes on the harbour front. There were dozens of mannequins in the window wearing bikinis with tiny shorts and a luscious rack of long cotton dresses to flick through.

'*Olá!*' a fresh-faced teenager called, from behind the till.

'*Olá,*' I replied, scanning the dresses for something appropriate. So many of them had pieces missing or were covered in sequins, or snake sized. I whipped the hangers along faster and faster as the rejections piled up and I could feel myself starting to panic. *No, no, no, no.* I *had* to find something to wear in this shop. Right now.

'English?' the young girl asked.

I nodded, holding up a bright orange minidress. *No.*

'I can help you?' she tried.

'I need a dress,' I said, pointing at my boobs and then my bum. 'For dinner.' I pretended to eat with a knife and fork. '*Grandez.* If… er… *possible.*' I'd run out of Portuguese words, so English with a bad French accent would have to do.

She disappeared off out the back as I flicked from gaudy nightmare to gaudy nightmare. There was a small selection of cotton dresses by the counter, but they looked like they were for children. I held a gorgeous emerald dress up against me in the mirror, but it was strapless and only went down to my knee. I hadn't worn anything like that for years.

The girl came back with a rainbow of dresses over her arm. Peacock blue, pink, cherry red and white. Cotton-soft maxi dresses that looked like they might work. Surely one of them would do.

'Oooh! *Mucho obrigado*!' I said, taking them and shuffling over to the 'changing area' – a mirror and a circular curtain. My muscles instantly relaxed as I kicked off my sweaty trainers and peeled off my dress, standing naked in the air con to cool down. I wanted to throw them in the bin, but I folded them into a pile instead. The blue dress was like a silk sheet on my skin, its plunge neckline and cap sleeves floating elegantly and landing in all the right places. They say dresses are like men – you know instantly when it's the one. When it's a definite yes.

I pulled the curtain back to give myself more space and stood in front of the mirror.

'Ahh! Is very nice,' the girl said, with a smile, her brown eyes shining. 'Is your colour.'

It ruffled around my cleavage and pulled me in at the waist, as if it was made for me. There was a slight whiff of chief bridesmaid, but I didn't have much choice. 'I'll take it, please. And a pair of those flip-flops in a medium. Both to wear now.'

'I have similar dress in red, here,' she said, holding up the cherry, which was equally beautiful. 'One is forty euro, both colours I do for sixty?'

'Erm... OK, go on then,' I said, wafting the material around like a flamenco dancer, then giving her a twirl. I loved it. 'And can I have a bag for my... er... other clothes?'

Would it be crazy to buy it in all the colours? *Yes*. But the costume change had unlocked something in me. I felt cheekier and lighter – a more excited version of myself. Was it the dress? Or was it going commando?

The island was a glossy mix of blues and greens with picturesque views in every direction. I walked through the main square swinging my shopping bags and as the breeze billowed through my new dress, that delicious holiday feeling hit me for the first time since we'd set sail. No expectations and nothing to think about, other than enjoying a new place. The square was teeming with people. Tiny bars served sundowners and snacks, while artists sketched portraits in charcoal and ink, and people meandered past, occasionally stopping to watch. The spicy sizzle of peri peri chicken mingled with the sugary cinnamon of churros, making me hungry, and I couldn't resist stopping for a quick glass of wine.

My phone pinged as I placed my order.

Heidi: What happened? Where are you staying? Have you booked a flight yet? When will you arrive? Keep me updated.

Completely hysterical as usual. Never one to underreact. I fired off a quick reply.

Me: Don't worry, Heidi, I'm fine. Yes, Leo has booked us on the first flight to Madeira, so we'll be there tomorrow. Wi-Fi is patchy but I'll be in touch.

HIIT Girls Group Chat:

Sara: I've just been reading about your pitch, Kat – isn't that Leo guy the one from Engelman?

Abi: Noooo? You're not stuck on a boat with him are you?

Me: It is. I am. I know – can you believe it? He's actually
not that bad so far

Me: And he looks pretty good in his trunks

I watched the world go by for half an hour with a cold glass of Vinho Verde and a handful of stuffed olives and emptied my mind completely. The bar was in the corner of the square and shaded by a beautiful old church, with crumbling stone walls and a clock tower. When the chime sounded for quarter to five, I popped in to light a candle, then made my way to the Harbour Club. I could happily have stayed here for a week, a month, even; I just needed propping up on a sunbed with a stack of books and to throw my phone in the sea.

Fifteen

The exterior of the Harbour Club was grand enough, with its huge windows and elaborately painted tiles, but it was nothing compared to what greeted me inside. Sumptuously styled with modern art on the walls, grey marble floors and linen curtains blowing in the breeze, this place was next level. Well-groomed guests in designer sunglasses wandered past in clouds of expensive perfume and my imposter syndrome was in overdrive as the concierge welcomed me into the cool. I made a beeline for Leo, who was sat waiting in the lobby. He looked straight through me at first and it was only when I was stood in front of him waving that he did a double take.

'Hey! Didn't recognise you there for a second. Nice dress.'

'Thanks. It's my new *Azorean lady* look,' I said, with a chuckle. 'Not my regular choice.'

'Luck be a lady, eh?' His eyes swept me up and down. 'Suits you.'

I felt myself blush and rifled around in my bag, pretending to look for something, but all that was in there was dirty washing. 'Shall we check in, then?' I mumbled. 'I'm desperate for a shower.'

'All done,' Leo said, handing me a key. 'You're directly above me, so keep the noise down please.'

'I'll do my best. You must need a lot of beauty sleep for that pretty face.'

'You think I've got a pretty face?'

I blushed again. 'No...' I stammered. This dress was knocking me off kilter.

'Charming. Well, can you bear to look at it over dinner tonight or have you had enough of me for one day? I totally understand if you'd rather order room service.'

'Oh, yes, there's an idea. I mean, no. I mean, it would be a shame not to eat in the restaurant, wouldn't it?' *Why was I getting so flustered?* He wasn't asking me out on a date, for goodness' sake. We were just two colleagues, two *rival* colleagues, on a business trip who needed to eat. It was *work* – and bloody hard work at that.

Leo looked confused. 'You lost me with all those double negatives.'

I took a breath and spoke slowly and deliberately. 'Yes. We should have dinner in the restaurant.'

'Agreed. Separately? Or on a table for two?'

I rolled my eyes. He was infuriating. 'Together is fine.' I wasn't used to being project-managed – usually it was me booking and paying for everything for Heidi and for the clients, and the team. And with men, now that I thought about it. Those half-hour dates didn't schedule themselves.

'It's a date. I'll see you on the roof terrace at eight.'

He sauntered off and left me panicking in reception. A date? *Was it?* I'd never been very fluent in 'man' language. *Man-guage.* I always took things the wrong way or laughed when they were trying to be serious. This was the problem with all my three-month relationships, I rarely got close enough to a guy to truly understand what he was on about and the more it continued, the less I bothered trying. What was the point?

I made my way up to Room 602 and nearly cried with joy when I walked inside. It was light and bright and HUGE. The balcony doors were already open, and a cool breeze rippled through the curtains. At last, some fresh air on my hot, sweaty forehead. I stripped off in the doorway and jumped straight in the shower, which was a full-on sensory experience, with wall jets and multicoloured lights, each one a different scent. Never had water felt so good. I wrapped myself in the fluffy bath towel and sat out on the balcony, watching the sun set, feeling snuggled and rested and like I'd been to a spa. It would have been rude not to crack open the complimentary half-bottle of Moët, and as I took my first sip I doubled down on that chilled-out holiday feeling: relaxed, excitable, and looking forward to a night out. I hadn't realised how stiff and swollen my body had been feeling, and it was such a treat to know I could just stop and relax. I swapped my towel for a robe and slippers and spent a full hour luxuriating in my suite, lying against the stack of feather pillows with my champagne and staring out at the ocean. I'd pop down for some dinner, then come back up and jump in the Jacuzzi. This was the life.

Eventually I had to get myself ready and it turned out the red dress wasn't all that similar to the blue. It was much vampier, with its silky batwings and plunging neckline, which was entirely fitting for such a glamorous hotspot. It had been a while since I'd worn a dress that showed off my curves like this and I almost didn't recognise myself in the mirror. It was slinky and sexy and made me feel like a different person. My blue dress was now washed and soaking wet on the balcony, so there was no other choice; the red had to go on.

Leo: I'm in the bar – would you like a drink?

Me: Vodka tonic please.

I wandered down to the lift, feeling completely out of place but rocking it in a red dress. Leo was sat on a bar stool, chatting with the maître d' and I suddenly felt shy as I walked over, relieved to see his cheeky face.

'There she is,' he said, his silver eyes shining. He looked every inch the *Azorean man* in his white linen shirt and tapered navy chinos.

The maître d' pulled out a bar stool. 'Good evening, madam, welcome to the Harbour Club – my name is Ricardo.'

'Thank you,' I said, quietly, hopping up next to Leo.

'The menus are here for you. For specials we have a king prawn with monkfish starter and a beef steak main with baked potato and feta cheese.' There were so many options to choose from. 'I'll leave you to enjoy your aperitifs.' Ricardo backed away, head bowed, as if we were royalty, shuffling his shiny shoes across the marble floor.

'Kinda nice here, right?' Leo said. 'Zach is livid. He's having dinner with Heidi and Brooke and not looking forward to another night in the bunk bed.'

'Unlucky!' I sang, toasting him with my glass. 'Poor Brooke, I wouldn't want to be in the middle of an angry Zach and Heidi.'

Leo laughed. 'Same. What is it with those two? They can't stand each other.'

I shrugged, not wanting to give anything away. 'They used to work together so I assumed it was just an ex-colleague thing.'

'Hmm. Seems deeper than that and Zach is being very tight-lipped about it. He usually tells me everything. All fuel for the competitive spirit though, eh?'

'True.' My vodka tonic was ice cold and sliding down far too easily. 'Leave them to it, I say. Why bring bad vibes when we're surrounded by all this?'

The harbour was crammed full of boats in all shapes and sizes; shiny, white and seemingly still, illuminated by floodlights. The chatter of yachty families and friends enjoying dinner buzzed through the air, as couples walked along the waterfront, going from menu to identical menu, trying to decide where to eat. That gorgeous holiday feeling of freedom, when you're in love or lust, or just full of expectation. When there's nothing to fill your mind other than where to sunbathe next, whether to swim or read, whether to have another ice cream and what flavour it should be.

Leo nodded. 'Agreed. Let's just enjoy it.'

He had a commanding way about him, and I felt myself surrender. It was time to switch off and forget about Heidi and Brooke and the pitch. To relax and enjoy myself for once. The ladylike swoosh of my skirt was helping, tickling my legs, which felt smoother and more moisturised than they had been in years. I was always rushing from one thing to the next, to and from work, dinner with clients, drinks with friends, squeezing some sleep in, then repeating it all again the next day. Being out here, I could shave and moisturise my legs to my heart's content. No more excuses. No more blaming the London life for being single, overstretched and hairy.

'So how is Amplify surviving for a week without their big boss and creative director?'

'I dread to think,' Leo said, his phone lighting up the table. 'I haven't had a minute's peace, that's for sure.' He switched it off and put it in his pocket.

'The constant interruptions drive me crazy. I especially love it when the American clients start calling just as I'm wrapping up for the day.' I picked up an imaginary phone. '*Kat's PR hotline, how can I help?* They must think I'm super-human. Sitting around waiting for them to call, twenty-four-seven.'

'How long have you been at Northstar now?'

'Oooh… coming up to six years.'

Leo gasped. 'Really?! Quite a while then.'

'Yep. I've only had two proper PR jobs since school – this was my first in London and I liked it, so I stayed. Loyalty is important to me.'

'Your first paid job you mean? Don't forget Engelman.'

'My first real job in London. I'm not sure Engelman counts; it was only work experience,' I said, dismissively. I didn't like to dwell on my failures.

'Of course it counts. That's been my favourite job to date. The pair of us dicking around and having fun. Remember that bloke Roger who was always accusing the receptionist of stealing his lunch?'

I chuckled, despite myself. 'Oh yes, poor Roger putting his sandwiches in the fridge every day – they'd be gone by eleven. He set up a camera in the end.'

'I'd have laced them with laxatives. That'd teach whoever it was – and would've been a fun way to do the reveal. He could have TikTok-ed it.'

'And that Christmas party where we dressed up as tube stations. We looked a right state at the after party – like a lost nativity scene. Angel, Parson's Green, all those nuns for Seven Sisters, Shepherd's Bush and didn't you come as Charing Cross?'

'No, I was an Ox with a clown nose for Oxford Circus. Janice decided on blue for Maida Vale and got mistaken for Mary.'

I laughed. 'Ahh that was a good night, wasn't it?'

'The best. Not a care in the world. Although I don't know what I'd have done if I hadn't got that job. Did you apply for a lot of others?' Leo asked.

'Hundreds. Well, it seemed like hundreds at the time. Having Engelman on my CV helped open some doors but I was fighting a losing battle to be honest. I did some freelance for a few years in the end, to bridge the gap.'

'Why?'

'PR is impossible to get into unless you know someone who knows someone – or at least it used to be.' I harumphed. 'How did you do it? Was it Mummy or Daddy who got your foot in the door? Or both?'

He frowned. 'I did it the same way you did – by applying and being accepted.'

'You must have known people in the industry though? You strike me as a man who comes from a well-connected family.'

'Some lazy assumptions there. My parents died in a car accident before I ever got to know them. My gran raised me and my brothers on a pension in Manchester.'

I sat back at that, stunned and completely mortified. 'Oh my God, Leo, I'm so sorry. I had no idea.'

'Why would you? We don't know each other *that* well.'

'But still, I shouldn't have said that.'

'Yeah. I know a thing or two about fighting for things as I've had to do it my whole life.' He gave me a cool stare, then seemed to change his mind and his face softened. 'It was hard, but we made it work. I had a hardship grant at uni and that Engelman job was a lifeline. I was up to my ears in debt, and any spare money Gran had went on my younger brother.'

I was gobsmacked. All these years I'd been incensed at the injustice of it all, convinced he had a silver spoon up his bum and I'd got him all wrong.

'I shouldn't have said any of that; it was presumptuous and rude. You always seem so… well put together. Your voice, your clothes. I just assumed.'

'Oh, that. Yeah, but it's all learnt behaviour,' he said, leaning in. 'My northern accent wasn't getting me anywhere, so I woke up one day and decided to try something different.'

'What, just out of the blue? That must have surprised your gran.'

'First day of uni,' he replied with a wink. 'New friends, new start, new me.'

'There's nowt wrong with a northern accent, lad,' I said, attempting one.

'Eh, that's pretty good is that,' he replied, much more convincingly, and my insides wobbled at his throaty timbre. Funny the things that remind you of home, and I was a sucker for a northerner.

'I think I'll stick with the Scouse, and my PhD from the University of Life.'

'She's a doctor, no less. Cheers to that,' Leo said, clinking my glass. 'More useful and much less debt.'

Ricardo came gliding over, all beaming smiles and teeth.

'Are you enjoying yourselves? How are your drinks?'

'Lovely, thank you,' Leo and I said in unison, then looked at each other and laughed. Were we similar in nature, or just PR robots?

'Are you ready for your table? I've got you the best view from the terrace as you are celebrating, isn't it true?' Ricardo said with a wink, snatching up our menus and marching off.

'Celebrating? Where's he got that idea?' I whispered, horrified.

'Erm... crossed wires. I said it had been a spontaneous decision to stay for the night,' Leo said, striding after him.

Ricardo stopped at a gorgeous table for two, overlooking the harbour and out to sea. A red and white chequered tablecloth with a candle wedged into an old wine bottle, and a vase of pink roses. The relaxing lull of water lapping at the boats could be heard over the chatter and it was *very* romantic.

'Please accept our congratulations and a glass of champagne on the house,' Ricardo said, as a waiter scurried over with an ice bucket.

Leo looked at me with a glint in his eye. '*Obrigado, Ricardo*,' he said and sat down.

It was against Scouse law to pass up a freebie – Mum would never forgive me. So, I followed Leo's lead and sat silently as Ricardo popped the cork.

Sixteen

Ricardo cleared the dessert plates and topped up our glasses. We'd both gone for the disappearing coconut foam and true to its name, there'd been nothing to it; melting on the tongue with an exotic fizz of flavour.

'Was everything to your liking?' he asked, beaming. 'No better place to celebrate your anniversary than the Azores I think. Is it true?'

Those crossed wires were now tied in a bow.

'Dinner was excellent, Ricardo, thank you,' Leo said.

I joined in, enthusiastically. 'Perfect table, delicious food…'

'…and wonderful company!' Ricardo said, with a wink. 'I can see it.' I was going to say wine, but same-same. 'I bring liquors and coffees for you, in *uno momento*, please.'

He fluttered off and Leo and I were left looking at each other across the table.

'Our anniversary now, is it?' I said, feeling giddy under his gaze. Guitar music floated in from the bar and the balmy air was scented with jasmine.

'It must be ten years since we first met – maybe that's what he means?' Leo said with a chuckle.

'It's been nice to spend some time together. I'm sorry for cutting you off after Engelman. I was devastated and wasn't thinking straight. That job was important to both of us and one of us had to get it. I was a sore loser and shouldn't have blamed you. It wasn't your fault – of course it wasn't.'

He reached over and put his hands on mine. 'I appreciate you saying that.'

'Feels like forever ago we were sitting in reception on our first day, doesn't it?'

'Another lifetime,' he said, with a wistful smile. 'I loved it there. Until you left.'

'What? I always imagined you spinning around in your leather chair feeling like the big winner.'

'Not at all. I missed my work bestie. It wasn't as fun without you there.'

How cute. 'Was I fun? I can't remember. I'm not sure my team would say I'm much fun now.'

'You were a lot of fun. You still are. I had a massive crush on you and it took me a while to recover after you left. The rest of the team really missed you too.'

My stomach flipped at that. I'd assumed it was an agency-wide rejection. I'd taken it so personally that I'd cut everyone off. It hadn't occurred to me that anyone would care or want to see me again. Least of all Leo. I'd never known anyone to have a crush on me before; men always treated me as the 'wham bam thank you ma'am' type, so it was touching to think of Leo harbouring a crush. I'd liked him too, but I'd been wary of getting involved with anyone at work – I'd been so obsessed with winning. Which made me feel even worse. Leo had felt a genuine connection while I was praying he'd fail. I didn't know where to look while my brain tried to work it all out. There was nowhere to hide from his confident gaze.

'Did it? Did you?'

'Yes! Wasn't it obvious? You promised we'd stay in touch no matter what happened with the job, then iced me out the second they offered it to me.'

I had no recollection of any such promise but I'd been so distraught when HR told me the bad news, I'd iced the entire world out. I'd felt too humiliated to go back and say goodbye.

'What?! I did not!'

Leo's expression went from confused to annoyed to hurt. 'Come on, Kat. You know you did. And I was gutted. I thought we were friends at the very least. I really did miss you when you left.'

I blinked at him, too stunned to speak. *What the hell was he even talking about?*

'I called, text, sent emails – tried to connect on LinkedIn with no reply. Eventually I took the hint and stopped trying. Either you'd deliberately given me the wrong phone number and email *and* had a fake LinkedIn profile, or you'd blocked me. Either way, you didn't want to speak to me, and I didn't want to be accused of harassment.'

'No one likes a quitter,' I murmured, in shock. Although, now he mentioned it, this did all sound kind of familiar. Had I misremembered our entire connection and every one of our interactions? Could it possibly be that I'd been the rude one? That I'd been jealous and childish, and he'd been perfectly nice? Had my memory distorted the facts to protect me from my own bad behaviour?

'I could never be accused of that,' Leo said, staring at me intensely.

'You must have moved on fairly quickly to already have a *one-word ex-wife*. What happened there?' I asked, to give me some thinking time and deflect the conversation. I needed to absorb this new information. That time in my life was such a blur.

'A silly and, as it turned out, very expensive mistake. Financially and emotionally. Victoria was my first official client at Engelman, and she was a junior as well, the pair of us were just starting our careers when we met. I was convinced she was the love of my life, but I was wrong. We were engaged, married and divorced in three years.'

He looked so forlorn, I was sorry I'd asked. I wasn't doing very well on the conversation front here.

'Wow. That's very... efficient.'

'Incredibly efficient. A word synonymous with true love,' Leo said with an eye roll. 'How about you? Married? Kids?'

I bristled. 'No. No weddings so far. Or children.'

'Anywhere close?'

It was a casual enough question, and no more intrusive than mine, but I felt a sadness in my gut, which caught me by surprise. The answer was easy enough; it was a straight no, but it felt like an admission of failure somehow. I'd never been anywhere close to having a significant other or *anything* other for myself – even my flat was rented. I'd been to friends' engagement parties and weddings and now we were onto the christenings, but I'd never had any of those celebrations myself. Just the birthday parties as I got older, and older. I had no problem landing a man; I could reel one in every day, twice a day if I needed to. But holding on to them was a different story and I'd learnt to like it that way. It was long enough to uncover their quirks (issues), preferences (kinks) and skeletons (crimes) and then I could move on to someone new. I'd learnt to enjoy men in quarterly bursts and then let them go.

'Not really. I still feel too young for anything serious,' I said, brushing the question away.

He frowned. 'What are you, thirty-five?'

'Thirty-four. Which is the new twenty-four, right? I'm barely out of education.'

He laughed. 'That's one way to look at it. Old enough to be married with fourteen-year-old twins is another.'

I gave a strangled chortle. He was right of course, but no need to say it out loud. 'Have you been talking to my nan?'

'I find it interesting to think about the possible paths. That generation – our grans – would have finished having children at our age. It's all a matter of perspective.'

'That generation also ate lard on toast and took it in turns to use the bath water, so excuse me for not living my life by their rules.'

'Garrafeira for you, *senhor*, and another for your beautiful lady with our compliments.' Ricardo set down two glasses of ruby-red liquid and two espressos. 'Our finest port, aged in wooden barrels – we call it a "vintage tawny" – and it is very famous for its delicious, syrupy taste.'

'Thank you,' I said, giving it a sniff and burning my nose hair. Jesus, this was strong.

'And your bill.' Ricardo placed it between us and Leo snatched it up, scribbled his signature and handed it back with a fifty euro note.

'Let me...' I started.

'Absolutely not. It can go on my room.'

Ricardo glanced between the two of us confused, presumably thinking Leo's room and my room were surely one and the same for our anniversary break. He settled on a smile. '*Obrigado*.'

Leo gently swirled his glass. 'Cheers,' he said, holding it up. 'Here's to making the most of a bad situation.'

'The very most,' I replied, looking up at the blanket of stars and the beautiful full moon. 'We're lucky aren't we?'

'Yeah, we could be queuing for the all-you-can-eat-buffet under pitch pressure.' A swathe of fairy lights glowed behind Leo's head, and it looked like he was wearing a halo. Saint Leonard, himself. Or Leonardo, or Leon. How strange to have been thrown back together like this. We clinked glasses, and took a large swig, then both nearly choked.

'*Eurghhh!* What the hell?'

'That'll clear out the cobwebs,' he said, with a shudder.

'Detonate the spiders, more like. It's not like any syrup I've ever tasted, and it smells like meth.'

We looked at each other in disgust, then Leo started laughing.

'Your face!' he said, doing an impression of me then laughing again. The sound took me back to our time working together; it was so joyous and familiar. He was right, we'd had a right laugh when we'd been work buddies. It was Engelman that had moved the goal posts on the job and it wasn't Leo's fault they'd chosen him. I just hadn't been able to stomach the rejection. It was easier to hide away.

I took another sip of my port and tried to keep a straight face. 'Just to be polite,' I said. 'I don't want to hurt Ricardo's feelings.'

Leo took a slurp of his. 'Yes, it would be rude to reject their *finest vintage*.'

Not to be outdone, I had another mouthful and we silently dared each other to keep going, sip by sip, and by the end of the glass, it wasn't nearly so bad.

'Winner!' I said, feeling light-headed as I finished my port and pushed the empty glass away.

'I didn't realise it was a competition,' Leo said, smiling. 'I'd have made more effort.'

'Isn't everything?'

'In that case I'll… race you to the lift!' he shouted, jumping up. He was halfway there before I'd even registered what he'd said, but I gave it a go anyway, chasing him through the empty restaurant. All the other couples had gone to bed without us realising and we'd been left alone. Not that we were a couple of course.

'You cheated!' I teased, as the lift doors opened and he waved me in.

'Ladies first.'

'Why thank you, sir. A cheat, but a gentleman – and a scoundrel to boot.'

'I got a headstart to save you the trouble. It is our anniversary, after all.'

The lift was small and we had no choice but to face each other to fit in, both breathless from the run, a magnetic heat in the space between us. Leo silently reached behind me to press the button and my nose brushed against his neck, his musky aftershave was intoxicating and I felt myself being drawn towards him. I leant back to counterbalance the attraction, and he reached his hand out to steady me, his touch making me tingle. He was so tall and strong, and I felt wobbly inside as I looked up into his eyes.

'Goodnight then,' he murmured as the lift pinged for my floor. I tilted my head back to kiss him on the cheek, but he went the same way at the same time and nearly caught me on the mouth. We stopped for half a second, his silver eyes on mine, and then our lips found each other, tentatively at first, then kissing more deeply as I pressed myself into the corner of the lift and the doors started to close.

'Goodnight,' I said, running my fingers through his hair.

He stroked my cheek, kissing me again, deep and slow this time, then pulled back to look me in the eyes.

'Goodnight,' he said throatily, and I realised he'd stuck his foot out to jam the doors open.

I held on to his belt as I backed out of the lift, pulling him towards me, and then pushed him back in. 'Happy anniversary!'

Seventeen

Tuesday 29th June

I woke up with a smile on my face, and my first thought was of Leo. That kiss had been something else, and it had taken every ounce of willpower I'd had not to drag him back to my room. His lips had drawn me in somehow and I'd been helpless to resist as he'd kissed me, his arms wrapped tight around my waist, holding me close. Or had I kissed him? I shivered in pleasure at the memory then ran into the shower to remember it some more. We'd talked our way through cocktails, dinner, coffee and port and it was only when the clock chimed one that we'd realised the time. I didn't want to go back to *Esmeralda*. I wanted to stay here with my pretend husband and enjoy our pretend anniversary break. I'd forgotten how funny and interesting Leo could be. And cute of course. So, *so* cute. I'd done my best to ignore all that when we worked together, to try and stay professional, but it was proving impossible on this trip.

I squirted the tiny toiletries onto the pouffe, lathering them up one by one, and luxuriated in the space one last time. I scrubbed my body, washed my hair, shaved my legs again and slathered myself in mini moisturisers. It was back to the peacock dress today; yesterday's outfit was still full of shale and festering in a carrier bag.

The cotton layers filled with air as I skipped down to breakfast and I felt light as a ballerina. These dresses were gorgeous – I shouldn't have resisted buying one in every colour; a rainbow of puffball dresses was exactly what I needed to brighten my wardrobe up. Although the carefree vibe wouldn't have been quite the same back in London; fighting against the December wind as I sloshed my way into the office.

Leo wasn't up yet – ha! – I'd finally beaten him at something. I poured us both an apple juice and ordered two espressos, then filled a plate with pineapple slices, apricots and a selection of mini pastries. He liked his fruit in the morning, and I wanted to do something nice for him to show my appreciation. The poor man had booked me into a hotel, paid for my flight and taken me for dinner, and I'd accused him of being a nepo-baby snob.

I heard a whistle behind me and turned to find Leo looking spick and span in a dark green shirt and matching shorts. His quiff perfectly gelled to one side.

'What time do you call this?' I teased.

'Mid-morning? I've already been up an hour.' He eyed up my breakfast display. 'Expecting someone?'

'Just you.' I gestured to the empty chair opposite. 'And me. Obviously.'

'Oh. Right. Thought you might be having a double breakfast for the hangover.'

'Now there's an idea. Perfect conditions for it – an all-you-can-eat buffet and plenty of time to kill.'

'Not masses,' he said, checking his watch. 'I'm an anxious traveller so I like to get to the airport early. Missing the boat yesterday was my idea of hell, especially running for it in front of all those people. Chris has booked us a cab for ten.'

'Cool, no worries. I'm ready to go when you are,' I said, even though I had the opposite philosophy when it came to travel and liked to leave everything to the very last second. Life was too short to wait around in airports.

We sat and ate our breakfast like an old married couple, passing each other the milk and sharing the jams and honey. It was the first time I'd had a holiday husband, and it was kind of nice. I only ever went away with the girls, but one by one they'd paired off: first my sisters, then Abi with Tony and Sara with Henrik. I was running out of single girls to go away with. There was nothing worse than seeing couples on holiday sitting in silence. Staring past each other into space or gorging on their phones, desperate for attention from anyone but their 'significant' other. I liked to gossip with the girls and fill in the blanks from the night before. It was all I'd ever really known. But being with a man abroad was quite an interesting experiment, and there was something strangely comforting about Leo topping up my juice and ordering us more coffee. He was looking after me in a different kind of way to my girlies; he was taking charge of our breakfast experience, and I liked it.

'You'll be pleased to hear I'm already packed,' I said. 'One handbag and two carrier bags.'

'Very chic. Minimalist.'

'Cruising through life.'

'Nice pitch. Cruising for a bruising is our latest line.' We both laughed. 'It's a shame we can't all work on it together,'

Leo said, with a smile. 'That would throw them. If we did a joint presentation and suggested they double the fee.'

'Heidi isn't very good at sharing. Stranger danger and all that.'

'You and I are hardly strangers,' he said with a wink. I felt my cheeks burn and didn't know where to look as his phone started ringing. 'Cab's here,' he said, turning the alarm off. 'Time to shoot.'

I wanted to soak up every last second of our fake minibreak, but Leo had already stood up and was eager to leave. He had such a commanding presence that I didn't bother trying to wangle another five minutes, downing my coffee and wrapping a blueberry muffin in a napkin for later. We left the beautiful, marbled reception of the Harbour Club, where Leo had already settled the bill, and a spotless Mercedes had us outside Lajes Airport in less than ten minutes.

'Is it even open?' I peered out the window at the tiny building. 'I hope the planes are normal-sized and not those toy ones.'

Leo leapt out and held the door, as I went to pay the driver.

'It's already sorted,' he said, offering me his hand. 'All part of the *Amplify* service.'

'Oh, right. Thanks.' *Not again!* He was exasperating! Every time I thought to do something, he'd already done it. Maybe he would run the Excalibur account more efficiently than we did – he was giving me a masterclass in client service, that was for sure. Unless this was how real men treated women? It certainly hadn't been my experience up to now; I barely got offered a drink these days – but then, maybe my lack of enthusiasm was showing. Too many bad dates to mention. Audition after audition until they all blended into one.

We had nearly two hours to kill and only a coffee hatch and a duty-free kiosk for entertainment. I wasn't really in need of a litre of vodka or a sack of M&Ms, so I settled into one of the plastic seats and sent Heidi a quick text.

Me: We're on our way – should be with you around 4 p.m.

Heidi: Hurry up. Doing both our jobs is exhausting.

As if. She was probably writing that from the spa while having her toenails painted.

'How are you at cards?' Leo asked, pulling a fresh pack out of his pocket and ripping off the cellophane.

'What are we talking? Texas hold 'em? Blackjack?'

'Er… Old Maid? Snap?' He turned the cards to show me the pictures and I laughed.

'You've found my level… I'm excellent at both.'

'It was all they had,' he said, deftly dealing them into two piles. 'But for the record, I'm a card shark in the casino.'

'Oh really? Casinos make me feel sick.' I tidied my cards into a neat pile.

'Why's that?'

'I just hate everything about them. The lights, the noise, everyone either off-their-face drunk or sober and desperate, slinging around money they can't afford to lose. The one and only time I've been, I stood at the roulette table for an hour and watched the croupier sweep up piles and piles of losing chips, while the punters mindlessly doubled down to try and win their money back. Money's *too hard earnt* to throw it away like that.'

'What about the people who win?' Leo asked.

'Does anyone really win? Don't they just gather up their chips and bet them all away again. Like kids on the two-pence machines, pushing coins into the slots, until they've all gone.'

'Keeps them quiet though, no?'

'Keeps them numb, handing all the money back to the only real winner – the big casino owner in the sky.'

'Interesting metaphor for the Almighty.'

'No, not God. The mafia or the mob.'

'Ready?' Leo fixed me with a competitive stare. I wasn't sure if I'd distracted him enough with my blathering to get the upper hand, but I gave him a solid nod and we started putting cards down one after the other, gathering pace. *Monkey, lion, panda, snake, dog, dog...*

'Snap!' we both shouted, Leo's hand on top of mine, as the lady sitting opposite jumped.

'Too slow,' I said, sliding the cards towards me.

'I let you have that one,' he said, with a devilish grin.

We played again and he 'let me' win again, and again, and again.

'Winner, Kat Brennan!' He chuckled as I snatched up the last few cards with glee. He was far too slow. 'Very impressive play. I can see you have a passion for the game. I'm more of a *slow and steady wins the race* type.'

'No room for that attitude in Snap,' I said, solemnly. 'Another game?'

'Go on then,' he said, with a cheeky smile. 'You're still as much fun as you always were, you know.'

'Am I?'

'I was dreading the pair of us being stranded on our own for the night and now I wish we could stay for a week.'

As if I was going to fall for such an obvious distraction technique as the cards started flipping. *Lion, penguin, tiger, flamingo…*

'And about that goodnight kiss,' Leo continued, as I watched the cards. 'I'm not sure who kissed who in the end, but we should probably keep it under wraps as far as telling the others.'

Cat, giraffe, giraffe…

'Snap!' I shouted, far too enthusiastically.

'Is that OK?' Leo asked, keeping his hand on mine until I met his gaze.

'I'm nothing if not professional,' I said, moving my hand and the cards out from under his. 'What goes on tour, stays on tour, right?'

'I didn't mean it like that. It's not some dirty little secret, we can still…'

Bing bong. 'Ladies and gentlemen, we will shortly start boarding flight 4765 to Funchal. If you are travelling business class with us today, please make your way to the front of the queue.'

Leo jumped up and grabbed our bags. 'That's us.'

'We're flying business?'

'Absolutely,' he said, with a frown. 'This is a business trip, isn't it?'

That told me, then. In case I got any funny ideas. The Amplify expenses bill was going to be HUGE whether Brooke paid it all or not. I'd barely ordered a milkshake outside of the official allowance, but Leo clearly couldn't care less about indulging in excessive *incidentals*. His confidence was a lesson in taking up space. We boarded the plane and settled into our enormous seats with a glass of champagne each.

'Pleasure doing business with you,' I said, then pressed the button to raise the privacy glass between us. Leo knocked and I sniggered into my drink, then lowered it slightly. 'Yes?'

'Hi. I was wondering if…'

'Not today, thanks,' I said, zipping it back up.

He knocked again and I slid it all the way down, revealing his cheeky grin an inch at a time.

'It's been fun,' he said, staring into my eyes and making me giggle with nervous energy. 'Here's to the rest of our *business* trip, eh?'

I put my feet up and clinked his outstretched glass. This was the life. 'You said it, mister. Back to the bunk-bed battleground we go.'

Eighteen

'Finally! The reprobates return,' Heidi said, as Leo and I walked into the lounge. She was sat on a velvet couch with Brooke and Zach, and they were tucking into the scone layer of their afternoon tea. Tiny lumps in different flavours: cheese, chocolate chip, cherry and sultana. My mouth watered just looking at the gold stands crammed full of goodies.

'It took a while, but we managed to give you the slip,' Leo said, with a charming smile, nudging in next to Zach.

'I'm so sorry, Brooke!' I gushed. 'There was an accident on the walk down from the volcano and we stopped to help. A lady fell and broke her ankle.'

'A pair of angels doing the Lord's work – how can I complain about that?'

'Exactly. Kat called the air ambulance and did a great job of keeping her calm while I carried her down.'

Not technically true, but I nodded along with Leo's version of the story. His eyes were on me, and my face was hot. I felt totally exposed. They were all going to find out we'd kissed and Heidi would be furious. She was very black and white when it came to business and would see it as defecting to the other side. I had to keep my professional wits about me and *act normal*. Sweating was not the answer.

The lounge had been decorated to look like the Orient Express, with wooden booths, crystal glasses and glittering silver cutlery. There were gold bells on the wall to tinkle if you needed more of anything, and barely a murmur as people stuffed their faces with smoked salmon sandwiches and cream cakes.

'We've got the whole day to explore Madeira,' Brooke said, cradling her cup and saucer. 'And I appreciate you all need some downtime, and thinking time – as do I, but Dahlia has managed to get us tickets for the island toboggan. Apparently it's an absolute "must-do" while we're here.'

'The Carreiros do Monte?' Zach asked, looking vaguely interested in the conversation for once. 'Yeah, count me in. How did she manage that? It's been fully booked online for days.'

'Where there's a Dahlia, there's a way,' Brooke said. 'She once got me on the front row for New York Fashion Week, three seats down from Anna Wintour. The girl knows everyone.'

'Tobogganing on water?' Now that was a safety hazard. I had visions of the five of us flying over a waterfall on a plastic sled without any brakes. *Red flag, red flag...*

'No, on the roads. Big wicker baskets on wheels, and two men push you down the hill by the looks of it,' Leo said, reading off his phone. 'Known as the gondolas of Madeira, it starts at the top of the island and finishes in Funchal.'

That didn't sound much better and I sensed Heidi recoil. 'How fantastic,' she said, with a well-trained smile. 'Although, unfortunately I'm allergic to er… wicker.'

'Are you, really?' Zach asked, in a sardonic tone.

'Yup. But I will absolutely cheer you all on from the sidelines.'

Leo frowned. 'Isn't wicker a weaving technique?'

'It's the bamboo or whatever they use,' Heidi said, smoothly. 'My skin is very sensitive.'

Brooke didn't even seem to be listening. 'We'll take the cable car up the hill, so grab whatever y'all need for the day and let's meet on the bridge in half an hour. OK?'

She marched off and I flopped down in her chair. I felt like I'd already done a full day's work and was shattered from all the travel but had to suck it up and get on with it. I ordered a coffee and a champagne and popped a scone in my mouth. Caffeine, sugar and alcohol would see me through.

Four black stallions with white plumes and plaited tails stood waiting for us as we got off the ship, held steady by a man in a top hat.

'You guys enjoy yourselves!' Dahlia called, helping the four of us into the cart. 'This is one of the excursions we are trialling for VIPs, so I want to hear all about it when you get back. Starting with a horse-drawn carriage up to the cable car and a queue-jump for the toboggan.'

'Are we allowed to do that?'

'Yep, all sorted. Here are your tickets for the cable car, then go straight to the front of the toboggan queue and show your Excalibur pass for the Carreiros do Monte.' She handed everything to me, as the responsible adult in charge. Heidi had of course reneged on her cheerleader promise under the guise of working on the pitch, so it was just the four of us on a double date. I sat opposite Leo in the carriage, clenching my thighs tight to avoid any physical contact. I could feel myself sweating at the effort, his pheromones buzzing around me as I tried to hold it together.

'Off we go,' Leo said, as the horses wobbled over the cobbles. The harbour was a beautiful web of pathways and roads going off in different directions and it was another gorgeous, sunny day. We passed the Mercado Dos Lavradores, the farmer's market, with its colourful fruit displays. Huge piles of bananas, mushrooms and potatoes out the front where sellers offered passers-by samples of tropical delicacies. A neat queue had formed outside the bakery, where the smell of fresh bread mixed with sugar and cinnamon lured people in. We clip-clopped past whitewashed buildings with ornate shutters and blue and white tiles, surrounded by lush green trees and flowers in red, pink and purple. It was the perfect way to see the island. I felt like I was in a musical and might burst into song at any moment.

'Ain't this the prettiest place?' Brooke trilled, handing out some mints. 'I just love Europe and I *extra love* that our cruises bring all these places to people. Or should I say all these people to places.'

On an individual level it was great for people to see so much in such a short space of time. And there was probably some sort of carbon footprint efficiency in so many people doing the same thing all at once. But we were like a swarm of locusts piling off the ship, in and out of the shops and restaurants and onto the cable car; eating, drinking, buying and spreading out to do and see whatever we wanted. Feeding off the island for a few hours before we got back on the boat and disappeared. It was hard not to see us as using and abusing the island's resources, even though logically I knew the locals relied on tourists to make a living.

We sank into the buttery leather seats of the cable car, enjoying the island view from another perspective, as it slowly dragged us up the hill. The flora and fauna laid itself out below like a vegetable medley with the layers of different greens in stark contrast to the icy blues and turquoise of the ocean.

'This is the life, isn't it?' Zach said, unzipping his jacket and making himself comfortable.

'Just missing a mini freezer with ice-creams,' I joked. 'And frozen daiquiris.'

'Great idea,' Brooke said. 'When we're curating experiences for our VIPs, we can add that into the brainstorm. I'll speak to Dahlia. For now, all I can offer is… another mint?'

Leo kept glancing over, sending me weak at the knees. This level of closeness was too much after last night. I needed some time and space to think about our conversation over dinner (among other things), not to be wedged into a tiny glass bubble with him, boinging about. It was a relief to reach the top of the hill and step out into the fresh air. Brooke and Zach must surely have sensed the sexual tension pulsating between the two of us. I could barely breathe.

'Well, take a look at all this,' Brooke squealed. 'Real-life HD.'

The colours were rich and vibrant; no filter needed – Mother Nature had already added hers. The cable car station opened out into Monte Palace and Gardens from the bygone days of Madeiran gentry. Butterflies danced in delight among the plethora of plants. Ancient trees and beautifully manicured rose bushes added a soft fragrance to the Japanese-style ponds, ornamental fountains and elaborate red pagoda. The gardens were mapped into separate squares and looked like red and green flags from a distance, slowly revealing themselves to be carefully curated plant combinations that would give Kew Gardens a run for its money.

'Ain't this just so magical?' Brooke said with a twirl and Zach rolled his eyes. His British disdain was on full show. 'Should we take a turn around the gardens? That's what they say in *Bridgerton* ain't it?'

'They certainly do!' Leo said, in a mock-posh voice, offering her his arm. 'Let's.'

Zach wasn't keen to follow suit and marched on ahead while I trailed behind full of jealousy at their closeness. I wanted to be folded into Leo's arms. Brooke had snuggled in way too close for my liking, but I couldn't very well burst through the middle of them and interrupt. I hurried to catch them up and linked her other arm instead.

'Have you ever tried Madeira? As in the wine? We'll have to drink some while we're here,' I said, grappling for her attention.

'Hell, yeah. Let's grab a couple bottles at lunch,' Brooke replied, getting into *The Wizard of Oz* vibe as the three of us walked in time.

'It's a type of port, isn't it?' Leo said. 'Count me out of that, thanks. I had enough last night to last me a while.'

'That tiny thimbleful?' I teased.

'It was enough.'

Zach was slowly waving in the distance. 'Hurry!' he shouted, and we ran towards him. 'How sick is this?'

We rounded the corner, and the toboggans came into view. A bunch of hot air balloons were missing their baskets somewhere out there. Huge wicker sledges on wheels were lined up in a row, and couple after couple were being helped in by men wearing white suits and boater hats. Two per toboggan, they circled the baskets, then pushed them along the road to gain momentum before leaping on the edges like the guys who ran the waltzers at the local fair.

Zach jumped in the front toboggan, while the huge queue huffed and puffed, giving the four of us death stares. 'Who's coming?' he shouted.

'Me!' Brooke ran over and got in, leaving me and Leo looking at each other.

'Alone again,' he said, wiggling his eyebrows as Brooke and Zach sped off with a whoop.

'We might get ten minutes if we're lucky,' I said, nudging him.

'Plenty of time.' He took my hand and helped me into the toboggan, then squeezed in next to me, his arm around my shoulder. 'Do you mind?'

'Not at all,' I said, snuggling into him. There weren't any seatbelts and his grip made me feel safe and secure.

'Ready for it?' a beardy man in white shouted, and we nodded.

'Then let's GO!' said another and they started rolling us along the road. My stomach dropped at the realisation I had no idea what was around the corner or what this whole thing was all about. It could have been a sheer cliff drop for all we knew; none of us had really questioned it, but it was too late now. We'd watched cart after cart fly off and disappear with abandon and I felt like I was inching up a rollercoaster track, getting ready to drop. Madeira looked spectacular, with her glittering white buildings shining in the sunshine, and a couple of donkeys hee-hawed at us from a nearby field. Leo gave me a squeeze as the cart sped up and the warmth of his hand gave me goosebumps.

We whizzed along the tarmac and I held my breath, but it was just a plain old road waiting for us – smooth and wide, with nothing to fear. The two men were riding the toboggan like a skateboard, steering with their bodyweight, their rubber shoes working as extra leverage to navigate the bends and whenever we started to slow, they'd paw at the road in sync to speed us back up again. This was no job for a couch potato.

'Flying down mountains is becoming our thing,' Leo said. 'Can you ski?'

'God, no. I'm a working-class Bootle babe! Although if Dahlia's got it planned in, I'll give it a go.'

He frowned. 'You can't go hurling yourself down a mountain without knowing what you're doing.'

'What do you call this?'

He laughed, as the sledge zigzagged, sliding us back and forth and pushing us even closer together. 'Fair point.'

'I don't mind taking chances, as long as I feel safe,' I said, smiling up at him.

'Oh yeah?' I melted as he kissed me, holding on tight, our legs glued together as we flew down the hill. The wind whipped through my hair, making my skin tingle as he pulled me closer, both of us knowing it was a risky move and we could only get away with it for a few seconds.

We felt the men in white pull on the brakes and sprang back as we rolled down the final part of the run. Traditional Madeiran villas with colourful tiled walls were now dotted in among the buildings in yellow and pink, as the centre of Funchal appeared. Brooke and Zach were brushing themselves off on the side of the road and Leo pulled his arm back to resume business mode and somehow caught my necklace on his sleeve. I felt it snap and tried to grab it but ended up holding the delicate chain and watching in horror as my beloved liver bird flew off behind us into a thicket of bushes.

'No!!!' I shouted, as the Carreiros Morris dancers screeched to a stop and I jumped out, running back to where I thought it had fallen.

'What's happened?' Leo called.

'My necklace, my Liverpool necklace…' I cried, already knowing it was lost forever. There was no chance of finding a tiny pendant in that huge hedge – assuming it had even landed in there.

'Oh no, I'm so sorry,' Leo said, scanning the road helplessly, as toboggan after toboggan flew by. 'Was that me?'

I shook my head. No point playing the blame game. It wasn't anybody's fault; it had just happened. Probably more my fault for sitting so close to him. Passers-by were staring at the ground as they walked past, trying to work out what we were looking for, and I clutched my hand to my neck, feeling naked without my lucky liver bird to keep me safe.

'Can you get another one?'

I shook my head again. Mum and Dad had bought it for my eighth birthday, and it was my most precious possession. 'They were a limited edition – only a hundred ever made and I had number eight. My lucky number. It's irreplaceable.'

Nineteen

Thursday 1st July

Dahlia blew hard on her whistle and everyone in the pool stopped and turned.

'Good morning, cruisers!' she shouted, passing a ball between her hands. 'Who wants to play some VOLLEYBALL?' She beamed as if she'd offered everyone a plate of free cocaine. The sporty-looking types cheered while the normal people – *my people* – slithered to the edge of the pool and made a sharp exit.

Leo, Zach and I were watching from the sidelines, hoping to get away with observing from afar this time. It was on the schedule, but we didn't need to physically *play* to engage with the idea. It was much better to view the experience from above, like an omnipresent creative force. Take it all in while enjoying a frappe or two. The relentless hum of *Esmeralda*'s engine pitched up a notch as Dahlia put the owners of abs and bikini bodies into teams. She did a head count then furrowed her delicate brow and checked her clipboard.

'Uh-oh,' Leo said, under his breath, as she scanned the sunbeds, then the bar, and then stopping when she got to us. 'Busted.'

The three of us looked in every direction but hers as she tried to get our attention and I took a slurp of my iced coffee. Then the shrill sound of her whistle made us jump.

'Kat, Leo, Zach! You're on my list!'

'What's that?' Zach called, while I took another mouthful.

'In the pool please, guys. Let's go!'

Zach reluctantly stood up and Leo pulled off his T-shirt. The two of them couldn't have been more different. Zach was a hairy bear, covered in tattoos, with the stomach of Winnie the Pooh and the dress sense of Rupert. Whereas Leo was smooth, muscular and in perfect proportion; he clearly looked after himself and didn't mind everyone knowing it.

'We'd rather watch if that's OK,' I tried, knowing it was too late to negotiate.

'Not OK, no. I need you to make up the numbers, otherwise there aren't enough players.'

I inwardly groaned.

'Where's Heidi?' Leo asked, his naked chest distracting me. I looked away, willing myself not to blush.

'Erm… she sends her apologies.' She couldn't be bothered but I wasn't going to tell them that – even though they already knew.

'Allergic to water, now, is she?' Zach said, then bombed into the pool, soaking the front row of sunbathers.

I was wearing my one-piece for maximum coverage but hadn't reckoned on doing any sports when I bought it. This place was starting to feel like a boot camp, but with thirteen pairs of eyes on me and Dahlia threatening to blow the whistle again, opting out wasn't an option.

'Just a second,' I called, peeling off my very elasticated jumpsuit.

Thank God I'd shaved my legs so closely in the Azores. There wasn't enough space to do them in our 'en suite' – which seemed ridiculous when we were on a thousand-foot boat. I'd have to do them in the changing room showers later. I put my swimming cap on and shimmied into the pool, shuddering as cold water crept into every crevice. I loathed swimwear and hated team sports, so all in all this was my idea of hell.

'Leo, take a blue bib, Kat and Zach, you're with the reds.'

'I'm not very good I'm afraid,' I whispered, already worried about letting the team down.

'I'll cover you,' Zach said, much to my surprise.

My survival strategy was to look busy and avoid the ball as much as possible. I lay low, snout out, with only the net between me and Leo, as he pointed at his eyes, then mine, and puffed out his chest.

'You're going down, Brennan.'

'We'll see about that!' I replied, knowing full well if I made any attempt to play I'd go so far down I'd drown. Seven of them and seven of us. Dahlia blew her whistle and a hench-looking man belted the ball over the net. Zach whacked it back, then Leo slam-dunked it in front of me for the first point and fist-bumped the girl next to him.

'Hey!' I said, getting a face full of water, the chlorine stinging my eyes. Idiot.

It was half an hour of terror. Palpitations whenever the ball came my way, Zach constantly leaping over to take my shot, me shrinking back and squealing. I was the last to serve and we needed the point. I threw the ball in the air and it boinged prematurely off my fist and smashed Zach in the back of the head.

'Oops,' I said, wincing. 'Second serve.' I channelled my inner Karate Kid and decided to go underarm to catch them unawares, pushing the ball up as hard as I could. Miraculously it went over the net, and I was so shocked, I bobbed in the water like a lemon while it bounced from player to player, both teams belting it as hard as they could to try and win the final point and the game. Leo smacked the ball and I sensed it heading in my direction as the team turned to face me. Zach swooshed over, but there was no way he'd make it in time. I threw my hands in the air, but I was too slow, and it clonked me on the head. I could almost hear the cartoon birds tweeting above me as I dunked underwater and swallowed a mouthful.

My head had inadvertently kept the ball in the game, and I came up for air just in time to see Zach bounce the ball over the net for the win.

'Yessss!' The red team whooped and cheered, jumping around and giving each other high fives. Zach held his hand up to me, but I was seeing double and missed. Feeling woozy, I pulled myself out of the pool and lay back on the cool tiles, my head pulsing in time to the music.

'You OK, Kat?' Dahlia shouted as I closed my eyes. My head was spinning as if I'd had a skinful, which only made the dizziness worse.

'The ball hit me quite hard,' I said, cracking one eye open and rubbing my forehead where a lump was forming.

'Coming through, coming through. Ship first-aider,' I heard her call as the crowd shuffled back to give her space.

'I'll be OK,' I said, sitting up and shading my eyes, embarrassed by all the attention.

'I'm fully trained. Lie back please.' Dahlia rolled me onto one side and put me in the recovery position.

'Is she conscious?' Leo asked.

'Yes,' I said.

I felt somebody gently lift my head and wedge in a pillow.

'Let me clear her airways.'

'They're clear!' I yelled weakly, the pair of them ignoring me while they argued it out. I didn't need mouth-to-mouth, and certainly not in front of the entire ship.

'If it's concussion, she'll need the nurse.' Leo brushed my hair back to look at the lump. 'Oh my God, Kat, I'm so sorry. I really whacked it.'

'I'm fine, honestly…' I closed my eyes as the sun was too bright and harsh without my shades on, and Leo's hand softly stroking my hair felt too good. Then suddenly a strong pair of arms was picking me up and a smooth chest was holding me in as I was lolled along the corridor. It was a sensation I hadn't had for quite some time, but wrapped in a towel and held tight, I felt safe and warm, and protected.

'Here we are.' Leo's voice was unmistakable, and I could see Dahlia running on ahead, flinging open the door of the medical centre.

'Urghgh,' I groaned. My head was killing me. It felt like it might split in two.

'Hi, Claire,' Dahlia said, pointing Leo towards the bays.

'Oooh hello, dear. Who have we got here, then?' The ship nurse smiled up at us from behind her desk, her pinafore and matching hat gleaming white. There was a waft of antiseptic in the air and classical music played quietly in the corner, giving the place a sense of calm. It felt like we'd crossed over into another dimension compared to the raucous glare and lurid colours of the rest of the ship.

'Kat Brennan. Room 1086,' Leo called behind him as he hurried in. 'She's been hit in the face with a ball.' He laid me down on the nearest bed. 'Will she be OK? It was my fault. I shouldn't have hit it so hard.'

'They were playing volleyball in the pool,' Dahlia added. Or not, as it turned out.

'Let's have a look at you, then.' Claire put a cool palm on my forehead, then felt for my pulse and checked her watch. 'You'll have a right shiner there tomorrow, lovey,' she whispered, flashing a torch in my eyes, then noting something down.

'She blacked out for a few seconds, so I brought her straight here,' Dahlia said. 'Was that the right thing to do? Or should I have gone in with mouth-to-mouth? I couldn't remember.'

Claire looked aghast. 'Good Lord, no. Mouth-to-mouth for concussion? What are they teaching in the first-aid sessions these days? Leave her with me, please, and I'll get her fixed. What's your name, lovey? Are you next of kin?' she asked Leo, who blushed at the suggestion.

'No. Er... no.' He cleared his throat. 'We're just friends.'

'Cruising *friends* then, is it?' she asked, knowingly. Was that a thing? Maybe we could use it in the pitch. My brain whirred into action. *Friends who cruise together... and booze together... fuse together.* There wasn't time to be lazing around in the sick bay – Heidi and I needed every spare minute to work on the presentation and come up with a winning idea.

'We're on the cruise together,' Leo said, slowly, searching for the right words. 'But we're not *together*, together.'

Claire tutted. 'These apps have got a lot to answer for, if you ask me.'

'They're with Brooke,' Dahlia interjected.

'Ohhhh. Gotcha.' She nodded. 'Head office VIPs. Well, if this is a test, she'll get nothing but top-class treatment from me, don't you worry. Now, out you go, both of you. Who shall I call when she's ready to collect?'

I listened in while pretending to be asleep.

'Me,' Leo said, handing over his business card. 'My mobile is on there. I'm in room 1085. I'll pop back in half an hour or so though and see how she's doing.'

Claire took it from him with a smile, then closed the door. 'Right then, lovey, I'm all yours. Now let's get some arnica cream on that eye, shall we?'

'For crying out loud, *what* is going on?' I could hear Heidi bellowing in the reception. 'Can I not just come in and see her for five minutes?'

'I can't stop you, but I'd prefer Ms Brennan to rest a while longer if possible,' Claire whispered urgently, racing after Heidi as she barged in.

'Kat? Are you awake?' Heidi called, loudly. Her bedside manner needed some work.

I opened one eye and nodded. The bruising was already coming through on the other eye, so it was best to leave it shut.

'What have you done to yourself?' she gasped, scanning my face over. 'You can't look like this for the pitch.'

'Go easy on the sympathy, won't you? I got smacked in the face by a ball.'

'Did you! What ball? Where?' She looked around the room as if she was expecting one to fire at her from the ceiling. 'Are you OK?'

'Yeah… it was an accident.'

'Who did it? You should claim on their travel insurance for assault!'

'Leo. But he didn't do it on purpose.'

She looked apoplectic. 'I bet. Trying to sabotage our chances, no doubt.'

'I moved at the wrong moment and got in the way of the ball. It looks worse than it feels.'

'Well, it's how it looks that matters.' Heidi huffed. She was raging. 'Appearances are everything in PR, Kat, as you know – especially in a pitch sitch. I don't want the Excalibur exec team thinking we're a pair of street wrestlers.'

'At least I've still got my teeth,' I said, baring them for her.

'And you haven't broken your nose… have you?' She stared at it and I shook my head. 'Let's see how you look in a few days and workshop it then. We can always wear matching sunglasses and do a *Blues Brothers*-themed presentation.'

Claire appeared at Heidi's shoulder with two glasses of water. 'The arnica cream is triple strength and works wonders on bruising,' she soothed. 'This time next week you'll barely notice it.'

'See? Plenty of time to get myself back together ahead of the presentation.'

'Thank you, Nurse,' Heidi said. 'That's reassuring. Well, in that case, let's use this as thinking time. If you're bedbound for the day, maybe you can sketch out a few ideas?'

I opened both my eyes at that, and Claire and I stared at her.

'Or... not.' She shrugged, then quickly changed the subject. 'Actually, Nurse, while I'm here. Could you have a look at my shoulder? It feels out of whack; I must have slept on it funny. Are you trained in shiatsu by any chance?'

Claire shook her head. 'I'm afraid not,' she said, pointedly. 'Not much call for shiatsu as a medical nurse, but they do a wonderful deep-tissue massage in the spa.'

'Great, I might pop and see her now, then,' Heidi said. 'I'll leave you to it, Kat. Feel better soon, won't you? Like, *really soon.*'

'I'll try. Enjoy your massage.'

She flounced out, taking all the oxygen with her and Claire gave a low whistle.

'Is that your... sister?' I could see her trying to work out the dynamic.

I laughed and shook my head. 'My sisters are *much worse.* No, that's my boss.'

'Ahhh, of course, you're both on a working trip. I'll remember for next time and stop her barging in to ambush you.'

She turned the lights down as a wave of exhaustion washed over me. The bed seemed enormous compared to the bunk, and the pillow was soft against my cheek. I sank into it and closed my eyes, relieved to have permission to rest. A momentary break from all the drama and pressure, not that it would stop me worrying completely. But I could dream about the pitch instead of actively thinking about it and maybe my subconscious would work it all out.

Twenty

Saturday 3rd July

Thiago dropped the anchor in the Jardim do Tabaco quay and the five of us took a boat taxi along the river Tagus and into Lisbon. The harbour was jammed full of yachts, with happy tourists breakfasting on sunny decks, while the crew knotted ropes around them preparing to set sail. Heidi was still in a huff with Leo about the state of my face, but it was just a black eye and some bruising – it would heal. I glanced across at him, lounging back on the other side of the boat, like a poster boy for the Mediterranean. All linen shirt and shorts with ironed on turn-ups, his mirrored aviators sparkling in the sun. He clocked me checking out his bulging calves and winked.

'I hear you've had another trip to the medical centre Kat,' Brooke said, her head on one side. 'That eye looks sore. How's your head?'

'Much better, thank you.'

'Can you all be more careful, please? We'll have to add danger money to the pitch budget at this rate.'

'Yeah, nice try, Leo,' Heidi piped up. 'There should be rules against trying to knock out the competition by physical force.'

'That would imply we see you as competition,' he shot back, without missing a beat, as Heidi gaped at the air like a fish out of water.

'It was an accident,' I said. 'If anyone's to blame, it's me, for getting in the way.'

Leo frowned. 'Are you sure you're OK over there? You look a bit peaky.'

'It's just so vast,' I muttered, closing my eyes and swallowing down my panic. I couldn't wait to get off this boat and onto dry land. The shore was so close now, I was half-tempted to dive off the side and swim.

'The Atlantic?' he chuckled. 'Yeah, you could say that.'

'There must be all sorts down there still waiting to be discovered,' Zach added, peering over the side.

'That's really helpful, thanks.'

'To think all human life started from an amoeba.' Leo shook his head. 'Unbelievable really, isn't it?'

'I can believe it with some humans,' Heidi replied, pointedly.

The driver's microphone clicked. 'To our right you can see the Lisbon coastline with the famous Castelo de São Jorge at the very top. Saint George's Castle, which is a very popular spot among tourists and one I would highly recommend to you all.'

It was a spectacular sight, set high up on the hill, watching over the city.

'Lisbon will be the jewel in *Esmeralda*'s crown,' Brooke whispered, leaning in to huddle us all together. 'It's our last official stop and we want to ramp it up a gear for the final few days of the cruise.'

'How so?' Heidi asked, taking photos of the shoreline.

'It's all on the app, but Chef has planned an exquisite Portuguese banquet on board; we've done a deal with the harbour restaurants for our guests to try a local dish, included in their cruise card; we have port tasting with grand cru vintners, a castanet show and a samba performance from Chico and Catarina, to mark the ship's final turn.'

'Sounds incredible,' I said, making mental notes.

'Peri peri chicken all round,' Zach drawled, sneaking a drag on his vape.

Leo laughed. 'The original cheeky Nando's.'

'I've never understood that phrase,' Brooke said, with a frown. 'How can a Nando's be cheeky? It doesn't make sense.'

'It's more *sneaky* than cheeky,' I said, confusing myself. 'A quick one… kind of a secret treat.'

Brooke was completely baffled. 'Secret chicken?'

Zach snorted then started to cough.

'Kat said it, not me!' Brooke said, affronted.

Heidi picked up the baton. 'It's more *covert* than secret. On the side… of a night out.'

'Or in the middle,' Leo added, catching my eye and daring me not to laugh.

'It's an unexplainable concept,' Zach said, eventually.

'Another one of your idiosyncrasies, eh? You funny old Brits.'

The river Tagus stretched out ahead of us and the driver pointed out places of interest from the front of the boat. The Belém Tower, the Jerónimos Monastery, the 25 de Abril Bridge. They all looked nice enough, but the only place I was really interested in was the hotel Heidi and I were checking into. We'd agreed our stay in Lisbon would be off-ship, and I was *so excited*, I couldn't wait. I was ready to power down with a large gin and tonic in the bath, followed by room service and a mindless flick through Netflix. Modern-day meditation in a big double bed. *Bliss.*

'On our left we have one of Lisbon's most famous landmarks, the Cristo Rei statue, inspired by Christ the Redeemer in Brazil. There is a viewing platform, which is accessible by boat across the river or taxi over the bridge – a wonderful spot to take panoramic photos of the city.'

The enormous stone Jesus gave us a wave as we floated by, his arms outstretched, sending out blessings to the world. The crew stopped for a beat and did the sign of the cross.

'I don't know about y'all, but I could do with a few hours to catch up on some work,' Brooke said, frowning at her phone. 'How's about we meet for lunch later and then take the evening for some personal time?'

'Great idea,' Leo gushed.

'Amazing,' I agreed enthusiastically, glad she wasn't one for sarcasm. I could feel Leo's eyes on me, but I knew I'd laugh if I looked at him.

'Glad y'all agree.'

'Gives us time to check in and get our bearings,' Heidi said, as the driver announced we were heading for the first stop.

'Check in?' Brooke asked.

'Yes, didn't I mention it? We've got a hotel for this final slice of the trip,' she said, hurriedly. 'Kat and I have a board meeting tomorrow before breakfast, so we need somewhere private to Zoom.'

'With reliable Wi-Fi,' I added. *And a double bed to loll around in.*

'The hustle never stops,' Zach said with a sly grin. 'Fair enough. You'll need your other clients when Excalibur Cruises comes over to us.'

Brooke shook her head, but the corner of her mouth turned up in a smirk. 'Now, now… let's all play nice.'

'We can get off here, in fact,' Heidi said, checking her map. 'Yes. This is the closest stop to the hotel.'

Not according to my calculations, but maybe there was a shortcut. Or more likely she just wanted to get on dry land and have some space as soon as physically possible. The pair of us smiled at the three of them as the boat took forever to bob to a stop.

'What say we meet at three at the harbour then?' Brooke tinkled. 'We can try a local wine or two and the Caldo Verde soup everyone raves about.'

Heidi nodded and Leo gave a thumbs up. 'Fine by us,' he said.

'Sounds like my kind of lunch,' I said, following Heidi off the boat. 'Late and liquid.'

We waved them off and jumped in a cab, both glad to finally be free.

'I thought we'd never get away,' Heidi said, with a sigh of relief. 'This trip is feeling more like an endurance test every day. I'm not sure I can take anymore.'

I nearly eye-rolled at her histrionics, she was never one to under-react. 'You're doing great. We'll be back in London before you know it, and I've been playing with a pitch line that might cheer you up.'

'Really? Go on…?'

'The split trip sparked the idea when we were all on Terceira Island. You and Zach were living it up at the Uzu Yacht Club, while Leo and I surfed down a volcano, having a polar opposite experience.'

Heidi smiled. 'You can say that again.'

'I've had *unimaginable moments* repeating like an ear worm in my mind ever since and been applying it each day as the trip has gone on. Cruising is like going off-grid for holidays – you can't really imagine what might happen – you just have to wait and see. Even now, you and I will have a different experience of Lisbon to the others.'

'Interesting,' Heidi said, tilting her head. 'I like it. Unimaginable meaning 'off the scale' but also doing things that haven't been done before. It certainly rings true for me; this trip has been non-stop surprises. I could never have imagined it.'

'And if that's our experience when the two of us have been sharing a room, think of the extremes we could show across *all* the guests and crew.'

Heidi's face shone with excitement as the taxi stopped outside the Hilton and bellboys descended on us from both sides. 'There's so much scope to play with, I'm already thinking of ideas to sketch up.'

'Brilliant. I've scribbled a few down too, so let's play around with some scenarios, then we can share with the team when we're back.'

Twenty-one

It was the third time my alarm had gone off, meaning my snoozing window was well and truly over. I'd faceplanted into bed as soon as I'd walked into the hotel room and I really, *really* didn't want to get up from my power nap, get changed and paste on a smile. But that was what PR was all about and these relationship-building opportunities with Brooke could make or break us. The relationship was half the battle when it came to a pitch. My phone screen was covered in messages, which I read with one eye open, and one still on snooze.

Life's a Pitch Group Chat:

Brooke: Ronaldo's is booked for 3 p.m.

Heidi: See you there.

Zach: Not feeling 100% so won't make it. Enjoy.

Leo: Rest up, man, I'll represent ☺

What *the hell*? That wasn't any kind of get-out surely? I hadn't felt more than eighty-five per cent for years. So now it was just us girls and Leo. I had no idea how I'd be able to handle myself in such close proximity to him in public. I couldn't stop thinking about the way he'd kissed me – I'd felt it all the way down to my toes. There was no answer from Heidi's mobile, so I dragged myself into the shower and stuck my head under the water to force myself awake. Showering on the boat was always quick and panicked, so it felt good to enjoy a full five minutes without worrying that the hot water might run out. I straightened my hair, which seemed to have grown five inches, then threw on my denim dress and corky wedges and felt like a new woman. I tried Heidi again, putting the phone on loudspeaker while I threaded through my dangly earrings, but no joy. She was probably in the bath, furious at the phone repeatedly ringing so I left her a voice note to say I'd see her at the restaurant. I was keen to get out and explore Lisbon on foot and didn't want to hang around.

There was a hospitable warmth about the city, and the cobbles seemed to glow as I walked along the main drag towards an arch in the castle wall. Crumbly old buildings with colourful facades and beautifully decorated Juliet balconies were wedged between shops and busy aperitivo bars. Potted olive trees festooned with fairy lights decorated the street and candlelit shrines covered with rosary beads served as a reminder of the religious foundations of Portugal. The rich history of Lisbon was on proud display wherever I looked. I absorbed the cool vibe as I wandered through the streets, watching myself move towards the harbour as a blue dot on Google Maps. A guitarist in a voluminous shirt crooned softly over samba beats, the sun highlighting the gold brocade on his waistcoat. Al fresco diners enjoyed the afternoon sunshine with drinks and Portuguese tapas – *petiscos* – and I felt a sense of contentment as a little girl wandered over with a bucket of orange roses.

'A flower for you, pretty lady? One euro.'

'No, thank you.'

'Please? Only one euro,' she insisted, picking one out for me and holding it up. 'Your husband will pay.'

'I don't have a husband.'

'Boyfriend?'

I shook my head, feeling sorry for us both. 'No boyfriend, either.'

Her puzzled little face said it all. I was far too old not to at least have a boyfriend.

'Hey, Kat! Wait up!' I turned to find Leo jogging towards me. 'Love the dress,' he said, checking me out.

'A rose for your rose?' A perfect bud appeared between us as we walked – she was a resilient saleswoman; I'd give her that.

'How much?' Leo asked, taking it from her.

'Two euro.'

He gave her a coin and handed me the rose. 'I'm so sorry about your eye, Kat. Honestly, I'm such an idiot for getting carried away and playing so rough. How does it feel? I've been worried.'

'A bit sore but I haven't cracked open the pirate patches yet. Honestly, don't worry about it – I should have ducked. I'm hopeless at sports.'

Leo looked sheepish, but he didn't push the apology. 'Dahlia's lovely, until you try and skip class and then she's like a dog with a bone. She won't take no for an answer.'

'Unless you're Heidi, who's said no to pretty much everything. Lazy cow.'

Ronaldo's came into view as both our phones beeped.

Life's a Pitch Group Chat:

Heidi: Mi.

Brooke: You OK, Heidi? Is that autocorrect for Hi?

Me: Oh no – that's our migraine code. Heidi can't see to type. DON'T WORRY, HEIDI. SLEEP IT OFF.

A thumbs up appeared next to my comment.

Brooke: Feel better soon! I'm running late myself. @Kat @Leo – shall we rain check and regroup back on the ship?

Leo and I scanned our screens then looked at each other.

'And then there were two,' he said, with a big grin. 'Smells too good to turn around now. Shall we?'

My stomach grumbled in reply. 'We shall. Out of respect for Brooke.'

'And to represent Heidi and Zach…'

'Absolutely,' I agreed, with a mischievous smile.

The restaurant was set back from the harbour, with a terrace full of packed tables. A spicy aroma filled the air and sizzling plates of chicken and prawns poured out from the kitchen in all directions, delivered at speed by a team of lads overseen by an old man. Presumably Ronaldo (McDonaldo) himself.

He ran over to greet us as if we were old friends, shaking Leo's hand, then kissing mine. '*Boa tarde*! Welcome both!'

'We have a table booked under Brooke Harris?' Leo said. 'Or possibly Excalibur?'

I was embarrassed to be rocking up as a two, while secretly delighted. Another date with Leo in plain sight, without having to make any excuses. They'd all cried off, so what else could we do? 'It was supposed to be five for lunch, but the others aren't well.'

'No problem for me,' he said, eyeing my rose. 'And more private for you. This way, please.'

He found us a table for two in the centre of the action and took our drinks order, returning promptly with a jug of rosé and a basket of bread. Leo poured a glug of olive oil into the hand-painted dish, and I poured out the wine. We were turning into quite the team.

'Do you think the others are having lunch without us?'

'Because we're so unbearable?' Leo said, a flirtatious glint in his eye. 'It hadn't occurred to me, but now you mention it…'

I laughed. 'I'm happy for them if they are. I didn't think we'd get chance to eat together again, just the two of us.'

'Like a date, you mean?'

I shifted in my chair at the thought of dating Leo. 'Erm… if you like.' How was he doing this to me? My whole body was full of warning bells, but I couldn't resist his cheeky, suggestive smile. I wondered if this was how the Dinky Drinks team had felt. Pinned to their seats and hypnotised.

He held up his glass to clink mine and the two of us were in our own private bubble again: the surrounding noise seemed to quieten to a murmur and all I wanted to do was sit and while away the hours together, getting closer and learning everything about him. It didn't get much more *like a date* than that.

'What do you fancy?' he asked, looking through the menu. 'Charcuterie? Salad?'

'Both?'

'Done.'

Leo ordered the food, while I sat and listened to the musical trio on Portuguese guitars. They were playing intricate pieces at such a pace I was surprised there wasn't smoke coming off their strings.

'How about after this I take you on a magical mystery tour of Lisbon?' Leo said, his voice low and full of suggestion.

'Sounds like a good way to while away the evening,' I said. 'What kind of tour?'

'Erm… *magical and mysterious*,' he said. 'There isn't a theme. Do you want one? Cheese? Ice cream? Wine?'

'How about a cheese-flavoured ice cream tour?'

'Mmm, tasty. Another impossible client brief – my favourite.'

I laughed. 'Aren't they all?'

'It's getting more and more that way.'

'How are you finding being a CEO? Amplify is getting bigger by the day, isn't it? There must be thirty of you by now, if all the job ads I keep seeing are anything to go by.'

'Fifty and growing. But honestly, being in charge is hard. I've been CEO for six months now and the pressure to bring in new business – but not too much – and run a happy team –

but not too happy – and make LOADS of money – is non-stop.'

'Like balancing a coin on a lemon in a bowl of water.'

His stressed face switched back to shiny. 'Precisely, i.e. virtually impossible.'

'Why don't you set up your own shop? If you can be CEO at Amplify you can be CEO for Kendrick PR... International... Limited.'

'That's got a nice ring to it.'

'Rolls off the tongue. Then you'd be bringing in the same new business but all for yourself.'

'I could say the same to you. Looks like you're doing most of the work at Northstar PR from where I'm standing.'

'Leo!' I pretended to be shocked. 'Don't let Heidi hear you saying that. She's convinced she does it all.'

'Of course she is. But does she? Hmm? How much does she really do?'

'I wouldn't want all the worries that come with owning a business, to be honest. I like getting a reliable wage each month and knowing the bigger picture is somebody else's problem.'

'I'm the opposite,' Leo said. 'I like to be in control of my own destiny, which might mean my own shop one day, but not yet. Heading up Amplify is perfect for me right now.'

'Just right, is it? Mr Goldilocks of the PR world.'

'Yup. It's not too big and not too small with a brilliant team and cool clients. Eventually I'll outgrow it, of course, but for now it's giving me every opportunity I need to learn, and I love it.'

His silver eyes turned serious when it came to work chat and a corporate sheen consumed him. These felt like well-practised lines. The words had been carefully chosen for maximum impact – as if he was being interviewed live on a podcast. He looked exhausted from trying.

'When you think we were both in the exact same place not so long ago, you've done brilliantly.' He gave me a bashful smile. 'Your grandma must be very proud.'

'She is. Granny Sal loves us boys.' He topped up our wine as the sun peeped out from behind the clouds. 'And the next layer down. Both my brothers have two sons.'

'Even better – Kendrick and Nephews PR.'

He laughed. 'Maybe. At the very least I want to instil a good work ethic in them. Although mine has always come from a place of panic. Knowing there's no backup.'

A shadow passed over his face, and I thought back to how it had been growing up back in Bootle. Dad had worked long shifts as a lorry driver and mum had done child-minding for extra cash, so there hadn't been much room for error when it came to month-to-month survival.

'It's one way to motivate yourself,' I said, reaching for his hand. 'I like to work, but I try to play equally hard these days.'

Leo looked out to sea as the waiter brought over our food and we piled up our plates.

'Work has always meant freedom to me,' he said, spearing a slice of salami. 'Or do I mean safety? Both probably.'

'I know how you feel,' I said, suddenly feeling vulnerable. 'At least if you only rely on yourself, nobody can let you down. I grew up knowing there wouldn't be any unexpected windfalls coming my way, so that's how I've always been as well.'

'It's empowering and frightening at the same time. If things go wrong, I've got nobody to blame but myself.'

'Aren't you past the things going wrong stage now, though? You're a CEO for goodness' sake. You're at the top of the tree.'

'It just means there's further to fall,' Leo said, soaking his bread in olive oil. 'I can't imagine the fear ever leaving me forever; it always needs feeding.'

'I have a different kind of fear, I think. Mine doesn't drive me forward – it holds me back.'

'In what way?' Leo seemed genuinely interested and glad the spotlight was off him.

'I outgrew Northstar years ago, but I'd never dare leave in case I couldn't get anything else,' I said, terrified at the thought. 'I'm too old to start again.'

Leo eyed me bemused. 'Too old for a new job, too young for a family – make up your mind. You're not too old or too young for anything – don't restrict yourself like that. There are enough people out there who will try and put walls around you, without you doing it to yourself.'

It was much easier to give advice than take it, but he was right. There was nothing stopping me taking my own medicine and starting Brennan PR International Limited. Apart from not having two pennies to rub together, of course.

Twenty-two

The tram juddered through the cobbled streets, slow and rickety, turning a wide corner before starting up São Jorge's hill. Lisbon was a muted palette of reds and whites, with the occasional orange flash as the sun hit, and seeing it from this angle was a real treat. Another unforgettable experience. I felt like I'd been on this trip forever. We'd visited so many different places in such a short space of time that I'd almost forgotten what my real home was like. The home before the home before the home. Leo sat next to me with his late-lunch espresso as we bounced along the track, and he leant in to take a selfie.

'Smile!' he said, pulling a funny face.

Not that I needed a prompt; I was already giving him big eyes from under my falsies. I held my cup up next to his, the pair of us flouting the Italian law of no coffee after midday.

'I'm glad we're getting to do this,' Leo said, kissing me on the cheek.

'Me too. Although I feel like the others could catch us at any second.'

'They'll do well to find us up here.'

It was stop-start on the final leg of the route, and I slipped my hand inside Leo's when we eventually reached the top. The tram doors exhaled and everyone piled off, following each other towards the railings where the view of Lisbon was breathtaking. Old-fashioned lamps marked out the castle perimeter, with gunmetal cannons pointing at the river on the terrace below. The history of the city was woven into everyday life as the locals returned from work, smartly dressed and carrying beautiful leather bags. Tourists sat on the castle wall and let their legs dangle free, as the bustle of city life played out around them.

'Fancy a jaunt around the castle?' Leo asked. 'We can pretend we're on a romantic minibreak.'

'Aren't we?'

The sun hovered on the horizon, spreading a peachy hue across the sky as we walked hand in hand along the castle parapet. Pockets of people queued for gelato and enjoyed sundowners from the pop-up bars, but we were tempted by neither as we strolled on by, eventually ending up back where we'd started. The light had shifted and the view seemed entirely different now the sun was lower, covering the city in a yellow glaze.

'The Cristo Rei is still keeping his eye on us,' I said, pointing out the statue across the water. The river Tagus was full of tourist boats and the city lights were gradually turning on. 'Impressive that we can still see him all the way up here.'

'Not bad, but it's no *Angel of the North*.'

'Similar vibe though, no? Albeit yours is the agnostic Geordie version.'

Leo chuckled. 'My grandad worked in the coal mine it stands over, so Gran would take us up to see it on his birthday every year.'

'You didn't mention him before – did he raise you and your brothers as well?'

'Nope. Just us boys and Gran. Twenty years in a coal mine wasn't the healthiest choice of career.'

I felt a pang of sadness for both Leo and his grandmother. 'It must have been hard for her without him. Without anyone.'

Leo gave a sad smile. 'Yeah, although she didn't ever say so – and she had us. All three of us grew up wanting to make her proud. My older brother Oscar is a musician, and Max is a numbers whizz.'

'The opposite of me then.'

'He's running some fintech that none of us understand and it blows my mind every time he tries to explain it. How about you? Any siblings?'

'Are you sensing eldest-daughter energy?' I teased. 'Younger twin sisters and they are a nightmare. An inseparable duo in their own little gang, so I'm used to being outvoted.'

Leo nodded. 'That explains why you're so confident and articulate – you've had to fight to be heard.'

I stopped at that. I'd never really thought about it before, but he was right. I had. He'd spotted a piece of me I hadn't even known was on show.

'Doesn't everyone?'

He shook his head. 'Nope. You can spot an only child a mile off because they assume centre stage as their right.

Brooke, for example. Whereas you and I are used to sharing, so we always check before we speak.'

It was an interesting observation, although neither of us knew she was an only child for sure.

'It must have been difficult growing up without your parents,' I said softly.

Leo shrugged. 'Can't miss what you've never had. Are you close with yours?'

'Yep. Mum has always been like a sister to me and Dad expresses his love through football. He's a season ticketholder at Anfield, so I always know where he is on match day. He used to take me every week when I was little, home or away. The twins were never interested so it was our daddy-daughter time together.'

'Exactly what I'll do with my children. Complete indoctrination from an early age. I'm from four generations of Liverpool supporters so it's in the Kendrick blood. There must be a Scouser in the family tree somewhere.'

'The best kind of people,' I said, in my best Scouse accent.

'I'm starting to think that too.'

He put his arms around me as we stared out at the city, the sun starting to set. We'd seen some incredible sights over the past two weeks, but Lisbon by night was pretty special. I leant back into his chest, which felt solid and safe, and the warmth of his body surrounded me as we stood in this magical spot. *Esmeralda* had brought me here and facilitated this perfect moment. I'd never in my wildest thoughts have imagined I'd be stood on top of a castle overlooking Lisbon with a potential new love interest like this three weeks ago. We'd both been transported here by Excalibur. A kernel of an idea was germinating. Almost like you couldn't have a brochure for it because the very nature of a cruise is so variable. *Unexpected perfection with Excalibur. Who knows what will happen on an Excalibur Cruise. Esmeralda – where will she take you next?* There could be something in it.

'What are you thinking?' Leo breathed in my ear.

'Just how random these last two weeks have been,' I said, trying to be honest without giving anything away. 'Like me and you in this moment right now. This whole trip has been so completely bizarre.'

'Hmm.' He nuzzled my back. 'Good-bizarre, though, right?'

I laughed. 'Yes. I also keep thinking about Heidi losing her mind when she finds out I've been fraternising with the enemy.'

'The enemy? I'll have you know I'm an upstanding member of the PR community. And not normally one for a holiday romance.'

'You're having a holiday romance?'

'Yes. With you,' he said, kissing my neck, then slowly turning me around. 'Although it is becoming somewhat of a distraction. I'm not used to having to think about anything other than work while I'm working.'

'So, I'm putting you off?'

'I've already told you this!'

I stopped in surprise and looked at him.

'In a good way. I'm far too easily distracted when I like someone. It doesn't mean I want the... er... distracting to stop.'

I softened as he stumbled over his words. For a man who worked in communications, he didn't half struggle with making himself clear.

'I see.'

He raked a hand through his hair, looking nervous. 'And I don't want it to end when the cruise is over.'

Neither did I. But I didn't want him to know that. Who knew how he might use it against me.

'End? It's barely started!'

'Exactly, and it's been a long time coming. I know we need to focus on the reason we're here and all that, but once the pitch is done, I'm taking you out. Properly.' His face searched mine. 'Would that be allowed?'

'Fine by me, but you'll have to ask Heidi's permission.'

Leo faced me and stared earnestly into my eyes. 'I'm serious, Kat, I like you. I've *always* liked you. I'm trying to stay professional in front of the others, but I'm not sure I'm carrying it off. I haven't had this much fun in ages.'

'I like you too,' I said, stroking his cheek. 'At the moment. I just don't know how far that feeling will extend if you guys win the pitch and I end up in the unemployment line.'

Leo's eyes widened. 'You won't lose your job, will you?'

'Of course I will. Excalibur *is* my job.' Surely he understood that.

'I assumed they'd move you on to another account.'

'Heidi hasn't mentioned it, but I can see for myself that there aren't any gaps. Excalibur is worth so much money to us, the agency would have to shed half its staff. I'll be the first to get the old heave-ho if we lose.' I shook my head. 'Sorry, I shouldn't be oversharing like this.'

'No, it's good for me to understand the situation, and I did ask you what you were thinking. Of course, you're going to be worried about your job and your team. I don't want to diminish that at all.'

'Not your problem though, is it? We both want to win and as it stands either of us could. So, we can enjoy this purgatory and each other before the pitch and let's review the ongoing situation once the results are in.'

'I'll take whatever terms you're offering,' Leo said, his brow furrowed and his expression dead serious.

'Really?'

Leo's eyes softened as he leant down to kiss me. 'Yes. Really.'

I pulled him close and we kissed again, his touch giving me goosebumps. Our bodies trembled as one, as we sent each other into a spin and it took me a second to catch my breath when we eventually pulled apart, my heart hammering in my chest. I was going to have to compromise on my 'work is work' rule – or ignore it entirely.

'I don't want my job to get in the way of this,' Leo said, quietly. 'Not again.'

He kissed both my hands and looked into my eyes.

'Heidi and I are staying at the Hilton tonight,' I whispered, letting the thought hang in the air. 'I could sneak you in later if you like?'

'Could you indeed...?' he said, stepping back with a devilish smile. 'I *would* like. I would like *very much*.'

'Then it's a date,' I said, feeling a thrill at taking charge of the situation. 'A secret second date.'

'Second date, already, eh?' Leo wiggled his eyebrows, then whispered, 'Will there be secret chicken?'

Twenty-three

I didn't want to like Leo as much as I did. Or at all, really. Out of all the millions of men in the world, *why did it have to be him*? It was hugely inconvenient. The phone rang out next to my bed and scared me half to death, lost in thought as I was, loudly reverberating around the room.

'Hello?'

'Good evening, this is Anjali on the concierge desk. We have a Mr Kendrick in reception for you.'

Arghhh! He was here. Which of course I was expecting and what I wanted, but still… *arghhh!* I adjusted my slinky dress to show more cleavage and cleared my throat. 'Send him up, thank you.'

Why did this feel so illicit? Like I was having an affair? We weren't doing anything wrong, but I was nervous and excited and terrified all at once. I downed a whisky miniature from the minibar, then poured myself a wine and sat on the edge of the bed. Then moved outside to stand on the balcony. He'd be in the lift by now, maybe even walking down the corridor. *Oh God*. My heart was pounding. What was I *thinking* inviting a strange man up to my room? I toyed with switching my heels for slippers. But then Leo would have shoes on, so I should too – I didn't want it to feel like some weird pyjama party. Was it too hot in here? I turned the air conditioning on and puffed up the pillows. Should I pour him a wine as well or wait and see what he wanted…? A sharp knock at the door made me jump. *Arghhh!* I checked my teeth in the magnifying mirror and spritzed on some Coco Mademoiselle. It was now or never as I eyed him through the spyhole, took a deep breath and opened the door.

'Room service,' Leo said, with a shy smile, holding up a bottle of red. He leant in and kissed me on the cheek, then pulled an orange rose out from behind his back. She'd got him again.

'Two roses in two days!' I said, smiling madly. '*Obrigado, senhor.*' It had been forever since a man had bought me flowers and now it was raining roses… one at a time. 'Come in.'

'What a great idea,' Leo said, looking around, then jumping on the bed. 'Zach and I should have done the same. Although I don't know what it says about how much you're enjoying the cruise.'

'I'm sure you can work it out if you try,' I quipped. 'It's not that cryptic.'

I beckoned him out onto the balcony and lit a citronella candle to keep the bugs away. 'Can I get you a drink, sir? Red, white, a beer?'

'I'll have whatever you're having,' he said, eyeing my wine. 'We can open the red later with some cheese.'

'Do you mean order some? I'm not sure there's any...'

He pulled a camembert from his inside pocket and some crackers from his coat. 'I took the liberty of swinging by the supermarket. I know you like a cheeseboard.'

He had me there. The cheese trolley at the end of each meal was always the best part of the night. 'I do! How sweet of you to notice. Cheesiness is next to godliness in my book.' I was entirely delighted. It was rare to find a man with cheese in his pocket. 'I've never been gifted a camembert before – more men should do this. Sod the champagne and roses.'

'Noted,' he said, taking the rose he'd given me and opening his jacket to tuck it away.

I snatched it back. 'Not that one, you big tease. Is this more of your PR-man polish?'

'Not at all. I just thought you might like it, that's all.'

'Well, you're right. I do.'

'I'll help myself to a wine then, shall I?' he said, disappearing back inside and rattling around in the fridge.

'Kat! Kat? Can you hear me?' A woman's voice floated through the air, but I couldn't work out from which direction.

'Hello?' I shouted, shading my eyes to focus. Was it a spirit?

'It's me! Heidi!'

My stomach dropped as I casually slid the balcony door shut and pulled the shutters down. *Arghhh!* I couldn't see her and had visions of her leaping over the wall or bungee jumping in from above. 'Where are you?'

'Over here!' she called, and her phone light turned on. She was stood in the shadows of her own balcony on the opposite side of the courtyard.

'Oh hi! How are you feeling?' I feigned concern and prayed Leo would take his time.

'Much better. I've been asleep all afternoon and I'm having an early night. Keeping my eyes closed is the only thing that stops the pain.'

Leo was trying to open the door behind me, and I stepped back to stand in front of it.

'Bath and bed for me too,' I replied loudly to hide the noise, holding up my wine as if it was evidence. 'After this one.'

'What's that, Kat?' Leo shouted through the glass. 'Are you talking to me? I can't get out – the door's stuck.'

'Shhh,' I side-mouthed.

'Already in your nightie, I see.' Heidi couldn't resist a barb, even with a migraine. Can't see well enough to type but can throw shade on me from a hundred metres. 'I'll leave you to get some rest. Goodnight!'

I raised my glass again and she turned, as Leo rapped loudly on the window. 'Can you hear me?' he shouted in a panic as I pulled the shutters up and slipped inside the balcony door, closing the curtains behind me.

'That was close,' I said, taking another whisky miniature from the fridge and downing it. 'Heidi's room is directly opposite. Five more seconds and she'd have seen you.'

Leo cracked a smile. 'How exciting,' he said, wrapping his arms around me. 'I thought you were trying to trap me in your bedroom.'

'Sorry to disappoint you, but you're free to leave anytime. You could have walked out the front door.'

He gave me a flirty smile. 'Why would I do that? I was warming to the idea of house arrest.'

'Not sure we can sit out on the balcony now. Shall we have cheese and crackers on the bed and watch Portuguese TV?'

'No,' he said, taking my wine glass and putting it down with his. 'We are in one of the most beautiful cities in the world and your boss is safely tucked up in bed, so let's go out.'

He had a masterful energy that was hard to resist and I was far too heightened to stay in the room with him now – I'd be buzzing about like a lost wasp. He was right; we needed to get out and explore. We jumped in a cab outside the hotel and Leo said something in Portuguese to the driver. 'There's a roof bar I want to check out, are you OK if we go there?'

'More than OK. It's nice to go along with someone else's plans for once – being away with Heidi is like being a single parent. I'm part business director, part PA.'

The taxi turned into a derelict side street and stopped outside a car park. Leo and I exchanged a nervous glance.

'*Chegamos!*' the driver said with a cheerful smile. 'Park bar!' He pointed to the barricaded entrance where there was a small door covered in graffiti. No doubt where the Grim Reaper was waiting to take our coats.

Leo googled and paid at the same time, while I locked my door. 'You take me to all the best places.'

'Looks different in the photos,' he said. 'But this is it.'

We got out and the cab sped off, which did nothing to reassure us. My inner voice was clearly telling me I was about to be mugged, but I ignored it and took Leo's hand, holding on tight as he knocked on the gross graffiti door. It creaked open to reveal a set of concrete stairs and he glanced at me and shrugged.

'In the words of Yazz...'

'The only way is up.'

And up was a bloody long way. Five flights of stairs later we arrived at the top, sweaty and panting. Which is how I'd imagined the night might have ended in the hotel, not in a multi-storey car park.

Leo opened the door onto the roof, and it was a relief to find Lisbon's answer to Club Tropicana hiding behind it. An open-air bar, full of sofas and high-top tables, where all the beautiful people were hanging out. The blood rushed back to my face as happy house music pumped out of the decks and a vigorous violinist grooved past. We were safe. I kept hold of Leo's hand as he weaved through the crowd, past groups of friends drinking colourful cocktails and couples dancing to the beats. Tiny candles flickered inside blue jars, and lamps with white globes had been dotted around to give the place a soft light. It was like being on set in a music video.

'What do you want to drink?' I shouted, trying to get control back of the situation.

Leo either couldn't hear me or ignored me, brandishing a fifty euro note at the barman who caught his eye. '*Dois champagnes!*' he said, holding up two fingers. How did he know what I wanted? I'd been doing dating all wrong – somehow I always ended up buying the first round. And the last.

We crammed into the crowd, eventually finding enough space to face each other as the saxophonist started playing 'Baker Street' over a beat from an old Chemical Brothers song. She had black corkscrew curls and was giving it some welly, so there was no hope of us having any kind of conversation. Leo looked at me unblinking, really looked at me, then smiled and clinked his glass against mine.

'Cheers,' he mouthed. He was tall enough to see over all the heads, while I was blocked in by necks and chests. A bloke barged through the crowd towards the bar and Leo put a protective arm around me as if I was his and the pair of us were one unit. It felt strange to be out with a man like this, rather than getting lashed with the girls or going on a pub crawl of average dates. To be out with a man I genuinely wanted to spend time with.

He leant down and kissed my cheek, but it wasn't enough; the connection between us was hot and electric and I wanted his lips on mine. I beckoned him back in, snogging his face off in the middle of the melee, the champagne adding an extra layer of fuzziness to the moment.

'Maybe going out wasn't such a good idea,' he breathed in my ear, starting to dance. 'You're getting me all excited.'

'Good,' I replied mirroring his moves. It was a very different style of dance to the silent disco – pumping his body to the beat. I tried to channel my old Ibiza days, when swinging arms were an acceptable dance move. The violinist appeared next to us and the crowd shrank back as the spotlight found her. Leo seemed to go up a gear, keen to be part of the show, whereas I wanted to shy away into the shadows. The crowd clapped along, egging us on, and Leo did some breakdancing spins, then dropped to the floor and launched into the worm. I shimmied next to him, then reverted to waving my arms. Basic and boring in comparison. The saxophonist piped up over the other side of the bar and the spotlight switched to her, our moment of fame over.

A couple of Portuguese bros slapped Leo on the back, with nods of admiration, and he held up his hands in thanks. I hovered in the background like a proud wife.

'Wow. Are you a professional street dancer? Where did you learn all that?'

He laughed. 'It's an evolution from trampolining in my youth to try and impress girls.'

'Well, it impressed me. Very cool. What other surprises have you got up your sleeve?'

'Ohhh… all sorts. There's loads of stuff you don't know about me – and I don't know about you. But that's half the fun, isn't it? Finding out.'

He twirled me round, then clasped my hips and pulled me close. I tried to think if there was anything out of the ordinary he should know about me. Had I been an Olympic athlete in my teens? No. Was I the child of a billionaire? No. Could I fold myself up into a suitcase? Not anymore.

We rolled into the hotel reception and nervously ran into the lift. Presumably Heidi was sound asleep in her bed, but better to be safe than sorry.

'I honestly don't mind going back to the ship, you know,' Leo said, putting his arms around me.

'Whatever you want. Just see me to my room, at least.'

'With pleasure.'

His voice was deep and gravelly and his eyes were full of desire as he leant down to kiss me. The lift jerked to a stop, pressing us into each other and the second the doors pinged open I ducked under his arm and ran up the corridor.

'Hey! I'm supposed to be accompanying you!' Leo called, chasing after me. He caught me up as I unlocked the door and I pulled him inside by his belt, popping his shirt open with my other hand.

'Can you accompany me any further?' I asked.

'All the way,' he said, picking me up and throwing me on the bed.

Twenty-four

Sunday 4th July

'I hope you don't mind me saying so, Kat, but you look dreadful,' Heidi said, sitting opposite me with her overnight oats.

I smiled sweetly and tried to muster some tolerance, while a vein pulsed in my forehead. 'Not at all! Why would I mind?' I'd piled on extra concealer to hide my black eye, but there was only so much Maybelline could be expected to do. And while I hated to admit it, Heidi was right – my face was getting worse, not better. I put my sunglasses on and pulled down my cap. 'Today must be the final day for the bruising to come out.'

'Let's hope so,' she said, unconvinced. 'Now. I've got some bad news to share. Sam was on the phone first thing this morning and he needs me home urgently.'

'Was he? Why? What's happened?' Another fake cat emergency no doubt.

'I'd rather not go into the details if you don't mind. I appreciate that it leaves you in the lurch somewhat, but needs must. I'm booked on a flight this afternoon.'

'To London?! This afternoon, as in *today*?'

'Yes, *today*,' she said, rolling her eyes. 'Urgent means urgent. I've explained and apologised to Brooke, but I've seen enough now to shape the pitch, especially now we have the unimaginable moments territory to play with, and you're still here to represent as the cruise wraps up.'

'Right.'

I tried not to look too pleased. I didn't want to let her off the hook completely, but my overwhelming feeling was one of relief. A couple more hours and I'd be free of her breathing down my neck 24/7, volunteering me for all the activities and skiving off. I could hide in my cabin and pretend to be working for the last day or two.

'I've sketched up a few execution ideas, so I'll send those over. And look, I'm sorry, OK? I'll make it up to you,' she offered, at least having the good grace to look contrite. 'I promise.'

Just as I opened my mouth to put a request in, Leo stumbled into the restaurant, and I nearly dropped dead in shock as Heidi frowned in his direction. 'What's he doing here?'

I shrugged dramatically. 'Morning!' I shouted, giving him the stink eye behind Heidi's back. Was this a wind-up? We'd agreed he'd leave discreetly, not follow me into the restaurant for a quick continental. He may as well wear a T-shirt with *Kat's in the bag* on the front and be done with it. He gave us one of his cheeky salutes, and my insides turned to jelly. That mischievous grin worked every time.

'*Bom dia*, ladies,' he said, piling his plate high with custard tarts. There was no further explanation offered, so Heidi leapt up and marched over, while I sat frozen to my chair.

'Industrial espionage for breakfast, is it?'

He laughed. 'Hardly. This place does the best *pastel de natas* in Lisbon according to the guidebook, so we thought we'd swing by and check it out.'

'We?' Heidi looked behind him. 'Are you with your imaginary friend?'

Zach marched through the swingy doors on cue and slapped Leo on the back. 'I'm starving,' he said, grunting an acknowledgement in our direction. He looked like he'd slept on the streets, with his pale face and wild, woolly beard.

'You're both here,' I said, relieved to see Zach.

'Obviously. We come as a pair.'

'A pair of jokers,' Heidi quipped and Zach gave her a withering stare. 'Bookends?'

'Aces more like. And we aren't *always* together; we bumped into each other down the street.'

'How romantic,' Heidi said. 'Well, if your plan was to sabotage our thinking time you're too late. We're done with our ideas for now and I'm flying home this afternoon. My stint on the *Esmeralda* is over.'

Zach frowned in disbelief. 'Since when?'

'Since I got a call from home, just now.'

'You're going back *today*?' Leo said and I stuffed a croissant in my mouth to stifle a giggle.

'YES!' Heidi huffed. 'So I'll say goodbye now and may the best agency win when we reach the other side. No hard feelings either way, eh?'

'Absolutely. A fair fight, no dirty play, and let's go for drinks either way,' Leo said, holding his arms out for a hug.

I couldn't decide if that was an accidental rhyme or something he said to everyone. An Amplify agency catchphrase.

'Let's not make promises we can't keep,' Heidi said, graciously dodging him and flouncing off to the omelette station.

'Left hanging!' Zach said, with a chuckle, going in for a hug with Leo instead. 'Worth a try though, mate.'

'It's my Manc manners,' Leo replied, flushing red. 'I can't help myself.'

'Lads, I'll take you for commiseration drinks once we're reappointed,' I whispered conspiratorially. 'OK?'

'And if you're not?' Leo stared at me, knowing the answer full well. 'I love how you're already planning to be a sore loser.'

'It doesn't hurt to plan ahead,' Zach said, stuffing a custard pie in his mouth.

'I'll see you boys back on the ship. Careful not to make yourselves sick.'

'How are your snake hips?' Leo asked, as we followed Dahlia into the Adonis Lounge for the salsa classes. The activities schedule was never-ending.

'Well... they don't lie, that's for sure, and they're telling me they'll need replacing in five to ten years. Overuse has sent them skewwhiff.'

Leo laughed.

'Jeez – oversharing much?' Zach said, with a look of disgust.

'How about you two? Are you dancers?' I asked, flexing my toes.

'Depends on the dance,' Leo said.

'Country dancing? Tap dancing?' I suggested. 'Lap dancing?'

'Oh yeah, all of that,' Leo said, with twinkly eyes. 'I'm known as the lap-dancing lion by the *Magic Mike* guys.'

'Nice,' I said, trying not to smile. 'Have you got a costume?'

'Wouldn't you like to know.'

'If it's breakdancing, I'm down,' Zach said, doing a cringey body pop. No one wanted to see that.

'I heard you can do the worm, Leo?'

'Maybe in my younger days, but it's been a while,' he said, with a wink.

The Adonis Lounge was wall-to-wall mirrors, with a barre running along one side and a shiny wooden floor. It took me back to my adult ballet lessons, which had served as a weekly reminder that I had the grace of an elephant. I eventually mastered the plié, which was really just bending both legs, but my swan lake dreams were crushed in week six when the teacher snapped that we were *supposed to be dancing*, not *clodding around like heavy lumps*.

Sculptures of noble heads sat on plinths at the far side of the room and there was a heavy black curtain at the back. I was surprised to see so many people mingling and chatting, waiting for 'class' to start.

The lights dimmed and there was an automatic hush as J-Lo's 'Let's Get Loud' started blaring from invisible speakers and Brooke ran in to join us.

'Ladies and gentlemennn,' Dahlia bellowed into a microphone, making me jump. 'May I introduce you to your dance teachers today, and this year's International Ballroom Dancing Champions, Chico and Catarina Enchalezzzzzz!'

The curtain whipped to one side and a perma-tanned couple burst into the room. The woman was in a silver bustier and froufrou skirt, and the man was trussed up like a space turkey in a ruffled waistcoat and silver trousers.

'Brrrrrrrrrrrrrr ow ow owwwwwwwwww!'

'Derrrrrrringgggg chicaaaaaaa chica!'

They screeched along to the Latina music, while spinning in the centre of the room, doing an energetic performance with a lot of bending, to get us all in the mood.

Leo side-eyed me and I could see his lips were twitching.

'Count me out for that,' I said, as Chico flipped Catarina upside down and held her up by her legs.

'Me too,' Brooke said, looking rightly horrified. She hadn't participated in any of the activities until now, but we were one down without Heidi, so she was getting a taste of her own medicine. A couple of the guests tapped their feet along, delighted, and I could see the hips starting to unconsciously move around the circle, but I don't think any of us had imagined salsa dancing could be so dramatic... and, er... gymnastic.

'Welcome class, it is our pleasure to teach you today,' Chico said, with an elaborate bow.

'Thank you each for coming on your LAST CRUISE SUNDAY,' Catarina added, and everyone cheered. 'We want to get you up and dancing straight away, so Dahlia, please hit on the music.'

'Everyone to stand on this side of the room,' Chico said pointing to the left, as he made his way over to the wall opposite.

'We will do some improvisation,' Catarina said, standing in front of us as Pixie Lott's 'All About Tonight' started over the speakers. 'Watch me first!' she shouted as she strutted over to Chico, waving her hands in the air and wiggling her hips to the beat. She turned with a flourish and pointed to Leo. 'You next,' she shouted, and my stomach dropped. *Oh please, no.* Were we all expected to do it? This was my worst nightmare. A much more embarrassing version of dancing in the middle of a circle of your own friends. Sober and in front of strangers. I really, REALLY didn't want to do it. Leo lapped it up though – of course he did – striding across the room wielding his air guitar, then dropping to his knees to do a solo.

Catarina clapped to the music and picked out her next victim. A tall woman in a velour tracksuit shimmied across to the beat, followed by a moonwalking man who was loving the whoops and cheers of the crowd. In the blink of an eye there were more people on the right of the room than on the left, and I had no choice but to launch myself forward. I didn't want to go last. I did a locomotion across the floor and nearly died of mortification, until Brooke grabbed my waist and made it a two-woman conga.

'*Fantastico,*' Chico exclaimed, once we'd all finished. He clapped loudly to quieten the chatter, and Dahlia switched the music to 'The Girl from Ipanema' and turned the volume down. 'Now, we have seen you can dance alone – some of you,' he said, glancing at Brooke. 'But dancing is really so much better as a shared experience.'

'Twice as nice for pleasure,' Catarina said, with an eyebrow raise.

'Can you all find yourself a partner and line up here, in front of me.'

I scanned the room in panic. Dancing with Leo would totally give us away, but Brooke and Zach had bagsied a brother and sister – same nose – and everyone else was taken. I looked around for any spares, but Leo and I were the only ones left.

'Quickly, quickly,' Chico shouted. 'Two by two here please: men this side, women on my left.'

Leo flashed me a smile. 'Me and you then, huh?'

'Not again,' I said, but I couldn't keep the smile off my face.

'Whoever leads, needs to position themselves like *this*,' Chico said, clutching Catarina to his chest.

'And to follow, wrap your leg around your partner, like *this*,' she said, lifting her leg thigh high and hooking it around Chico's back. 'If you cannot lift so far, then nuzzle in together, is OK.' The velour tracksuit lady looked relieved.

'Let's stick with the PG version,' I said, standing opposite Leo.

'Are you sure?' he murmured, making my insides melt.

The lights were shining in my face, and I was conscious of my sweaty palms as we held hands. We were the total opposite of Chico and Catarina's hot, Latino dirty dancing, with at least a foot between us. We looked like we might start country dancing instead.

'Okaayyy now everyone to follow us please as we lean nice and sloooow, then unfold, stay pressed together and GO; one two cha-cha-cha, three four cha-cha-cha.' They were rotating their groins as one, in a never-ending circle. I smothered a giggle at the thought of Leo and I dry-humping in public and had to really concentrate on the solemn-faced plaster bust over his shoulder to hold it together.

We stepped back and forth feigning disinterest, but the distance between us made it worse somehow. A palpable vibration fizzed through our bodies as they connected and the space between us was alive with energy. We were like two magnets attracting, and no matter how hard I tried to keep my distance, I kept getting closer. I couldn't resist him. It was excruciating.

'You might need to come forward a little,' Leo whispered, trying to follow the steps. He moved towards me and put his hand on my back. His hands were soft and cool, but the heat between us was interfering with my chi. I hadn't danced cheek to cheek with a man like this in… well, in forever.

'You two get closer, much closer please,' Chico called over, squeezing his hands together to make his point. 'This is your holidays, enjoy yourselves, fall in love *all over again*. Brrrrrrrr, reeeeeee,' he screeched over the music. Like Speedy Gonzales on speed. Was Speedy Gonzales on speed?

It was pointless trying to explain that we weren't on holiday together and had never been in love. Chico didn't care, he was already on to the next couple, suggesting they sniff each other's necks to activate their pheromones.

Leo's back felt smooth and solid through his shirt, and he flinched as I accidentally scraped my nails against him.

'Sorry,' I breathed in his ear.

'I liked it.' He held me close as our bodies moved to the cha-cha rhythm, his heartbeat next to mine. If Brooke or Zach looked over, they'd instantly know there was something going on. It was impossible to hide it while clinched together like this and I ached for us to be alone, feeling almost dizzy with desire as he held me up. My breathing grew shallow as I looked everywhere but in his eyes to try and distract myself.

Catarina clapped loudly, breaking our moment. 'Now we do the conga! Everyone in a line.'

'Thank fuck for that,' Leo murmured as he held my waist. 'You'll have to go in front of me I'm afraid.' I grabbed the nearest person to join the human chain, running to catch up with the others who were concertinaed together. Leo crashed into my back, his grip strong and firm on my hips and it felt even more intimate him holding me from behind. I was having a hot flush.

'Take it to the floor!' Chico cried, once we'd circled the room, kicking out our legs in awkward unison. The Latina version of 'Oops Upside Your Head' started blaring from the loudspeakers and we sat in two lines. I was mortifyingly conscious of sitting so snugly against Leo's crotch in public as two exuberant Irish sisters led the moves. This was the weirdest dance class I'd ever been to. They chose side-to-side floor slapping to start with, followed by the front to back wiggle and I had to use every muscle in my inner core (of which there were none) to stop myself lying back in Leo's lap. And I was sure he was shuffling himself forward – he felt so close.

The music eventually stopped, and the public torture was over.

'Let's get out of here,' I whispered in his ear and he nodded.

A sweaty Brooke came over, out of breath, with Zach in tow, but Leo and I were a different kind of hot and bothered.

'Wow-weeee! That was more like a spin class than a dance class,' she said. 'I haven't crawled around on the floor like that in years!'

Leo laughed. 'This is what all the activities have been like. You've had us jumping through all sorts of hoops.'

'The ultimate test of resilience,' I said with a grin. 'Not that we can't handle it, of course.'

'Well, I can't deny it, I do like to be entertained – it's the only child in me, I reckon.'

Leo gave me a knowing look. He was good at this people thing.

'Nothing wrong with checking how much we want your business,' Zach said, pointedly.

'There's no doubting any of you in that regard,' Brooke said, dabbing her sweaty brow with a tissue. 'Excuse me while I run to the little ladies' room and freshen up.'

'You still want their business then, huh?' Zach pushed, his tone suddenly much less professional. 'After all these years?'

'We've already got it, remember?' I replied, good-naturedly. 'Which is why it's impossible for Heidi and me to compete with your level of—'

'Client service?' Leo interjected.

'No.'

'Creative excellence? Financial acumen?' he tried again.

'No and no,' I said with a smile. 'Your level of *desperation*. It's difficult for us to be hungry for something we've been eating every day for years.'

'I'd rather be a pick-me than past my sell-by date,' Zach snapped, walking off.

'Did I hit a nerve?'

'Possibly, but I back Zach entirely – we are both proud to be desperate and getting Brooke's sympathy is key to our pitch plan.'

I rolled my eyes. *Idiot.* 'Good luck with that strategy. I've been waiting to get you on your own to talk about this morning – what on God's green earth were you thinking bowling up for breakfast at the hotel?'

'Oh yeah, sorry about that. I saw Zach on my way back and panicked, then had to pretend I was up early, on the hunt for custard tarts.'

I laughed. 'Obviously – what else would you be doing?'

'It was the best I could do on the spot – my sleep-deprived brain wasn't the sharpest – and it was the only hotel I could think of to suggest.'

'Hmm. I suppose it almost sounds plausible,' I said, chuckling at the thought of him bumping into Zach on his walk of shame. 'I'll miss that big hotel bed tonight.'

'So will I,' he said, wistfully. 'Among other things.'

'You can always sneak over when Zach starts snoring. I've got the whole room to myself.'

'The *whole room*, eh?'

'All two metres squared.'

'Sharing a child-size bunk bed with you instead of Zach, you say? Now there's a proposition.'

I giggled at the thought of us wedged in a single bed together. There wouldn't be much sleep happening in that tiny space either. 'It's a once-in-a-lifetime opportunity,' I said, from under my lashes.

'Then how can I say no?' he whispered, sending a shiver down my spine.

Twenty-five

Monday 5th July

My stomach was a cocktail of last-day-of-school excitement and end-of-holiday blues. I'd been awake and full of butterflies for what felt like hours; not least because I had a big, sexy man in my bed (good butterflies) who I'd crossed the business-pleasure boundary with once again (bad butterflies). My cardinal work rule had been broken for the fourth time in a week. *Ooops.* At least there was only one day of professionalism left to navigate before I could hide away and think about what I'd done. Leo looked so cute with his head on my chest, snoring gently. I had a horrible feeling it was well into breakfast time, but I didn't want to risk waking him up to lean over and check my phone. Just a few more minutes of snuggling and then I'd get up.

An alarm started screeching and made us both jump, then Leo lay back down.

'Is that mine?' he mumbled, as it carried on.

'Either that or there's a fire. Quick! Zach will hear it through the walls!'

He barely moved, reaching one hand under the pillow to turn the alarm off. 'I didn't think it could get any tighter than a bunk bed under Zach – yet here I am now sharing one with you.' Leo pulled me in tight and one of the mattress springs popped.

I giggled. 'It's a lesson in gratitude.'

'Yep. You don't know what you've got until you've only got half of it.'

We unravelled ourselves and wriggled out from under the bed, standing and stretching at the same time. Leo could almost get his elbows on the ceiling as he swayed, opening his eyes fully and accepting the inevitable – morning was upon us.

I couldn't resist kissing his bare chest. 'You can rest when you're home.'

'True. Sleep was never promised. I'll be back in my own bed tomorrow night. My soft, comfy double bed with two pillows. I'll be a physical wreck if I stay here much longer.' He stretched again and checked his watch. 'Shit! It's nearly ten!'

'Is it?' OK, that was later than I'd thought.

'Zach and I have got a call – I better run. See you later for our final "test" – whatever it might be.'

He hopped into his jeans and threw his T-shirt on, hitting his head on the doorframe as he left, and the room felt instantly colder without his sunny energy. I flicked on the radio to fill the void and Spanish guitar music played an appropriate lament while I got ready for our last day on the ocean. I hated goodbyes and this was potentially the beginning of a goodbye relay – *Esmeralda*, the crew, Brooke, the Excalibur account, my job, life as I knew it… and Leo.

Dahlia was stood on stage dressed as a chicken when I arrived on deck, scrutinising the tables of guests in front of her and scribbling on a clipboard. Her expression was so serious and her costume so ridiculous, I wasn't sure if she was in the middle of an arthouse performance. I tiptoed over to where Brooke was sitting with Leo and Zach so as not to disturb, and Dahlia picked up her microphone as soon as she saw me.

'OK! That's everyone here,' she called, with a grin. 'Welcome one and all. It's our last day together here on the *Esmeralda*, so let's make it a good one, shall we?'

Everyone cheered as I slid in between Brooke and Zach.

'Mornin' Kat,' Brooke said.

'Late again,' Zach *joked*. I gave him a filthy look and he laughed.

'Am I?'

'Only a touch, honey,' Brooke said with a smile. 'These boys get up when the birds start tweetin'.'

I nodded over at the chicken. 'What's going on?'

'Dahlia's announcing it now,' Leo said.

'We have the activity to end all activities here on the ship today. If you are not on a table of four then please get up and move. This is a team game, and each team needs four players.'

I smiled around the table. 'Sorted.'

'I hope it's not a triathlon,' Leo said. 'I haven't got the energy.'

Zach shook his head. 'Nah. Not enough activities.'

'A quadathlon then.'

'Any ideas for a team name?' Brooke asked.

'How about the group chat?' Zach said. 'Life's a Pitch.'

We all laughed.

'Brilliant!' Brooke said, delighted.

'The keen-eyed among you will have noticed I'm dressed as a chicken,' Dahlia shouted.

Squawks and pock-pocks emanated from the crowd as she continued. 'Which is a big clue to today's challenge… "Crown the Portuguese Cockerel".'

'Crown on the cock!' someone heckled.

'Thank you – I prefer my title. I thought of it myself. One of you will be the team cockerel and will stay where you are for the entirety of the challenge. The rest of you will have one hour to dress your teammate up as the *Galo de Barcelos* – which is the official name.'

'Not a chicken then?' someone else shouted.

'No. There is a photo of what we're looking for on each of your tables, but to make sure everyone is super clear, we have a full-size version being modelled for you by none other than… the fabulous Barbie Queue!!!'

Barb strutted on stage wearing a voluptuous black dress, a feathery cape and platform boots. She had a beautiful yellow beak made from cardboard, white tissue paper to mark out the wings, a rubber glove red crest and shiny blue tights.

'Alright, cockers?' she shouted, stalking up and down like America's next top model and pouting at the audience. There were wolf whistles galore as she flapped her wings and pretended to lay an egg. She pulled a paper bag from between her legs and started throwing Cadbury's Cream Eggs into the crowd, shouting: 'It's a miracle!'

'The winning team will get a voucher for a future cruise of their choice,' Dahlia shouted.

'Subject to availability; terms and conditions apply,' Barbie Queue quickly added.

There were excited oohs and aahs from the crowd and the noise level went up as teams started discussing tactics.

'I'll be the cock,' Brooke announced. 'You guys work as a team and let's see what we can do.'

'Is it bad form for head office to win the holiday?' Leo asked.

'Definitely,' I said.

'Why? We're here as guests!' Zach said. 'All's fair in cocks and cruises.'

'No, good point… it'll look like a fix. Let's gun for second place just in case,' Brooke said. 'We can have a free cruise whenever we like, after all – within reason.'

'Everyone ready?' Dahlia shouted. 'Starting in THREE… TWO… ONE… GO!!!'

She sounded a Klaxon, and everyone started running except us.

'Shall we write down the colours we need then split out and gather?' I said, pulling out a notebook.

'Blue legs, black body, yellow beak, white and yellow patterns on the wings…' Zach reeled off the list. 'Red crown.'

'I'll take black and white,' Leo said. 'Zach – black as well? And red?' Zach nodded as Leo turned to me. 'Any ideas for blue and yellow?'

'Yellow, yes…'

'I've got a blue feather boa that will work for one leg,' Brooke said, handing me her room key. 'Top right in my wardrobe.'

'Barb has one too,' I said, thinking back to her treasure-filled wardrobe. 'Is it cheating to borrow from her?'

'No such thing,' Zach said. 'All's fair in—'

'Alright, alright,' Leo said. 'Let's go. Back here in twenty minutes, yeah?'

Brooke gestured to the waiter for another drink and the three of us raced off in different directions.

I ran to my room and dragged my work bag out from under the bed, along with a pair of Converse trainers Heidi must have forgotten to pack. I had a lump of Post-its for brainstorming, which would make a brilliant beak, and I whipped the mustardy laces from the trainers in case we could use them too. Then on to Barbie Queue's dressing room. Her 'Enter at your own risk' sign hit different going in alone. It was her private space after all, and it was a bit cheeky to 'borrow' without permission. But it was a feathery emergency. She'd understand. I knocked a couple of times even though I knew she was at the cockerel contest, then slipped in and grabbed two feather boas in turquoise and navy, before making my way to Brooke's suite.

How the other half live. Even her key was a posh electronic bracelet and made a satisfying tinkle as I bleeped my way in. Her room was cool and calm, with a gorgeous flowery fragrance and the air conditioning on full blast even though no one was home. Brooke had one of the corner suites, with dual aspect and a panoramic view and her bathroom alone was bigger than mine and Heidi's room. She had a four-man Jacuzzi blowing steam into the air, waiting for her to get back.

I almost forgot we were on a timer as I stared around the room gobsmacked, the four-poster bed, the floor-to-ceiling mirrors, the beautiful furniture, the chaise longue. I mean, I'd seen photos of the suites before – of course I had – but they'd taken it up a notch on *Esmeralda*. This was like a mini hotel-for-one on the sea. I opened her wardrobe and took in the rail of beautiful dresses, black with feathers, gold pinstripe, icy blue, chocolate strapless... and all the shoes! Eight different pairs on show, each one unique and immaculate – my shoes looked like they'd been chewed by dogs in comparison. It was all too beautiful and neat to go ferreting around. I stood on the chair from her dressing table to get a closer look and spotted a bundle of feathery blue at the back. I made a grab for it, pulling the boa out like a beautiful soft snake. The feathers were so fluffy, they felt real, not like the gaudy sparkly numbers from Barb's box of tricks.

The boys had already started dressing Brooke by the time I got back and she was stood in a long black shirt and a New York Yankees baseball cap. Zach was sellotaping cotton wool to her 'wings' and Leo was fashioning a red crest out of four packs of Rennies.

'She's back!' Zach called.

'She sure is and she brings gifts,' I said. 'I've got three feather boas and Post-its or laces for the beak. Wow, people are really going for it!' I looked around the room at the different teams and their dressing-up efforts. One cockerel was covered in a black blanket, another was wrapped in bin liners, with beaks made out of pegs, pencils and rubber ducks, and legs wrapped up in cling film. Dahlia was blasting out a chicken-themed playlist, and we all did the actions to 'The Birdie Song' as we worked.

'This is lookin' fine y'all,' Brooke said, as we made her up. I wound the feather boas around her legs and stuck the Post-its on her nose. The three of us kept adding to our creation, sticking bits on to create a very avant-garde version of the famous Portuguese cockerel.

'I'd say we've given more of an overall flavour than a replica image,' Leo said, as the three of us stood back to admire our handiwork.

Zach took a couple of photos and Brooke squealed with laughter when she saw the state of herself.

'I think she likes it,' I said.

'Seems that way,' Zach agreed.

'Like it? I love it! This is going to be my new look. Animal vibes.'

'And antacids on tap,' Leo said. 'The ultimate business outfit.'

'Time is UP, ladies and gentlemen,' Dahlia shouted, sounding the Klaxon again. 'Dressers, please finish whatever it is you are doing and then can all cockerels make their way to the front here, and join me up on stage.'

Brooke shuffled forward and Leo and I fussed around her, smoothing down stray feathers and brushing on a final layer of bronzer.

'Go forth and represent!' Zach said and Brooke nodded.

'I'll try my best,' she said, waddling off.

'Winner, winner,' I shouted.

'Chicken dinner!' we all chorused, repeating the chant as she followed the other cockerels onto the stage. Then we collapsed in our chairs to have a well-deserved rest.

'Martinis for the workers?' A waiter came over with a tray-full as Dahlia got back on the microphone.

'We have twenty wonderful cocks to choose from,' she shouted.

'Chance would be a fine thing,' Barb called from the back of the stage.

'Well done, all of you. You've done a fantastic job. And as we all know, it's not the winning but the taking part that counts.'

'Boooooo!' Barbie Queue appeared behind Dahlia and the cocks. 'What are you on about, you? We're innit to winnit – am I right?'

'Yessss!' everyone shouted in glee.

'We need a parade and a public vote, just like they do on *Strictly*, don't we gang?'

The audience cheered and whistled.

'Do you want a cock parade?'

'Yessss!'

'Subject to availability,' Barb added, with her tongue in her cheek.

'Alright then!' Dahlia wailed. 'Come on roosters, let's see you STRUT.'

Madonna's 'Vogue' kicked in and Dahlia ushered everyone to the back of the stage to wait their turn, before striding along the stage in her classic chicken costume to lots of whoops and applause. Then Barbie Queue took another turn, freezing in different poses to show off her outfit, followed by each of the cockerels one by one. Some walked, some danced, one punched his way along as a fighting cockerel, another ate a custard tart to prove he was Portuguese; all of them looked fabulous.

Brooke was last to go, and we clapped and cheered at the tops of our voices as she flapped her wings and waddled like a pigeon. We did our best to influence the clapometer, which seemed very hit and miss – and was really just Arlo pressing a button behind a curtain.

'Thank you,' Dahlia said, gathering all the contestants together to take a bow. 'All of you. You are all winners in my eyes.'

Everyone cheered.

'But there has to be an official winner for the grand prize and according to our clapometer the gold star Portuguese Cockerel prize goes to...' she reached into the contestants and pulled out one of the cockerels to present to the audience '...you! Whoever you are!'

'Give me an hour, then let yourself in,' I whispered, slipping Heidi's key into Leo's pocket. I wanted our last night together to be extra special and I'd had an idea.

He gave me one of his dark, intense looks and I nearly forgot where I was. We'd give ourselves away if I sat here much longer. *I'd* give us away. 'I'm not sure I can wait,' he said.

'Try,' I murmured. 'It'll be worth it.'

The pull between us felt stronger than ever, and I found it difficult to physically draw myself away. 'Night, both,' I called to Zach and Brooke, who were deep in conversation, before speedwalking off down the corridor. I had to ready the room and myself, and even an hour was cutting it tight.

I dragged both mattresses onto the floor bringing the pillows and the blankets down with them, fluffing them all up to make a cute floor bed. The two strawberry-shaped tap lamps gave a soft light from on top of the bed frame, and I spritzed the air with some perfume. It wasn't the Four

Seasons, but it could almost pass as a double futon in a cosy studio apartment, if we half-closed our eyes. Anything was better than another night in the bunk. That tangled-up sweatbox was fun as a one-off but as a romantic experiment it was not to be repeated.

My battery was dead again, but my inner clock told me I had at least another half hour, so I plugged in my phone to charge, had a long shower and put on the one decent set of underwear I'd brought with me. I spritzed my hair with sea salt and gave it a good brush. Mum always said if I brushed it one hundred times, the blonde would turn to gold. Which wasn't entirely false, as it was always much shinier by the time I'd finished. Although I think her source was Rapunzel. I twisted it into a long plait and would shake it all out once Leo arrived. The original non-heat beach waves.

Were heels too much? It was our last night after all… I popped on a pair of wedges to give myself some height, then did a full face of make-up including false eyelashes. And then worried I'd overdone it. I sprayed perfume onto the bed sheets, with another spritz into the air for good measure, then wafted it about.

It must have been another thirty minutes by now… I slathered my arms and legs in a citrus moisturiser and reapplied my lipstick. My phone was still black. I needed a new one; the battery was forever powering down when I needed it most. There was so little space in the room that it was easiest to sit on the floor in my new bed. Leaning against the bunk bed ladder in my underwear while I waited was far too weird. Leo would be biding his time, so as not to be too obvious. Keeping up the ruse. He had a key, so he'd get here when he could, I'd just have to be patient.

I put the radio on for some mood music and lay down in the bed, which was surprisingly snuggly. Having the weight of both duvets and the softness of two pillows made all the difference. It was warm and comfortable, and a wave of tiredness hit me as soon as I lay down; I was zonked from running around all day. I'd just rest my eyes for a second or two, maybe even have a power nap to recharge. Leo could wake me up when he got here.

Twenty-six

Tuesday 6th July

I woke up in my makeshift double bed, but there was no Leo. My frilly knickers and matching bra were still pristine and even my false eyelashes had stayed in position. I couldn't have been more ready for a good send-off; I'd had everything I needed – except for Leo himself. I reached for my phone, and it was still black and blank. *What the hell was going on with it?* I took a closer look and realised I hadn't switched it on at the socket. User error. I plugged it into the battery pack instead and waited for it to boot up. It must be morning by now… it felt like morning. I pulled up the black-out blinds and it was light outside, so I threw on my dressing gown and tiptoed to the door to see if people were bustling about. It was docking day after all.

No one. It must be earlier than I thought. Unless there'd been some mass exodus and I'd been left alone on the ship. I felt suddenly panicked, with no Leo and no proof of life anywhere. I needed to find some other humans, so I threw a dress on, grabbed my phone as soon as it had a sliver of charge and wandered down the corridor in my slippers. The crew were buzzing around as usual, so there hadn't been an apocalypse. We hadn't been captured by pirates or zombies. Phew. It was just too early for most people to be awake: quarter to six according to the restaurant clock. I'd walked around the boat in a loop and stopped when I realised I was just down the corridor from Brooke's suite and her door was opening. What was she doing up? *What was I doing up?* I didn't want her to see me lurking around in my slippers, so I hid behind a large urn to let whoever it was pass. I waited a few minutes and nobody walked past, so I peeked out and spotted a figure walking the other way. I watched from a distance as a dishevelled Leo sauntered off down the corridor, his hair mussed, shirt crinkled, and his suit jacket slung over one shoulder. The same jacket he'd worn in the bar last night. I couldn't believe my eyes. Not only had he left me alone and wanting when he'd promised he was on his way, *he'd slept in Brooke's suite*. After his big speech about honesty and trust, he'd almost fooled me into thinking he was one of the good guys.

How could he? This was so much worse than being ghosted; I'd rather have had my usual three-month fob-off than catch actual feelings and be cheated on. That was something that never happened. I was shocked and humiliated and devastated all at once. I tried to swallow my feelings, but it hurt. For the first time in I couldn't remember how long, I'd left my heart slightly ajar and it had taken a direct hit. Well, it was time to close it up again. I watched him stop mid-stride and pull out his phone, swiping and tapping as I loitered behind a water butt. Then my pocket vibrated as the battery came back to life.

Leo: I might not make it to your room tonight – Zach wants to play cards and I can't see a way out of it. Can I make it up to you when we get back to London?

He'd sent that at midnight, but it had only just come through.

Leo: Morning, beautiful. Land ahoy! Sorry about last night I got waylaid and couldn't get away – I'll tell you all about it at breakfast. One final fry-up at our usual table?

The absolute *cheek* of him. Rifling through women like Barbie Queue flicks through frocks. There was only one way to deal with a man like that. Delete and block. I felt like such an idiot. I'd let myself get distracted and now the pitch was only two weeks away, with only one solid pitch idea around unimaginable moments.

Me: Hey. I'm still packing. Don't think I'll make it down.

I marched back to the room, my stomach grumbling; there was a packet of Hobnobs in my case somewhere… I'd have to make do with tepid tea and biscuits to keep me going. I kept my head down as I tunnelled along the corridor and nearly collided with Brooke as she overtook me on the corner.

'Oh!' she said, jumping back. 'Good mornin', Kat! Lovely day ain't it?'

'Hi! Yes!' I said, with false bright eyes, feeling awkward. She wasn't to know I knew, and I knew she didn't know about me and Leo, so it wasn't like she'd done anything wrong. Girl code made me want to share but client-agency code meant I couldn't. There were a lot of different boundaries at play.

'You comin' for breakfast, doll?'

'Already done!' I lied. 'I've been up since six, making the most of these final few hours. Leo is heading down there though.'

'No surprises there. I swear that man has a double,' Brooke said, with a titter. 'He's everywhere!'

Ain't that the truth. 'He keeps himself busy – I'll give him that.' Bedding the client and the competition in the same twenty-four hours was no mean feat.

'Nothing but the work will sway me, honey, don't you worry. And Greg is just the same.' Leo probably had plans to bed Greg pre-pitch as well.

Thiago's velvety voice interrupted us over the Tannoy. 'Ladies and gentlemen, I am sad to say it, but we are nearing the end of our time together on the *Esmeralda*. I hope you have enjoyed cruising with us – thank you for joining her maiden voyage. We are on time and due back into Dover Ferry Port at twelve noon. Please leave your bags outside your rooms by nine-thirty and the crew will take them to the departure deck. Thank you.'

'See you later!' Brooke called as she carried on down the corridor. I pulled out my phone and fired off one final text to Leo as I walked back to my room.

Me: Brooke is on her way down though, if you're keen for company.

Knock yourself out, Leo. I didn't want to look churlish, but I couldn't resist.

Leo: Eh? I'm not keen for just any old company – I want
to have breakfast with you!

I switched my phone off. He didn't know I knew and my
mind was too full to think of an appropriately cutting reply.
Best to ignore and get myself packed ASAP. Then I'd just have
to hide around the ship and avoid him until we got back to
Dover. He was just another disappointing man, but it wasn't
his fault – they were all like it. If I'd met him on Tinder my
expectations wouldn't have been so high; that was what made
it so gutting. He'd convinced me he was different, one of the
good ones. I rolled my clothes up and stuffed them in my
tiny suitcase. All but one – the dress Barbie Queue had loaned
me for the captain's dinner. *Ivy* had been hanging out in our
wardrobe ever since, so I left my suitcase outside my door and
took her down to Barb's dressing room and knocked gently.

'Come back tomorrow!' *Eek*. There was no tomorrow on
this cruise but Barb clearly wasn't in the mood for company.

I hung *Ivy* on the doorframe with two feather boas
dangling off her shoulders, and tiptoed away. I was halfway
down the corridor when the door flew open and she emerged
in a cloud of raspberry vape, fully made up in a gold catsuit.
The dress toppled and landed on her head.

'What the pissin' hell's going on…?'

'Sorry Barb, I was just returning your dress. I should have
brought it back ages ago. I didn't mean to interrupt you…'

She scoffed. 'What're you bringing it back for? It's yours
now, love. It was made for you. Take it.'

I wouldn't get much wear out of a crystal-covered ball
gown back in Camden, but I didn't want to seem ungrateful.
'Are you sure?' I asked, more tentative than delighted.

'Yes, darlin', you enjoy it. Wear it somewhere fabulous with that boyfriend of yours.'

'Who? I haven't got one…?'

She snorted. 'The fella who's always staring at you. That confident one – with the quiff.'

'Leo?'

'That's him. Put it on and go for drinks at The Ritz. Do it for Jane. Hop up on the grand piano and make a show of yourself. Promise me you will?' She eyeballed me fiercely. '*Ivy* is a glamorous goddess, and she deserves to have a good time – please don't hide her away in a plastic bag.'

'I won't, don't worry,' I said, imagining myself slithering around on a piano like Marilyn Monroe and an army of security guards throwing me out. 'I'll take her to The Ritz and send you a photo.'

Barb closed her eyes and nodded dramatically, and I couldn't tell if she was being real or it was all part of her act. It must be hard to slip in and out of character. 'Come back and see us soon, Kat, won't you, love?'

My stomach churned. 'If we win the pitch, I'll be back; I can promise you that. And if we don't… well, then I'd like to audition for The Crustaceans.'

She rolled her eyes and sucked on her vape. 'I'm not sure you've got the rhythm, love. No offence.'

I laughed and gave her a hug, which was all boobs and trying to avoid her foundation.

'Think about it.'

I was sad to walk away from my holiday sister – not that I needed any more sisters – but I'd felt like we'd bonded. Or was it just me who felt like that? Barb would do the same gig with the next group of guests and forget all about me.

The transient life of cruising crew. Working on the ship for months at a time, performing under the spotlight night after night. Never really having any privacy. Your life on show for all to see – every minute of every day.

I wandered back to my room, more out of habit than anything else as the cleaners were already in there getting it ready for the next person. It was time to give my sea legs a rest and change my cruising status to *disembarked*. Despite the relentless activities schedule and Heidi breathing down my neck, the past few weeks had somehow made me feel extra holidayed and extra rested. If I hadn't been here because of work, PR would have been the last thing on my mind. What a funny thing cruising was. A blip of time where a microcosm of society goes on a boating holiday together. And soon we'd all be gone again, like dandelion seeds on the wind blowing in different directions. Light, tiny and quickly forgotten. I turned the corner and froze at the sight of Leo standing outside my door with a plate of pastries and a tropical crush. I wasn't ready to face him yet, so I tiptoed back out of sight and waited until he gave up, my heart thumping with sadness, already broken in two.

Twenty-seven

Esmeralda slowed to a standstill, chuffing smoke into the air as the crew ran around throwing ropes and the engines shut down. I was glad to be back on British soil – well, almost. Our big cruising adventure was finally over, and we were back in Blighty. Back to real life and real work. How depressing. I'd been hiding in the loos to avoid bumping into Leo and had emerged cautiously as Thiago announced we'd reached the shore. Heidi had been right all along: he'd been trying to distract me from the pitch and I'd fallen for it hook, line and sinker, and I hated myself. I stood at the back of the pool bar, silently observing the other passengers as they lined the decks and readied themselves to disembark. It was a mighty sight to see everyone in one place and humbling to be one among so many. Leo was stood with Zach and Brooke, the three of them watching as the drawbridge eased down and people inched closer, ready to make a run for it. He kept checking his phone then glancing around and had already sent me three texts.

Leo: Where are you? I want to say goodbye properly.

Leo: Have you fallen overboard? Drop me a pin and I'll come and find you.

Leo: I'm starting to worry. Are you OK?

I debated ghosting him but didn't want him calling out the RNLI.

Me: Just coming.

Leo: Thank God. Don't do that to me. We are by the drawbridge.

I forced a big smile and marched over, channelling my inner Barbie Queue. I was a professional woman and could ab-so-lute-ly handle this situation. Bryce was in my ear – *You've one hundred per cent got this. You know exactly what to do.* I'd say a quick toodle-oo and be on my way.

'Hey, you three, I thought I'd missed you!' I said, grinning from ear to ear. 'Where have you been?'

'Same spot as always, sweetie,' Brooke said. 'In the coffee lounge.'

Leo frowned. 'Where have we been? Where have *you* been?'

I carried on smiling, ignoring the question. 'So, this is the end of the road then, huh?'

'It sure is,' Brooke said, giving me a hug. She was so small and fragile – I could easily have lifted her off the ground and popped her in my pocket.

'Thank you for being such a fabulous hostess and letting us experience *Esmeralda* first-hand. It's been an incredible trip.'

'Not at all. It's the Excalibur way – expect nothing less.'

Zach shuffled awkwardly, while Leo tried to catch my eye. 'It's been great getting to know you both,' I said, deliberately shaking Zach's hand first.

Leo gave me a strange look. 'You too,' he said, waggling my hand like a leaf of limp lettuce. 'Pass on our regards to Heidi. I hope her emergency... got resolved.'

I met his confused expression with a tight smile. Firm and professional – he deserved nothing more. 'Sure thing.'

The rows of cars waiting to board ferries at Dover port brought the reality of home flooding back, not to mention the biting-cold wind and drizzle. The taxi rank wasn't too far away; I just needed to locate my luggage and I'd be on my way. I headed for the conveyor belt where Arlo was dishing out suitcases and waited patiently in the queue. I could see mine on the trolley behind him, but he was stressed enough with everyone shouting and pointing so I took a step back to let the paying customers get in there first. Then I felt a tap on my shoulder.

'What was all that about?' Leo whispered in my ear.

'All what?'

'You blanking me then walking off!'

'How is me shaking hands and saying goodbye blanking you?'

I wanted to be anywhere but here right now, but there was no escape.

'You know exactly what I'm talking about. Going cold and vacant as if I'm nothing to you. I deserve more than that.'

'And I deserve more than to be lied to, waiting around for you in my room like a fool. Although I've got to admit I'm almost impressed – it was a clever way to get rid of me on the last night and have Brooke all to yourself.'

'I text you last night and I've been trying to find you all morning to explain. Zach and I ended up playing cards all night and I couldn't leave without raising suspicion. Especially as I didn't stay in the room with Zach the night before. I didn't think you'd want me to take any risks.'

He seemed so genuine and apologetic – what a performance. I couldn't believe he could lie to my face so convincingly.

'You were playing cards with Zach?'

'Yeah. Not just Zach, there were a few of us. Thiago, Arlo, some other staff and a couple of the guests.'

'OK, fair enough,' I said. There was no point engaging, he was obviously a compulsive liar. I just wanted my bag and to get in a taxi so I could go home.

'Why are you so angry? I don't understand.'

'This is who I am, Leo. Sorry if that doesn't work for you. I've got a pitch to prep for. I haven't got time to mess around with the opposition. Real people are relying on me – their jobs are at stake.'

'*Mess around with the opposition?* Are you serious? Is that all I am?' He looked genuinely crestfallen, but it was clearly just another level in his 'act', and I wasn't one of those naïve, gullible types. I wouldn't stand for it.

'We both know it's all about winning the competition for you,' I said, flatly, while trying to catch Arlo's eye. 'You're addicted to that feeling of success and will do anything to get it.'

He stared at me, mouth agape. 'Where are you getting all this rubbish from? I'm not a win-at-all-costs type at all. Just goes to show how well you know me.'

I had to stay strong, however convincing he might be.

'Kat – is this one yours?' Arlo held up my battered old suitcase and read off the Excalibur label. 'Kath-er-ine Brenn-an?'

'Yes!' *At last.* I could have kissed him.

'Back to business then, is it? Just like that. The party's over?' Leo followed me and picked up my case as I signed for it. 'After all we've been through?' He lowered his voice. 'After the bottom bunk?'

'Words no man should ever say to a woman,' I said, as my mask nearly slipped into a smile, but then I remembered how he'd made himself at home in my hotel room and crammed himself into my bunk bed, manipulating me into developing feelings while he was star-fishing away in Brooke's emperor-penguin bed. Who knew how many cabins he'd 'tested out' in the name of *research*.

'You're so cold,' he said, looking me straight in the eyes as I tried to wrestle my suitcase off him. 'I can't believe you're doing this to me again, but then I'm the idiot to have let it happen.' His gaslighting made my blood boil, but I wasn't going to get into an argument with him here. There were too many people around and it could seriously harm our chances with Brooke if she knew I knew. Or even worse, found out Leo had been staying with me too. For the sake of my future and the people who worked with me, I needed to keep schtum and shut the conversation down.

I marched off towards the taxi rank and Leo chased after me with my suitcase.

'Where to, love?' the cabbie asked, jumping out to take my case.

'The station please.'

'Kat, let's not end on a weird note like this. Talk to me – what's going on? Zach and I are getting a car back to London, you can jump in with us.'

'No thanks, I need some time on my own.'

'Can I call you tomorrow?' he pleaded, a look of abject confusion on his face. He was putting on a good show; I'd give him that.

'I don't know what more you want from me, Leo. I've said goodbye; what else is there to say?' His face was a picture of hurt and confusion, but I wasn't falling for it. This was what narcissists did – I'd had fair warning from Bryce in episode forty-four: 'Mirror, mirror'. I wasn't going to play his game by offering up an explanation; he knew what he'd done. I'd keep my powder dry until the pitch was done and won.

I got in the taxi and sat back in relief.

'Bye then, Kat. Good luck with the pitch, yeah?'

'You too,' I said, not meaning it even a little bit. 'Goodbye.'

I closed my eyes as we drove off, glad to be on my way.

'Been away on holiday, have you, love?' the taxi driver asked.

'A work trip.' I really didn't feel like talking, but I didn't want to be rude.

'Oh right. Nice work if you can get it,' he said, chuckling to himself. 'Do you work on the cruise boats then?'

'We do their PR,' I said, and burst into tears. How much longer would I be able to say that? My whole life was hanging in the balance, and the pressure was too much.

Twenty-eight

I was *so* happy to get home, I could've cried. The London leg of the journey had been gruelling, and I felt like a human husk when I eventually arrived back in Camden Town. I'd been on endless escalators in Victoria station, wedged myself onto two sweaty tubes, then walked the final ten minutes to my flat. I'd have been back hours ago if I'd accepted Leo's offer, but I'd chosen my principles over a free ride and exhausted myself in the process. Every part of me ached: my bones, my head, and most importantly my heart… and my social battery was flashing red as I pushed my front door open.

Home sweet home. My bedsit was enormous compared to the cruise-ship cabin I'd grown accustomed to, and as I kicked off my shoes and threw my keys in the coconut shell, it was like I'd never been away. My flat was painted in four shades of yellow, so it always felt warm when I arrived home, like a queen bee hanging in the hive – or more realistically, a weary worker bee bringing home a pouch full of honey. There were evergreen flowers in every vase, and I had two different Lego bunches in the 'lounge', a bouquet of metal roses in the kitchen nook and a paper daisy chain in loops across the window. I'd wanted to fill the place with flowers that would last. Space was at a premium, and I'd done my best to be clever with what went where, but really that just meant everything was out on display. Dressing gowns on hooks with slippers in the pockets, saucepans and kitchen gadgets hanging from the ceiling, a cheese grater, a colander and a spatula tied together on one piece of string. Necklaces on every doorknob and my long dresses either end of the curtain poles. Wherever you were in the flat, you could pretty much see all of my possessions at once and it was lovely to be surrounded by it all again.

My double bed was the ultimate space-saver, folded back against the wall when not in use, pinning my duvet and pillows in place. I pulled it down and jumped on it, staring up at the plastic stars on the ceiling and glad to be back in my own space. The sheets had been sprayed with lavender sleep mist, and I felt my body sink into the duvet as I inhaled its soft smell. I closed my eyes for thirty seconds… and woke up three hours later.

Mum: Are you home?

Mum: Well?

Missed call: Mum.

Mum: Call me please. You should be back by now.

Missed call: Dad.

Eek. I dialled Mum with one eye open; the lavender had knocked me for six.

'Kat?' she shouted. 'Don't ever do that to me again! It is you, isn't it? Kat? Kat?'

'Yes, it's me! If you'll let me get a word in. Sorry, I fell asleep.'

'I'm not surprised; you must be exhausted. Have a bath and go back to bed.'

'I need to unpack and do my washing,' I mumbled, eyeing my suitcase by the front door where I left it.

'Leave all that for tomorrow – you can take your time then, rather than rushing to do it in between sleeps. You need a tech-free duvet day to get yourself organised.'

'There's nothing tech-free about the office.'

'You're not going in tomorrow, surely? You've only just got back!'

I let out a deep sigh. *If only.* Heidi would expect me in the office first thing, on my A-game and brimming with ideas, so there was no time for any rest and recovery.

'Of course I am, Mum – that's how work, works, isn't it?'

'That place is ridiculous. They work you like a dog. You should have two weeks off in lieu by law for the time you've been away; the least she can do is give you a day to recover.'

'And pigs might fly.'

'Well, do a power hour now, then go to bed for twelve hours. The duvet day will have to be a duvet weekend once Heidi's had her money's worth.'

The air was stifling and I felt hot and sticky. I ignored my body screaming at me to let it snuggle down and got in the shower, turning the water cool and washing my hair. This was London life – keep on keeping on. Mum was right; I could sleep at the weekend – if Heidi didn't have us all in working on the pitch. I put my pyjama shorts on in front of the fan and tied my hair in a high pony. London was hotter than Lisbon and I was missing the sea breeze on my body. I knew if I got back into bed then that would be it until morning, so I flicked on the radio and cranked it up loud to keep myself awake. The flat needed freshening up and re-energising so I threw open the windows to get some air circulating, then watered the row of thirsty herb plants on the window ledge. They had miraculously survived two weeks without me, just about, and the smell of rosemary and basil was comforting as I pulled off the dead leaves and left space for the others to grow.

The great thing about a bedsit was you could do most things from one spot. I watched the fish zoom around with excitement as I sprinkled over a pinch of flakes, their tiny mouths open and hungry. Funny to think these golden dots had come from the same ocean as the humpback whales. Would they be happier in the wild, or didn't they know the difference? These pampered goldfish wouldn't last five minutes out there. My sea legs and sea stomach were wobbly from being on the ship, and my head was scrambled. How could I possibly go to work tomorrow and be in any state to contribute creative energy when I felt like this? I needed to get my balance back – in all areas – and everything felt so confusing. Leo had looked genuinely hurt as the taxi pulled away and I couldn't get his sad eyes out of my mind. What kind of brilliant actor was he? And to what end? Whatever he was trying to pull, I just couldn't understand why he'd put so much effort in, and I'd run out of energy to try and work it out.

HIIT Girls Group Chat:

Me: I'm back, bitches.

Sara: There she is!

Abi: How was it with Leo in the end? Awks or OK?

Me: OK, then good, then amazing and finished v weird.
We kinda had a thing…

Abi: Another one of your things? I bumped into your LA
fling-thing in Target last week.

Me: I thought this might be more than a fling-thing – like
something real. But it turned out he was keeping it real
with the client as well.

Abi: Putting his little thing about.

Sara: WTF??? Isn't that against the rules?

Probably, but who was I going to complain to? I wasn't
really in a position when I'd done the exact same thing. I
could try and seduce Greg and play fire with fire, but that
was a sixty-something bridge too far. I had to accept Leo
wasn't the man I thought he was and move on, and the best
way to do that was to stay busy and focus on the work. I
unzipped my suitcase and tipped everything onto the floor
to force myself to sort it all out. Putting a load of washing
on while I could still be bothered. The quicker I did it, the

quicker it would get done and no one else was going to do it. My passport went back in my 'shoebox of important things,' which was hidden under a loose floorboard, and I fished around in the front pocket for the cruise paperwork to chuck it away. My fingers caught on something smooth and hard instead, and I pulled out a small envelope with my name scrawled on the front. My birthday was coming up, but who would know that to pop a card in my case? Surely not Heidi being a thoughtful sweetheart out of the blue...

'Angels' started playing on the radio and Robbie Williams' chocolatey voice took me straight back to Leo being straddled by Barb on stage. He certainly got full marks for participation and was so much more relaxed than I'd remembered. He'd almost had me fooled. I opened the envelope carefully, so I could keep it, and pulled out a postcard with a breaching whale on the front.

Hi Kat,

I haven't seen you for hours and I'm starting to worry that I won't for some reason before we leave. Has something happened? Please talk to me. Let's not have another decade-long misunderstanding. I've tried to call but you aren't answering, and it feels like the end of our internship all over again. In case of any miscommunication here – I don't want this to be the end of our story. These past two weeks with you have been so much fun. I've loved getting to know you again and remembering why I had that crush on you all those years ago. Please can I take you out for dinner when we get back to London? I want to explore what this might be, and I hope you feel the same.

I know we've got the pitch to consider, and we're both professionals, but can we keep business and pleasure separate and give this a try? I can if you can.

We can wait until after the pitch if you'd rather – so we don't have that hanging over us. Whatever you want to do – I'm in.

I'll pop this in the post to you at work if I don't see you before you go.

Please call me and let me know you're OK.

Leo xx

Twenty-nine

Tuesday 13th July

A week later and I still felt gutted. All I could think about was Leo. His eyes, his smile, his stupid jokes. And how he'd somehow managed to stitch me up again, *in plain sight*. I was furious and humiliated, but also incredibly sad. I'd let him get in my head and maybe my heart, just a tiny bit, and he'd broken it and left. My one saving grace was that he didn't know I knew. Player's gonna play. I wanted to block him on everything and lock him away in my WhatsApp prison but I didn't want him to know I cared that much. No, it was better to ghost and ignore. I wanted to hurt him as much as he'd hurt me, but it was impossible when it was all so one-sided. The only way to kick him in the metaphorical goolies was to win the pitch and wipe that overconfident smirk off his face. He was so sure they had it in the bag. Offering me a job?! The cheeky bastard.

'Talk me through where you're up to,' Heidi said, mascara smudges under both eyes. We'd been working round the clock and were all exhausted.

Scott, Natalya and Andy stood behind the boardroom table ready to present the ideas.

'I've got the pitch deck,' I said, pulling it up on the big screen. 'I've kept it clean and simple and we've only got an hour, so let's get onto the creative as quickly as possible.'

'Agreed,' Heidi said.

Natalya cleared her throat. She had been creative director at Northstar PR for nearly ten years and knew the Excalibur account inside out. If there'd been space for more than two on the cruise, she'd have come with us.

'Who knows if past knowledge is a blessing or a curse, but that's what we have on our side so let's use it to our advantage,' she said. 'We've mapped out the key audiences using age, income and attitude to holidays, and then visualised the potential cruiser personas.'

She pulled up a photo of me, retouched to look ten years younger, wearing pantaloons and a crop top and we all cracked up.

'Love it, guys. Where do I sign?'

'This is Kat as a young Gen Z,' Natalya said. 'Obviously.'

Heidi nodded. 'I like that as a way in. Keeps it light and fun, but personal. Good thinking.'

'Then we ask – what does Kat want from her holiday?'

Thinking about myself in the third person was strangely confronting. What did I want from my holiday? A highlights reel of the cruise flashed through my mind: playing water volleyball with enthusiastic strangers (before I got hit in the face), whale watching at sunset and tobogganing through the streets of Madeira. Beautifully cooked food and every type of cuisine. The fake anniversary dinner with Leo under the stars... I don't know about twenty-something Kat but the two weeks I'd had on *Esmeralda* had been close to perfect for the real me – accommodation aside. I felt my breath catch in my throat as all those magical moments crashed together. Younger Kat couldn't have asked for more.

'Kat, you can then answer directly. Run through the demands of Gen Z to set up the creative ideas.'

'Brilliant. Some theatre to reel them in.'

'We've used a selection of the photos from the trip,' Andy said, laying them out on the table blown up to poster size. The group shot of the five of us in Madeira was full of colour and joy. It was a textbook holiday snap – we couldn't have looked happier. And it encapsulated what cruising was all about. The five of us hadn't known each other before we set sail, but we'd bonded over too much food, plenty of booze and a bizarre selection of activities. And now we had a shared experience that we'd remember forever.

'These are perfect,' I said, studying the images. 'Moments we could never have imagined before we set sail,' I said, as I looked at it.

'Correct,' Heidi said, snapping her fingers. 'Gen Z want adventure, to live life to the max, to get full bang for their buck and to connect. More than anything they crave connection. We all do.'

'We can invite stories from people who have met on cruises and had hilarious, unusual and bizarre encounters, using *unimaginable moments* as the hashtag,' Scott added. 'Then use the best stories to pitch for the mags and rags and get a word-of-mouth campaign going.'

There was a knock on the boardroom door, and an enormous bunch of pink peonies walked in, shielding our receptionist. The top of her pixie cut was just about visible, bobbing along behind them.

'Wow!!!' Heidi said, her tired eyes shining. 'They… are… stunning! Sam is getting serious husband points; he can be *such* a sweetheart sometimes. Put them in my office, Jules. Thanks, love.'

'Erm…' She set them down on the table. 'These are addressed to Kat… marked as urgent and sent by courier.'

I was flabbergasted. I'd never had flowers delivered to work in my life. 'For me? Are you sure?'

'Oh,' Heidi said, turning her back. 'Someone's a dark horse. I didn't even know you were seeing anyone.'

I laughed. 'You know me… anyone and everyone.' I grabbed the card and opened it.

What happened?
Where did you go?
Call me.
L

x

'Anyone we know?' Heidi asked, trying to nosy over my shoulder as I stuffed it back in the envelope.

'My mum,' I said, my heart racing. There were at least thirty stems in the bunch. It wasn't a mum-bought bouquet by anyone's standards, and none of them believed me.

Heidi raised a sceptical eyebrow before turning back to the presenter. 'Right, well let's get back to it. Chop, chop. I like where you're up to. Put the creative into the presentation and let's regroup and run through it in an hour. See how – and more importantly *if* – it works.'

The peonies were open and fluffy and weighed a tonne as I carried them back to my desk. I'd never even seen a bouquet as big as this before; they were almost cartoonish. Was this what they called love bombing? Whatever it was, I couldn't help but smile. They looked like little pink pompoms, cheering me on as I got back to work. Brooke had probably had a similar bunch delivered. Buy one get one free.

What happened? Exactly my question, Leo! You tell me! I'd been ignoring his messages ever since we'd gone our separate ways, but I decided to have a quick check through.

Tuesday: You were so annoyed when we said goodbye. I don't understand. Can we meet?

Wednesday: Obviously not. Can we at least talk then?

Thursday: Obviously not.

Friday: Are you getting my messages? I've just realised they're all unread.

Saturday: Have you lost your phone?

No, Leo, I haven't lost my phone. I hadn't been getting his messages, but eventually he'd got mine as the daily texts had stopped. But now this. The old BRG – big romantic gesture – if that's what this was.

I had to acknowledge it.

Me: Thanks for the flowers. Nothing's happened my side – how about you?

Leo: There you are! I've been worried. You disappeared. What's going on?

Me: Working hard on the pitch.

Leo: Yeah, us too. Back to business as usual then, is it?

Typical narcissist, making me feel guilty for breaking it off when he knew exactly what he'd done. I didn't mind pretending to be the bad guy if that's what had to happen. I'd seen him leaving Brooke's suite with my own eyes, and there was nothing he could do about it. He didn't deserve another second of my consideration. I one-word replied.

Me: Yep.

Then deleted him.

Thirty

Wednesday 21st July

The cab pulled up outside Excalibur Cruises head office and Heidi turned to me.

'Remember when we're in there: we're a team and we back each other up. Nobody knows this account like we do – and we are going to WIN THIS PITCH.'

'You said it, boss,' I said, holding my hand up for a high five.

'Let's hope I'm still saying it this afternoon,' she said, handing the driver a twenty and opening the door. I took a deep breath and channelled my inner Bryce to manifest a win. *Act as if the deal is already done.* The brain doesn't know the difference between words and the truth. But the bank does. And there was the small matter of 'doing the work' in the middle – and how the hell would Bryce know, anyway? He was ten thousand miles away in Australia somewhere, knocking out podcasts in a tin shed. Oh God, I was unravelling. Nonetheless, I tried to envisage us as the winners. We'd worked so hard on the presentation and done everything we could. The deck was slick, and the ideas were sharp and ambitious.

I bundled out onto the pavement after Heidi, with the laptop and the boards, like her personal packhorse. I was wearing stockings under my red Azorean dress for secret sexiness, and it felt freeing and exciting. Barbie Queue would be proud. I smiled to myself; this pitch was ours to lose.

Leo and Zach were already in reception drinking coffee. Of course they were. They'd probably stayed overnight so as not to be late.

'Morning,' Heidi said into the air, without looking at them.

'Morning,' they chorused.

'Hello, Kat,' Leo said, looking wounded.

I ignored him and half-smiled at Zach in his yellow, surfing T-shirt and white jeans, with a tailored jacket to smarten himself up. His tiny specs were nestled in his woolly hair and he looked like an affable cartoon character. Leo was the total opposite in an uber-fashionable blue suit and crisp white shirt, with shiny brown shoes. The classic PR man with his creative sidekick.

'May the best man win, eh?' Zach smirked at his own joke.

'Good luck,' Leo said quietly. 'Hope it goes well.'

I looked straight through him. Sleazebag.

'And for you,' Heidi said with a chuckle. 'Break both legs and all that.'

There was a high-pitched squeal as Brooke appeared through the swinging doors in a bright pink power suit, her hair tonged into ringlets.

'Howdy there, friends!' She hugged Zach then Leo with a beaming smile. 'And here are my girrrls,' she said, giving me and Heidi exaggerated air kisses.

'Exciting day,' I trilled, enthusiastically, my game face firmly on.

'Sure is! Can't wait to see what y'all have got for us.'

I waggled my boards. 'Plenty of ideas in here.'

'Well, what are we waiting for? Let's get goin'!'

The four of us trooped through the security turnstiles and followed Brooke down a maze of corridors, eventually landing outside the boardroom. Greg was sat at the head of the table, flanked either side by officious-looking women, one blonde and one brunette – both with clipboards.

'Good morning,' I said, smiling at them all and walking over.

'I've met some of you before, but not all,' Greg said, with a smoker's gravel. 'I'm Greg, the chairman. This is Mindy, my PA, and Elizabeth, our COO – and my wife.' It was a cat's cradle of arms as we all shook hands, one after the other, until I realised I was shaking hands with Leo. The smooth, soft hand that had held me as we'd danced, and traced patterns across my back in bed. I dropped it as if it were on fire, ignoring his hurt expression.

Brooke stood in front of the screen and took control. 'OK, good morning everyone, thank you to both agencies for coming in today. We are excited to see how you've approached the brief. Greg's team have cleared three hours in his diary for the presentations, including time for any questions, so we should get right on with it.'

Heidi and I sat opposite Leo and Zach, all four of us fake smiling to play nice in front of the grown-ups. Leo's eyebrow twitched as he looked at me, and I couldn't help but think he was mocking me somehow. Bastard.

'Amplify have asked to go first if you gals don't mind,' Brooke said, giving us no choice in the matter. 'Zach needs to dash once they've finished presenting.'

'Absolutely fine,' Heidi said with a smile. 'Shit before the broom,' she side-mouthed.

Leo leapt straight into presenter mode, while Zach fiddled around in the background.

'Thank you, Brooke. Then let me begin. Ladies and gentlemen, we are here today because we want your business. We make no bones about that. Amplify are the marketing brains behind several holiday companies as you know: Tui, Hilton Hotels, Virgin Holidays...' As he said the names, Zach flashed the logos up on screen. 'And we want to add a cruise company to that list. Not just any cruise company – the best in the market. Excalibur Cruises.'

Oh, he was good. His whole demeanour said *I'm your man* and it was difficult not to get on board as he nodded slowly to himself then smiled at each of the clients, pausing when he reached Greg. I nearly started nodding myself.

Zach lay their boards face down on the table, while Leo trotted through the strategy slides, outlining the thinking that had led to their *big idea*. Then once he'd whet their appetite and they were desperate to see the creative, he paused.

'Time for the show,' he said, gesturing to Zach, who started turning the boards over like a game show host. Brooke got up and walked to the front to get a closer look, as I scanned the copy underneath the illustrations. I couldn't help but gasp as the words came into focus. Their line was our line. It was our idea.

'*Unimaginable moments*,' Zach said. 'Two simple words, but a rich creative territory to play with.' He flashed a photo of the four of us at the silent disco and then another of Leo and I whale watching. A montage quickly followed. Photo after photo, each telling a different story. The dining room at sunrise, a couple snorkelling with manta rays. Thiago in full captain regalia on the bow of the boat. Barbie Queue performing at the drag cabaret. A sunset over Madeira. 'We've taken hundreds of photos from our trip, showing the richness and range of moments we had on our cruise. Two weeks that could easily be mistaken for six months.'

Oh my God. I glanced at the clock. We were on in fifty minutes, I needed to think fast. How could we spin our presentation to be something entirely different in time for our slot? I opened my notepad and pretended to take notes, scribbling so Heidi could see.

WTF???? Shall we revert to Phileas Fogg?

She shook her head and picked up her pencil.

'A new generation of cruisers' or 'Cruising for a new generation' Do the opposite of this. Go practical for the audience he wants. 'Generation Cruise'.

We needed to agree.

What about existing customers?

They'll be dead soon. I'll talk around it.

I pushed my chair back slowly, trying to be quiet, but it scraped across the floor and six sets of eyeballs turned to look at me. 'Apologies,' I winced. 'I need to use the bathroom.' I left as quickly as I could, bashing my hip on the table and knocking one of the boards over as I reached the door. 'Sorry, sorry.'

'She's having some trouble,' I heard Heidi whisper as I left. Honestly, was there ever a scenario where she wouldn't feel comfortable throwing me under the bus? My hands were shaking as I pulled out my phone to call the office.

'Hello? Natalya? Are you there?'

'She's just in a meeting – can I help? This is James.' He was a freelance designer we'd hired to work on the pitch.

'Hi, James, it's Kat. We've got a nightmare problem, and I need some new designs for the Excalibur pitch.'

'Say that again? You're cutting out, which pitch?'

'Ex-cal-i-bur,' I said, nice and slow.

'Sure thing. I can jump on it after lunch; I'm just finishing an urgent job for...'

'This is *more* urgent,' I hissed. 'The most urgent of urgent jobs.'

'Right. OK. No problem.'

Bollocks. Robo-designer did not understand the severity of the situation.

'Is Natalya interruptible?'

'Say again?'

'Can-you-get-Natalya?'

'Natalya? Erm... I'm not sure. She's with clients so...'

'No, no, it's fine. I don't have much time, so I need you to write all this down. Then get Andy and Scott to help you. Heidi and I are in the Excalibur pitch, and the other agency have presented a similar idea to ours.'

'OK...'

'I need you to go into the presentation and rework the creative slides.'

'The slides? Right.'

'As fast as you can. The headline needs to be changed to say "Gen Z Cruising" with an image of young people having fun on boats and the Excalibur logo and website at the bottom. Can you do me a few different options then email me the updated deck? We're on in forty minutes.'

'Forty minutes?'

'YES, James. We are here right now,' I hissed through gritted teeth. The receptionist glanced over, and I needed to go back in before my absence became suspicious. 'Is that OK? Can you do it?'

'Sure.'

'And you'll email it to me?'

'Yep. Did you say it was Kat?'

Jesus Christ. 'Yes. Kat Brennan. One of the business directors of the agency.'

'Right you are. I'll take a look at it now for you.'

I didn't hold out much hope. How the hell were we going to pull this off? I went back into the boardroom and silently took my seat. Mindy gave me a sympathetic smile across the table. Heidi had probably told them I had cystitis, or an STD. The room was now covered in boards and far too many photos of me for my liking.

'I don't remember signing a model release form for all these ads,' I joked, seeing myself on top of a volcano, swimming in the sea, drinking cocktails with Heidi and Brooke, and on the tram in Lisbon with Leo.

'They're just positionals,' Zach said, dismissively. 'Obviously, we'll use proper models for the campaign, if we're appointed.'

'Unless you're interested?' Leo said, twinkly eyed.

'Let's see who's appointed first, shall we?' I said, sweetly.

I scribbled on my notepad and Heidi frowned.

James is on it.

James who?

Freelancer. Others were in a meeting.

'…and we'd suggest getting your message out there on hot air balloons. You can run a competition on social with different words on different balloons and have people work out the message.'

I was already thinking through the slides we'd need to delete from our presentation – at least half of them. Heidi could do the set-up and talk through the business side of things at the front, while I untangled the back. I tapped a message out to Natalya, under the table.

Me: Hey – urgent – I've briefed James. Need the Excalibur creative updating ASAP.

Natalya: Already on it.

I flashed the phone at Heidi, and she nodded in relief. It was the best we could do under the circumstances. Those cheating bastards.

'I like it,' Greg boomed, when Leo eventually finished talking. 'But if we can be anything to anyone – how do we focus in enough to sell one vision? Sounds expensive to have hundreds of different scenarios.'

'The beauty of the product you're offering is that variety is a genuine truth. We can run a photo shoot on one of your cruises and get enough imagery to target eight different audience segments at once,' Zach said.

'We wouldn't need to do lots of set-ups and scenarios, and incur model fees,' Leo added, gesturing at me. 'The idea can flex to work within any budget. A couple of models for the hero shots, and real passengers or crew for the rest.'

'It can run for years. As many campaigns as there are cruises.'

My phone lit up with an email from Natalya. God love her. She'd be getting a fat Christmas bonus if she pulled this one out of the bag. I clicked on it to have a quick scan through, as Brooke coughed pointedly and gave me a look. I'd have to wait to check it. She stood up and beamed at Greg, then turned to Zach and Leo.

'Thank you so much for that excellent presentation, guys. It's clear to see a lot of thought and work has gone into the ideas, plenty of food for thought. Can you email me the deck?'

'Already done,' Leo said, with a smile.

'Always one step ahead. OK – let's keep the energy UP. I'm conscious of time, so let's have a quick comfort break and replenish coffees, while Heidi and Kat set up pitch two. That sound good to you, gals?'

Heidi and I nodded, like cartoon rabbits, as all the chairs squeaked back and everyone scarpered. To the loo, to vape, to check phones and have a few minutes to themselves, while Heidi and I had a professional meltdown.

Thirty-one

'Quick, open it!' Heidi hissed, grabbing my phone to see.

'Let me connect my laptop and we can look at it on the big screen.' I pressed a button, and the presenter went blank. 'Hang on, I just need an adapter to...' Leo had presented on a PC, and I was using a Mac. I rummaged through the leads looking for the right one but couldn't put my hands on it. 'It's in here somewhere.'

'Hurry up!' Heidi snapped. 'Or give me the code for your phone?'

'It's eight-two-zero... here it is!' I said, putting my hands on the adapter and plugging my laptop in. The presentation flashed up on screen, and I quickly flicked through the slides. Heidi and I in our power suits, the logos of our clients, our background story and the awards we've won along the way. Blahdy, blah, blah... then into the creative.

Heidi gasped as I put up the first slide.

A boat full of twenty-somethings in bikinis and budgie smugglers, with cocktails and pints stood under the headline: 'The new Booze Cruise.' I flicked onto the next slide. 'Cruising and Boozing for a new Generation'. I felt the blood drain from my face. It looked like a drug-fuelled full moon party.

'What the fuck did you brief them?' Heidi asked, aghast.

'Not this!' I replied, increasingly bewildered as I flicked through the deck, desperate for anything that might save the situation. One visual that we could pin our pitch on and talk around. I got to the final slide, which was arguably the worst, as Brooke walked in.

'Client alert,' she tinkled, then stopped dead in the doorway. I stabbed at my computer to turn it off, but the screen had frozen on 'Cruising for some boozing?'

'Holy smokin' hot bananas, what is that?' she said, looking at the boat made of vodka bottles.

'Wrong presentation,' I said, frantically pressing escape. I was getting a migraine.

'But that's our logo?' she frowned, fixated on the image.

'Some confusion with one of our freelancers,' Heidi said, standing on tiptoes in front of the screen to try and block it as I pulled out the power lead.

'OK, dolls. Well, I'm countin' on ya to put on a good performance here. My neck is on the line if you don't shine. I want both pitches to be possible winners, ya hear me? I'll leave you gals to it.'

She flounced out while I messaged Natalya.

Me: These designs are insane????

Natalya: James said you needed Gen Z Boozing?

Me: CRUISING.

Natalya: Ohhh. That makes more sense.

Me: Can you knock me something else together? I can't share these. We're on in 5 but won't get to the creative for 20 mins. Cool couple on the *Esmeralda*. Use the shots we took or pull something from Instagram.

Natalya: *Thumbs up emoji*

Heidi was all tits and teeth, grinning like a mad thing. 'I'll do my slides, then leave the creative conversation to you.'

'Great – thanks.'

'Change the strategy slide to say we are focusing on new audiences.'

'Mm-hmm.' I clicked through to the strategy slide and quickly updated it. My hands were shaking as adrenaline coursed through my veins. We needed to be convincing with an entirely different approach. New audiences... Which new audiences? Young people, groups of friends, men. Anyone but old couples. I scanned our opening slides to check they still worked, and was deleting the creative at the back of the deck when everyone piled back in. I switched to the start of the presentation, showing our agency logo with *WELCOME* in white letters on dark green.

Brooke clapped her hands together and made me jump. 'OK, let's crack on. Everyone got a coffee?'

'Oooh...' Heidi flashed me a look and I changed tack. 'I'm cool with water.'

No coffee for us, then. Not that I needed the caffeine with all this panic pumping around my body.

'Greg, Brooke, Mindy, Elizabeth, hello,' Heidi said, with a maniacal grin on her face. 'It's a pleasure to be here today, talking about the account we love so much – and have loved for such a long time. To present our thoughts for its next phase of evolution. I'm sure you'll agree that no one knows the marketing side of your business as well as we do.'

Sycophantic with a sinister undertone. Weird choice. I flicked to the next slide, where the two of us were beaming out from the screen.

'We need no introduction – we've known you all forever. I'm Heidi Caddel, the owner of Northstar PR. Thirty years in business and have worked with the likes of P&O, Thomas Cook and Sandals, to name a few,' she said with a modest smile.

'And I'm Kat Brennan. Business director and client lead for the Excalibur account. Six years working at Northstar PR.'

Greg gave a little nod.

Heidi started waffling through her slides as my phone vibrated. Natalya, *thank God*. I surreptitiously clicked it open on the seat next to me and even from a distance, on my small screen, I could see the image was much better. A couple in shadow, close and intimate on deck. The background a vivid, blood orange as the Madeiran sun set on the horizon, with tiny boats in the distance and the silent disco in the background. A perfect balance of calm and chaos.

'…and now I'll hand you over to Kat to talk through our creative hook. We didn't want to ambush you with executions as we really wanted your buy-in on the thinking at this stage, but we believe driving new-to-cruising customers is the right strategy to take Excalibur into its next phase and build market share.'

I swallowed hard. Time to strap in.

'We had hundreds of brilliant ideas – as you can imagine…'

'Sounds like we'll have to.' Greg chuckled.

'The team are always thinking about *what's next* for Excalibur; that's just the way we are with our clients: proactive, curious, one step ahead. But the pitch has given us all extra permission to go big on the creative.' I fiddled around with the laptop to add the new slide into the deck, then blew it back up to full screen.

Mindy drew a sharp breath and Greg tutted, as I looked behind me.

'Oh, er… hang on… sorry, that's the wrong slide.'

'Cruising for some boozing?' Greg uttered in disbelief. 'I have never in my life… seen anything like it.'

'Is this what you think is next for us?' Elizabeth added, her smile faltering.

'No, not at all,' I clicked onto the next slide. 'I must have accidentally left one of the old ideas in…'

'Modern technology is always a nightmare in these situations,' Leo said, taking the attention off me, as all four clients turned in his direction. 'It wasn't so long ago everything was on paper or projector slides, so the presenter was always in control. The laptops are always trying to catch us out.'

'So true,' Brooke agreed, softening. 'I was mid-presentation last week when an email flashed up reminding me of a waxing appointment.' Everyone laughed while I put the correct slide in place.

'Here it is,' I said, giving Leo a grateful smile. 'We believe Excalibur need A NEW GENERATION OF CRUISERS and we want to re-launch you to Gen Z as the ultimate way to travel.'

Brooke nodded encouragingly.

'The TikTok crowd always seem to be on a countdown to death – do you know what I mean? You only get eighteen summers with your kids, you only get fifty summers yourself, you'll be dead before you know it – that kind of thing.'

Zach sat completely still, like a bird of prey waiting to pounce.

'We wanted to lean into that mentality.' I was impressing myself with my own bullshit. 'Cruising gives the young people exactly what they want. It's the only mode of travel that allows them to easily work through their bucket list. You don't have to wait a year between holidays; you can tick off several places at once and TikTok all about it.'

Greg steepled his fingers with a smile.

I flicked the new slide onto the screen. 'This is just one way we could juxtapose young people partying with a sophisticated couple enjoying cocktails against the ocean backdrop. Excalibur is the only destination they'll ever need. Their portal to the rest of the world.'

'With a nod to the old A to Z maps,' Heidi added, spit balling. 'Travelling across the world from A to Gen Z.'

'Interesting,' Brooke said, thoughtfully. 'So, is the idea about a new generation or multi-destinations? Or the ship as a gateway?'

'It encompasses all of those thoughts,' I said, floundering.

'I'm confused,' Mindy said.

'It's very simple.' Heidi smiled. 'Gen Zs mapping their way across the world on a cruise ship via multiple destinations. AKA the cruise is their gateway.'

I caught Zach rolling his eyes at Leo and inwardly seethed.

'I like it,' Elizabeth said, and my shoulders dropped in relief. 'But it's a sector ad; it isn't Excalibur-specific.'

She had a point. I tried out one of my NLP techniques and nodded to agree with her.

'You're right. And that's because as the market leader, you do a lot of heavy lifting for the sector. We've been working hard to shift perceptions on cruising for years and in owning that leadership position, you've become the go-to brand for cruising. When people book a cruise, they consider you first. The original, premium, classic.'

It was a word salad, but I delivered it confidently enough to get them all thinking.

Heidi joined in. 'And we can layer on the specific activities that only Excalibur offer... and drill down into the individual boats. This could be the *Esmeralda* execution, for example.'

'I see,' Brooke said, scrutinising the shot. 'And you only have one execution to share with us today?'

'Yes, we felt this was the most powerful representation of the thought. The young couple sharing an intimate moment in the shadows, the party going on in the background, the boat on the move to its next destination.'

'Is that you in the photo?' Mindy asked.

I whipped round to look at it. 'Erm... No... I don't think so?'

'Good spot, Mindy!' Greg said, putting his glasses on to take a closer look. 'With Leo, if I'm not mistaken?'

'Hardly Gen Z then, no offence,' Elizabeth piped up. 'Clearly you're enjoying yourselves though. Remember when we were like that, Greggy?'

The photo had the couple in shadow, but it was definitely me and Leo. How had I not instantly realised? My cheeks flushed as I lost my train of thought. Someone must have captured that moment after the Salsa class when we very nearly lost control of ourselves and kissed on the boat. How had this photo ended up in the presentation?

'So it is,' Leo said, chuckling awkwardly, his eyes burning into me as he slowly raised his eyebrows.

'It's… er… just a positional,' I said, desperate to flick on to the next slide, but knowing there wasn't one. 'We'd use much younger models to get the vibe right.'

'There's definitely a strong vibe coming through,' Brooke murmured, and Mindy and Elizabeth giggled.

'The point is that a focus on the younger audience is essential,' Heidi said, trying to get the conversation back on track. 'They need to be front and centre.'

'Even though you haven't shown a younger audience in your one piece of creative?' Greg batted back, sharply. 'Is that the end of the presentation?'

'We'd like to invite any questions,' I said, feeling weak. I switched my laptop off and the buzz of technology stopped, leaving us all in silence.

'No questions from me. Anyone else?' Greg asked, standing up and making it clear the meeting was over. Brooke, Elizabeth and Mindy shook their heads. 'Excellent, well then, thank you all for coming in and you'll hear from us very soon.' He shook our hands, one after the other. 'Ladies, gents. Brooke will see you out.'

And that was that.

Thirty-two

Friday 23rd July

'I don't know what you gals were thinking with that pitch, but I had some fast explaining to do once you'd gone,' Brooke said, exasperated.

It hadn't taken long for the jury to deliberate.

'A couple of slides got mixed up,' I said, glumly, not even bothering to fake smile.

'Well, however bad you thought it was, double it. I was mortified. Greg made me walk him through the whole pitch process to prove you'd had the same brief as Amplify because he couldn't believe it. Your work made him question my professional capability.'

'I'm so sorry we put you in that position, Brooke.' Heidi was furious.

'Too late for apologies now. It was a horror show, but what's done is done. And with that said, I hate to deliver bad news, but you must be expecting it. We've appointed Amplify as our agency of record going forward. I'd have been sorry either way as I was rootin' for ya'll on both sides – I really was.'

Brooke had waited till 5 p.m. to put us out of our misery. We'd known the 'thanks, but no thanks' was coming, of course, but to hear it officially confirmed was still a gut punch. And just the beginning of a whole world of shit. Telling the team, making people redundant, handing all our files over to those smug-faced cheats, and then finding a new job myself. I had a few thousand in savings, but that wouldn't get me very far on London rent.

'Needless to say, we are very disappointed to hear that,' Heidi said, pulling the spider phone close. 'And this isn't my normal approach in any situation, let alone a pitch, but I feel compelled to tell you there's been some dirty tricks at play with Leo and Zach.'

I pulled a panicked face, worried what she might say next. Not that it could do any more harm than had already been done.

'Dirty tricks? In what way?'

'We didn't want to cause a scene in front of Greg, so out of pure professionalism we kept quiet during the meeting, but I'm sorry to say the idea they presented was ours.'

'What?' she shrieked. 'How can it have been?'

'Your guess is as good as mine. I've left messages for Leo, but he's not returning my calls.' Heidi said, clicking her tongue. 'Funny that.'

'We thought you should know before we take it any further,' I added, trying to soften the tone.

'That's the real reason our pitch was such a shambles.'

Brooke tutted. 'Now, now, Heidi, darlin', you gotta take feedback as a gift in this game. Amplify won the deal fair and square, and nobody likes a sore loser.'

'It's true!' I blurted. 'That line was mine. I said it to Heidi myself. I don't know how they knew what we were working on, but *unimaginable moments* was our line. With very different executions of course.'

'*Very different* is one way to describe them. I've never been so embarrassed. Look, ladies, it's a valiant attempt to switch the conversation up but I'm afraid the decision has been made. I need to run as I'm on another call in five.'

'Can I just…?' Heidi tried.

'Sorry, sweetie, I really have to go,' Brooke said firmly. The conversation was over. 'But let's grab dinner next week, hey? I want to thank you both properly for all the work you've done for Excalibur Cruises over the years. No hard feelings, y'all. Bye for now.'

'Byeee!!!' We put our best cheery voices on as she hung up, then Heidi slammed her hands on the table and screamed. She looked about ready to hurl her coffee cup at the wall.

'Over the years?' Heidi spat. 'As if Excalibur has been an insignificant side project – not the bedrock of my business and ten years of my life. Get me Leo on the phone. NOW.'

I jumped at that. I couldn't help but think this was all my fault somehow. Leo must have seen something in one of my notebooks or maybe I'd said something that gave our idea away. The only in-the-flesh connection between their team and ours was the two of us. This was my comeuppance for fraternising with the enemy. But I couldn't let Heidi find out on a conference call or through some other random route. I'd be losing my job now anyway, so there was nothing more to lose. She may as well hear all the bad news at once.

I put the business card he'd given me in Madeira on the table and traced the outline with my fingers.

'Go on then, hurry up! What are you waiting for?' Heidi shrieked, standing up and striding up and down the boardroom. I'd never seen her so angry.

I shrank back in my chair, feeling like a total traitor. 'Before we call him, there's something I need to tell you.'

Heidi whipped round to face me, her eyes glassy. 'What?'

Eek. This didn't feel like the *ideal* time for a tell-all confession, but it was too late to change my mind now. I had to put my big-girl pants on and do it.

'I've been racking my brains trying to work out how they could possibly have known what we had planned and I can only think of one thing.'

Heidi's eyes widened, as she waited for me to continue.

I smiled, nervously. 'It's a funny old situation really...'

'Cut to the punchline.'

'Leo and I got together on the cruise,' I blurted out as fast as I could to get it over and done with. 'I'm so sorry, Heidi, I know it's a huge no-no and I feel awful about it. He must have seen something when he stayed at the hotel with me in Lisbon.'

She stood completely frozen, so I carried on babbling.

'Although the timing doesn't feel right as I thought we'd only briefly talked about it by then. I can't work out what he would have seen. But maybe I'm misremembering. It was a hectic two weeks; I can barely remember what happened when. Shall I just get him on the phone and we can ask him ourselves?'

Heidi nodded, seemingly much calmer despite my revelation, and I silently dialled his mobile while she drummed her nails on the table. We sat and listened to the phone ring out until it clicked into voicemail, with Leo's charming voice and affable invitation to leave a message unintentionally rubbing salt in the wound. There was nothing we could do today, we'd have to wait.

'They're probably out celebrating,' I muttered, feeling sick at the thought.

'Those fuckers!' she screamed, ripping Leo's business card into tiny bits.

'I'm so sorry, Heidi, this is all my fault.'

'You've got nothing to apologise for. You're not the sneaky rat who stole someone else's idea and palmed it off as your own. Leo has played you like a fiddle and first thing Monday morning we're going to have it out with him. Let's meet outside their office at seven.'

I nodded. 'Good idea. This conversation needs to happen face to face. I want to watch them try and lie about it.'

'They can ignore our calls, but they can't ignore us setting up camp in their reception.'

'I'll bring our original pitch boards and anything else I can find,' I said, thinking of all the flipcharts we'd scribbled on in the brainstorming sessions, then threw away. Not that we needed to prove anything to them. They bloody well knew. It was Brooke we had to convince.

'I need a drink,' Heidi sighed, putting her head in her hands. The rest of the office had cleared off for the weekend, and it was just us left.

'I've got a bottle of Zinfandel on my desk,' I said, feeling weary. 'For emergencies.'

Heidi wrinkled her nose. 'Cheap pink plonk? It's not that desperate, is it? No, let's go next door.'

There was a wine bar on the corner of the road and it was impossible to walk past without popping in for a quick glass. There was always someone from the team sat in the window, beckoning me inside. Not that I was ever hard to convince – not normally anyway. I loved a few wines and a Nando's on the way home.

The Farringdon pavements were teeming with red-faced city boys, swigging pints and shouting at each other through clouds of smoke. The air was thick and gloopy, and I was hot, bothered and *fucked off*. It was officially the weekend and I wanted to be out with my real friends, not sat in a sweatbox listening to Heidi bitch and moan.

Heidi pushed her way to the bar, and the beardy barman with the tattoo sleeves served her immediately. There were occasional perks to the amount of money we all spent in there. She passed an ice-cold glass of wine through the crowd, and we found a spot of wall near the loos to lean against.

'Cheers!' she said, sarcastically. 'Here's to working our bollocks off and getting no reward.'

'They don't deserve us,' I said, taking a sip and closing my eyes. It tasted a lot better than a mug of warm rosé. Ordinarily I found the hubbub in the bar buzzy and exciting, but tonight it was noisy and annoying – what I really needed was some peace and quiet. I couldn't wait to get home, kick off my shoes and sink into a bubble bath. My wine was delicious though, and I could make my excuses after one glass and head off. Heidi was drinking twice as fast as me anyway, so we'd be done in half an hour if I stayed focused on necking it.

'I need to talk to you about a couple of things, Kat,' Heidi said, suddenly serious, and my stomach clenched. 'This is hardly the ideal setting, but having reflected on your confession it needs to be said so it'll have to do.'

Was she going to give me notice right now? *In the pub?* I took another gulp of wine to prepare for the inevitable.

'First of all, I haven't been entirely honest with you about my relationship with Zach, and I think it's time to come clean.'

'Your relationship?'

Her ears turned pink as she nodded. She swallowed awkwardly. Almost as if she was… *squirming*. I'd never seen this side of Heidi before. 'We… er… used to work together, as you know,' she started, slowly. 'Years ago, though – yonks and yonks. It must be… well, ten years now.' She lifted her glasses and narrowed her eyes, studying her wine glass intently.

'Right…?'

'It might even be fifteen,' she said, rubbing at an imaginary lipstick mark. She laughed in shock. 'Yes. Blimey. Time flies.'

'Righttt…?' *Jesus.*

'Right,' she said, snapping back to reality. 'And we were kind of together at one point. Living together.'

I choked on my wine. 'What? You were together? *Together* together?' She nodded coyly. 'I thought you hated each other?'

'We do now. Sort of. I didn't like to mention it before as… well, I didn't think it was relevant or… appropriate. And neither of us wanted to make things awkward.' She took a large gulp of wine. 'Anyway, that part isn't important.'

Like hell it wasn't. 'What happened?'

'Well, that's the thing. We were both creative directors at an agency at the time and the executive creative director

– Orla – announced she was retiring. We both applied for her job and had to present our ideas for the future of the department.'

She stared off into the distance wistfully.

'I'd happened upon one of Zach's suggestions when I was tidying up one day and couldn't get it out of my head. I thought about it so much, I couldn't think of anything else and ended up evolving it into a better version and presenting it as my own.'

I stayed quiet, letting her get it all out.

'I didn't mean to steal his idea. I'd convinced myself it was different enough to get away with it, but it meant I got the job. My ambition got the better of me and screwed over my relationship. I mean… *I* screwed over my relationship and betrayed Zach in the worst possible way.'

'Did you tell him?'

She shook her head. 'No. We agreed me being his boss wouldn't work and it was best to focus on careers in different agencies. So, I convinced him to resign.'

'Savage.'

'I didn't want him finding out what I'd done. I wanted to keep both the promotion and my boyfriend and if he wasn't around, he'd have no reason to suspect foul play. He just assumed I'd got the job through a fair win. I told him I'd presented something completely different.'

At least she had the good grace to look embarrassed.

'How did he find out?' I asked, feeling sick. *When people tell you who they are – believe them.*

'Zach needed a reference and some career advice, and Orla assumed he knew why I'd got the job over him. We were living together after all. She talked him through where he'd gone wrong and I'd gone right. Just to rub salt into the wound. He was livid.'

'Sounds like he's been waiting a long time for payback,' I said. 'Do you think he had something to do with it then, rather than Leo? How would he have found out though?'

Heidi looked me straight in the eyes and took a deep breath. 'Well, that's the other thing I need to tell you. We er... reconnected during the trip. At the hotel in Lisbon, and while you were in Madeira.'

'What!?'

'I know, sorry about that. He left his trainers in our room, and I was convinced you'd find them after I left.'

'Oh, the Converse are Zach's. I brought them back for you but that makes more sense. Tell me you didn't do anything in the bunk beds though, please?!' I pretended to be outraged.

She nodded. '...and at the Uzu Yacht Club and in one of the dressing rooms...'

'Heidi! This is outrageous salaciousness. I am shocked!'

'Yes... big reveals all round. Sam and I have been in an open marriage for a while now, so he's fine with it, but Lisbon was especially wild and I needed to get home to him after that. It was getting too intense.' *Too much information.* 'But all this is to say Zach had plenty of access if he'd wanted to snoop on our ideas.'

'Access all areas, in fact, and a more likely culprit if he had an axe to grind.'

'Whatever the motive, and whoever did it, they're not getting away with it. I admit I was in the wrong all those years ago, but two wrongs don't make a right. Me and Zach both know what he did, and he knows I know. It was your idea, so I know you know too. I just need to find out where Leo stands in all this and convince Brooke we're telling the truth.'

'That ain't going to be easy,' I said, finishing off my glass, my mind whirring. 'Because I'm pretty sure Brooke chose Amplify for more than just their idea.'

Heidi's eyes narrowed. 'In what way?'

'To add to an already complicated triangle, I caught Leo sneaking out of Brooke's suite the morning we arrived back in Dover.' Her jaw dropped. 'I know. He didn't see me, and I didn't bother confronting him. I was too shocked.'

'Seduction tactics. Well, well, well – a feisty competitor to the end. Doing whatever it takes. I can't lie, I'm kinda impressed.'

'Heidi!'

'What? If the client had been a man I'd have been on him like a rash. Not physically, and no sleepovers, obviously, but nothing wrong with using your womanly wiles to get what you want in life. Although it does pose a different kind of problem, if she's into him.'

'I'm not even sure she is. She strikes me as more of the loosey-goosey type. Into everyone for a little while. Give your flirtation tricks a whirl – you never know.'

Heidi rolled her eyes. 'This job will be the death of me. But we're not letting them get away with it. Too many jobs are on the line.'

Thirty-three

Monday 26th July

'**L**adies! How lovely to see you,' Leo said, when he finally arrived for work at ten past ten. 'Can I get you a coffee?' We'd been sat in their empty reception for nearly two hours, listening to the receptionist repeatedly answer the phone with a sunny '*Amplify, good morning!*' I needed more than a coffee. I needed a Valium.

'At last,' Heidi said, curtly. 'Can we go somewhere private to talk? With Zach as well if he's around?'

'Sure. Follow me.' Leo looked fresh and fit in charcoal jeans and layers of hoodies. Back to his non-client wear, although the Amplify offices reflected his sharp, cool vibe. The team had standing desks with walking treadmills, like hamsters on wheels; presumably being forced to generate their own power. With its slick jute flooring and huge paper lampshades it was like being inside an art installation. Leo led us into their boardroom, which overlooked St Paul's Cathedral, and gestured towards two boucle chairs around a large black table. 'Did you say yes to coffee?'

'Black, two sugars.' Zach appeared in the doorway, looking wary. 'The Northstar PR team on the premises, no less. Here to congratulate us I presume?'

Heidi ignored him and addressed Leo direct. 'We're not here for coffee or pleasantries. Let's cut the bullshit, shall we? It's just the four of us now and we all know what happened.' I couldn't bring myself to speak just yet, so I sat with my arms folded, glaring at Leo.

'What bullshit?' Zach sneered. 'We don't know what you're talking about…'

'Talk us through what you think happened and let's take it from there,' Leo said, gently.

'You stole our idea, you smug prick.' *Eek*. Heidi wasn't pulling any punches.

Zach folded his arms. 'Well, that's something you'd know all about, isn't it? You've got some nerve accusing *us* of that.'

'Why would we steal your ideas when we had hundreds of our own?' Leo added. 'Including the one that won us the pitch.'

'That was ours – you cheated.' I couldn't stay quiet any longer. 'I literally said those words to Heidi. *Unimaginable moments*. They came from my brain.'

'Yeah,' Heidi chipped in from behind me. 'It was a private conversation between the two of us.'

'And yet Zach also said that very sentence to me,' Leo countered.

'Yeah, right,' I said, rolling my eyes, although it did cause me to stop and think. Leo didn't strike me as a liar. Was it possible Zach and I had come up with the exact same idea at the exact same time?

'When?' Heidi squeaked.

'When, what?' Leo frowned.

'When did he say it to you?'

'Don't answer that.' Zach marched over to the door and flung it open. 'We don't need or want your interrogation. We won the pitch fair and square, and that's all you need to know.'

'Hang on,' Leo said. 'I'm happy to have the conversation and resolve this. We've got nothing to hide.'

'Mate, they aren't the police,' Zach scoffed. 'Just a pair of sore losers. What's the pitch score between us now?'

'It was in Lisbon,' Leo said, snapping his fingers. 'You'd finally got a good night's sleep, and we went to that hotel for the *pastel de nata* breakfast – the one you girls were staying in. You were delighted with yourself.'

Zach shook his head. 'I don't remember exactly when the idea came to me.'

'Sounds like it was *in Lisbon*.' Heidi repeated, giving Zach a look. She stepped in front of me to confront him face to face. 'That's interesting timing, isn't it?'

He shrugged then started fiddling with the coffee machine, fixated on making himself a flat white. The grinding noise filled the room, drowning out Heidi's questions.

'I happen to know Zach barely slept at all the night we stayed in Lisbon. He was awake for most of it, in fact,' Heidi said. 'Because he was in my bedroom, in bed with me.'

'What?' Leo looked at her in shock and then over at Zach who pressed the coffee button again.

'Which is by the by. It's more that I'd sketched a few iterations of the "unimaginable moments" idea onto my notepad, which was in my room. Kat and I had had the conversation on our way to the hotel.'

'In the cab,' I added, thinking back.

Leo watched like a hawk as the conversation unfolded.

'The two of us had had such a different twenty-four hours on Terceira Island,' Heidi continued. 'Our experiences were unrecognisable to each other even though we were on the same cruise.'

Zach necked his coffee with a scowl. 'You can't copyright an idea, Heidi, we both know that.'

'You admit it then?' she said, furious.

'I ain't admitting nothing, sweetheart,' he replied.

'Is there any truth to this?' Leo asked, sliding his eyes from Heidi to Zach, who shook his head.

'Wait a minute, I can prove the idea was mine!' I said, fishing around in my handbag. 'Here.' I slapped down the coaster from the bar in Madeira, with my original scribblings. 'These were the lines I was playing with before settling on "unimaginable moments".'

Holidays as unique as you are.
See the world your own way, with Excalibur.
Greek for breakfast, Italian for dinner.
Excalibur Cruises: too good to imagine.
Unimaginable moments.

'You could have written those down anytime,' Zach said, swallowing hard.

'Could she, Zach? Really? To what end?' Heidi said. 'Why would we lie?'

'You tell me. It's never stopped you before,' he said, glaring at her across the table.

'OK, I don't know what's going on here, but this is either an unbelievable coincidence, and you both had the same idea at the same time, or one of you is lying,' Leo said, picking up the coaster and looking increasingly confused. If he was in on it, he was delivering an Oscar-worthy performance.

Heidi was livid. 'Why won't you just admit it, Zach? You won through cheating – which isn't fair on any of us.'

'Now you know how it feels.'

'I knew it. I *knew* you weren't over it. Is that what this is about? Payback for all those years ago?'

'You say it like it was nothing. You ruined my career! I couldn't get a job for months after you forced me to resign.'

'Wow, I'm sorry, OK? But I thought we were way past all that.'

'*You* might be, but I'm not. And no, it is not OK. A quick sorry after all these years doesn't even come close. How does it feel to get a taste of your own medicine, eh? To have your livelihood threatened?'

'Aha! And there we have it,' I said, jumping in.

Zach shrugged. 'I had been thinking along the same lines, myself. It's not exactly ground-breaking creative territory, is it? It all comes down to the execution.'

'Except we couldn't present our executions, because you'd used our line.'

Leo, who had been quietly observing, stood up and looked me in the eyes. 'I've heard enough. Ladies, would you mind leaving us, please? Zach and I need to have a conversation.'

'Absolutely. Although I will need to communicate the situation to Brooke,' Heidi said, grabbing her handbag haughtily. 'I can't stay quiet on the matter forever. I'll give you till the end of the day.'

'Much obliged,' Leo said, running a hand through his hair and following us to the door. 'Thanks for coming over to see us.'

I almost felt sorry for Zach as he watched us leave. He looked completely defeated. How to piss off your boss, your client, and your side-shag in one fell swoop.

Heidi poured herself a second glass of wine. 'We've got them by the balls, Kat,' she said, eyes gleaming. 'By. The. BALLS.'

I didn't want to think about Zach's balls. Or Leo's for that matter. We'd stopped at the first pub we could find for a debrief and miraculously bagged a table for two amid the lunchtime rush.

'Do you think Leo knew?' I asked, twizzling my gin and tonic.

'Inconclusive. He did seem surprised at the suggestion but no doubt they're concocting some bullshit story to cover their arses as we speak. I've half a mind to phone Brooke right now, before they can get in front of it.'

'Give him a chance,' I replied, feeling suddenly protective. If Leo was innocent in all this, then it wasn't fair to go over his head before he'd had chance to deal with it himself. 'Zach didn't seem too bothered about the accusations.'

Heidi had said she liked wild and imaginative men, but I'd assumed she meant windswept and rock-star-ish, not Zach's poor-man version of Dr Who.

'He doesn't think he's to blame – that's why. He sees it all as a big game and obviously feels vindicated.' Heidi took a gulp of her rosé. 'Fancy holding a grudge your entire life like that. Weirdo.'

The busy hum in the pub went up a notch, as tables filled with hungry punters ordering ploughman's and Caesar salads. It was a roasting hot summer's day and impossible to resist a pint or two. I didn't know what to think anymore. I was officially on notice if the Excalibur Cruises account went to Amplify, so what happened next was critical. It was the difference between life carrying on as it always had and polishing up my CV to start looking for a new job. But would Brooke really care either way? She obviously had more than one reason to appoint Leo and Zach, and maybe she just wanted a change, regardless of who had the best pitch. Heidi's phone started bouncing around the table with *Leo Kendrick* flashing in big letters.

She pushed it towards me, wide-eyed. 'You speak to him!' she squealed. 'I've had too much wine.'

I grabbed it and ran outside.

'Hi, Leo, it's Kat,' I said, smoothly. 'Heidi is currently indisposed.'

'Sure. OK, fair enough.' I heard him suck in a deep breath before speaking again. 'Once you'd gone, Zach admitted it all. He didn't see it as a big deal – well, not until I lost my shit. He's packing up his desk right now and will be suspended without pay until I decide what to do with him. I wanted to speak to you and Heidi in person, but I didn't want to leave you hanging. Please believe me when I say I knew nothing about this and would never have presented the idea if I had. I can only apologise for the whole situation. For putting you through so much stress in the pitch and for not believing you as soon as you raised it. This is not the way I do business, I can promise you that. I'm so pissed off with Zach and absolutely mortified.'

'Hmph. Well, thank you for at least having the decency to admit it and call us so quickly.'

'I've also spoken with Brooke to remedy the situation.'

I inhaled sharply. That was fast work.

'I couldn't have it on my conscience another minute. She was very understanding and kind, but almost dismissive – as if it didn't really matter. I couldn't have that, so I resigned the account.'

'You did?' I exhaled in shock, more impressed by the second.

'Yup. We can't go ahead under these circumstances – whatever Brooke says. If the idea was yours, then it's yours. We have no right to the business.'

'What did Brooke say, then?'

'She wanted to meet up and discuss it, but I told her we were taking a step back. You guys should at least have the chance to present your original pitch before any further conversations are had.'

'That's very chivalrous of you.'

'I can't bear it when things are unfair. It's one of my many foibles. If we don't have integrity, then what's the point?'

'Honour among thieves.'

'Something like that. Brooke said she'd call you, so Heidi might not want to be *indisposed* for too long, hey? You know how these clients can be.'

'Thanks, Leo,' I said, a lump in my throat. 'I thought you wouldn't care. This industry is so cut-throat – it's nice to know some people still have morals.'

'Sure. Just not Zach though, right? Good luck when you speak to Brooke and who knows what will happen – we might all end up working together.'

Thirty-four

Wednesday 28th July

Thirty-five years old and barely surviving – certainly not thriving. I'd had a weird day at work where nobody had remembered it was my birthday and I hadn't bothered to remind them. I couldn't be doing with all the fuss. Brooke had officially given us the green light to deliver our original pitch, and half the agency were reworking the presentation at double speed to get it ready for next week. It was a relief to be home before midnight, let alone in time for my birthday party Zoom with Sara and Abi. At least *they* wanted to celebrate me. I'd stupidly decided to dress up for the occasion and slipped Ivy on, and now I felt like an idiot, with my glamorous white dress and three strings of pearls. Like an Audrey Hepburn reject hosting a murder mystery. I put the finishing touches to my femme fatale make-up, poured myself a glass of Savvy B and dialled in.

Abi and Sara were both sat waiting in *Happy Birthday* hats. They blew their party horns as soon as I arrived then started singing out of sync.

'Happy birthday to yooou, happy birthday to you, happy birthday dear Kaa-aat, happy birthday toooo yoooou...'

'What are you wearing?' Sara said, peering into the screen. She was in a plain cream dress that looked like it was made from a sack. The simple life in Norway suited her.

'Oh yes,' Abi said, stopping to stare. 'You look bloody gorgeous, darlinggg! Should we have dressed up?'

'You mean you haven't?' I said, zooming in on her slash-neck silk dress. 'Everything you wear looks brand new, so I thought I'd make an effort. It's the closest I'll get to a birthday piss-up this year, and I can't see this dress getting out much otherwise.'

'Absolutely,' Sara said. 'Dress for the occasion, not the location.'

I glanced around the flat and thought back to the promise I'd made Barbie Queue when she'd given it to me. To wear it to The Ritz and make a show of myself, drape myself over the grand piano. How ridiculous. Well, at least I hadn't stuffed it in a plastic bag and hidden it under the bed.

'Thanks for coming out to play, girls,' I said, raising my glass in a virtual *cheers*. 'Happy birthday to me. Thirty-five and living the dream.' Sara had a red wine on the go and Abi was sipping an Aperol Spritz.

'Yes Kat!' Sara said. 'We are in our international girl gang era.'

'We sure are,' Abi said. 'I'm dreaming of Italy while sweating in LA.'

'You guys are the international gang; I'm in the same place I've always been. Dreaming of anywhere and everywhere while sweating in London.'

'Well, I keep offering... You know you're welcome anytime. Quit your job and move to Norway with me and Henrik.'

I laughed. 'Henrik would be delighted at me rocking up.'

'He probably wouldn't care – he's very relaxed about stuff. There's no sweating here – just clean, healthy fun.'

'That sounds like the opposite of fun,' Abi said.

'You can see for yourselves when you come and visit,' Sara said. 'It's my turn to host so get your asses over to Norway for some group hygge.'

'Remind me what that is again?' I said, sipping my wine.

'It's lounging around wrapped in blankets and eating carbs.'

'Is it?' Abi frowned. 'I take it back. That's exactly the kind of fun I'm looking for.'

I laughed. 'And me. That's three yeses – you're going through to judges' houses.'

'Speaking of carbs, I've made you a cake.' Sara held up a chocolate cupcake, with gold glitter icing and a pink candle in the middle. 'Well, Henrik did.'

'That looks delicious,' I said, salivating. 'If only I could eat it.'

'I know,' she said, faux sad. 'It's such a shame. Oh well, I'll eat it for you.'

'You're such a good friend. Please don't sing again.'

Sara lit the candle and the three of us watched it flicker for a second. 'Make a birthday wish and I'll blow it out. Just tip me the wink.'

I closed my eyes and took a deep breath. I wished everything would go back to normal. That we'd win this pitch and life could carry on how it had been before.

The front door buzzer made me jump and I opened my eyes in alarm.

'I'll take that as my sign,' Sara said, blowing out the candle.

My unexpected guest held the buzzer down for far too long, then held it down again.

'Bloody hell! Who is that? Sorry, girls, I better get it.' I ran to the intercom, already irritated. 'Hello?'

'Delivery for Kat Brennan,' a gruff voice replied.

'A what? At this time of night? I thought there was a fire. OK, just a second.'

I ran down and there was a delivery driver on the doorstep. He looked me up and down when he saw the dress. 'Miss Brennan? Sign here please.' I hated that 'Miss' so much – it made me sound like a nursery rhyme. I scribbled my initials and he handed me a long thin box, covered in red ribbons. 'Thank fuck for that. I've been driving all over town to get this to you.'

The girls must have timed it to arrive while we were on the call together. They were so bloody sweet. I LOVED getting presents and I so rarely did these days. How exciting. I carried it upstairs carefully – maybe it was a long necklace or a wand...

'You guys! What is this?'

They glanced at each other on screen, and I could see them both typing.

'Erm... I don't think it's from us,' Sara said, looking unsure. 'Is it, Abs?'

Abi laughed. 'You're giving yourself away there, but no, it's not.'

'You pick the gifts and I transfer the money; that's how it's always been,' Sara said, laughing. 'We make a good present-buying team. From my perspective, anyway.'

'Don't leave us in suspense,' Abi called, slurping on her cocktail. 'Get it open.'

'The label says "Care of Northstar PR" so Heidi must have sent him here.'

I slid a knife along the Sellotape and opened it up. Mum and Dad had sent me some money, and the twins were taking me for a birthday steak, so it wouldn't be from them. If it wasn't from the HIIT girls, then who…? I pulled the lid off and there inside sat a single orange rose.

'What is it? What is it?' Sara called.

'SHOW US,' Abi shouted.

I turned the box around to show them then spotted an envelope tucked inside the purple tissue.

'Roses are orange…' Sara said.

'Orange is the new black,' Abi added.

'Do you mean it's really a black rose?' Sara said.

'Shhh, I wanna hear what it says. Read it out.'

I pulled out a bright white card with one line written in black ink:

From one Leo to another: happy birthday, Kat xxx

Thirty-five

Monday 2nd August

'Here we go again my darlin's,' Brooke trilled from across the boardroom where she sat starry-eyed next to Greg. I was starting to wonder if she was an AI bot. 'This is a truly bizarre situation, and please allow me to apologise to y'all for dismissing the idea that Amplify had cheated. It's just not in my nature to think badly of people and I truly believed those boys had the purest of hearts.'

'Not at all,' Heidi said, graciously.

Greg harumphed. 'Can we please get on with it.'

'Sure thing, sugar,' Brooke said. 'I'll hand it over to you gals then. Please, take it away.'

Our boards were in position, and I stood up ready to reveal them one by one. We were going to blow their minds.

'Cruising is having a moment right now,' Heidi said, flashing them both a smile. 'Once purely the realm of the rich and retired, the perception of cruising as a see-it-all have-it-all option for the younger generation is starting to emerge, and we need to double down on it in our PR.'

'Amen,' Brooke said, stirring her coffee.

'We all know this generation live on their phones. They can travel the world without ever leaving the house through their tiny screen. All they need do is type a city name into the search box on YouTube or Tik Tok and someone out there will have been there, filmed it and shared it. They have zero attention span and a desperation for the "new". The untouched. The space where no one else has been – where no one could even imagine to be. And we can give that to them. *You* can give that to them.'

Greg looked about ready to nod off. We weren't telling him anything new.

'And so, we propose a global PR campaign to get people talking about those hidden gems, to reconsider cruising beyond the obvious.'

I turned the first board, like a magician's assistant.

'*Unimaginable moments from Excalibur Cruises*. You already love the line, now let me walk you through the executions.'

I turned the second and third boards, which were full of beautiful faces.

'Fronted by influencers and YouTubers and the many different celebs out there who use crew, crews and cruise as part of their identity. Lana Cruise, Annabelle Cruz, The Surf Shack Crew… all brands in their own right, with access to ten million subscribers between them – and that's allowing for a generous amount of crossover.'

'Never heard of them,' Greg barked, his silver hair glinting under the fluorescent lights.

'These are the people influencing the next generation,' Brooke said, gently. 'And we do need to meet the young people where they are.'

'One payment, one cruise, a hundred ways to look at it. I'll let the work speak for itself. Kat?'

I was poised and ready to postulate. 'Absolutely. *Unimaginable moments* can't be pre-planned, so this becomes a game of one-upmanship that can be accessed by anyone. It's not about money, but experiences, available to all – and everyone can play.'

Heidi jumped in. 'This audience use firsts as their currency – they don't just want to live their best life – they want to be seen to be living it. Social media is their proof platform, and this campaign will help them see cruising is the best way to do that. There is no frame of reference for what might happen on an Excalibur cruise.'

Greg's face started to soften, despite looking at photos of kids he'd never heard of and an idea that felt alien to his generation.

'The beauty of this campaign is its stretchability. It works at all levels from your average nine-to-five Gen Z on minimum wage all the way up to major celebrities. We target the audience with the stories that will resonate most.'

'For example…?' Greg said, steepling his fingers.

I pulled out our hero image and Brooke gasped. A couple swimming in bioluminescence, under the stars. 'Wowzers!'

I smiled. 'Exactly.'

Greg put his glasses on and leant forward. 'Wow, where is that?'

We'd got them both.

'On an Excalibur cruise of course,' Heidi chipped in, delighted with their reaction.

'Is it?' Greg looked a little closer. 'Oh, yes. I see it now.'

'*Esmeralda* has docked in the background,' I said, pointing to the image with my pen. 'And this couple have found a little piece of heaven for an on-shore swim.'

I pulled up another board and handed it to them. 'Then here we have a group of friends volcano screeing in the Azores.'

'That looks incredible,' Greg said, turning to Brooke. 'Is this possible to do?'

'Sure is. And it wouldn't be the kind of thing our regular passengers would go for.'

'We've got hundreds of ideas on this, but the real stories will come from our customers and that's where the crew idea can stretch beyond influencers. Cruising with your girl crew, your uni crew, your rowing crew – and of course we would showcase *Esmeralda*'s crew as well. They'll have some stories to tell.'

'Hell yeah – plenty of juicy tales to be shared there. Barbie Queue alone is a whole TikTok waiting to happen,' Brooke said.

'How does this translate into PR?' Greg asked with a frown.

'And how the hell are we gonna afford Lana Cruise?' Brooke guffawed. 'She won't be handing us her ten million audience for free.'

'We can work on the influencer list depending on the budget. The most important consideration is landing on what Gen Z want in a holiday. What is the sell here? And the answer is simple. On a macro scale they want the same as we all do. Value for money, experiences they can boast about, and to make the most of their annual leave. On a micro level, they want to be with like-minded people and have some guaranteed fun. Whatever fun looks like for them. The genius of cruising is that it gives them all of this and more. Like a skeleton key, it fits all locks, and our PR campaign will help them see that for themselves.'

I turned the next three boards over and propped them against some books.

'Message in a bottle. We will ask our current customers to write a message to the cruisers of the future and put them in a small bottle. The first thousand people to find these bottles aged between twenty and thirty will get to go on a "voyage of discovery". A free cruise where they can blog and post and share their journey. A viral campaign on a global scale to encourage a whole new audience that wouldn't otherwise have considered cruising, to do so.'

Heidi joined in. 'We want *Esmeralda* to speak for herself. We don't need to do a hard sell on cruising; we just need to turn the experience inside out. Most people see these behemoth boats on the water and have no idea of the box of delights inside. Of how delicious the food is, how friendly the team are, how much adventure you can pack into two weeks when you're on the water. Excalibur are best in class after all, so why not let the product do the talking?'

Greg sat back in his chair, arms crossed, then slowly started to nod. 'I'm an old man these days, and I know nothing about tikking and tokking, but I do know that we give our customers a damn good time at a damn good price. Our reviews tell us week after wreek.'

'But they ain't getting any younger,' Brooke said. 'We'll take their dollars while they've got 'em, but we need to keep fillin' that funnel full of fresh young cruisers. We must find a way to get a new audience in.'

'And this could absolutely be it,' Greg said with a snap of his fingers. 'I'll write one of the letters myself. As a top prize ticket. They can sit next to me at the captain's table... or if that's not exciting enough for them, next to Lana – whoever she is.'

'The ultimate Cruise,' Heidi said, turning over more boards. 'Our crew, your Cruise.'

'We plan to hide some of the bottles in the virtual world as well,' I said, revealing the final board. 'In the spaces where this audience spends their time. Fortnite, Minecraft, they will stumble upon the bottles with instructions on what to do with them. It will be like finding a VIP ticket to the Superbowl in your pocket.'

Greg slammed the table and stood up. 'I love it. Brooke – I'll leave you to wrap up and sort contracts.' He shook my hand firmly, then Heidi's. 'Excellent stuff, ladies. Good to have you back on board.'

'We never left,' Heidi said, her voice trembling.

Brooke chuckled to herself as he stalked out. 'Well, there's your answer ladies. No room for misinterpretation there.'

'Really?' I asked, too scared to believe it.

'Really. You've got yourself the Excalibur Cruises account back.'

Thirty-six

We stepped out into the fresh air grinning like idiots. 'Thank fuck for that,' Heidi said, giving me a high five. 'Well done, Kat, you did an amazing job.'

'So did you.' I couldn't help the tears of relief and exhaustion as I pulled Heidi into a hug. 'What a journey, eh?' I couldn't believe it was over and we were finally on the other side of it. I felt physically and mentally spent. The non-stop adrenaline rushes had left me weak and tired, and I couldn't wait to get home and crawl into bed. I hadn't realised how much angst I'd been holding on to inside and now it was all finally done, I felt like I might collapse. I wanted to scream into the sky and then sleep for a week. This whole process had thrown my inner peace off kilter in so many ways, but it was worth it to eventually win. It had been a sharp lesson in staying vigilant and protecting what you've got. There was no room for complacency in PR.

'I need a large… something to celebrate.'

I nodded at the pub over the road. 'Bucket of rosé?'

'Vodka.'

'Sounds good,' I said, picking the pitch boards up off the floor.

'Two large vodkas, hold the tonic,' a voice called behind us. Leo was stood on the corner of the street with his arms folded. 'Celebration or commiseration?'

'Celebration,' I said, archly. 'They came to their senses in the end.'

'Thanks to you,' Heidi gushed. 'Resigning the account was a truly honourable move. Not many people would have done that.'

'I can't abide cheats,' Leo said. 'Without trust, what is there, really?'

The *audacity* of this guy. My goodwill towards him was dissolving now we'd taken back what was rightfully ours. I was so hurt and angry I could barely look at him.

'How come you're here, anyway?' I asked. 'Lunch date with Brooke?'

'I wanted to buy you both a drink or two, or five,' Leo said, tentatively. 'As many as it'll take to show there are no hard feelings – and to congratulate you on your win, of course.'

'There's really no need...' I started, feeling ambushed.

'Absolutely you can,' Heidi cut in, talking over me. 'It's a small world in PR and always better to stay friends.'

I dragged my feet behind the two of them, trying to think of a good reason to go home. Leo looked heartbreakingly handsome in a charcoal suit and tie, his hair combed into his trademark quiff. I couldn't sit opposite those silvery-grey eyes and play nice knowing he'd slept with Brooke – and God knows who else – while I'd fallen headfirst for his seduction technique.

Heidi stopped to answer her phone while Leo and I walked into the empty pub. Crammed with antique tables and chairs, the afternoon sun shone through the dust in the air and there was a whiff of freshly sprayed furniture polish.

'A Guinness and two large vodka tonics please, mate.'

'Sure. Take a seat and I'll bring them over,' the barman said with a nod.

'Crisps and nuts?' Leo asked. We were alone, together, for the first time since we'd parted ways at Dover.

I shrugged. 'Why not?'

He waved a bag of smoky bacon and some honey-roasted cashews at the barman then handed them to me. Which was annoying because that was exactly what I wanted – it was like he'd read my mind. We sat in the bay window, with the sun in our faces, making it difficult to see, and I felt a deep tiredness in my brain and in my bones. I'd given everything to this process.

'You must be relieved it's all over,' Leo said.

'Relieved to still have a job,' I said, busying myself with opening out the crisp packet and then the nuts and popping one of each in my mouth. 'Even though it's the same job I had before this whole palaver started, so nothing much changes in the grand scheme of things.' My thumbnail had a small chip in the corner, and I checked the others as I ate my nuts. They needed a fresh coat of polish.

'You can stop the dismissive "I'm too important to bother with you" act now, Kat. You've won. It's over.'

I smarted at his change in tone. He wasn't usually the snarky type. That was my job.

'The what?' He silently raised his eyebrows in answer. 'That's rich coming from the best showman in history. How dare you accuse *me* of putting on an act.'

Heidi came rushing in. 'Guys, I'm so sorry but that was Sam on the phone and Penfold has been in a street fight. I've got to go and meet them at the vet's.'

'Oh no! Poor old Penny in the wars again. He's making good use of his nine lives,' I said, standing up to leave. 'I'll come with you.'

'Yeah, we can do this another time,' Leo said as the barman slid our drinks onto the table.

'No, no. Absolutely not. You'll have to celebrate for me,' Heidi said, gathering the pitch boards. 'I'll take these in case of any prying eyes. We don't want to give the game away twice.'

She waved her phone at us in goodbye and dashed off, leaving me exactly where I didn't want to be – on a pseudo-date with the enemy.

'You look worried,' Leo said archly, clearly amused. 'I won't bite... unless you ask nicely. But feel free to get a takeaway cup if you can't bear to sit with me.'

'I'm worried about Heidi, not you,' I said, snootily. 'And... Penfold.'

'Yeah, right.' Leo took a long drink of his Guinness and was left with a white moustache. 'Can we address the elephant in the room here?'

'If you must,' I shot back, feeling very self-righteous.

'What is your problem?' he said, wide-eyed. 'You heartlessly led me on, slept with me, waited until I started to catch feelings, then dropped me like a hot potato. No explanation, no communication, barely even any eye contact since we left the cruise. Don't you think I deserve some kind of apology? Or an explanation at least?'

I drank down the first vodka tonic in a rage. I was almost too angry to speak. 'How you've managed to spin the narrative like that is beyond me,' I hissed. 'The scary thing is you seem so genuine. If I didn't know better, I'd swear you were telling the truth. That I was the baddie in all this.'

'Neither of us are baddies, Kat. But you've got to admit – your behaviour has been totally uncalled for.' His eyes searched mine, seemingly bewildered.

'You're a fascinating study, you know. Is this compulsive lying or is it pure schadenfreude? I can't work out if it's deliberate or not. You don't even seem to know you're doing it.'

'Doing *what*?'

'I *saw* you, Leo.' I paused to let him hear the words. To let it sink in that Mr silver-eyed, silver-tongued charm school himself had been caught out. 'I saw you with my own eyes.'

'Is that the end of your big reveal or are you going to tell me what you're talking about?'

'The day we left. The morning after the night you went missing and I was waiting for you in my cabin. I saw you leaving Brooke's suite as I walked down for breakfast.'

He frowned. 'And...?'

'And what? You're complaining that I dropped you with no explanation – well this is the explanation. I know you were knocking off Brooke while we were also... knocking... ourselves... off.'

Leo's mouth dropped open. 'I think this is what they call putting two and two together and coming up with three hundred and twelve. I have not been "knocking anyone off", thank you very much! Certainly not Brooke, and definitely not you.' He scoffed. 'Where do you get this stuff from? Believe it or not, I actually like you, Kat. Like, really. And stupidly, I thought you liked me too.'

He liked me. He actually *really* liked me. *I knew I hadn't been imagining it.* I felt butterflies in my stomach at the thought, but I squashed them down. It was too late for all that now. I had to stick to my guns.

'I did! Before I realised I was one of many. That I was queuing up for you like the old dears queued up for the Chinese banquet on the ship.'

Leo laughed. 'I am not an all-you-can-eat buffet. And if you'd just asked me, I'd have told you why I was coming out of Brooke's suite.'

'In your tuxedo from the night before.'

'In my tuxedo from the night before.'

'After blowing off our last night together.'

He turned to face me and my heart wobbled. He'd taken his jacket off and his chest was straining against his shirt, reaching for me.

'In fact – I already did tell you this,' he said, looking confused. 'I was playing cards. Dahlia put a poker night on for some of the crew and Brooke insisted Zach and I join in. We used Brooke's suite since it's so big. It was a sort of wrap party once the guests had all gone to bed and I tried to get out of it, but she insisted. Obviously we wanted to keep her happy, and I didn't want to make her and Zach suspicious by saying no, so I thought I'd just go along for an hour or two and then call it a night. I'd planned to come back to your room but I kept winning, and I lost track of time. Suddenly it was five in the morning, and I didn't want to disturb you.'

I eyed him suspiciously.

'It's the truth. Ask Barbie Queue if you don't believe me. She was there.'

The second double vodka was softening my resolve, and I did start to wonder if maybe that made some sense. More sense than him sleeping with her.

'Did you win money?' I mumbled.

'No. I was winning big, then lost a couple, then started chasing the losses and Thiago won the lot. It cost me three hundred euros.'

'Oof.'

'I'll claim it on expenses. All part of the client immersion – am I right?'

I half-smiled. 'Why didn't you tell me all this at the time?'

'Because I had no idea that was what you were thinking and we haven't been alone together for a second since! You've ignored my calls and messages – exactly like you did all those years ago when we were interns.' His face was full of hurt and confusion. 'I didn't want to look like an idiot again, so I decided to face facts... and the obvious explanation was you'd used me to get ahead in the pitch.'

'I'd used you?!' That he could even think that about me was galling.

He shrugged. 'None of it made sense so I chalked it up to a weird sales tactic on your side.'

'OK well it seems we might have both jumped to conclusions then,' I said in a small voice.

'I'll say,' Leo replied. 'You've always thought the worst of me, and I've no idea why. Give a guy a chance, eh?'

I tipped the nuts in with the crisps and faffed about, mixing them all together. My cheeks were burning, and I wasn't sure if it was shame or because I'd had four shots of vodka in under twenty minutes.

'Sorry,' I said, offering him one of his own nuts. 'Although, in my defence, it did look dodgy. What was I supposed to think? It looked like the walk of shame to the untrained eye. Anyone else would have thought the exact same thing.'

'Anyone else wouldn't be you though, would they?' Leo said, taking my hands. 'I was starting to hope you might see the good in me.'

'I did! I do,' I tried, earnestly. 'But you fooled me once and I walked straight into it with a trusting heart. I couldn't bear to think it had happened again. I didn't ask for an explanation as it seemed obvious there could only be one.'

'Well now you know the truth.' He took the nuts gently from me and placed them on the table before taking my hands in his. He stroked his thumb over mine, and I felt the butterflies spring back to life.

'Maybe I've been looking for reasons to say no, instead of reasons to say yes,' I said, suddenly shy.

Leo kissed both my hands, then held them to his heart. 'There are so many reasons to say yes,' he said. 'It's always been a yes for me.'

Thirty-seven

Marylebone high street was buzzing as our black cab crawled along in the heat. It was packed with people wandering around in the sunshine, mooching in and out of the shops, and the pubs and restaurants were teeming with hungry tourists and after-work drinkers. This part of London held a special place in my heart and always felt exciting. Full of good vibes, it was the closest thing to a physical act of apology I could think to do. I looked over at Leo and couldn't believe we were here together, out and about in London on a real date. Finally.

'Just here please,' I said, and the cabbie lurched to a stop outside the best restaurant in London – Chez Margot.

'Can you round it up to twenty?' Leo said, with his card already out.

'I'm getting this,' I said, handing the driver the cash. 'I'm still apologising, remember.'

We climbed out of the cab and I pointed towards the restaurant. 'This is my favourite place to eat,' I explained, taking his hand. 'And by me bringing you here you are now privy to classified information that only the HIIT girls know.'

'Got it,' he said, zipping his lips. 'I don't want to upset the hit-girls. I assume they're like hitwomen but younger. Snipers?'

'Close. They're my exercise group. Although we don't really exercise anymore. We met at HIIT classes a while ago and one of the girls, Abi, brought me here and I've been coming ever since. She's in LA now, but her other half is Italian and his family supply some of the wine.'

'Sounds complicated. Can you draw me a diagram?'

I rolled my eyes and pulled him along. 'If you really need one.'

'We'll order a bottle or two,' Leo said. 'To support your friend's other half's family.'

'I suppose we should really,' I agreed, beaming like an idiot.

I pushed open the door and kept my fingers crossed Margot would have a table. The restaurant was vibrant and busy, despite it being a Monday, and the open windows welcomed in a warm breeze, as people enjoyed their steak onglet and charcuterie boards with large glasses of wine.

'Ahhh, *bonjour, Katarine, ca va*?' Margot came bustling over with a big smile and a triple kiss. 'It 'as been a while! And who 'ave we got 'ere? Welcome to you both.'

'Margot! I'm very well, *ca va bien*! This is Leo, a friend… kind of thing. Can you squeeze us in?' I looked around hopefully, but there weren't any empty tables. No such luck.

'But, of course! A pleasure to meet you, Leo,' Margot said, double kissing him warmly. 'A cat and a lion, together, eh? How is that working out?'

'I'm more of a kitten, Margot, we both know that.'

'*C'est vrai*. You are that – a cute little kitty cat.'

'I hear this place is London's best-kept secret,' Leo said. 'Not that you'd know.'

Margot tinkled with laughter. '*Zut!* I wish it 'ad been better kept! Where 'ave all these people come from?'

'Your food is too good, Margot,' I said, my stomach rumbling. 'We can just sit at the bar if that's OK?'

'*Absolutement*. For a few minutes at the bar but I will find you a space, you know that – 'ave an aperitif on me while I pressure someone to leave.'

I laughed as we followed her over to the ornate, mirrored bar, and hopped up onto the stools. The shelves were packed with every spirit you could imagine, but I only ever went with Margot's wine recommendation. She automatically poured me out a glass of white, while smiling at us both. 'Is it wine for you too, Leo, or can I get you something else?'

'Yes, please. I'll go with the flow.'

'We like that in a man, don't we, Kat?'

I nodded. 'We sure do. But it's a sound decision. Margot has the best wine selection in London. What are we drinking tonight?'

'Ahhh, I 'ad a fresh delivery from Tuscany just this week – from Abi actually – and this one is from there.' She pushed two straw-coloured white wines in our direction. 'It is like a honey. *Salut*. Please enjoy and I will get you a table as soon as I can.'

'*Salut!*' I said, clinking my glass with Leo's.

'*Salut* to you too,' he replied, with a smile, our legs touching as we sat side by side.

The wine was deliciously light and drinkable. Just how I liked it.

'I was hoping we might get some alone time together as it happens,' Leo said. 'I got you a little something just in case.'

'Did you?' I asked. 'What if I'd told you to sod off even after you'd explained?'

'Call me a hopeless romantic, I guess,' he replied, pulling a small box out of his pocket.

I eyed it in surprise. 'Are you about to propose?'

Leo laughed. 'I'm not that hopeless.' He opened the box and there, wedged into a red velvet ring slot, was my liver bird necklace.

I was speechless. 'How did you even…?' I picked it up in shock; it was like a magic trick. He must have hired a fleet of detectorists to find it. There was no possible way it could be…

'It's not your lucky number eight I'm afraid,' he said. 'But I managed to track down another.'

'There were only ever a handful made. How did you…?'

He turned it over in my hand. 'Luck must be on my side. I know it's not the same, but by some miracle I found number eighty-eight. Double your lucky number for twice the luck,' he said, with a shy smile. 'I know how much it meant to you.'

The gold was glossy and the chain was slinky and delicate. Leo put it on for me, then kissed my neck, and it sat in the exact same spot as my old liver bird, next to my heart. It felt right.

'I don't know what to say,' I whispered, holding on to it tight. 'This is so incredibly thoughtful. Thank you doesn't feel like enough.'

'It's enough,' he said, softly. 'I'm glad you like it.'

'I do.'

'Now your lucky moments can remind you of me, too.'

'Why would I need reminding of you?' His smile dropped and I lifted his chin with my finger. 'This isn't the last time we'll see each other, is it?' His eyes searched mine, hesitant and slightly fearful, as though I was about to pull the rug out from under him again. 'I didn't mean for that to sound like a question,' I said, changing tone to make it a statement of fact. 'This isn't the last time we'll see each other, is it.'

'I hope not, but as I said, this whole situation has been very confusing. I've never been entirely sure where I stand.'

'Mr Leo Kendrick feeling insecure? Now I've seen it all. Hold the front page of *PR News*.' His neck flushed bright red. I hadn't seen this side of him before, and I felt mean toying with his emotions. 'Let me tell you where I stand – or where I want to stand – and maybe that'll help. When we worked together as interns I couldn't think about anything but getting that job. I liked you – of course I did – but you were the competition, and all I could think about was beating you. Then when you got it instead I couldn't bear to stay in touch as the loser. Any reminder of you made me feel like a failure.'

'No!' he said, looking genuinely concerned. 'You were the smart one, the creative one – the one with all the brilliant ideas. I just put the decks together and talked them through. I was convinced that whole summer that you'd get the job and I'd be out on my arse. It seemed obvious to me that you were the right choice.'

'Yeah, right.'

'It's true! And then when they offered it to me, I couldn't believe my luck. I felt like the cat who'd got the cream – the job and maybe a chance with you. I'd planned to ask you out properly once the dust settled and you'd been snapped up by a competitor, but you disappeared. You never got back to me when I reached out. How could you ever feel like a failure? I was the fraud – I should never have accepted the job.'

'Of course you should. You got the job for lots of different reasons; it was never just down to the work. You're cool and relaxed and charming. I'm none of those things.'

'You're all of those things!' he said, reaching out to squeeze my leg under the bar, as if to emphasise his point.

'Well, I'd never describe myself like that, and that's the truth. YOU have an innate belief in yourself that I've never had and seeing you after all this time has reminded me of that.'

'I'm glad it appears that way, because inside I'm full of jelly. The imposter syndrome is real.'

'For me too, and if I'm honest, this pitch brought up those same feelings of failure again – knowing you could take my account from me and having you right there in my face. However much I liked you as a person, my livelihood was at stake. But amid all that, I started to develop real feelings and the more they grew, the more I just wanted to be with you.'

'Same,' he said, leaning in.

'I was almost looking for a reason to shut it down, you know? Maybe my subconscious needed to believe the bad in you to be able to focus on the pitch. Maybe it was the same thing all those years ago as well – to justify the loss. I was devastated and it was easier to blame you than to consider I might be at fault somehow.'

'Wow,' he breathed, looking at me tenderly.

'But as of now, I stand sorry and hopeful we might be able to sort this out,' I said, giving him a friendly nudge. 'I feel embarrassed about the whole situation and... I've missed you.' I paused. 'What about you? Where do you stand? Or where would you like to?'

He pretended to think for a second.

'I'm not sure I want to stand anywhere at the moment; I'm pretty happy sitting right here.' He leant forward and kissed me, sending tingles down my spine. Leo came up for air and pulled himself together. 'But if you insist on an answer, then I'd like to stand next to you in the American Bar in The Savoy and drink dirty martinis,' he said, stroking my hand. 'I'd like to stand in the crowd at Wembley with you and watch Liverpool win the FA Cup.'

'Haha, we wish!'

'I'd like to prop up the bar with you in my local pub, where they have a lock-in on a Thursday and then queue up with you for my favourite curry house on Brick Lane where the poppadoms are bigger than the plates.'

'Bagsy the mint yoghurt dip.'

'See? We're yin and yang. I'm mango chutney all the way.'

'Keep going,' I said, drinking my wine and enjoying this glimpse into his mind.

'I'd like us to carry on learning salsa together and I want to whisk you away to New York to see *Hamilton* on Broadway... and a million other things. Being on the cruise together was such a laugh. It's been like living in black and white ever since we got back. I've been lost without you.'

'Have you?' I asked softly.

He nodded. 'It's the first time I've ever felt lonely on my own, if that makes sense. The cruise was so full-on, wasn't it?'

'We were kind of… thrown together and left to get on with it,' I said, putting my hand on his leg and snuggling in. 'It was like a social experiment at times.'

Leo laughed.

'Come, come, follow me!' Margot cooed from behind us. 'I 'ave a table for you now. The best in the 'ouse.'

'You say that to everyone,' I said, giving her a hug. 'Thank you, Margot.'

'Your man is very cute!' she whispered into my hair. '*Tres bien.*'

I couldn't stop the smile spreading across my face.

There was a small charcuterie with fresh bread and butter already on the table and Margot topped up our wine and left us with the menus.

'I do mean it,' Leo said, staring into my eyes. 'I want to wine and dine you.'

I laughed. 'And the rest.'

He smirked. 'Yes, that too. All of it. I knew from the very first time I saw you, all those years ago, that there was something special about you, Kat Brennan. You took my breath away and still do. I don't get nervous around people very often; it just isn't in my nature. But with you, I start second-guessing myself.'

'I feel the same,' I said. 'I was gutted when I thought you'd spent the night with Brooke. I didn't want to believe it, but I'd seen you with my own eyes – what else could I think?'

'I'll say it again – you should have talked to me,' he replied earnestly. 'We work in communications for God's sake – we should be good at this stuff. But for the record,

I'd never do something like that. Cheating on you, cheating the process… It's not who I am. Not to mention it would overstep every professional boundary there is.'

I nodded. 'You're right; I should have known there'd be an explanation. I'm sorry.'

'As long as we're cool now, that's all I care about. My feelings for you are real and I just hope you feel the same way about me.'

'I do.'

'Can we seal it with another kiss? Just to make sure?' His eyes searched mine, a cheeky smile on his lips.

'Leo and Kat the kitten together at last?'

'I've always seen you as more of a lioness.'

I smiled at his handsome face and leant forward to kiss him. His lips felt soft on mine, and the charge between us was electric as we finally surrendered to each other, giving in to what fate had planned for us all along.

Epilogue

Six months later

'I didn't want to tell you before all the details were confirmed, but I've been working on a secret project.' Leo handed me a press release as The Heathrow Express hurtled through a tunnel.

Amplify CEO set to launch PR Cubs and Kittens.

'You're not in PR News, again? Honestly, I don't know how they'd survive without all the free content you feed them. Cubs and Kittens? Sounds like a strip club.'

He rolled his eyes. 'Yes, that's exactly it – I'm opening a strip club, and I thought I'd wait until we were on the way to the airport to tell you.'

I laughed. 'What is it, then? You'll have to read it out; the copy is tiny and the words are jumbling together.'

Leo cleared his throat and shuffled the paper like a BBC newsreader. 'Today marks the historic occasion of London's coolest and most successful PR agency – Amplify –'

'Some big claims there…' I interrupted.

'It's my press release, I can claim what I like,' he said, going back to it. '…Amplify launching its new intern programme, Cubs and Kittens. They are inviting applications from those aged sixteen to twenty-five, and particularly welcome school leavers and graduates from underrepresented backgrounds.'

I felt a lump in my throat as Leo continued in his clipped English accent.

'Leo Kendrick, CEO, said, "This is a subject close to my heart. I was one of the lucky few to get an internship when I left university, but these opportunities are incredibly rare these days. We'll be taking three interns on each year and giving them the experience they need to get an entry-level role in the PR industry."'

I took the press release back and scanned it. 'You are amazing, Leo. Do you know that? What a brilliant thing to do.'

'Well, I figured there's no point me being CEO if I'm not going to make a difference. It's up to us to help the next generation.'

'True enough. All of us, not just you. Why cubs and kittens?'

'Isn't it obvious? I've named it after us. From cubs and kittens, lions and cats grow.' He growled in my ear, and I shivered as he kissed my neck, purring in reply.

I was stunned into silence as the train started to slow down; the internship was a nod to our time together at Engelman and I felt proud to be associated with it in some small way.

'Can Northstar get involved as well?' I asked, suddenly having a flash of inspiration. 'I'm sure Heidi would take three interns on if we spoke to her about it. We could make it a cross-industry initiative. A legacy for all the CEOs and leaders out there.'

Leo's eyes lit up. 'Love that idea. Sure, why not. The more the merrier, right? Send her a copy of this press release and if she's up for it we can do a joint call to arms for other agency leaders to get on board.'

The idea of giving a younger version of myself a step up gave me goosebumps. That Leo and I could be the reason someone somewhere had a slightly easier time of it than we'd had. The next generation out there, trying to get on the bottom rung of a slippery career ladder with no 'connections' to help them. We could be their connections – it didn't have to be the same story on repeat for all of time.

Leo leapt off the train, grabbed both our cases and started running towards the check-in desks. We were only going to Barcelona, so why we were travelling from terminal five was anyone's guess. I ran after him, realising I had the passports in my bag; he wouldn't get very far without those. I rounded the corner and scanned the crowd for his cowboy hat, only to spot him sat on a chair with his legs crossed, suddenly very relaxed.

'What is going on?' I said, out of breath and clutching both passports.

'I've got a surprise for you,' he said, with a smile. 'Come and sit down next to me and close your eyes.'

He'd lost me. 'I can't have a surprise today – it's your birthday. It's my job to do all the spoiling and the presents.'

'It's for both of us – you'll see.'

'OK, but our flight goes in an hour, and we don't even know the gate number yet. Can we do the surprise once we're through departures?'

Leo shook his head. 'Nope. It's happening right here, right now.' He patted the seat next to him and I did as I was told, unzipping my coat and shoving my gloves in my pockets.

'Do I really need to close my eyes? You're not going to run off, are you? Because my make-up is in that suitcase and if you disappear with it, I'll be devastated.'

Leo gave me a look, so I closed my eyes and sat quietly, while he shuffled about.

'Keep them closed, no peeking,' he instructed, and I felt his headphones cover my ears. 'OK, you can open them now.' He handed me his phone where Brooke's face filled the screen.

'Hey there, love birds!!!' she squealed, and I blinked in disbelief.

'Brooke! How are you? Where are you? What's going on?'

Leo pressed pause. 'It's pre-recorded,' he whispered.

'Oh.'

Her bleached blonde bouffant was piled high on her head and her lips shimmered pink with gloss. 'Greg and I wanted to say a huge happy birthday to you, Leo, and that we're so damn happy to hear you guys found love on the *Esmeralda*. Another unimaginable moment, brought to you by Excalibur, hey? That line really does just work for every occasion, don't it?'

'It sure does,' I said, nestling into Leo's chest as he watched on in delight.

'Leo has probably spilt the beans by now, but just in case he hasn't – Kat, we've got a surprise for you both.'

I looked up at Leo who was grinning from ear to ear.

'I'm sorry to be the bearer of bad news, but you've missed your flight to Barcelona.' Brooke pulled a faux-sad face. 'Because there isn't one!' she squealed in delight. 'Instead, Greg and I are sending the pair of you on an all-expenses-paid trip to Barbados to sample the *Princess Aaliyah*.'

I nearly dropped the phone in astonishment.

'Pretty cool, hey?' Leo said. 'She figured they owed us a holiday after the bunk-bed trauma. To compensate us for any back trouble – mine will never be the same.'

'Greg has said I can put it down as mystery shopping,' Brooke continued with a wink. 'You both deserve a rest after everything we put you through on the *Esmeralda*. Those rooms, that crazy schedule, and all the running around Dahlia made you do.' She giggled. 'Although it was a lot of fun to watch y'all play along.'

'That woman is seriously twisted.'

'I wanted you to meet another one of our cruise ships in person – and *Aaliyah* is just the ticket. Absolutely gorgeous. If you thought *Esmeralda* was beautiful, *Aaliyah* is going to blow your freakin' minds. Don't have too much fun without me – can't wait to see the photos!' Brooke gave a frantic wave and the video froze.

'Is this a wind-up?' I said, completely confused.

'Nope. It's real.'

'So we're not going to Spain?'

Leo chuckled. 'Gotcha,' he said, nudging into me. 'I wanted it to be a surprise.'

'Barbados!' I said, dreamily. Leo was always organising little surprises, but this was huge.

'I've never been to the Caribbean before – and the *Aaliyah* looks amazing, but why would they give us a free holiday? What's the catch?'

'There isn't one, and I've been promised it won't feel like an Excalibur holiday. I don't want you thinking about work the whole time. The Caribbean ships are quite different apparently – with fewer people and much bigger, plusher bedrooms.'

'Bigger and plusher than those staff cabins? Surely not?' I said, kissing him in delight. 'And I know all about the *Aaliyah*, silly, I do their PR, remember?'

'Apparently they're testing out a new model for honeymooners.' Even the word gave me palpitations as I tried to remember what I'd packed. 'It includes a couples massage, water-skiing, quad bikes so we can get around the island and a meal for two on the beach.'

'The snorkelling is supposed to be incredible out there, as well,' I said, my mind racing. 'This is *so* cool. How long until we fly? Can we watch some of the match?'

I snuggled into Leo's big arm for extra warmth. The Liverpool game was about to start, and we were wearing our football shirts in solidarity for the boys.

'Oh yes, one other detail Brooke forgot to mention,' Leo said, pulling two tickets out of his pocket. 'We're flying business class!'

'No??!'

'Yes.' He smiled, as my mouth dropped. 'So, we can watch the match in the lounge with a bottle of champagne.'

I threw myself at him and screamed. 'How is this happening? Thank you so much!'

'You're worth it. There is one more thing I've been wanting to talk to you about before we go through, though,' Leo said, his expression suddenly serious.

My stomach clenched. 'What's that?'

'Do you know what today is?' he asked, unfurling his arm.

Oh no. A test. 'Other than your birthday,' I said, knowing that couldn't be the answer.

'Yesss, other than that.'

I pretended to think for a moment before shaking my head. 'No idea,' I said, honestly. I was rubbish at remembering dates and anniversaries and what happened when.

'It's exactly six months since you introduced me to Chez Margot and we finally got together.'

'Is it?' Had it really been six months? 'Is that something we should celebrate?'

'Yes. It's our half-anniversary, and I wanted to mark the occasion with a question.'

Another question. This was starting to sound like a *Cosmopolitan* quiz. *How well do you know your other half?*

'OK… go on…?'

'I love you, Kat,' he said, taking my hands and turning me towards him.

'I love you too,' I said, my heart skipping a beat. *I really did love him,* and I'd say yes to whatever question he wanted to ask.

'Good,' he said. 'Because I can't stop thinking about you and "us" and the future – our future – and I just really want us to be official.'

I looked at him, bewildered. 'I thought we already were?'

'More official than that. To take the next step.' The emotion in his eyes was more than I could bear, and it was all I could do to stop myself from wrapping my arms around him. 'I want to at least put the idea out there because I know it's what I want, but no pressure at all if you're not there yet.'

'If I'm not where, exactly?' I wasn't entirely sure where this was going.

'If you're not one hundred per cent all in, I get it. It's just that I am and I'm impatient and if you are too then I'm ready for us to get going with the rest of our lives.'

My stomach clenched again, but for a different reason this time. I knew exactly what he meant now, because I felt the same way. Dating back and forth these past six months had felt like a weird waiting game. The preamble to us getting started.

'I'm excited too, you know,' I said, softly. 'And I am all in, Leo. Two hundred per cent. I want to do life with you.'

He kissed my hands, eyes shining. 'Really? Well, then I can ask you my question.' He stopped and took a breath, staring at me intently. 'Kat. How would you feel about moving in with me?' I nearly broke. He looked so vulnerable, scanning my face in earnest for an answer. Wearing his heart on his sleeve for all to see.

'Oh, wow,' I said, taken aback. 'I don't know what to say.'

'Say: *yes, Leo, that sounds amazing, I'd love to move in with you.*'

'Right.'

'Only if you want to, of course.'

'Of course,' I repeated, feeling totally overwhelmed. 'That does sound amazing. And very grown up and slightly terrifying. I've never lived with a man before. What if I hate it?'

He beeped my nose and grinned. 'Then you can move back out again, and we'll go back to life as it is now. Don't worry, I won't hold you against your will, but the question you should be asking is *what if you love it*?'

That was another way of thinking about it... what if it just worked out?

Leo pulled a shiny key out of his pocket, attached to a crumbly hunk of stone. 'Recognise this?'

Again, he'd lost me. I shook my head, while the washing machine in my stomach went on fast spin.

He chuckled. 'No reason you should. It's a piece of volcanic rock from the Azores. I picked it up when we walked up Monte Brasil and brought it back.'

'Oh, wow, that's very cool.'

'I had it treated and made into keyrings.' He pulled another piece from his pocket and put the two halves together. 'My key has a lion etched onto it and yours has a kitten.'

I took a closer look and could see the tiny images. 'That is so cute and thoughtful!' I said, planting a kiss on his cheek. 'And very us.'

'Uniquely us.'

Living with Leo was the scariest, most wonderful thing I could ever imagine. But was it too soon? I was only thirty-five after all and far too young for that level of commitment. Except of course I wasn't – not even slightly. Would it work or would we argue all the time and eventually grow to hate each other? Maybe we'd laugh all the time and become obsessed with each other? There was only one way to find out. My heart was shouting yes, but my head was in panic mode, loitering in maybe-one-day territory. But I knew what I wanted to do and I wasn't going to let irrational fear get the better of me. It was time to be brave and venture into the unknown.

'Let's,' I said, simply, taking the key and feeling a pulse of energy from the volcanic rock.

'Really?' he whispered, barely breathing. 'Do you mean it? Do you really want to?'

'Yes! I really do.' I threw my arms around him and held on tight. 'In fact, I can't think of anything I want more right now. Happy birthday, handsome.'

Acknowledgements

Huge thanks as always goes to my agent Rosie Pierce and editors Aubrie Artiano and Holly Humphreys. This book has been so much fun to write, and you have all helped me every step of the way. To Yasmeen, Pippa and the rest of the team at Head of Zeus – thank you for everything you have done to get the book into the hands of readers. Thank you to Gemma Gorton for another gorgeous cover design – I love it! And to my copy editor Helena Newton for finessing the final version and deleting anything I could be sued for before the book goes to print.

A big thank you to my writing friends who have been a brilliant sounding board while I've been cruising around on an imaginary ocean liner. To the Romantic Novelists' Association – especially the Essex chapter who are always so open and kind, with special shout outs to Julie Haworth, Lizzie Chantree, Lorna Cook and Carrie Elks. To Cressida McLaughlin for reading an early copy of the book despite a mountainous TBR pile. To Hannah Dolby and Joann Smith for all the cruise ship tips and for answering my many strange questions about how it all works. To Helen Lederer and the Comedy Women in Print gang who are always on hand for advice and a gossip. To my Faber writing girls, friends and family for reading early versions and for your brilliant and thorough feedback – Sarah Lawton, Liz Webb, Marija Maher-Diffenthal, Rachel Lyon, Helen Jamieson and Claire Lucas.

Thank you Mom for your unwavering support and daily pep talks. I love you very much. Thank you again to my favourite sister Claire, for your positive vibes and plotting advice. I love you very, very much. Thank you to my husband Rob, who is incredibly patient and understanding and brings me cups of tea and Twirls on the regular. I love you very, very, very much. And to Ziggy and Bruno, my best boys, who have tried very hard not to bark while I've been working and have kept my feet warm.

And finally, to my readers – can I call you Walkies? – thank you for reading and reviewing and sharing. Thank you for your lovely messages – I read them all. Thank you for joining me on this wild ride.

If you enjoyed this book,
you'll love...

Escape to the Tuscan Vineyard

...where it's always wine o'clock!

CARRIE WALKER

Escape to the Tuscan Vineyard

After getting her heart broken in her early twenties,
Abi Mason vowed to live by a simple (but non-negotiable)
rule: no second dates. Who needs a boyfriend, or
anything else for that matter, when you have
a career to think about?

But life has other plans: with some unexpected time on
her hands, Abi finds herself on holiday in Tuscany. Among
sun-dappled vineyards and olive groves, Abi meets dashing
American Tony, and it seems the universe is conspiring to
force her out of her comfort zone...

**If Abi can break her own rules, could this unexpected
Italian fling lead her to a happiness she never
dared to dream of?**

Available to buy now

Discover more holiday romance from Carrie Walker

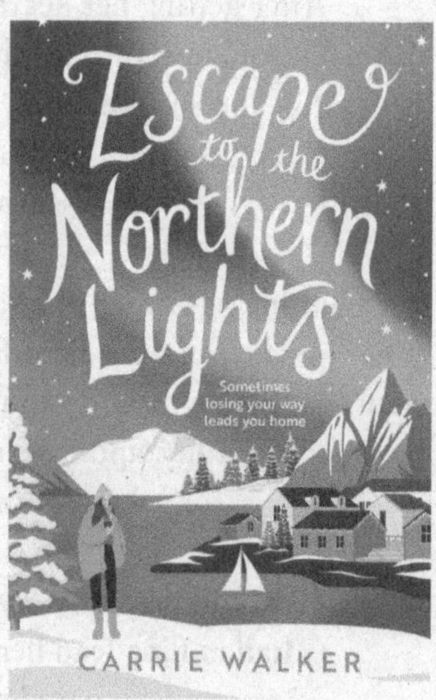

'Carrie Walker will whisk you away with this fabulous destination romcom...
An irresistible delight!'

Sandy Barker

About the Author

CARRIE WALKER is a romantic comedy writer with a lifelong passion for travel. She has lived in a ski resort, on a Greek beach, in the country and the city and tells stories inspired by her adventures through Europe, South America and Asia.

Longlisted for the Comedy Women in Print prize, Carrie is the author of Head of Zeus' Holiday Romance series, which includes *Escape to the Swiss Chalet*, *Escape to the Tuscan Vineyard*, *Escape to the Northern Lights* and *Escape to the Turquoise Seas*.

Previously CEO of a global disability inclusion movement, a board director of a brand agency, a newspaper editor, a football mascot and a fancy-dress carrot for the BBC, she is now writing novels in Essex where she lives with her husband and two dogs.

Thanks for reading!

Want to receive exclusive author content, news on the latest Aria books and updates on offers and giveaways?

Follow us on X @AriaFiction and on Facebook and Instagram @HeadofZeus, and join our mailing list.